THE MISTS OF ARLTUNGA

1989

508-479

~ Ferreira

Eliret/3   7/3

4/13

THE MISTS OF ARLTUNGA

Roger Jones

Greencup Books

Greencup Books
PO Box 4945
Chattanooga, TN 37405

ISBN: 978-1-943661-42-8

Printed in the United States

The boy sat high on the camel's back, his head lolling with the dips and sways of the long- legged gait. A loose end of the lungee wrapped around his head swirled in the hot gusts. He was barely a boy, a squat child, no more than a bump among the tied-on bags and boxes.

On the camel in front of him sat another boy, taller and more erect, his lungee pulled tight around his face. Beside his camel walked a tall man, a European from his clothes, under a broad, flat-brimmed hat with a puggaree flapping down his neck. He carried a leather satchel, moving it from one shoulder to the other at intervals to avoid the soaking of sweat.

The loaded camels walked along the track in two files of eight, the head Afghan cameleer astride the lead camel of the left file, three pullers moving along the sides, dark faces looking out from robes and lungees, poles in their hands. No one spoke. The only sound was the creak of ropes and cinches, the chuff and thump of camels' feet across rocky soil, the *whish* of wind. The air shimmered from the heat in a broad band above the horizon, flat as a griddle. Only a ragged run of hills to the northeast gave any sense of distance.

The camels and men walked. The squat child swayed under the sun. It would be hours until they rested.

They came to the water hole as the sun settled into a glimmering red ball on the western horizon. The head Afghan led the two files into separate staggered circles, one within the other among the scrubby trees. At his soft word his camel knelt, front end down one leg at a time, then the back, all the legs folding under in full crouch. He dismounted as the pullers went to the other camels in turn, grasping their nose lines and speaking a word, touching their knees with a pole if necessary. With camels down, knots and cinches were loosened, and bags, boxes, and crates slipped off the humped backs onto the red dirt.

The two boys and the man stood and watched this ceremony, as they had each of the last fifteen days since leaving Oodnadatta, the man swaying slightly from dehydration and exhaustion, the boys dazed and unfocused. Away from the water hole the desert stretched around them, ragged hills raking the horizon on three sides now, a beard of hard scrub over all.

In the center of the two rings of chewing camels the Afghans' close fire boiled water for tea. The camels had been fed first, a gruel of mashed oats and water. Heads erect, the camels chewed, lower jaws sawing side to side, gazes steady, contemplative. The boys unwound their lungees and squatted like the Afghans, staring into the fire. The smaller boy's head flamed copper, his mop of blond hair casting back the red of the setting sun. The taller boy's close-cropped brown hair threw auburn highlights. The man did not remove his bush hat but wound the puggaree back up around the crown. He pulled a flat rock against the gnarled bole of a tree and sat, his long legs stretched before him, his satchel at his side.

The water boiled in the pot over the fire, and one of the Afghans stood, mixed in tea leaves, and after a few moments poured the brew into chipped, enameled iron cups—serving the tall man first, the blond child, the brown-haired boy, the head Afghan, then the other two pullers, who passed guttural comments in their language. Neither the man nor the boys spoke.

One of the camels gave a long groan. The Afghans glanced over but didn't rise. The blond child did, though, leaving his tea cup on the ground and striding over to the camel, which did not look at him, but groaned again. The child fidgeted for a moment, the sitting camel's head taller than his, then drew in his breath and groaned back, more of a bleat than a groan, but still a remarkable sound from a small boy. The camel looked at him. The Afghans looked over as well. One laughed, then the others. The child bleated again. The camel made a new, softer sound. The child replied.

The head Afghan rose in his robes and approached the man on his rock. The boy sounded like a new camel, he said, a *bay-bee*. The groaning camel was female; she had responded to the boy's sound. It was unusual. The man on the rock nodded. The Afghan returned to his group. The child bleated again, but the camel did not look at him. After a while he returned to his cup.

"What else you talk to?" said the man.

"Anything," said the child.

With the setting of the sun the air grew chill. Swags were unrolled, the Afghans spaced close to camels around the outside circle, the man and two boys in the center. As the light died, the sky filled with a sparkling powder of stars. A dingo barked to the east, answered by another. The boys slept a dreamless sleep, buried in their swags. The camels sat, heads up, eyes open, chewing, chewing all the night.

The mountain came into view on the morning of the nineteenth day. At first it was just another ragged edge to the northern horizon, the width of a thumb held at arm's length, no more distinctive than twenty other rocky jumbles they had approached and passed by. The tall man gave no sign of recognition until one of the walking Afghans slipped beside him and gestured forward, finger pointed, murmuring. The man nodded and gazed out under his hat.

As the day progressed the ragged edge widened to a mountain occupying a full third of the forward vantage. The land turned from the gray of distance to close-up rust, expressing iron in the composition of soil and rock. But the mountain remained gray, looming higher and wider. How wide? *Surely six kilometers around,* the tall man thought. *Up three thousand meters.* It was no mountain such as the tall man had seen in his own country, gradual slopes through foothills to ascending peaks joined in a chain. This was a giant isolated extrusion in the vast flat country, an enormous, bare growth that had erupted out of the plain...without a summit. The mountain was flat-topped, as though it had been cut off.

That night, as the boys and Afghans slept and the camels chewed, the man sat erect in his swag, stiff blanket over his shoulders, gazing north to the jagged rise, an edged hump at the base of the starry sky. He fingered the satchel, held it under his arms crossed over his chest.

They walked past the pools at the mountain's foot before they stopped. The pools were twenty feet in diameter, four-foot sides of vertical wooden planks bleached gray by the sun, crusted yellow-white with dried chemicals. The stench was terrible in the heat. The mountain had its own smell. That smell had been with them for hours, by now hardly noticed. But this was different, industrial, biting at the nostrils. Half a dozen men in stained, sweat-soaked overalls and broad hats moved among the pools, alternately roiling the yellow-green mash within with long rakes, then stooping over vats beside the pools, prodding the contents with paddles. The men must have seen the camel train approaching long before. They did not look up now as it passed.

The track ran between the pools, five on each side, to a yard fronting a low stone building from which came the sound of grinding, as of a wheel turning in a mill. From the doorway of the building a man stood and watched them, one man, his clothes without chemical stains, his eyes deep in the shadow of his hat. Along the wall beside him stood long rows of burlap bags, three rows, ten, twelve, more in a row. Behind the building the gray stone of the mountain rose up and out.

The head Afghan turned the camels aside and swung into a large corral, rock-edged at a low height. A camel could easily step over, but they would not. The man in the doorway stood and watched while the camels circled, knelt bleating and groaning, the Afghans moving among them. When all the camels were crouched and composed the Afghans went to work on the ties, hands flying among the ropes, loosing and lifting the bags and boxes onto the stony ground. The man in the doorway watched, and the tall man, standing aside with the boys by the corral entrance, watched him.

They both turned when a rattling sound came from a cleft up the mountainside. Two men appeared, guiding an empty two-wheeled wooden cart down a stony path. Another cart followed, then more, all rolling down the path and turning until five carts were lined up outside the corral entrance, ten new men standing beside them, waiting. The man in the doorway kept his eyes on the cleft, the Afghans too, and after a few moments an eleventh man appeared, in clean khaki clothes, a tan hat and spectacles, a clipboard with papers flapping. A murmur passed over the Afghans. The man in the doorway walked toward him.

The spectacled man strode past the carts into the corral and straight toward the head Afghan. He was close when he saw the tall man and the two boys. He stopped, looked at the Afghan, then turned and came toward them. He stopped six feet away, sun behind his head, moved his hands to his hips. He was not so tall as the tall man, but far more solid.

"Who in the bloody hell are you?"

The tall man looked at him, his face shaded by his hat brim, his satchel on his shoulder. The taller boy looked too, squinting up, his lungee tied tight around his face. The child did not look up, scuffled a foot along the ground.

"I have a letter," said the tall man. "In here." He gestured to the satchel. "It explains."

"A letter," said the spectacled man, his mouth twisting into a scowl. "Who would it be a letter from then?"

"From MacReedy Mining, from a big man there, in Perth."

The spectacled man hesitated. "And who are these?" he said, gesturing to the boys.

"They have come with me," said the tall man. "They have come to work."

"To work?" The spectacled man snorted, twisting his mouth again. He looked at the boys, shook his head. "I'll talk to you at the top. You follow the carts up."

He turned and strode back towards the head Afghan. "Ha, Achmed," he said loudly. "Let's see what you have for me."

The cart before them creaked with the load, steel-shod wheels rasping against the stone of the path. The two men pulled the cart with harnesses strapped around their chests, leaning forward with the strain. Three carts more had gone ahead. One stayed behind, loaded with supplies for the pools. The spectacled man had moved among the bags, boxes, and crates, probing, prodding, consulting with the head Afghan and the man who had come from the doorway, making notes on the paper on his clipboard as the carts were loaded. He started back up the mountain as soon as the loading was done. Many parcels were left behind, more hauling to come.

The tall man had approached the head Afghan, stood before him, taken off his hat and dipped his head, held out his hand. His hair was blond, like the younger boy. The Afghan regarded him a moment, then took his hand in a limp grip.

"I thank you for bringing us here, for guiding safely with your camels," the tall man said. He shook the Afghan's hand, then released it. The other Afghans were watching. The leader stood, black eyes bright against his dark skin, beard darker, lungee loose around his head. He bowed slightly and salaamed.

"It is good," he said. "It is okay." He dipped again.

The tall man, his hat back in place, bowed at the other Afghans as he passed them. They dipped their heads in return. He put a hand on each boy's back, to hurry them along. The last cart was rolling out of the corral.

The track wound up through the cleft, onto a narrow shelf, then into another cleft. The man walked tens steps behind the cart, a boy on either side. Twice on the track they came to shallow steps cut out of the gray rock. The men pulling the cart brought the wheels up against a riser, then with a blast of breath and effort, pulled them up and over. Above, other carts were doing the same, a din of metal on stone. The man and boys walked heads down, huffing from the exertion.

They barely noticed when the cart paused, but after a few steps more they stopped, looked up...and stared. They were standing on a broad natural shelf in the mountainside, and the whole great mountain was hollow inside, a great jagged bowl two miles across. Behind the shelf the rock face continued up another six hundred feet, but at the edge before them it fell away. How far? They could not see, because the view was shrouded in mist, yellow mist flowing all about them, filling the vast hollow of the mountain, mist that brushed with the wind up and over the edge. The stench of the mountain was in this mist, more pungent here than below, an acrid stench that cut a newcomer's nose when he breathed, his throat when he swallowed. The tall man looked down at the boys. The younger child had unwrapped his lungee from his head, twisting it around his neck to leave the two ends dragging along the ground. His mop of blond hair was matted and streaked. The older boy had left his lungee tight. He looked up at the man, a question in his eyes.

"The smell is bad," said the man. "But it's a rare site, this is. This was a huge volcano much, much ago. We are inside the volcano, in the caldera."

"What does that mean?" the child whined. "We are not inside anything."

"I will explain later," said the man. "I will draw you a picture."

The line of carts moved across the shelf and stopped at the center. Men unstrapped their harnesses and laid down their handles. The spectacled man was there with his clipboard as parcels were unloaded. The tall man stood, waiting, watching.

At the back of the shelf three layers of rectangular rooms stepped up against the rock face, the lower walls blocks of the gray stone of the mountain, the upper, adobe bricks. Ladders laced the structure between levels, up from the ground to flat roofs providing access to higher-story doorways of gray-weathered wood stained yellowish like the pools below. Only the door left of center of the lowest level was painted, a shade of blue darker than the sky.

Before the layers of houses was another corral as below, a low square ninety feet on a side edged with piled rock. A track crossed the shelf below the corral, one side to the other. After a low lip the shelf tilted down in a succession of terraces, walls of quarried stone three to six feet high filled with earth brought in from…where? Far outside, surely. Plants filled this earth: corn, beans, cabbages, vines bearing squashes, low apple and nut trees. Joining the terraces, beside paths between them, were troughs scooped from the stony soil and lined with flat stones: water passages, a system of irrigation from springs up the mountain. Two low sheds, stone-walled and plank-roofed, lay along the eastern edge of the shelf. Adjacent was another corral, narrower and higher than the one in the center, containing chickens and goats and a ram with long, curved horns. The shelf itself went beyond the terraces, ninety feet more before it dropped into the mist.

The younger boy pulled on the man's trouser leg and sat on the ground. "When is food?" he asked.

"Two hours," the tall man said. The sun was below the edge of the ridge to the west. The light…It was hard to judge with the mist. The child sighed.

"Tell me again where you say you came by this letter."

The spectacled man had taken off his hat. He was sitting behind a wide table, at the end of the long room. The room was behind the blue door, almost the whole left half of the ground floor in the stack of houses. The boys were sitting on a bench against the inner wall. The spectacled man had read through the letter twice and held it like a brick.

"From a big man, an important man, in MacReedy Mining in Perth," said the tall man. He had taken off his hat too, holding it in his hands. His satchel lay on the bench beside the taller boy. "A big stone building, marble on the floors—"

"'McLoughlin,' it says," said the spectacled man. "Angus McLoughlin. I don't know any Angus McLoughlin at Mac-Reedy Mining." He looked up at the tall man.

"He is a big man. He said it. It is on the letter. Vice President, MacReedy Mining Limited."

"Aye. I see that." The spectacled man looked at the letter again. "Vice President." He looked up. "You are Janescz Boruski?"

"Yes, I am," said the tall man, dipping his head. The spectacled man looked at him, then over at the boys.

"And the boys with you, they are Plietor and Davik Boruski?"

At the sounds of their names the boys looked up.

"Yes, they are."

"Which is which?"

Before the tall man could answer the younger boy said, "I am Davik." The older boy said nothing.

"You are their father, are you?"

"Yes, I am."

The spectacled man looked at the boys again, then back.

"And what is it brings you all the way out here with your two sons, Mr. Janescz Boruski?" The spectacled man's mouth was twisted somewhere between a scowl and a sneer.

"It is to work," the tall man said, with force. "It is on the letter. I come here to work. For MacReedy Mining. The boys come too. They can work." He paused. "They have no place to go."

The spectacled man looked at the boys again, shook his head, then back to the letter, scowling hard.

"Mr. Angus-McLoughlin-Vice-President says here I am to treat you fair and give you separate lodging, separate—

bloody—lodging." He snorted, then brought his hand down forcefully on the face of the letter. "I treat everyone fair. I don't need Mr. Angus McLoughlin to tell me that." He shook his head. "As to your lodging. Does Mr. Angus McLoughlin think we have flats in this Camp standing empty? Why should I give you a flat, when other men have worked here half a year, sleeping on a cot in the bunkhouse?"

"It says on the letter," said Janescz. "From MacReedy Mining. All the way from Perth. From the big stone building—"

The spectacled man stood, his chair tilting backward. "Yes, it does!" he said. "I see it does." He pursed his lips into a hard line, glared at Janescz. "This letter…" He stabbed it with his right forefinger. "This letter is the last I take any direction on your behalf from anybody, Mr. Angus McLoughlin be damned. I am Overseer of this Camp, and from this moment forward your personal welfare—your every breath, all of you…" He swept his arm backhanded to take them all in. "Is entirely dependent on me. I am Mr. Dobbins. Mr. Angus McLoughlin is a thousand miles away in Perth. When I say something, it shall be done. Is that clear to you?" He glared into Janescz's eyes. Janescz looked back, steady, then looked down.

"It is clear," he said.

"Good," said Dobbins. He looked over at the boys. "Good." He pulled his chair back to the table, sat again, and looked up at Janescz. "Karski will show you what's what: the bloody flat for you, the bunkhouse where you will draw clothes—"

"'The flat' you said," said Janescz. "There is a flat for us then?"

Dobbins glared. "I said there was, didn't I then? If I say it, it is."

Janescz looked down, keeping expression from his face. "Yes, sir."

"So," said Dobbins, then drew breath and barked "Karski!"

The blue door opened, and a man came in.

"This is Karski," said Dobbins. He glanced at him, gestured with his head. "These are the Boruskis, father and sons. Karski will show you your work. You, Janescz Boruski, will work over the Shelf, down in the pits. Karski will take you to the super there. These boys will work on the Terrace." He looked at Karski. "Take them to Bartosz, so he will know what he is getting."

Dobbins looked hard now at Janescz. "You work tomorrow. All of you. All day. Full day. No room for sluggards here." The tall man nodded. "Out the door then. Karski, you stay."

Janescz looked to the boys. The older boy slid off the bench, reached back to pull the arm of the younger. Dobbins snorted. "Welcome to the Arltunga Mining Camp, Janescz Boruski and sons."

1.

A dog was howling. A shrill undulating howl, hardly pausing to draw breath, somewhere out on the street. He heard it through the window, through the cracked panes.

"See what that bloody *psia* wants," called out the woman's voice from the next room. She said the word in her language like *sha*. He had heard it before.

He went, pressed his nose against the lowest pane, looked down into the dark street. A shiny black dog tied to the lamp post lifted its muzzle, howling into the dark sky outside the pool of light. He couldn't tell what the dog wanted.

"Well, what do you see then?" called the voice.

He was drawing breath to answer when the front door of the flat rattled under a hard hand.

"Bloody hell," said the woman.

Plietor's eyes snapped open into the thinnest of gray light. He was on the bed, mattress ticking lumpy under his hips, his left hand numb under his cheek. The dog was still howling the shrill undulating howl, not pausing for breath. Except it wasn't a dog. It was the wind.

Plietor moved his numb hand, worked the fingers to get the feeling back, felt the tingling, then the abrasive powder of dust. He put the hand to his face—dust, all down his cheek.

They had seen the dust coming the evening before, a red-brown wall of mist in the west, the west wind rising. When the west wind was strong enough in the dry time it brought the dust. There was nothing to do.

There would be no flying today, no work on the Terrace. Maybe repairs on the gliders. Janescz would decide that. Wood could be cut and shaped in the dust. But no glue, no fabric work.

Plietor pushed up on an elbow. Nobody on the other beds. They would be down the ladder in the main room, into the morning tucker. He pulled on canvas trousers, a rank singlet, stuck his feet in thongs. From a chest at the foot of the bed he took a long cloth, wrapped and twisted a lungee around his head, only his eyes showing. It was what everyone did when the dust came.

Everyone but Davik. In the main room, as Plietor stepped off the ladder, Davik was pacing the wall bareheaded, his blond mop reddened by the flickering candle light. Janescz was sitting at the table leaning on his elbows, a bowl and mug in front of him. Coals from their charcoal ration glowed red in the fire grate. Plietor's own bowl and mug were at his place, covered with a cloth. Janescz lifted his mug to his lips, almost invisible among the folds of his lungee.

"So," said Davik. "At last he comes."

Plietor took his mug across to the grate and poured from the jug there, the hot fumes fragrant.

"Why should he come before?" said Janescz.

Plietor felt the tea run down his throat. He carried the mug to the table, returned with his bowl to the pot of porridge on the stone hearth.

"We will go to the sheds, dust or no," Davik pronounced. "There is good work to do. I need to make the cable to my rudder tight."

Plietor sat down with his bowl and glanced to Janescz, who did not look up, applying himself to his own porridge, his spoon disappearing into the cloth. Dust made halos around the candle flame. Plietor ate. Davik paced. Janescz sighed.

"What is it, pa-pa?" said Plietor.

"We will work today," said Janescz. "We will work. But it is not good. The light is not true. The dust dulls the tools. These wraps—"

"*Acch,*" said Davik. "So. It is enough that we work. I will tell a story when the mob is all there. You will see. We will get good work done. The gliders will be better. It is not the first time for dust."

Plietor was thinking the usual expression: *Nor will it be the last.* But he didn't say it. Better to work in the sheds, whatever was done, than be cooped up in their flat all day with Davik. Maybe he could go to the plant sheds. There would be inside work there to do too.

Janescz was placing mug and bowl into the bin, Plietor following, when the sound of beaten iron came over the wind's howl, the fast strokes of alarm.

Davik started up. "Go!" said Janescz. "Go and see."

Davik pushed the door with his shoulder. Dust swirled in as Plietor squeezed through behind him.

As soon as they were out they knew what the alarm was for. Reddish glow suffused the sky to the west, brighter than the gray morning glow to the east. Fire. How could there be fire on the mountain? There was nothing to burn. But fire there was through the dust, and a smell on the wind different from the usual rank smell of the mist from below. There were two ladders to take them from their level to the ground.

Karski was still swinging the iron around the triangle at the top of the corral in the Yard when they approached. Lungeed men were slipping down other ladders all over the Stack. Faolán Carnahan, Overseer, tall in his long coat and red lungee, stood beside Karski. Davik and Plietor wedged into the gathering crowd, backs to the wind, glancing around every few seconds to see the glow.

Karski gave three great wangs of the iron and stopped. Wind howled alone in the Yard as the ringing faded.

"You can see and smell it as well as I," shouted Carnahan into the wind. "It's fire to the west. Must be a great roaring thing to be seen through the dust, and the smell is like burning oil. We need to know what it is."

He paused. Men looked around, into the wind and dust, looked back quickly. "I'm sending a party of four men to see what's what. It needs game lads, good on the rocks."

Davik pushed forward. "I'm to go," he said.

Carnahan didn't pause. "Yeh, Davik," he said. "Jump to ill times, as always. Plietor, you go too, keep him out of trouble. Who else?" Several men called out. Carnahan pointed. "Rozum. Musil. Best if it's flyers I'm thinking, with your kits and all. Not you, Fergus, not with your leg. The rest, get yourself up, overdaks and goggles."

Davik was already turning away, pushing back through the crowd.

"*Eh,* Davik," called Carnahan. "Don't be in a rush. Flyers is best to go, but I sure and don't want to lose none to this." The wind whipped Davik's hair. He nodded, up-down, and moved to a ladder.

Fifteen minutes later the four were gathered in the Yard at Carnahan's blue door, fully covered in canvas oversuits, boots, gloves, balaclavas, goggles on their foreheads. Davik banged on the door. Carnahan pushed out, looked them over. Plietor had picked up a swag bag as he went out.

Carnahan noticed the bag and nodded. "Don't take chances, blokes. I just want to know what's what is all. Don't want a great blasting fire coming down on us in this wind. Go see and come back straight, is what. You got that, Davik?"

"Yeh, I do," said Davik.

"I'm putting Plietor in charge. You'll do what he says now, or I'll know the why of it."

Before Davik could reply, Plietor said, "Let's go then." He turned away, pulling down his goggles.

In a hundred yards they were in the rocks, the ziggurat of the Stack, the Terrace, the sheds lost in the dust. The hillside was all rocks, angular gray-black, room-sized boulders down to pebble fields that cut at their boots. They moved west, into the wind toward the red glow, clambering where they could not walk. Davik picked up speed, jumping straight from boulder to boulder, but Plietor caught up and pulled him down, yelling into his face what Carnahan had said: "Don't rush." They'd be hard pressed to carry him out if he slipped and his leg broke.

It was heavy going into the wind and dust, up and over and around the rocks, hands and feet. But there was no mistaking the way. The red glow strengthened, the smell more pungent, and now they could feel the heat. Plietor had his head down when Rozum called out *"Hai!"* in front of him and stopped. A lull in the wind slackened the dust for a moment, and they all stood up to see. A quarter mile away a tall tongue of flame leaped thirty feet in the air, encased in a vortex of swirling back smoke.

"Fuken 's truth," said Musil, his voice muffled inside his balaclava.

Plietor turned away from the wind and pulled the cloth down from his mouth as the other three gathered.

"Let's go easy now and all together," Plietor half-shouted. "We don't want any one caught up." He looked at Davik and was glad to see Davik nod.

They spread out in a short line, four arms apart, and moved forward, looking sideways as they clambered to keep their spacing. The heat and smell were coming and going more intensely now, but they could see nothing but dust ahead and above, rock below.

Davik was far right past Rozum. Plietor saw him move off suddenly away from the line, disappear into the dust, reappear, lifting something in his right hand.

"*Eh* what!" Davik shouted. "Here's a bit."

It appeared to be a part of a blackened metal cylinder, one curved portion, the rest a jagged mess of ripped edge. The others looked at Plietor. He gestured forward. Davik tossed the metal away. It rang against rock.

Musil was next to call out, twenty feet to Plietor's left. He clambered toward Plietor, drawing the others in.

"There's a whole bloody engine down slope there," Musil said, pulling his balaclava from his mouth. "Great bloody thing with shards of propeller. Looks ripped away. Do you want to go and see?"

"No," Plietor said. "But we know we're getting close. Hear it now."

Under the howl of the wind, they could hear the fire, a lower eddying roar. The smell of burning oil was strong. The blowing dust waxed and waned red and black. They spread again and moved forward.

And then it was before them. A tall metal girder rose up from the rock, a crisscrossed welded structure of blackened steel three-feet wide, broken off at the down end, up thirty feet to disappear into the swirling reddened dust. And just behind it, now emerging from the dust and smoke, now disappearing, was a vast radial spiderweb of metal extending out from a nose cone, a circular web enfolding a mangle of scaffolding bending back into the dust out of sight, bending back into the fire.

"*Kurwa mać!*" said Rozum.

"Yeh," said Musil. "*Kurwa* bloody *mać*. What the bloody hell is it, or was it?"

"I don't know," Plietor said, "though I have a guess. But we have to get round it to find the fire. Let's go to the right. Davik, you lead."

Davik moved over a boulder and off, the others following in a ragged line alongside the enormous metal frame rising up twenty times their height, a myriad of crisscrossed girders and trusses bent like a broken toy, blackened but still connected, leading ever backward, fifty yards, a hundred, two hundred. Debris littered the rocks everywhere they turned, lengths and corners of metal, splintered and burned pieces of wood, charred swatches of leather and cloth. The heat was growing intense, the roar of the fire louder, the frame beside them now warm to the touch.

"A shirt is here," shouted Davik, ten yards in front. "A suitcase. Clothes. There was people here." And then, "I see the fire."

The others caught up to him. The frame before and above them was burning. No, not the frame. The frame had been covered by heavy fabric, and the fabric remaining was burning, flames rearing up twice the height of what was the tail of the frame, a pointed completion surmounted by four of what were surely rudders. The fabric was burning with an intensity impossible for fabric by itself, and even as they watched a burst of flame erupted in front of one of the rudders, a great jagged ball that zoomed skyward into the dust, casting its heat back on them so that they turned away.

"I know this thing," shouted Davik into the roar. "This is the Zeppelin, the bloody fuken Zeppelin we see flying high over Camp. And that is gas, light Zeppelin gas. The Zeppelin gas is burning, burning everything." He swept his arm back the length of the great metal frame.

"Yeh. Too right," Plietor shouted back. "It is the Zeppelin. It must have got driven down into the mountain by the wind, burning the light gas and petrol from the engines. Poor buggers on board. At least we know the fire won't go any further than here. We can go back and tell Carnahan."

"What about people?" shouted Davik. "Where are the people?"

"Thrown out, I suppose," responded Plietor. "Or burned up."

"We should look," said Davik.

"Don't want to take the chance," said Plietor, flinching with the others as gas ignited from another ruptured cell in the tail. "Carnahan told us not to take any chances."

"Hell with Carnahan," shouted Davik. "If there's people here, I will find them." He started off. Plietor was about to reach for him when Rozum stepped up.

"Davik's right on this, I say. Maybe someone is alive. We should see. Musil and me, we are careful." Plietor looked at Musil, who nodded.

"All right," Plietor shouted. "Davik, you hear that?" Davik half turned, waved his hand. "We meet at the front in fifteen minutes. I don't want to be looking for anybody." He paused, shouted again. "Don't anybody go into the frame.

Too dangerous, people or no people."

Plietor didn't like it, separating in all this dust and roar, nobody able to see or hear one another. He never knew what Davik would do. But if there was anybody alive….

Rozum followed Davik around the tail of the Zeppelin. Musil moved straight out and away. Plietor headed back to where Davik had found the suitcase.

It was a man's leather suitcase, sprung open as it hit the rocks, but not burned. Maybe it had been thrown out before the Zeppelin hit. Plietor bent down and shuffled through the contents: trousers, two white shirts, fancy jacket, underdaks and singlets, a shaving kit, a belt, necktie. *Formal bloke,* he thought. Sort of bloke would book on the Zeppelin. Where was he now? Plietor stuffed everything back into the suitcase and closed one latch, unslung the swag bag from his shoulder, folded the suitcase inside, slung the bag up again. *Five minutes gone,* he thought. Moving away from the wreck, he saw more structural metal and wood fragments, a scattering of kitchen ware, spoons and forks bright against rock, an aluminum bowl and pot, *bloody dear, that.* But there was no point in stuffing his swag bag. It would be worth a salvage expedition after the dust was done.

The first body he saw was wedged between two boulders, flung like a rag doll. A man in a uniform, dark blue, stripes on the sleeves and shoulders. *One of the crew,* Plietor thought, bending over him, but there was no life there. Two more bodies in uniform were nearby, one sprawled on his back over the top of a rock, arms out, mouth agape, the other doubled over on a pebble bed. Plietor reached around and lifted his head, only to see a great gash upon his forehead, bone at the bottom, blood down the side and over his collar. Plietor's stomach gave a twinge. *Ten minutes gone. Time to rendezvous.* Nobody could have survived this crash and fire.

Carnahan would have to send a crew back, for salvage and to deal with the dead.

As Plietor stepped back toward the hulk, a glint in the rocks caught his eye. *Glass.* He reached into a wide crevice and withdrew a heavy brass instrument, splintered wood from a mount still screwed into its bottom. It was a compass, foot-round glass face cracked all across, but case intact. Yes, there would be salvage, but he would take this. He stuffed the compass into the swag bag atop the suitcase. Time to rendezvous for sure.

At the girder in front of the hulk, Musil was there already, nothing in his hands. Rozum emerged from the dust a moment later. He and Davik had found bodies, he said, three, badly burned. Davik had sent him back, but gone out away by himself, up hill. Rozum glanced at Plietor's bulky swag bag. "Salvage," said Plietor. They stood, backs to the wind and dust, shuffled and waited. Five minutes. Ten. Plietor was thinking they would have to go back and look for Davik, when they heard *"Hai! Hai!* Here I am." They turned.

Davik was walking out of the dust, carrying something in his arms. He stepped up a great rock and down the side, not leaping, but carefully, searching for foot places.

"I got a sheila here," he shouted. "She's alive, she is."

They scrambled toward him, clustered around. It was a young woman, limp in his arms. Much of her clothing had been burned, and with it the skin of her forearms and lower legs, red, puckered, charred. And her head. Her hair hung down over Davik's arm, blowing in the wind, auburn in places, but more charred and frizzled. Musil put a hand out and a fistful of hair came away.

"Eh! You leave her alone," Davik said, swinging aside.

"How do you know she's alive?" asked Plietor.

"She was moaning, like," responded Davik. "And I listened in her mouth, my balaclava off. I could feel her breathing." He looked at Plietor. "We got to take her back."

"Of course we do," said Plietor. "But we've got to cover her up first, protect her skin and her head, keep her from breathing all this dust. There's clothes in this suitcase."

He unslung the swag bag, but Davik had turned and was charging away from the wreck, already down the far side of a boulder.

"We can help you!" shouted Plietor. Davik didn't turn. "What if you kill her taking her back?"

"Bloody hardheaded bugger," said Musil.

They took less time getting back to the Camp than they had getting over, wind and dust at their backs, wreck and danger behind them. Davik led the way, leaping up and down rocks, staying ahead even with his load. Nobody was in the Yard when they walked in. Rozum banged with his gloved fist on Carnahan's door. They waited, and in a moment Carnahan pushed out, tying his lungee around his eyes.

"It's the bloody fuken Zeppelin," shouted Davik before Carnahan had fully emerged. "Crashed in the rocks, all the Zeppelin gas burning. I got this sheila here. She's alive. We got to get her inside." He moved around Carnahan toward the door.

"Not in my rooms you don't," responded Carnahan, stepping in front of him, turning toward Plietor. Plietor glanced to Davik, shrugged, but described the wreck—the location, the source of the fire. There was salvage to be had and bodies to be dealt with. He unslung the swag bag, untied a corner to reveal the compass inside. Carnahan glanced at it, back at Plietor.

"No danger to us then? None at all?" he asked. Plietor nodded, but Davik interrupted.

"*Eh* now, what about this one?"

Carnahan turned to the girl, looked her over quickly, shook his head. "She's not long, and no responsibility of ours—" he said, but Davik exploded in his face.

"Gott damn you, Carnahan. She's alive and breathing this moment. What are you saying, man?" Plietor moved in tight to Carnahan, Musil and Rozum shifting into place beside him.

Carnahan held his ground, looked at Davik for a moment, then said, "Take her to the clinic then. Tell Wetkin to do what he can." He looked over their heads. "We'll talk about the rest when the dust goes." He shouldered through them, looked out west, the red glow down, invisible in the morning light. He spoke without turning around.

"There's work in the glider sheds today, Boruskis. See you get to it. Musil and Rozum, back to the bunkhouse. Janescz will call you if he has need." He turned suddenly. "Off now, all of you. Leave that bag, Boruski."

2.

"So, it was seven bodies you found," said Carnahan.

Plietor Boruski sat before him across the table at the end of the Long Room. Carnahan, as Overseer, had the Big Flat in the left end of the Stack on the ground level. Outside the Long Room was where the Camp gathered on Mid-Week afternoon to hear him speak the Overseer's Report, then back inside to down one nobbler each, the Company ration, which generally led to dancing and singing. But there was no Gathering that night. Just before Karski rang the five strikes out-ringing, Carnahan had sent him with the summons.

Carnahan himself had spent the day alternately raging and pondering, six-feet-two of him, red hair sticking out over his ears, red-blotched scalp above that, perpetual scowl on his ruddy face. He wanted to get more details from Plietor, but he had no doubts about what had happened, and didn't like any bit of it. The bloody Zeppelin had crashed into their mountain. There was only one secure way across the middle of the continent and that was by the Zeppelin. There was only one Zeppelin. And it had crashed on their mountain.

Carleton Dobbins, the previous Overseer, had told Carnahan he would see the giant airship flying over the Camp, way up, on its run from Cairns to Perth. The thing was filled with light gas, Dobbins had said, gas that would burn like Hades itself if it was sparked. Dobbins knew the ship had been given up by Germany after the war, but he had no idea how it had got to Australia. The circular Dobbins had from the Zeppelin transport company didn't say anything about that either, the circular Carnahan had dredged from back of a pigeonhole in the desk that morning, after shaking the desk almost to pieces looking for it. The Zeppelin was a huge thing from the picture on the front of the advert, men standing around it on the ground like bugs. What in the name of Mary was it doing crashing at his Camp?

The times Carnahan had seen the Zeppelin over the Camp, times when a south wind blew the mist north and cleared their air for a bit, it looked like a fat cigar, silvery, way up there. Mr. MacReedy, the mine owner, had told Carnahan he booked on it now and then from his business in Perth to Cairns, seeing to shipping there. "I'll be looking down on you, Carnahan," MacReedy had said. "Don't you forget that."

Lor. That was what stopped Carnahan, thinking on it this morning. What if Mr. MacReedy was on the bloody Zeppelin? What in bloody hell *if*? Because it had bloody well crashed, crashed on the mountain in the bloody dust storm, and now he had to think what in the buggerall world was to be done about it.

The circular lay on the table between him and Plietor now. Plietor's eyes strayed toward it as he spoke.

"Yes sir. Seven bodies is what we found, or six and the girl. But I can't say as there weren't more. We didn't look well." He looked up at Carnahan. "With the dust and fire, we didn't like to separate, and you said not to take chances."

"Aye, but you did separate," said Carnahan. "Davik off by himself found the girl. You said so yourself."

Plietor looked down again. "Well, yes sir we did. But

only that once."

"Tell me again, then," said Carnahan, as though the telling might change this time. "Three men in uniform you saw yourself. Rozum and Davik saw three more. And then the girl." Plietor nodded. "And the three Rozum and Davik saw, all men?"

"I don't know that, sir," Plietor said. "Rozum didn't say, just that they were bad burned."

"And Davik didn't say neither?"

"No sir, said Plietor. "Davik was taken up with the girl."

"Did you and Davik speak on it today, in the sheds?"

"No sir. Davik was going on to Janescz and the other men. You can't stop him when he's going on, you know."

Carnahan gave him a look, started to say something, stopped, scowled, then said "All right then. Off with you."

"We need a party to go back," Plietor said. "There's gear all over, kitchen gear, pots, all kinds of metal. We can look for more bodies then."

"I sure and don't need advice from you," said Carnahan, without looking at him. "Off." He waved his hand. "And close the door fast."

After Plietor had gone, Carnahan sat stewing. Yes, a party would have to go back, and he would have to lead it. A two-mile scramble through the rocks would be a bugger of an outing, but there was nothing for it. The advert claimed a crew of sixteen for the Zeppelin, and as many as twenty passengers, so there was bound to be more bodies, though they could be all over the mountain. It was unlikely that Mr. Mac-Reedy was on the Zeppelin, and unlikely if he were that they would find his body. But, if found, he—Carnahan—would be able to identify it. Sure and no one but himself could do that; he was the only one had ever laid eyes on the man.

But what were they going to do with bodies they did find? Were they to bring them back to the Camp and lay them in the Camp cemetery? Plenty of bodies there already, lain on the stony ground in rock-pile mausoleums. But why bring these back? Why not just pile the rocks over them there?

And what about salvage? Could they take what they wanted? That got to the nub of it right off. And the nub was who should be told about the crash, and how. That was what had aggravated him so the whole day.

To notify anyone he would have to send men to Stuart-town, nearly sixty miles southwest. The telegraph was there and two policemen. Sending meant at least two men, better three, on a three-day walk in the bush. That was a serious risk. The desert bush was a difficult place at best, and though land between the mountain and Stuart had been part of a cattle station, walkers were as like to strike blackfellas as mounted men from the station, if there were still any, and blackfellas and their spears were bloody unpredictable. He could not afford to lose men.

If he did send men, and they got through, they would have to talk to the Mounted Constable. Carnahan had no use for policemen, a bloody useless lot altogether. He could see the Constable riding into the Camp all aflame to "secure" the wreckage, wanting a detailed accounting of the dead, accusing him more than like of illicit salvage, at the least needing himself and his horse—or bloody camel—to be fed and housed while he strutted about with his notebook and questions. The end of that all back in Stuart would be telegraphs out to the Zeppelin transport company and MacReedy Mining, and wouldn't Mr. MacReedy just like getting a telegram from the Stuart constabulary announcing the actions of his Overseer at the Arltunga Mining Camp with respect to the crash of the Zeppelin AS-1, or whatever the bloody thing

was called.

No. If Carnahan was to send men to Stuart, they would have to telegraph Mr. MacReedy right off and take his instructions before any bloody policeman got involved. But Mr. MacReedy didn't like a bit anyone poking into his business, certainly no Constable coming out to the Arltunga Camp. What could his instructions be, all the bloody way from Perth, and the telegraph man sitting there lapping it up?

The more Carnahan thought about it, the more he thought no word about the crash should go out at all. The other mining camps away down the Caldera couldn't possibly have seen it, not with the twenty hours of buggered blowing dust. Themselves had only seen the glow from the fire, and not three miles from the burning. The advert said the Zeppelin was "in continuous wireless radio communication with eager ears on the ground," but Carnahan knew that was just advert talk. The Outback was huge and empty. They were five hundred miles or more from any "eager ears on the ground" with a wireless. Nobody would have known where the bloody Zeppelin was, storm or no storm, more than where it was supposed to be on a Cairns-to-Perth line drawn on a map. Stuart-town would have sent a telegraph about the storm, but nobody would know that the Zeppelin had gone into it. With the winds, it could have been blown off course, or gone way around Hades on purpose to get away. Nobody would know nothing except that the bloody thing didn't arrive where it was supposed to arrive and when.

So Carnahan's thoughts had gone all day, round and round, all leading to the same conclusion. The best course was for no word to go out from the Camp. He had the Camp to run, and that was bloody hard enough as it was, without outsiders poking in. Bags of powdered threnium oxide

passed out of the Camp with the camel trains. Nothing and no one else left, not hardly ever, excepting Dobbins of course. That was the way Carnahan was going to keep it.

Having reached the same conclusion yet again, he got up from the table and walked to the window. The dust was still blowing, but a man could see farther than the end of his nose now. Soon the mist would be coming back, and the world would fix again at the edge of the Shelf.

What about this girl, this young woman, the one Davik had brought in? Likely she was dead already. She had looked bad burned and barely breathing. But he hadn't had a report from Wetkin, so maybe she was alive yet, and if she was, Davik was probably over at the clinic now, browbeating Wetkin about her. She was a trophy of the expedition for Davik, and he wouldn't like to give her up. He'd come barging over with some demand or other about her, any excuse to challenge Carnahan, with three or four of his mates behind him. If it wasn't for Plietor and Janescz keeping a bit and a rein on Davik, he would sure go over the line sometime and Carnahan would have to take him down.

Carnahan scowled deeper at this line of thought, but it wasn't anything he could do about then. What he could do was plan an expedition to the crash site. A sizable group would be called for, ten men at least, with tools, rope, and bags. Lucky tomorrow was Mid-Week, with no work in the afternoon and the evening Gathering. He'd ring a meeting this evening and set up the party to go out in the morning. He could afford to lose half-day's work. There sure and would be no shortage of volunteers. His scowl slackened, thinking on it. He was looking forward to seeing the crash site himself.

3.

"Twenty-one bodies we found," Davik said, "counting those before."

He was pacing, back and forth along the wall at the end of the table in their house, the shutter slit in the window showing the full light of mid-day. Plietor and Janescz sat at the table, tearing pieces of flat bread and dipping them into dark soup, sipping root tea.

"How many crew?" asked Janescz.

"Ten, we thought, twelve maybe," said Davik.

"Some we just couldn't tell," said Plietor. "Too burned, clothes, even shoes. The three I saw the first time were maybe the flyers, from the flying box at the bottom of the ship. The compass I brought back was nearby to them, a wheel, maybe for turning the ship, electric boxes—"

"The sheila was on the other side," said Davik. "Eleven others there. An old sheila, not too burned, with gold rings on her fingers."

"How many did you bring back?" asked Janescz.

"Five," said Davik. "Five we could carry, that were not too bad."

"We will have to rig litters, wood and rope, to bring several at a time," said Plietor. "Some..." His face twisted momentarily. "Some cannot be carried...without a litter."

A moment of silence.

"So, Carnahan is going to bring them all back here?" asked Janescz.

"There is no place there—" began Plietor.

"Yes, he must," said Davik, his voice rising. "It is decent. It is what must be done. Carnahan thinks only of quota. But he must do this. They will go in the Camp ground, with the others."

"It is going to mean many trips," said Plietor. "Carnahan understands...I think he understands, that we must search for papers, for identifications. Sometime, others will want to know—"

"Acch," said Davik. "Carnahan don't care what anyone wants to know. He cares only for production. He will go back for salvage, as many times as it needs. But we will bring them back, for the Camp ground. We will do that."

Davik paced, turning at the wall, paced and turned. Plietor and Janescz dipped their bread.

"The girl is alive, you know," said Davik, stopping in the corner. Plietor looked up at him. "Karski told me this morning. I asked Carnahan, but he told me nothing. He said I was not to go to the clinic again. But Karski told me. She is alive. I saved her."

Janescz looked up too. "One night..." he began.

"One night is good," said Davik. "It is good that she is alive. It is good that I saved her."

After a moment Janescz went back to his soup, swiped the last of it with a bit of bread, got up to take his bowl to the bin.

"You might go yourself, once, over the rocks" said Plietor to Janescz, "to see it, to see if there is anything for the gliders, something you could use."

"Maybe I will," said Janescz.

Almost the whole Camp was gathered in the Yard in front of Carnahan's door, forty-three men, nine women, dressed in party clothes for the Gathering. Julia the nurse was not there, presiding over the burned girl in the clinic. The doctor, Wetkin, would tell her any news. The mist flowed over them, lighter today than sometimes. Three men coughed, a ragged, raspy sound. The acrid stench that so cut the nose was so familiar as to be unnoticed.

Carnahan towered before them on a box, the sun, even through the mist, turning the hair under his hat the color of blood. Karski rang the iron twice.

"I am sure and you are all aware of the crash of the Zeppelin on our mountain yesterday, in the dust and the fearsome wind," he said in his oratorical voice. "The Zeppelin was designated AS-1 and was the sole airship of Colonial Airship Transport Limited. I'm sure you have seen the Zeppelin before, flying over the Camp, transporting it was between Cairns on the northeast coast and Perth on the southwest." Carnahan had made full use of the circular he had resurrected from the desk. Now he consulted a card in his hand. "The flight of over two thousand one hundred miles occupies but a single twenty-four-hour day." He stared at the card. "Bloody amazing, that." Snorts and shuffling came from a group of men at the rear. Carnahan looked up. The shuffling stopped.

"The crash was a great tragedy. The Zeppelin was destroyed, consumed by fire. Souls were lost, as our preliminary expedition yesterday morn determined. This morn I led a larger expedition, a difficult scramble over two miles of pathless rock. We discovered bodies numbering twenty-one, and brought back five, at my direction." A snort from the group of men again. "Brought—them—back," said Carnahan, "to lay with those of our own in the Camp ground. They have been interred this afternoon. May they all rest in peace." A murmur ran over the group. Carnahan drew breath. "A mob will be pulled off other work to continue recovering these bodies, until all are, so, recovered." He nodded, as though agreeing with himself. "We also recovered items and materiel that will be of use to our operations here. We will continue to do that too."

"When are the johnnies coming?" The voice came from the unruly group in the rear—Davik's voice.

Carnahan's mouth hardened. "The nearest Constable is in Stuart-town, sixty miles. I have no wish to send any of you on a three-day walkabout in the bush to the town for an...uncertain result." A murmur over the group. "I'll send a proper letter out with the next camel train, with proper inventories and...descriptions."

"But that's a bloody month!" Davik said. People stirred.

Carnahan raised his voice. "I have said what I will do. The crash of the Zeppelin is a tragedy, for all those..." He drew breath. "I will not make it a tragedy for this Camp. We are a mining camp. We have our work. We will do that work."

"What about the sheila?" said Davik. Heads turned toward him. Carnahan's mouth hardened more.

"There was one survivor to the crash. Davik discovered her and brought her in, as he will sure and no doubt be willing to tell you." Eyes turned to Davik, who smiled and made a gesture with his hand.

"She is bad burned and has taken smoke and fire into her lungs. Dr. Wetkin tells me this." He gestured to the doctor, standing near the front of the group. "But she has lived the night past and this day. She will get the best care Dr. Wetkin and Julia can give, the care we give our own." He raised a hand for emphasis. "The outcome is in the hands of the Lord."

"He better get them hands moving, then," said Davik. Loud laughter from the group around him. A murmur from the rest.

Carnahan's eyes were angry now, his mouth a hard line. He drew breath again to speak, decided against it, then raised both arms.

"We gather inside, for dance and song," he said, loud, with an effort of conviviality.

"And a stiff nobbler," called Davik back.

Carnahan looked away, scowling, stepped off his box toward his front door. Karski rang the iron one solid whack.

It was hotter than outside in Carnahan's long front room, hot and close with the smell of moving bodies, the breath of shouts and calls, the rasp of coughing, the grind of boot soles on the dusty floor. Clothes were saved for Gatherings but washing in the Camp—bodies or clothes—was a luxury. Oil lamps along the rear wall contributed their own odor to the room, along with wavering yellow light. Strange, that other odors should be noticeable in a world where the yellow mists filled every day with stench.

Carnahan's wide table was pushed tight against the east wall, under the now-dark window. Karski sat at the end, three tumblers before him, a bowl of water, a quart bottle of Irish whiskey two-thirds gone, a clipboard. Dancers swerved alongside the table. Karski sat, protected his wares, drummed his feet to the music.

The music came from the far end of the room, four players at their work. A tall, gnarled man in an alpine cap cradled his tiny dorma high on his chest, his left hand flying over the strings, his pick hand a blur. A much shorter man to his left wailed on his clarinet, cheeks pinched with effort. To the clarinetist's left a sallow fellow sawed his concertina, his gaze fixed over the heads of the dancers. Behind him a rotund, rosy-cheeked chap in a checked shirt intermittently *oompa-hed* a base line from a crockery jug or raked a wash board with metal knuckles to scratch out a percussive rhythm.

In between Karski and the musicians the dancers stomped and twirled through polkas, paced through ragged schottisches, gathered in circles for rough mazurkas. Men lined the walls, waiting for a chance with one of the women, shouting with the choruses or with demands to change partners.

Plietor dodged his way to the wide table and leaned over Karski. "I'll have my nobbler now," he shouted over the din. Karski took up the clipboard and drew the stub of a pencil from behind his ear. He located Plietor's name near the top of a page and added an oversize check-mark beside it to others already there, then drew one of the tumblers to him and poured it half full of the whiskey, lifting it up with a gesture to Plietor. Plietor took the tumbler, returned the gesture, and took a long sniff of the liquor, smiling at Karski, who smiled back, and stood up to shout in his ear.

"Drink it up lad, or your brother be breathin' down your neck to double his share." They both looked down the room. In front of the musicians, Davik was arm-and-arm with a frowzy red-haired woman, her broad skirt flying, his blond mop gleaming in the oil light. But he was indeed looking back at them, and when their eyes connected he raised his off arm high, as though holding a glass. Plietor raised his own glass high, brought it down and drained it, his cheeks going rosy with the heat of the liquor, his eyes watering. Karski clapped him on the back, took the tumbler, and rinsed it in the water bowl before returning it to the table.

"Get yourself a sheila," he shouted. "Go take ol' Gwen from Davik there."

Plietor struck him playfully on the shoulder, stood for a moment, then turned and set off down the room, weaving among the dancers as the polka was ending. Amid the clapping and shouting, he made a sweeping bow before Gwen and Davik. Davik thrust her hand into his.

"You may take her, me brother," he shouted, "But have a care. She's a hot one." Gwen let out a squeal and threw her other arm around Plietor, who staggered back. Then the clarinet wailed, circles formed, and they were off into another mazurka.

Plietor was soon lost in the motion and the music, the turns, the steps, the quadrilles. Gwen moved away from him for a woman's center step, then back, with a smile and a warm hand as they kicked around the circumference. He had not noticed she was so pretty before, her breasts so ample. He admired the skin, reddened with exertion, above the line of her bodice. His stomach and blood were warm. He moved smoothly with Gwen, gracefully, the room flowing around them. He hardly noticed the sweat.

Abruptly the music halted, a sudden long chord from the concertina, and the circle of couples was broken by a phalanx of men, pants and shirt arms rolled up, flexing and strutting, Davik at the fore. Plietor knew what was coming and moved to the wall with a spark of anger, watching Gwen retreat into a group of other women. Hoots and whistles swept the walls as the musicians took up a slow Cossack dance and the men began to stomp and kick in rhythm, arms linked over shoulders, a line of sweaty beef turning, turning. The music sped and the men began to bounce, still in their line, the stomping now ceded to those along the walls. As the fingers flew faster over the instruments, the dancing men finally separated and began to jump, to twist in the air, legs flying high, then stoop and kick, each one an acrobat, none more so than Davik. His gleaming hair flew out in a blond plate as he whirled, stood up as he jumped, swung as he kicked. And he whirled faster than any other, jumped higher, kicked out farther.

"Yeh, Davik!" called out men's voices from the walls. "*Aye! Aye!*" women shrieked. Whistling screeled over the wailing of the clarinet. The floor shuddered with stomping. Now the men were squatting and kicking, arms crossed high, one leg out, then the other. The music became a driving cascade. The stomping from the walls could not keep pace, and neither could the dancers, missing a step and falling over, one after another. Except for Davik. Men sprawled around him, one doubled over with coughing, but still he bounced and kicked, his face flushed a crimson roil of sweat, his arms locked high.

Plietor stood and watched from a corner. Davik, this brother of his, what he could do with his body. A man so densely formed, yet so strong in his weight, so agile. Plietor looked for Janescz, found him with Karski at the table at the other end of the room. But Janescz was behind Karski and he was not watching Davik, not stomping and clapping, not shouting into the din. He was looking out the window, hands clasped, peering into the dark.

The music collapsed before Davik, rushing off a cliff of crescendo into a ragged final chord. "Davik! Davik!" swept the room as Davik balanced on his forefeet for a moment, then toppled theatrically over backward, spreading his arms and legs as he did, to lie prone on the dusty floor, his great chest heaving, his hair around his head like a halo. Sprawled around him, other dancers rose, clapping and whistling.

Davik lay a moment more, basking in the cheers, then sat up smiling a huge smile, made a wide gesture with his arms, and bowed to the floor between his knees.

The musicians mopped themselves with handkerchiefs,

joined the flow to the door. In the dark Yard a few matches flared at the ends of precious cigarettes. Women flounced their skirts for air. Men loosened collars. Talk was low or loud, nothing in between.

Inside at the table Karski sat, nursing his own nobbler. Janescz sat beside him, neither speaking.

Plietor came back into the nearly empty room and over to them. "I saw you looking out the window, old man," he said to Janescz, "while Davik danced like a Russian." Janescz looked up at him, one eyebrow raised. "What did you see?" Plietor asked.

"He saw the pope and forty angels," cracked Karski.

Janescz snorted. "I saw everything...and nothing," he said, a smile on his lips.

"Ha! A riddle," said Plietor. "I know the answer. You saw everything in the reflection, nothing outside. That is the way of glass."

"That's as may be," said Janescz.

"*Acch,*" said Karski, smacking his lips over the last of his whiskey. "A couple of priests you are. Can't understand a word of ye."

Men and women were trickling back into the room. The concertina player wheezed a few chords. The clarinetist blew a long raspy breath into his instrument to clear the spit. There was a half hour of dancing to go for those who stayed, Plietor knew, decorous dancing, most of the men's energy expended. He would seek out Gwen again.

"Gott damn you, Fergus!"

Davik's shout from just outside doorway broke into his reverie.

"You can just take your bloody kraut ways..." Plietor heard Fergus shout back. And then there was bedlam as the group of half-a-dozen men at the door erupted into shouting, shoving, grasping, and swinging. The women already in the room fled to the far side, while other men inside and out collapsed on the fighters. A man fell over a bench near the door, bringing down two other men with him. Plietor saw Davik's blond head in the melee, his face red-splotched with rage.

"Enough! Enough, I say!" Carnahan's bellow from the inner doorway across the room rose over the din. Carnahan conspicuously absented himself from the dancing and singing of the Gatherings, but he was never far. And now he appeared, striding out of the doorway in all his magnitude and authority, brandishing a long-barreled revolver over his head. The jostling men around the outside doorway froze in a tangled tableau.

Carnahan stood before them, glared, and waited. The men slowly, carefully, separated themselves, no one meeting the eyes of another, no one looking toward Carnahan. Men adjusted their clothes, wiped sweat and spit from their faces.

"And who is it here in the center of things but Davik Boruski himself," growled Carnahan.

"It was Fergus—" began a voice from outside.

"Fergus it may'd be," Carnahan said, "as it was Nowak last time and Kaminski before that. But it is always Davik Boruski."

Davik swiped his hand across his mouth, squared his shoulders, and looked up at Carnahan. The men around him shifted uneasily.

"Take him home, Janescz," Carnahan said. "Him and Plietor too. I'll see him before me at the in-ringing of the morning." He took a step backward, looked around to take them all in. "And all the rest of you sods. Gathering's over. To your beds. We lost the day yester to dust, this morning to the expedition. We'll make up for it tomorrow. We have quotas, we do, and we make our quotas here, come dust or fire." He half turned to Karski, lowered the pistol he had been holding chest high throughout. "Put the room back together, Karski, and shut the door on your way out." He turned and strode back to the inner door, his boots echoing on the hall floor after he had disappeared into the gloom.

"He'll send you to the pools, you know," said Janescz, leaning over his bowl of porridge at the table the next morning. "For a week. Maybe more."

Davik paced the wall, his steaming tea mug in his hands.

"And if he does, what'll be with his bloody quota?" said Davik. "One flyer the less'll be no good for that. The others can't up take up the production, no matter how the bastard pushes."

Plietor, at his own place at the table, spooned his porridge. "You're right there," he said. It was true enough what Davik said, regardless of what Davik was implying about his own flying skills.

Davik glanced at him as he paced. "So what's the bloody good of it?"

Janescz shook his head. "You can't go challenging Carnahan at every turn, no matter what the flyer—or dancer—you are." He shrugged. "You go strutting about with your mob, you don't think Carnahan notices? It's a battle you can't win, *chlopiec*."

"Maybe I can," muttered Davik.

"What?" said Janescz. "What's that?"

Plietor looked up too, his spoon half way to his lips.

"Nothing," said Davik. "Nothing. I need to go, to see Mr. Carnahan at the in-ringing."

"Yeh," said Janescz. "'Mr. Carnahan' it is. You'll get more with respect than another way." He paused, squinted up at

Davik. "There's no place to go, you know. It's day after day. And the pools…the pools is a way to get to a bad place faster. Mind what you've got, *chlopiec*."

Davik looked away. Janescz got up with his own mug and bowl, stacked Davik's where he had left them on the table. "I hope to see you at the glider sheds."

"Don't expect it," said Davik.

4.

The glider sheds were right below the Terrace, built facing out toward the edge of the Shelf, of the same gray, volcanic stone as the base of the Stack and the plant sheds, the same plank roof. There were three stalls, each fifty feet wide, thirty feet deep, and a single enclosed room, the fabrication room, they called it. Davik called it "the fob."

The in-ringing iron was still vibrating as Janescz and Plietor paced down the walkway between the terraces, the sky to the east ruddy pink through the mist. The wind was light, the mist barely moving. They didn't even notice the eternal acrid smell. The *drtskis* were well at work, backs bent, Bartosz the Terrace super moving among them, the only one upright. Water coursed through the troughs alongside the walkway, threading its way into smaller troughs parallel to the terraces, and thence through gaps in the up-hill sides of the terrace walls into the earth of the gardens. Watering was at first and last light. In between, the heat of the sun evaporated water too fast to let it run over the surface.

Janescz moved to the door of the fob while Plietor walked to the stall beside it. The fronts and sides of the stalls were open, hung with parallel strips of canvas a foot wide, roof-beam to ground, weighted with sewn-in stones at the bottoms to keep them taut. Plietor parted the hanging curtain at the front and looked in. Two monoplane gliders were nestled, staggered side-by-side on their single wheels, the wing of the rear glider across the back of the front. The gliders completely filled the space, only a few inches beyond the wingtips to the side curtains. Plietor backed out and moved to the next stall, and two more gliders. The last contained only one. The sixth was being repaired in the fob, a hard landing by Fergus the week before.

Inside the fob, Janescz was releasing clamps from the previous day's gluing. Fergus had stalled the glider five feet off the ground, flaring too high was what Janescz said. Fergus blamed a last-second gust. Whatever the cause, the glider had hit tail first, breaking the body—the *fuselage* Kemper had taught them—just in front of the tail pieces, which Kemper called the *empennage*. These were French words, Kemper explained, but all flyers used them. Plietor liked to say them to himself, real French words.

Janescz and Walter Prokop had the wings off and were rebuilding the fuselage from the wing back to the empennage. It would be a slow process.

Plietor walked back into the first stall. The gliders there were the ones he and Davik flew, Davik's in front, with a red rudder. Plietor's rudder was blue, all the rudders different colors for identification. The paired gliders had to be pulled out together, but Plietor wouldn't do any pulling until the others arrived—Fergus, Rozum, Karpiak, Musil, and maybe Davik. Maybe not. They each checked over their gliders every day: wood, fabric, controls. It was life or death for them.

Standing in the pink mist, Plietor remembered the first glider in the camp. It had come in parts four years ago, two great crates all the way across the ocean from Germany, with Horst Kemper. It had been comical, the crates like sheds on wheels, each pulled by a camel.

Carnahan had come with Kemper too. Dobbins had

been sick, the coughing lung sickness that had taken so many others. But even so, there had been a great row. Dobbins didn't believe in gliders, didn't believe in "aerial collection"—the first time anyone of them had heard that word; nobody knew what it meant—and he didn't trust Germans. Dobbins had told everybody what he thought at the Gathering, with Kemper and Carnahan standing there. And the next morning Dobbins was gone, gone with the camel train, back south to the rail station, and Carnahan was Overseer. Janescz said Carnahan had a letter from Mr. Ian MacReedy himself.

Kemper. Now there was a man. Blond, but not blond like Davik; ashy blond, straight as a pole and as hard, but a man who could tell a story, in his funny German way of talking. What stories he told: of flying up into the bottoms of clouds, flying over the green German countryside, little villages of white walls and red roofs, church steeples and dark runs of forest. Some of the olders couldn't get enough of Kemper's stories. "Just like home," they said, over and over. "I remember. I remember." Germany must be beautiful. Plietor had wondered if he would ever get to see a world like that.

But all that was after. After they knew what the glider was for.

Kemper had put the first glider together himself, on the naked Shelf below the Terrace, cracking the crates at first light when the wind was calm enough so he could control the broad, light surfaces inside, spiderweb frames of wood covered with tight white cloth—linen, Kemper said—painted with clear paint. Janescz had helped. He had risen in the working order from sopping at the pots on the inside of the Caldera to raking the pools on the outside, to super for the grinding, and then up to the Shelf when he showed he knew wood. Kemper needed someone to help him who knew wood and tools, and Carnahan gave him Janescz.

Plietor remembered watching Kemper and Janescz out on the Shelf with the glider pieces. Everyone working on the Terrace was watching, despite Bartosz calling out names. The wing they bolted together was so long, mounted atop the body right behind the hole where the flyer sat. Plietor hadn't believed a man could fit into that hole, but Kemper had squirmed his way down, only his head to be seen, turning back and forth.

The next day Kemper waited for the wind to come up to fly the glider. He had brought the long rope, two hundred feet, with a stretchy section in the middle, "Gum rubber," he had said. Ten men from the pools had come back up, to anchor the ends. The mist was flowing up the Shelf with the wind. Everybody was watching; everybody on the Terrace anyway, all the *drtskis,* and Carnahan, standing big, his arms folded across his chest.

Plietor ran his hand over the wingtip of his glider, relishing the memory. The tail of Kemper's glider was staked right below the lowest terrace, tied with a cord. Kemper had pulled on a tight leather hat that fit his skull and covered his ears, buttoned it with straps under his chin, not the full overdaks and balaclavas they wore now. And goggles; Kemper had goggles. First goggles Plietor had ever seen. Kemper worked down into the hole, moved the panels in the wing and tail, and shouted *"Fort!"* The men on the ends of the ropes marched out toward the edge of the cliff, stretching that rope into a great V, leaning into it, until Kemper yelled *"Halt!"* A breathless pause, then Kemper shouted *"Weg!"* "Vek," he said, and Janescz cut the tail cord.

The glider just leaped off the Shelf into the air. Plietor now knew well the feeling of that leap from inside the glider, remembered the rush the first time he had done it. But this was something that no one of them there had ever seen, had any idea of. There was a great gasp from the throats of them all. Plietor remembered the sound.

The glider had mounted into the wind, into the mist, up and up, almost as high as the ridge behind, sailing out over the Caldera. Everyone had looked hard, arms up and fingers pointing for glimpses through the thickness of the mist. Just when they had thought they could see it no more a wing came up, up and then over, the nose went down, and the glider dived, dived like an arrow back towards them, down, down below the level of the Shelf, to disappear altogether into the mist. Many had rushed from the Terrace to the edge, thinking the glider must surely strike the rocks below, and they had waited for the sound of the crash. But no! In front of their faces the glider had risen out of the mist, its nose reaching upward, risen so fast that they gave another great shout and turned and craned as it rose up over their heads again. It was now flying the opposite direction from the first, and so fast, down the wind. Plietor had worried it might go into the cliff face behind the Shelf, but then the wing came up and it rolled back into the wind, high like before, and sailed back out over the Caldera. That was the first "cycle," as Kemper said it later. Kemper flew four more cycles before he raised the panels in the tops of the wings and brought the glider down softly, rolling its one wheel on the bare stone of the Shelf where a dozen men laid hold of it to keep it steady.

How many plunging cycles into the mist had they all flown since that day? But that was the first time anyone of them had seen such a thing, and it was wonderful.

Kemper was careful. Before that day was over he had attached a long streamer of fine net to the gilder tail and repeated the plunges. He had brought the net with him, bridal lace it was, from Belgium he said. When he landed, the streamer was wet with a froth of yellowish jelly from the mist, and Kemper was glad to see it. Knowing he could fly with the streamer, Kemper had doubled it to make a loop and plunged with that, setting the glider down with more jelly on the loop than with the straight streamer. Carnahan had come down from the Yard to see the loop with the jelly too. None of them on the Terrace knew what they were watching, how it would change things.

That was how it started. Carnahan sent men to Stuart the next day, to the telegraph. And a week later at the Gathering, after the men returned, he said the Camp would be moving to "aerial collection," with more gliders coming from Perth, and materials for building sheds. And Kemper would be super for the whole thing.

Plietor could hear voices, Karpiak and Musil, and Fergus. Would Fergus be flying Davik's glider? Davik never let anyone touch his glider, except Janescz. But Davik was…where? Down at the pools already? Still facing Carnahan? Plietor didn't know. But Davik wasn't there yet. And Fergus was.

Plietor and Davik had been the first flyers picked by Kemper. "Small dogs" they were, Kemper had said, small dogs who could be taught new tricks. Four years ago Davik was only sixteen, already strong, but compact. He could fit in the glider's flying hole, the *cockpit* Kemper had called it, nobody knew why. Maybe because the hole looked like a pit, Plietor thought. But for *cock*? Janescz said it was for chickens. Fergus, sniggered, said look in your pants. Plietor looked into Davik's glider now, the cockpit bigger than in his own. Davik had grown. Janescz had enlarged the cockpit opening after the nose on the glider had been crushed. Davik's bad landing, back in the early days.

Fergus was arguing with Karpiak. Plietor heard their

voices raised, Karpiak coughing. He remembered when it had been just him and Davik in gliders, and Kemper for a while, before Kemper had gone back with the camel train, and Carnahan made Janescz super. The first two new gliders had come in their crates from Perth, and he and Davik were ready for them. Kemper had trained them in the desert, out beyond the pools. Carnahan had moved men off production to clear a wide, straight strip in the dust, to chop brush, move stones. Then men came every day to stretch the rope. And he and Davik sat in the cockpit and flew Kemper's glider, wiggled the control stick—that's what Kemper called it—pressed the pedals. It was exciting, terribly exciting after their years as *drtskis* on the Terrace. For many pulls they barely got off the ground, learning the controls, keeping the glider going straight, the wings level, rolling on the wheel. Then Kemper had the men stretch the rope tighter, and they got well off, ten feet, twenty, flying the whole length of the strip.

And then Carnahan! Carnahan wanted to fly too. He had been watching. One day he told Kemper. Kemper said he was too big, too heavy. They argued in front of all, standing in the desert. But the next morning Kemper said Carnahan was to fly. It was hard for him to get into the cockpit, twisting and squirming, his knees back almost to his elbows. Kemper strapped a board at the back of the fuselage for "balance" he said. The glider was sluggish with Carnahan inside. The men with the rope pulled hard for only a few feet of air. But Carnahan flew up and down all one morning, while Kemper stood aside, looking sour.

The real flying though...the real flying was for the two of them, him and Davik. They jumped from their beds in the morning to fly at first light, before the wind. When they went fifty, a hundred feet above the ground, learning to turn, learning to use the panels in the wings to land, they felt like birds, ready to fly away.

Musil's voice now joined Fergus and Karpiak in the argument. *They must be standing above the sheds,* Plietor thought. Why didn't Janescz come out and see what was what? If he didn't, Bartosz would come down soon enough. Everyone could hear them.

Plietor took a deep breath, ran his hand over the cloth-wrapped edge of Davik's cockpit. The day they had first gone off the edge of the Shelf...He had thought his heart was going to explode from his chest. Then, after the leap into the air, the wind was so strong, like a great wave pushing him up. He had remembered, even in those moments, the first time he had seen Kemper fly the glider; it had seemed like a miracle. And now he was doing it too.

"Gott damn you, Fergus." Karpiak was fully shouting now. "If Davik was here—" He broke off into a spasm of coughing.

Plietor turned and ran from the shed, around the side of the fob. Fergus had a hand on Karpiak's chest, pushing him away, Karpiak shaking his fist in Fergus's face. Musil was standing beside Karpiak, his jaw jutting. Plietor looked up the Terrace as he ran. Vol Rozum, seriously late, was running across the Yard from the Stack. Walter Prokop, late as well, but in no hurry to face the argument below, was sidling down the main path. Bartosz was rapidly gaining on Walter, shouting *"Hai! Hai!"*

Plietor, slowing, was pushed in the back, a hard push that made him stumble. Janescz rushed past him.

"Cholera! Gott damn you mob all!" Janescz roared. "I am gluing and cannot come. Where is Prokop? And what is this!? All this shouting?"

Bartosz arrived then and pulled Fergus roughly backward, while Janescz got between the men and pushed

Karpiak.

"He thinks he can use Davik's glider," Karpiak shouted in Janescz's face, backing away with his cough. "Him with his sorry landing."

"You look to your own landing," Fergus shouted back. "We need gliders flying for production. Carnahan would say so."

"Davik will kill him if he touches his glider," said Musil, from the edge of the fray.

"Yeh, now!" said Janescz. "I'm the one speaks for Carnahan here. And I say…" he looked back and forth at the two men, at Bartosz, "I say Davik's glider will not be flown today, except if Davik comes."

"He ain't coming," snarled Fergus. "Carnahan has sent him to the pools for being a bastard."

Janescz turned and slapped Fergus hard across the face. Fergus struggled, but Bartosz had a firm grip on his arms.

"A word from me and you'll be at the pools yourself, or back to the pits, better," hissed Janescz.

"Carnahan'd never stand it." Fergus wasn't giving up. "He won't sacrifice that much production—"

"I said I'm the one who speaks for Carnahan." Janescz said. "Maybe we will all go up to Mr. Carnahan tonight, and see who he wants to listen to." He glanced at Bartosz, as Fergus returned a dark look. "In the meantime, Plietor, Karpiak, and Musil…and Rozum, by the grace of God…" Rozum had rushed up, panting. "See to your gliders. The wind'll be up in an hour. We don't want to sacrifice no time, no time at all." He jerked his head, dismissing them, and they moved off, leaving Fergus still in Bartosz's grip.

"And you, Eoghan Fergus," Janescz said. "You'll be in the fob with me and Walter, all the day 'til out-ringing. There's much sweeping up to be done and sewing of nets. And maybe, if you cool down, you can work on your own glider, the sooner to get it back into the air." Plietor didn't turn around to see Fergus's expression.

5.

Ginna MacReedy rolled over on the lumpy mattress and groaned. With waking came knowledge that she was no longer in the clinic, and the pain. She knew when she moved the pain would be worse, so she lay still a moment longer in the dark. But the pain in her left ankle where the right ankle touched it grew great, and she had to move. Then came the daggers in both legs, her arms, her head. She groaned again, trying to keep her breathing shallow, for anything more than a shallow breath hurt deep within her chest.

Julia came every day with salve and fresh bandages and that helped, though the washing after the old bandages were removed was excruciating. *Dear Julia.* She said her name, "Youlia," and she wasn't English, rather something Slavic, but she was very gentle. The all-over pain never left Ginna, though, changing with every position, every arrangement of her limbs. It was hard to think of anything else.

What else was there to think of? Her memory surged back to the Zeppelin, and she pushed away the image. She couldn't think about that now, certainly. The smell. She could think about the smell, the unearthly smell of this place, this house. She had understood from her father that the Camp was bathed in the threnium-oxide-rich mists. That's what made it such a special mining site, made the collection with the gliders possible. But she hadn't understood what that

53

meant to the nose, to the throat, to the eyes, to the lungs. The stench was constant, at once organic and metallic, fecal and industrial, something like sulfur, like lye. Ginna's only previous experience with such a pervasive pall had been in south London on a cold, coal-smoke-fog-shrouded day.

"You do get used to it, Miss," Julia said, assuring her that it was much worse down among the pools, and had been altogether worse in the Caldera among the bubbling pits when the men worked there, before the gliders, when collection had been made with great sopping cloths.

However bad the smell was out on the Shelf, as Ginna had learned the broad Camp plateau was called, it was worse in this house, where it mingled with smoke from the fire, rancid food waste, reek from the latrine hole, and the smell of unwashed men's bodies. Three men lived here, or ate and slept here, as it were. "Boruskis" they were called, Carnahan had said, when he told her she must leave the clinic.

Carnahan. Now there was someone to think about. Faolán Carnahan, her father's Overseer. She had never met him before. Her father had found him when Ginna was in England at Girton College. He had come out with Horst Kemper, she knew. Some trouble with the other Overseer, Dobbins. When was that? At the end of 1920 it would have been, her first year away from Perth.

The pain in her left forearm woke her this time. The pillow was touching it, like a hot iron. Gray light was coming through the shutters in the one small window, shutters that bulged and creaked in the wind, the infernal wind from the north that blew all the time, swirling the mists over the Camp, and the stench. There it was, the stench. But it hadn't been the first thing she noticed. Maybe that was progress.

What had she been thinking before she drifted away

again? *Carnahan. Well, Girton.* But there was no point to thinking of Girton. *Carnahan:* a great, ruddy Irishman who loomed over her in his broad hat and told her she must leave the clinic.

"So you've lived to see this day, have you?" were the first words to her out of his mouth.

Dr. Wetkin had pronounced her out of immediate danger, Carnahan said, so she must go, leaving the clinic ready for others. Julia had protested that she was still subject to infection, that her burns and wounds must be cleaned and dressed, that she was weak and unable to look after herself. Carnahan had stood for a moment, then announced that Julia could attend her once a day where she was to lodge, so long as nothing more pressing was required of Julia at the clinic. He had looked at the doctor, who had nodded, saying not a word.

"There is only one place for you in the Stack," Carnahan had said then. "You'll lodge with the Boruskis. They have a room that may be freed." He scowled down at her, her head all swaddled in bandages. What must the man have seen? A nameless female invalid thrust upon him? He could have no idea who she was. Julia would take her to the Boruskis the day next, Carnahan had said. Julia could call on someone named Karski for help, if she needed it.

They had brought her on a litter. She could not stand on her own, nor walk, certainly, surely not climb the ladder to the second level of this stack-of-stone structure, nor the two ladders to this room on the third level of the Boruskis' flat, this little stone room, this bare little room, with the wind bulging the shutters...

She woke again to the buffet of heavy feet on the ladder that rose to her floor. She knew the sound and was a little pleased to hear it.

"Hai, and are you awake, Miss?" said the man Davik, his solid silhouette filling the rectangular opening in the wooden floor.

"Yes, I am," she said weakly, "though I am not moving much."

"You don't need to move none," said Davik. "I've just brought you tea and a bit of porridge."

Even in the dim light his hair gleamed. His round face was serious. He seemed to fill the room. "Did you pass the night well?" he asked.

"Well enough," she said, smelling the tea, a faint pleasant wisp against the stench. She was on her back. Now she worked her arms under her and pushed to elevate her shoulders, her gown bunched under her, the rough cloth sheet slipping away down her chest. She clenched her mouth but could not stop the sharp inhale of her breath as the pain struck.

"Here, can I help now?" asked Davik, placing the tea and bowl hurriedly on the floor and moving beside her.

"Maybe," she said, "but, slowly, slowly," remembering his big hands, strange hands on her yesterday.

Davik was one of two Boruski sons, she had learned three days ago when she came here. "Boys" was what Janescz Boruski had called them, "My boys," when introductions were made in the kitchen downstairs, before Davik and Karski hoisted her litter up to this room. But they were certainly men, men her age she thought, though their skin was browned and toughened. Plietor might have been the older, his eyes wide below a high forehead, brown, short-cropped hair. Davik was compact, with powerful shoulders that pushed at his shirt sleeves, and the mop of gleaming blond. Janescz had introduced them and himself with some formality, a man her father's age maybe, gaunt and leathery, but with an element of the courtly about him. He pronounced their names carefully for her, "Brooski," he said, rolling the "r." She had given only "Ginna" in return. No more seemed required, and she did not want to offer her last name.

Who are these people? Ginna thought, when Davik had gone back down the ladder. She was half sitting, drinking her tea, the bowl of porridge in her lap. Davik had taken her chamber pot with him, would send it back up with Julia, who came in the mornings.

Who were these, her father's people, in this wild place? She knew that men who worked at her father's mines were recruited from port cities all over Australia—from Darwin, Cairns, Brisbane, Sydney, Exmouth, Perth, of course. Her father sent his finders out to the docks, the rooming houses, the saloons, offering a year of employment, a good salary put up in the Perth Building Society, room and board, transportation in and out. Her father laughed when he said "saloons," but he was quite serious. The men in these places, no matter their qualities, her father said, were desperate, men who had arrived on the shores of Australia with few or no options, outcasts from societies all over the world—England, Ireland, China, since the War increasingly the lands to the east of Europe. He gave them a chance. They signed for a year, but stayed on, almost always stayed on. "We bury more than we send away," her father said.

The Boruskis were surely from the east of Europe, "Slavic," Ginna said to herself, with their names and accents. Ginna had never met Slavic people before, had never met any real miners, just the men in the office at Perth, businessmen like her father and their families. These were the people she had grown up with, all the people she knew before the trip to Europe with her father, before Girton. Then there had been all kinds of new people…and Horst.

Davik came again at the end of the day when the light behind the shutters faded out, ten minutes after the five strokes of the iron. Ginna understood the ringing of the iron to announce the segments of the day, like church bells did in Catholic places. This was no bell, nor a gong, rather a sharp, percussive sound. Five strokes came just past first light, the in-ringing, Davik had said, when she supposed all were to be at work. Three strokes were struck twice, about half an hour apart for midday and a break to eat, she imagined. Five strokes came near last light, the out-ringing that sent the men…where? Back to their flats in the Stack, she supposed. *Where else would there be to go?*

"Hai, Miss," Davik said, his head emerging at floor level, "Are you well this afternoon?"

She had heard him on the ladder, his smell entering before his voice.

"I am not well, Davik," she found herself saying, "but only well enough."

"I will ask you 'well enough' next time, be sure," he said with the barest chuckle, twisting from the ladder to sit on the floor.

Ginna shifted in the bed. "I didn't mean to be rude," she said. "Only the day is long, and I am not…comfortable." Then, feeling she *was* being rude, and that it was somehow the right thing to do, she said, "You must call me Ginna."

"Yeh, then, Miss Ginna, how could you be comfortable, as bad burned and cut as you are?" When she didn't reply he went on. "It was a terrible thing, the fire with the Zeppelin, all the twisted metal, the other…"

"Don't! Please!" she cried, her chest heaving, her breath a scythe. She was not ready for this, but images flashed up before she could push them away: her great friend Eloise so happy, Ginna's own flirtation with the German pilot of the Zeppelin, her entreaties that they fly over the Caldera despite his concerns about the dust storm. Ginna had so wanted to see the Arltunga Camp, to see the gliders at work, to understand the Caldera and the location of the other camps. She wanted this partly out of her own curiosity, but also—she had to admit—out of a desire to have something to tell the man in Sydney, the man from the Admiralty. She was to send in letters in hand, to a post box. She had had nothing to say to him.

But then they had gotten caught up in the storm, and all curiosity, all thought, had been overwhelmed in the sickening motions of the Zeppelin, everything inside flying about, Eloise screaming, the crash, the other screams, the explosions of fire....

Davik was hovering over her, his hands alternately reaching to her and drawing back, a stricken look on his face.

"Oh! I'm so sorry. So sorry. I am so stupid to say this. Of course to remember is a bad thing. I only...I only..." Ginna worked to compose herself, willing her breath to slow, relaxing her hands clenched from the pain, sinking back in the bed. "I only wanted to say," said Davik, "how you are lucky to be here at all. And I saved you, you know. I, Davik, did. I found you and carried you back."

Ginna looked up at him, not able to take that image in. "I didn't know," she said softly. "I don't know anything after...after..." She lifted her hand, all rolled in bandages. He touched it with his fingertips.

"There's no need for talk about it," Davik said, paused. "Did Julia come up today, with the bandages and all?"

6.

Ginna didn't know if she would have wanted to see the Arltunga Caldera had it not been for the men who came seeking her at Girton College. That was something she could think about the next day, to pass the time in her stony room. She had rehearsed the conversation many times before, but now…could she distract herself by setting the full scene? She took a careful breath.

She had returned from town on her bicycle, she remembered, remembered feeling warm and convivial. What had it been, just tea with friends? So many of her occasions had seemed momentous that last term, so many warm. A raven had called as she stood under the pointed gateway arch, and she had looked up to the square tower four stories above her head, all red brick balconies and arched windows, the diminutive crenellated thumb on the top. Four years and the rigorous neo-gothic look of the place still amused her. What had she been wearing? Could she remember? Perhaps her long gray skirt, a white ruffled blouse. That was often her cycling costume. And her hair: she would have been tucking strands of hair in her bonnet. *Oh!*

Ginna winced, pain and anguish together. What had become of her hair, her lovely auburn hair? She moved her head, felt the pain, the bandages. She had never asked Julia. Would she ever have hair again? She couldn't think about that. She must think about Girton, the day the men came.

The sky. The sky that day had been clear blue, set off with the white puffy clouds she had learned to call *cumulus*. Reading Natural Sciences she had learned the names and natures of so many things, most of all plants. She knew the Latin names and annual cycles of every tree and shrub on the Grounds, in Old Orchard, in the ornamental and kitchen gardens. She had loved her hours in the nursery, despite the mock-horror of her friends at the dirt sometimes beneath her nails.

She loved a good deal of her life at Girton, and that day she would surely have been thinking of the last of her examinations, of leaving the lanes and paths of the gardens, of leaving the days of cycling into Girton-town, of drinking tea in the afternoons in the Tower Wing Commons. She felt tears in her eyes. She couldn't wipe them.

She breathed in. What then? What would she have done that day, arriving back at college on her bicycle? Surely she had wheeled the bicycle around the back of the tower to be recovered later, then gone in at the Portress's Lodge.

What had Emily Hills, the Portress, said to her? She remembered that. "There are two gentlemen here to see you. They have been waiting an hour in the library." Ginna had asked Miss Hills if she knew who they were. She was feeling a little flushed from her ride, not eager to face visitors.

"Messers Kingston and Whitower," had said Miss Hills. That's how they had registered in the guest book, representing themselves. A matter pertaining to her father, they had said. Only that.

Ginna remembered a flush of irritation. Men with whom her father did business had occasionally appeared at College, at her father's request. They offered to take her to tea or dinner in the town, asked general questions as to her health and progressions, established, she had been sure, opinions as to her state of mind. Then they departed, following with a telegram to her father in Perth. He would be satisfied, at least for a time. Encounters such as these had not been terrible for her, but she had resented her father's long-distance scrutiny at the same time she understood it. She was his only child.

Ginna sobbed then, a halted breath that wracked her chest, her eyes filling again. She had never known her mother, who died in her birth. It was only she and her father. Her poor father. What could he be thinking, the Zeppelin lost, she lost with it?

She cried, gulping and wincing, tear rivulets stinging the wounds on her cheeks. She couldn't think about her father. She must think about the men at Girton.

She drew a painful breath. She remembered having been surprised that no note had been sent arranging an appointment, wondered if the men were just down from London on business in Cambridge and thought to stop by, as a surprise to her father. She had gone to find them in the library.

She focused her mind, trying to recapture the scene. The men had been seated at the corner nearest the door of the large common table in the center of the room, their bowlers on the table before them. Light from the high bay window opposite the door was coming onto the book-lined walls, the cobalt-blue center panel casting color on window seats. There had been no one else in the library.

The men had risen as Ginna advanced, holding their hats awkwardly. They appeared not fifty, she thought, a bit younger than her father. One was taller than the other, with a mustache. The shorter man sported ginger muttonchops at the edges of a mottled face.

The tall man introduced himself: Francis Kingston, she remembered, pleased that she did. The shorter man was

Whitower. Kingston had asked if she were "Miss Ginna Mac-Reedy of Perth, state of Western Australia?" She remembered that, an officious question. She had affirmed herself, but been entirely unprepared for him to go on with, "And are you the daughter of Mr. Ian MacReedy, also of Perth, principal owner of MacReedy Mining Limited?" Her heart had started beating faster. Was this some sort of official inquiry? Should someone representing the College be there?

The shorter man, Whitower, had stepped in then, all reassurance. All very informal, he had said. He had waved his hat. Most informal indeed. They worked for the government, and sometimes erred on the side of excessive formality. He provided a smile. *Worked for the government.* She should have known something then.

They sat. How had it been that they sat? Kingston had been by himself on one side of the table. She had sat a chair down from Whitower on the other side. The men had placed their hats under their chairs. And then, baldly, with no pre-amble, Kingston had asked...she remembered the words, even now drifting as she was, exhausted by pain and emotion.

"Are you aware of the nature of the materials produced by your father's mining operation in Central Australia?"

Just like that. She had been startled then again, but this time paused only a beat. "You mean the threnium," she had said. "Threnium oxide, to be precise. I am aware that the mining operation at the Arltunga Caldera produces an impure form of threnium oxide, which is transported by camel train four hundred miles south to the railhead in Oodnadatta, where it is loaded onto rail cars to be transported one thousand miles west to Perth."

"Indeed," Kingston had said. He had raised his eyebrows, bushy brown eyebrows.

"I have read Natural Sciences here," Ginna said. "I have completed the course in Chemistry. And my father shares with me many details of his business."

"Precisely," said Whitower. "That is why we are eager to speak with you."

That should have been a warning to her too. But she had simply sat for their examination.

Kingston, again. "Are you aware of the dispensation of the threnium after it leaves Perth?"

"I *am* aware," she had said. "I am aware that my father operates a smelter in Perth where the threnium oxide is purified. The threnium metal produced there is shipped here, to England."

Kingston nodded, a prompt for her to continue.

"And I am aware that here in England, in Sheffield, the threnium metal is alloyed with other components to produce a steel of superior tensile strength." What else could she tell them? "It's something about the threadlike character of the metal. It's terribly strong along the length of the thread. That's what provides the tensile property of the steel when it goes into the mix."

"Remarkable," said Whitower.

"Rather," agreed Kingston. "Your knowledge is detailed and accurate."

The men had exchanged looks. Ginna had felt smug, a little defiant. Kingston had cleared his throat.

"We are extremely fortunate," he had said, paused, begun again. "England is extremely fortunate to have had, and to continue to have, such a source of threnium for the manufacture of this exotic steel alloy. Your father, and the other mining operations in the Caldera, have provided a commodity valuable to England's national interest."

Well, of course she knew that. And when he had begun

to go on about the rarity of threnium, about the only other mining site, in South Africa, she had interrupted, giving the South African mine owner Bekker's name, denigrating the purity of his product, emphasizing the advances in purity from her father's operation, especially since he had begun to use the gliders. No one had said anything about the gliders before that. She had been a little full of herself.

That's what she thought when she had considered the conversation later, for when Whitower had broken in and said, "We are trying to come to a common vantage point," she had responded, "And what do we hope to see?" That, she had reflected, was impertinent. Kingston's face had hardened.

"It is not only England that has an interest in threnium-alloyed steel," he said, a dark tone. "At some future time England may be prepared to share this resource with our allies, but we have no desire that use of this material become widespread, or, indeed, that use of this material spread at all."

Ginna should have understood what he was saying. She had blushed every time she had recalled it, her leaping to what she thought she understood, trying to maintain control of the conversation

"You want to corner the market," she had said, rushed on. "But you won't be able to because the two other mining operations at Arltunga have two other owners with their own ideas, not to mention the South African operation."

Kingston's eyebrows had knit this time, a dark look to go with his tone.

"We have information that another national entity is extremely eager that we not corner the market. Another nation. Germany, to be specific. Our concern," Kingston said, even more darkly now, "is for the potential use of threnium-alloyed steel in the manufacture of armaments."

Our concern. That should have been the key. She should have stopped, right at that moment. She should have tried to extricate herself. Maybe it wouldn't have made any difference. But she had been so foolish, walking right in....

What she had done was to sputter about the war's being over, the world no longer divided into allies and enemies, the Treaty of Versailles, Germany's desperate state. Horst had talked so much about this, at their dinners with her father and her, the days on the Wasserkuppe with the gliders. Horst was eloquent in describing Germany's ruination, the bleeding of her wealth in reparations, the draconian conditions of the Treaty. As to "information" on Germany, she had told them, if anyone were trying to buy threnium, her father would surely know about it.

Kingston and Whitower had gazed at her. Would "implacable" be too strong a word? And when she had halted with that ringing declaration, Kingston had said, so softly, "Would he discuss that with you?"

And then she knew. Not everything, but enough to see her vulnerability. She had tried to regain control, asking what agency in the government they worked for. Kingston had answered civilly: the Admiralty. And what did the Admiralty do?

"It is the job of our agency to find out things in other countries that may be important to England's strategic interests," Kingston said. "I'm sure a well-educated young woman such as yourself can understand what that must entail."

She had felt the blood rise in her neck. *Secrets.* Secret intelligence. That's what these men did. There was a girl at Girton whose father...The girl talked about it only in whispers.

What did they want from her?

"We want," said Kingston, "your cooperation." He had looked at her from under his eyebrows. "We would like to know such details of your father's business as might be important to England's strategic interests."

Her hands were cold, she remembered, freezing. "You want me to be a spy. Against my father." She had barely been able to choke it out.

Whitower had almost leaped from his chair. "Oh, no," he said. "Oh, no. Not at all *against* your father." He had exchanged a look with Kingston. "You may be able to be his biggest ally if..." Now he gazed down at her. "If others have plans for...for his assets."

Then her cold hands had started to tremble. "Is he... in danger?" she had asked. Another look between the men. Whitower had shrugged. "Is someone trying to seize the Arltunga Camp? You must tell me!" She had looked at Kingston.

"We do not know," he said.

She had to stand, to move. She had pushed her chair back abruptly, walked to the bay window at the end of the room, looked out. Two girls in gowns had been hurrying into the dining hall. It was Served Dinner that night. The girls would be early, she thought, then wondered if perhaps there was some ceremony she had forgotten. So many ceremonies that time of year.

She turned. The men had not moved. They sat, staring at her. How rude that was, she thought. But then...

"What if I am unable to 'cooperate,' adequately?" she had asked. "What if my father does not discuss these matters with me?"

"It would be in both your interests for you to discover what there is to know," said Kingston. "You could be...resourceful." Both men had sat, fixed.

Resourceful. That's what spies were. Resourceful in finding out things others didn't wish them to know. Who might not wish her to know? Her father? Or...others? *Horst.* Would Horst not wish her to know? She had shivered. She remembered that, shivering at the idea that Horst could have been an agent of the German government. Horst had been at Arltunga. He knew everything about the mining operation. Could her father...could he really be in danger? She couldn't complete ideas then, neither on the many past rehearsals of the conversation, neither now.

"If I did have information, how would I transmit it?" she had asked, finally. The briefest of looks had passed between the men, merely a slanting of eyes.

"You would be contacted periodically," said Kingston, "with the utmost discretion, I can assure you. We have other...'cooperators' about."

Emily Hills had come in then. Ginna had wondered if she had been lurking outside the library door. "Dining is at six, Miss MacReedy, as you well remember," Miss Hills had said. And Ginna had replied, "I do remember. I shall not be late."

"I cannot be late for Served Dinner," she had said to the men as the Portress had departed. They had nodded, stood holding their hats.

"I will cooperate," she had said. "I will do my best."

They had nodded again, half bowed. She had left them then, standing with their hats. Emily Hills had been just turning into the Portress's Lodge, at the end of the hall.

Ginna closed her eyes in her stony room and slept.

7.

Ginna passed three more days in and out of sleep, floating in a sea of pain beset by sharp reefs. The light waxed and waned through the creaking shutter. She brought up scenes from Girton, from her childhood in Perth, again the fateful conversation. She thought of the man from the Admiralty in Sydney. "Best wishes on completing Cambridge B.A.," his typed note had said. A post office box. She was to send any reply in hand. She had done so, to indicate her "cooperation." But she had had nothing to say to him. Until now. What would she say now?

That Davik came at first light with tea and porridge before in-ringing? That Julia came mid-morning for a wash and application of salve and clean bandages, once providing a clean gown? Janescz came at noon with soup, Davik again for a look-in after out-ringing, then with more soup and bread for dinner.

The brother, Plietor, came once with Janescz with a special dinner, an egg and boiled cabbage to go with the soup and bread. They all came, up the ladders, Janescz in her room with the tray, Plietor's head at the floor, Davik at the ladder's base below, as he announced. She had asked about the tea that night, a strange tea, with the taste of licorice. "Sassafras," Plietor had volunteered, brewed from "immature rootstock," he had said, "chipped and dried."

"Immature rootstock," Plietor's voice repeated from below, though his head and shoulders were above the floor. Then Davik's own voice. "Yeh. There's Plietor for you, there is."

The fourth day of this convalescence Ginna was restless. Julia suggested she try standing and moving around the bed, and when that was more successful than Ginna anticipated, they agreed for her to try going down the ladders. This was painful and slow, but Ginna persevered. *At least to the latrine hole,* she thought, and shrugged inwardly. On the first level, after the latrine, they walked the kitchen, Julia opening the shutters to the wind and the mist, Ginna registering the rank smell with no particular reaction.

Below the block of flats they could see an area marked by a low wall, a post in one corner with a great iron triangle suspended from an arm. "The Yard," said Julia at Ginna's side, "and the iron you know." The block of flats they called "the Stack." The whole shelf of rock spread before them, simply "the Shelf." It widened out, descending gradually with terraces of built-up stone, terraces filled with soil and growing things. Ginna couldn't see what was growing, the mist covering everything, ebb and flow. She did see workers bent over, kneeling among the crops, men walking in the lanes.

"What do you grow in the terraces?" Ginna asked.

"Everything we eat fresh," said Julia. "Onions. Cabbages. Beans. Peppers. More. We grow round the year. You will see, when we go out."

"Maybe we can go out tomorrow," said Ginna.

"Maybe," returned Julia. "We need clothes for you. I will ask."

Ginna had a sudden thought. "Are there other women here?"

"Of course," said Julia. "Where there are men there are women."

Ginna didn't know what to think, what to ask. What kind of women would be in this place? Where would they have come from? What would they do? What work? What... with the men?

After a moment, Julia said, "Women work on the Terrace, good *drtskis*. In the plant sheds. With the animals. One with Janescz sometime, in the glider sheds, to sew cloth. And one," she gave a sort of laugh, "one Youlia, in the clinic."

Ginna looked quickly at her. "Of course..." she began.

"Not so many women here," Julia went on. "But good women. Maybe...not all good. But like men, some good, some not so good."

"I didn't mean..." Ginna tried again.

"What can you know of us," said Julia, her voice a little hard now, her eyes out the window. "What can you know... from the Zeppelin?"

"Oh!" said Ginna, as though from a pain. But it was a different pain from those of her skin and chest. Her father had never spoken of employing women at his mines.

When Davik burst from the ladder into the front door of the house the next afternoon, five minutes after the out-ringing, Ginna was sitting in the kitchen, at the near bench beside the table.

"*Hai!*" he said, stopping short, as a grin flared across his face. "It is you!"

"It is indeed," said Ginna. Julia had found her a dress— very old-fashioned, green-checked gingham, but with three-quarter sleeves that went over her bandages. The neck was cut a little lower than she would have preferred, particularly without proper underclothes. But it was a dress nonetheless. The dress had an odd aroma, partly human, partly medicinal, but aromas were nothing to Ginna now. There she sat, her hands swaddled in bandages up to her elbows, her legs likewise up her calves, a scarf wrapped over the bandages around her head. Julia had found the scarf too. Ginna smiled at Davik, her smile pulling the skin at the salved scabs beside her mouth and on her neck, but she smiled nonetheless. "Good afternoon, Mr. Boruski."

Davik smiled even more broadly, shook his mop of hair, spread his arms, and took a step back into a deep and perfect bow that surprised Ginna very much. "Good afternoon, Miss Ginna. I hope to find you well enough."

Ginna would have laughed, but she truly could not.

Two nights later when Davik sprang into the door, she was standing at the cooking shelf shredding cabbage, water boiling in a pot on the grate. Davik scraped a bench back and sat down.

"*Hai!* And are you well enough again today, Miss Ginna?"

"I think, Davik, I may say today that I am simply well."

Davik laughed. "Well that's a good thing, that is."

Julia had taken the wrapping bandages off Ginna's legs and hands, leaving only those still adhered. Unlaced boots covered those on her feet; brown cotton gloves, her hands. The scarf wrapped her head like a lungee pulled tight.

Davik sat for a moment, then sniffed loudly and said, "What delec-ta-bels"—he stumbled on the word—"are on the table this night?"

"I think," said Ginna, not turning from her work, as though in deep concentration, "I think we shall eat leek soup and flat bread, with cabbage cooked with onions, and tea, of course, sassafras tea."

"*Ahhh,*" said Davik. "Sassafras. Well, all that…is most unusual."

Tonight Ginna was able to laugh. "Indeed," she said, "most unusual."

A half hour later, Janescz entered the door from out of the dark…and stopped. Plietor was right behind him, head down, and bumped into his back, saying *"Oof!"* Then, "What?"

The dinner was served on the table: three mugs, three plates of steaming cabbage with discs of flatbread, three bowls of soup. And where Davik usually sat, the iron skillet, the soup pot, and the tea pitcher. The candle wavered in the center. Ginna stood in the shadows at the grate, her gloved hands clasped in front of her, a smile on her face. Davik sat a little apart from her, on a rung of the ladder.

"Wel-come," said Davik grandly, standing up. "Wel-come to the dinner at the home of Boruskis." He gave a half bow to Ginna. "Miss Ginna has made it all for you, and for her, and for me." He gestured to mugs, plates and bowls and to the pot, skillet, and pitcher, finally spreading both hands to take in the whole table. "For this we are most grateful."

Janescz looked from Davik to Ginna, to the table, and back again to Ginna. Ginna couldn't read his face. It was a smile, but also a frown. Had she done something wrong? She looked at the table. It was Davik's idea to use the skillet and pot.

Plietor moved from behind Janescz. "Here. Here," he said. "This is fine. Davik, I'm sure, was a great help." He looked at the skillet and bowl. "Or, if he wasn't before, he will be in the eating."

"Ha!" said Davik.

"We *are* grateful," said Janescz, looking seriously at Ginna. "We are. Plietor and I will wash and then…" he looked uncertainly down at the table again, "we will eat. And Davik can wait until we do."

They moved beyond the main room into the little wash room. A deep bowl was there, for washing, a bucket in the corner filled with water. Ginna didn't know where the water came from. The latrine hole occupied the other corner, with its small bench to sit.

Ginna heard Janescz and Plietor conversing in low voices in the wash room. Davik reclined grandly on his ladder rung, smiling at her whenever she glanced at him. They waited.

Finally Janescz and Plietor emerged, Janescz twisting his hands to dry them. Davik stood up from the ladder, and they all approached the table. Everyone smiled at everyone, and they sat.

They ate in silence for a bit, Davik and Plietor together on the inner bench toward the grate, Janescz and Ginna on the other side. Davik made a show of extracting cabbage from his skillet with his fork, dipping his spoon deep into the soup pot, lifting the tea pitcher two-handed to drink, with a smack and an *"ahhh."* His performance kept him at the table, but finally he could sit no longer. He pivoted his legs over the bench and stood.

"Most fine," he said. "This food is most fine."

"Oh, it's the same food we eat every night," began Ginna. "I just put it upon the pl—" She stopped, blushed, and faltered on. "Not that it's not fine food. It is. Davik is right." She smiled uncertainly at Janescz and Plietor.

Plietor smiled back, Janescz more slowly, finally saying, "It is fine food." Then, "It is what we have. It is our ration. Everyone eats the same, except Carnahan."

Ginna sat still. *Ration?* "I'm sorry…I don't—" she began, and stopped.

"We take our week's ration at the plant sheds, Gathering Day," said Plietor quickly. "Everyone, the same day, the same ration. Food, and charcoal for cooking. We bring it here, and we eat. It is very simple." He smiled at her again.

Ginna still wasn't sure what was being said. "What is Gathering Day?" she asked, a safe question.

"The week's middle," said Davik. He was leaning in the corner, in the shadows, his arms crossed across his chest. "We talk in the Yard. Carnahan talks to us anyway, says of production. Says of us we are to work harder. Ha!" He wrinkled his nose, as though he had a sour taste. "Then we go in the Big Room, for singing, for dance." He smiled broadly, "For a nobbler too."

"A drink, you mean?" said Ginna.

"Yeh. We get a ration of that too," said Davik. "Just enough to make a whistle. Carnahan is tight with that, with everything."

"Ah…" broke in Janescz, quietly. "Yes. And speaking of this ration. You must see, like Plietor said, we get the ration of the week Gathering Day." He looked at Ginna who was looking back, eyebrows knitted. He shrugged slightly. "It has to go the week." He looked at her intently. "You understand, the week."

"Oh!" said Ginna. "Oh, I see." She looked quickly down at the table. "Are you saying that I—"

"He's not saying," said Plietor. "This was fine food this night, everybody agrees." He looked at Janescz and Davik. "Tomorrow is Gathering, and all is enough. But we do have to have our mind on the ration is all he is saying." He smiled at her again.

Ginna blushed up her neck into the scarf around her head. "I understand," she said quickly. "I do understand. How presumptuous of me to go into your larder." She looked down, paused a moment, "Surely your ration is increased…for me, while I am here."

"Ha!" snorted Davik, prowling along the wall. "You do not know Carnahan. 'No more production, no more ration,' says he, the bastard. He will make us pay—"

"But that's not fair!" interrupted Ginna, only to be interrupted herself by Janescz, who stood up suddenly. "*Acch!*" he said. "We have our ration. We can adjust. It is not forever. Only," he softened, "you must understand."

"I do understand," said Ginna, her head up, looking at Janescz, nodding. She pressed her lips together, thinking that she would certainly speak to Carnahan about this, when she was better, when she could stand up in front of him.

"Heh, now," said Davik, taking a big stride out of the corner to lean over the table on his straight arms. "It's all fine. It is. Janescz has said it. Plietor has said it." He looked over at Plietor, then turned to Ginna, a smile crinkling his eyes. "Besides, I know what the cabbage was thinking and saying to the onion, on the Terrace there, in this afternoon."

Ginna looked at him blankly. "I beg your pardon?" she said.

Davik stepped back, squinching up his face. "Oh now," he said, in a rough, low, but unmistakably feminine voice. "Who's this sheila come looking after us with a purpose in her step?"

He grinned at her, then assumed a different squinch, his voice shriller, more nasal, but still unmistakably feminine. "Can't say," he trilled, "but she's got a knife with her, and that like means I'm to shed my skin and go all to ringlets."

Ginna stared at him, her eyes wide.

"Ha! You'll shed your skin for a sheila soon enough, knife or no knife," said Davik in the low voice.

"You'll be shedding a leaf or two yourself, if I know anything" the higher voice retorted. Davik's face morphed from one expression to the other as he spoke, his eyes on Ginna.

Ginna continued staring, her mouth open now, transfixed.

"What would you know about sheilas anyways," said the low voice. "You no sooner shed your skin than they cries big tears. You're worst than the mist!"

"*Ohhh,*" trilled the high voice, shriller than ever. How could such a voice come from a man as sturdy as Davik? "With your leaves all shed, why what's left of you?"

"Don't you nag. My leaves are me best part."

"That's what I'm saying."

Ginna couldn't contain herself. She snorted, giggled, then laughed out loud, cringing as she did so, her hand going to the scabs at her mouth.

"Oh, I'm sorry," said Davik in his normal voice, bending forward.

"No. No," said Ginna, giggling again. "It's nothing. "It's just…your voices, they are so…almost surreal." She looked at Janescz and Plietor, both smiling half smiles.

Well," Davik, said, "I don't know as about that."

"She just means," said Janescz, "that she can hardly believe them."

"I can hardly believe them myself," said Davik. "Two old sheilas on the Terrace like that, making up to you and all."

Ginna giggled again. "Making up to me. A cabbage and an onion." She snorted delicately again. "I can't laugh. I can't. But it's…screaming." Her chest shook. Little tears rolled out of the corners of her eyes. Plietor looked at Janescz.

"See. See what I said would happen with the bloody undressed onion," said Davik.

8.

"And then he said that the cabbage and the onion were making up to me," Ginna giggled.

Her legs, bare to the knee, lay before her on the bed, Julia stooping over them, applying salve. Here and there scabs were coming off, the skin beneath them red, stretched, thin. Ginna tried not to look, tried not to think what the skin on her face would look like, on her head, how her hair would grow. She touched her head bandages.

"That's Davik's way, that is," said Julia, "particular with the ladies." She gave Ginna a sidelong glance. "He is wont to make people laugh, specially if there's a bad moment, you know. Does this hurt, Miss?"

Ginna shook her head.

"That's good. These places are coming along good."

"How does he do the voices?" asked Ginna. "Whose voices are they? They sounded like women's voices, so real."

"Oh, he can do real voices," said Julia, gesturing for Ginna to hold out her arms. "He can do our voices so we don't know it's not us. Zofia—she's the longest here—she says he has since the beginning, when he was just a *drtska* on the Terrace. He did it then, he does it now, to make people laugh, but also to poke people, to get under the skin, to make them sound stupid, you know, in their own voice."

"*Hmm,*" said Ginna. Most of the back of her right hand

81

was new skin, stretched and puckered. "What will this be like," she asked quietly, "when it's...as it's going to be?"

Julia did not look up from her work. "It will not be as it was, not like your other. These places..." She gestured to the long scab on the inside of Ginna's left forearm. "They will be part of you, part of the terrible thing that happened. But... they will be your skin sure, and they will serve, they will, as well as the rest."

Ginna looked down, away from her arms, felt a shudder rising in her, but suppressed it.

She took a deep breath. "Well," she said, decisively. Then, "There *was* a bad moment, Julia, before Davik told about the cabbage and the onion. We were talking about the food ration for the household."

Julia stretched tape at the edges of an arm bandage.

"It seems the Boruski household is to get no greater ration to account for my presence here."

Julia taped on.

"I feel," said Ginna, now conscious of Julia's silence, "that is unfair, that I should do something about that."

"And what would you do, Miss?" said Julia, not looking up.

"I thought you might advise me," Ginna said. "I don't know how things operate here, how things...are exchanged." Julia glanced briefly at her, then focused on cutting another bandage. "I thought," said Ginna, into Julia's silence, "I might speak to Mr. Carnahan about it."

Julia didn't meet her eyes, concentrated on the tape and the bandage. "Hold your arm just so, please, Miss," she said, bending Ginna's elbow.

"Do you think that's a good idea?" said Ginna.

Julia finished with the arm. "Your head next, then," she said, reaching up.

"Please, Julia," said Ginna. "I have no one else to advise me. It is unfair for me to be taking food from the Boruskis. Surely I can do something."

Julia took a step back, looked squarely now at Ginna. "I'll just say this. You'll be speaking to Mr. Carnahan soon enough, at his bidding. He'll be telling you what's what, and that'll be as it is. There's no asking with Mr. Carnahan." She moved back in, to Ginna's head, plucking tape off the wrap of bandages. "And that's all you should hear from me."

The ladder from the first story of the flats to the ground was awkward, the steps wider apart than those of the ladders between the levels of the Boruskis' flat, and more of them. Ginna went down facing the steps, Julia below her to watch for an insecure foot. The shoes Julia had found for Ginna—light boots really—were clumsy, too large, though serviceable with the laces drawn tight. The wind blew the long skirt of the green gingham dress. Ginna was conscious of the lack of a petticoat.

"Well," said Ginna turning at the bottom, smoothing the skirt, "Here we are." Behind them in the Stack was a blue door. Before them was the Shelf, Ginna's first steps upon it. The mist swirled up into their faces.

"We'll just walk about a bit, and I'll show you things," said Julia.

They walked across the Yard and angled below it to strike the path through the center of the Terrace. Hatted figures stooping among the plants looked up, then stood as they approached, mostly men, but a few women, wearing light-colored narrow shifts, tied with a thong at the waist. Julia wore a similar dress, with the addition of a white apron.

Ginna was able to identify everything she saw: tall corn plants, low squash vines, cucumbers, several kinds of peppers, cabbages of course, and onions, beets, garlic, turnips and radishes, two varieties of beans. Ginna thought about bacterial inoculants, a little smugly. Beans needed specific soil bacteria to grow; it was part of their nitrogen-fixing ability. Since the soil filling the Terrace must have been brought in, the inoculants must have been brought in too. Someone here knew about beans.

But what did they know about fertilizer? The plants all had an unhealthy look, full-leaved enough, but yellowed and a little withered. Ginna noticed the troughs for irrigation. Did the settlement have enough water, for people and plants? A gust of wind pulled at her skirt, pushed at her head scarf. The mist swirled.

The mist. Of course, the mist. Ginna had hardly been conscious of it; it was just always there. But what would be its effect on the plants, the continuous bath in the swirling chemical mist? No wonder the leaves were yellowed. And yet…the plants were eaten. All the harvest from the Terrace was eaten.

The food. The air. The water. All were bathed in the mist. Ginna monetarily felt giddy, a little sick. She stumbled. Julia put a hand on her arm. She would speak with Julia, Ginna said to herself, ask of diseases of the lungs, of the digestive system. Surely there must be effects. Would Julia talk about these things? How did the men—and the women—bear up? If, as Ginna suspected, illness was common, why did they stay?

"They have no options," her father had said. They were outcasts from their own countries. And now that they were here they could not go. As she could not, for a time, at least. She needed to talk to Carnahan about going.

"Look! There's a glider," said Julia, looking up. Ginna's heart jumped. Finally to see a glider! She squinted into the hazy orb of the sun. The glider was not two hundred feet overhead, long monoplane wings angled in a steep right turn into the wind, its trailing streamer of net undulating sluggishly behind it. *Aerial collection.* The phrase formed in Ginna's mind, her father's phrase. How often she had imagined it. The airbrake panels atop the glider's wings were open, and they brought it down swiftly, not twenty feet over their heads as it passed the Terrace with a whishing sound she could hear above the wind. Ginna looked quickly to the Shelf edge, not very far at all for a glider to land on, without going over. There was something odd at the edge, though, a pattern she could not quite make out for a moment, then did. It was a net, a low, wide-gapped net, stretched all the way across the Shelf from the sheds to the far rising stone. *To keep the gliders from going over,* she thought. *Insurance.*

The landing glider bobbled once in a gust before leveling into a soft touchdown on its single wheel, nosing over hard onto its skid for a quick stop. Ginna let out breath she hadn't realized she was holding. Images of Horst landing his glider on the Wasserkuppe bubbled up in her mind, the feel of her own landings on soft grass. She turned smiling to Julia.

"Aerial collection," she said. "Now I have seen it." And as soon as she said it she wished she hadn't.

"What's that?" Julia was looking sharply at her. "What have you said?"

"I am happy to have seen a glider, that's all," said Ginna quickly.

"Those were not your words," said Julia. "And what do you know of gliders then?"

Ginna inhaled. "You said to look up to see a glider, just now. And so I did, and so it was. And...and it was a beautiful thing, with its long wings, and its net." *Its net.* She shouldn't have said "its net."

Julia narrowed her eyes. "And so I ask you again. What do you know of gliders, of us here in the Camp?"

"Who is it then, there!?" It was a challenging male voice, a deep voice behind them, moving forward. Julia looked around quickly.

"Bartosz is super, for the Terrace," Julia said under her breath, then called out, "It's Youlia, Mr. Bartosz. And the Zeppelin lady." Ginna noticed that Julia rolled the "r" in "Bartosz" the way Janescz had when he pronounced "Brooski."

Bartosz strode up to them, speaking before he had stopped. "Hai, Julia. Not so often you're out here." He peered at Ginna, tilting his hat to see better. "And this, this is Davik's sheila, is it?"

"My name is Ginna," said Ginna firmly, extending her gloved hand. The man lifted his own hand to pass across his chin, but made no effort to take hers, and after a moment she dropped it.

"That may's be," Bartosz said, shaking his head. "It's all the same to me, is what it is. You can't be out standing here in the Terrace, though, you know, interrupting work." He looked around, and half a dozen standing figures stooped back down to their plants.

Ginna had the urge to say that he was the one interrupting work by accosting them, but Julia was looking down under Bartosz's gaze. "I was just showing the lady around a bit," she said. "We'll be going then." She turned back up the Shelf without looking at Ginna.

"Indeed we will," said Ginna, setting off in the opposite direction, toward the sheds stretched along the right lower edge of the Shelf.

9.

"That was a very smooth landing!" Ginna called out. With Julia trailing behind, she had walked not to the sheds, but straight out to where the glider perched. Bartosz had not followed. Two handlers had run from the sheds to the glider before it stopped rolling, one to secure each wing. They drew cloths from pouches fastened at their waists and began to wipe. A third handler had gone to the rear of the glider and was collecting the net, folding it carefully into what looked to be a two-gallon bucket.

*The fly*er was still sunk to his neck in the cockpit, only his white-clothed, goggled head visible. At Ginna's call he pulled his goggles down, wrenched a balaclava over his head, and looked about for the voice.

"Here I am," Ginna called out, behind the glider's left side. The flyer struggled for a moment inside the cockpit, releasing belts, Ginna thought, then twisted around to see, extending an arm in a semaphore wave when he caught sight of Ginna.

"Oh!" she called. "It's you, Plietor. I'm so happy."

"A moment!" Plietor shouted. "And I will come to you."

He levered himself up from the cockpit, elbows on the edges, then hands, one leg over the side, then the other.

"I didn't expect you here," he said, finally standing before her.

"Julia was kind enough to offer to show me around," Ginna said, giving Julia, now standing beside her, a pat on the arm. "*So we* came to see the gliders. To see you at your work."

Plietor spread his arms in a welcoming gesture. "So I am. At work," he said, making a little bow with his head.

"I like your costume," Ginna said, as Julia shifted beside her.

"My...costume?" said Plietor, looking down at himself. He was enclosed from neck to boots in a suit of dirty white canvas, buttons down one side, a stain of deep mustard yellow *in a band* below the neck.

"Your suit, your all-over suit," said Ginna.

"Oh!" said Plietor. "My overdak. It can be a little cold in the glider, you know. So we wear the suit. And these." He pulled the balaclava—more mustard-stained canvas—quickly down over his head, adjusting it so the opening was to the front, pulled the goggles up over his eyes. "Now," he said, spreading his arms wide. "Now I am the flyer, in full costume." He laughed inside the cloth.

"I would never recognize you," said Ginna, clapping her gloved hands. "But your goggles are all streaked."

Plietor pulled them up over his head. "It is the mist, the chemical in the mist. We fly deep down into the mist, where it is so thick." He rubbed the goggles absently on the front of his suit. "It comes on everything." He gestured to the top of his oversuit and the balaclava, waved a hand over his shoulder, where the wing handlers were wiping hard. "The glider too, of course." He held up the goggles. "I will clean them better, before I go again. It is better on the goggles than in the eyes, though."

"Oh yes, I'm sure of that," said Ginna. She felt a pressure in her side from Julia's elbow, and looked around to see

Janescz walking purposefully down from the sheds. Plietor saw her look and looked around too.

"Acch. I must go. To clean the goggles. To go...to the latrine." He smiled a little smile at her. "Then fly again. That is what we do, fly again, all day."

Ginna felt Julia's hand on her arm, pulling her away. Ginna pulled back. "Can I stay and see you launch?" she asked.

Plietor's eyebrows raised for just second, then he said, "It's okay, I think. Come to the sheds." He turned and started toward Janescz.

"Hai! Hai!" one of the wing handlers called out. Ginna looked up to see another glider, low over the Terrace, just past their position on the Shelf. There was not much room for it in the Shelf's width. She lifted her skirt to follow Plietor.

"Please, Miss," said Julia, in a voice that belied the "please." "We must go. We must be gone from here. We are not for this work."

"We won't be in the way," said Ginna, moving quickly past her. "Plietor said it was okay."

"He said it was—" began Julia, but Ginna was out of hearing in the wind.

Ginna followed Plietor and Janescz back to the sheds, ten paces behind them, Julia five paces behind her. Plietor and Janescz were in animated discussion, with strong gestures. Ginna saw no need to be closer to them.

Just before the main shed door Plietor turned back to them—Julia had caught up—and said they should stand at the far corner to watch. They could watch one, two gliders go, he said, but then they should go back to the Stack, taking a route on the east side of the Shelf, past the plant and animal sheds, to stay away from gliders, coming and going. They should not go in the sheds. Janescz had said this, Plietor said. Janescz was super for the gliders, if she did not know that.

Ginna had nodded through all this, Julia fidgeting beside her. Janescz stood against the door of the main shed, looking across at them, his hat pulled down.

"I will see you in the evening," said Plietor, waving as he moved toward the doorway. Ginna waved back.

Out on the Shelf, another crew of handlers had secured the second glider and were beginning to wipe. The flyer had emerged from the cockpit and was striding over to the sheds. Ginna couldn't tell whether it was Davik or not, but she was not going to call out, or go over to the door, where Janescz was still standing.

After a short time, Plietor came out the door again, giving them a look and a wave as he pulled on his balaclava. His glider had been wiped and moved back up the Shelf as far as it could go, to the base of the lowest terrace. Ginna saw a man stoop near the tail to attach a clean net and something else, a securing cord, she thought. This was all familiar, the process Ginna had seen many times on the Wasserkuppe, had experienced herself from inside a glider. On the Wasserkuppe it had been green grassy slopes, blue skies with cumulus clouds, soft breezes. Here, the glider rested on naked stone, facing the edge of a precipice descending Ginna had no idea how far into a volcanic floor, buffeted by swirling winds carrying chemical-laden mists. Still, the process was the same.

All six handlers moved to take up the long, thick rope, the elastic launching rope. Three to an end they moved symmetrically out away from the nose of the glider, where the rope attached to a cockpit-releasable hook. They reached the taut point and stopped, looking back at the glider. In a moment Plietor's arm waved and he shouted, "Fort!" *Odd,* thought Ginna, *to hear the German word*. But then, Horst had trained them. The two groups of men moved forward and away, stretching the great V with the rope, leaning into the stretch, approaching the edge of the Shelf before Plietor shouted, "Halt!" A breath-holding pause, the rope quivering with tension, then Plietor shouted, "Weg!" and the glider leaped forward and up into the wind, climbing at an impossibly nose-high angle for a few heart-stopping seconds before nosing over, leveling off and…disappearing. The mists closed around it, and it was gone, as though it had never existed. Ginna let out her breath and inhaled again, suddenly conscious for the first time in days of the stench of the mist, her hand pressing her skirt against the swirling of the wind.

Out on the Shelf the handler crew were readying the second glider for launch. "Hai! Hai!" came a call, and Ginna saw another glider low over the Terrace, aiming at the space Plietor had just left. Two more men emerged from the shed doorway, hurrying out to greet and stabilize the incoming craft. Janescz remained standing in the doorway, watching Ginna and Julia, his face invisible under the shadow of his hat.

"Hai! So you were at the sheds today." Davik burst through the door of the flat in the evening half-light, five minutes after the out-ringing, speaking without preamble. Ginna was at the food shelf chopping carrots, tipping them from a board into a boiling pot on the grate. She turned, smiled, and went back to her work.

"Yes, I was," she said. "Julia and I went out. She showed me around, the plants in the gardens, and then the gliders." She wondered if she should say anything of her encounter with Bartosz, the Terrace super, decided she would not. "We saw Plietor land and be sent off again." She was careful not to say "launch."

Davik scraped a bench from under the table and threw one leg over it, straddling. "Yeh. And you admired his costume, he said."

"I did," said Ginna, smiling to herself. "I have never seen anyone dressed like that before." Davik was silent long enough for her to scold herself for saying something else that invited questions. But he didn't ask.

"Yeh. Fine overdaks we wear. Keeps the jelly out."

"Jelly?" Gina asked, though she knew what he was speaking of. She finished with the carrots and took up a stalk of celery.

"Yeh. You know, the chemicals in the mist. What we troll for. Looks like thin, yellow jelly with hair in it, it does. Like snot!" He snorted, blew out of his nose as he said it.

Ginna cringed, then turned her head and smiled. Davik rose from the bench and began walking the room in front of the door.

"Yeh. Jelly goes over everything. Up here too, but nothing as down in the mist, where we fly for the jelly, nets filled with jelly."

"How…extraordinary!"

"Yeh. I forget, you don't know about us, what we do here. Has Julia told you much?"

"Not much," said Ginna.

"Well, it's mining we do here. Strange mining it is, not in the ground, like most mines." Davik paused a moment. "I don't know much about mines, but it's what fellas say." Ginna turned and smiled at him, then back to her celery, with leeks standing by.

"What we want is in the pits down below, hot pits bubbling, terrible smell." Davik snorted. Ginna turned, laughed. Davik smiled back. "We used to sop the pits with great cloths. But no more. Now we get the jelly with the gliders, like I say, in the nets. You saw the nets."

"Yes, I did," said Ginna. "But I didn't get close, to see the jelly."

"No need to get close. Take my word on it."

"I'll be happy to take your word." Ginna smiled, moved to the leeks.

Davik stood a moment in the doorway, looking out into the darkening sky. The wind swirled in his hair. "Valuable snot it is, though," he said, almost to himself.

"I beg your pardon?" Ginna said.

"The jelly," said Davik, turning back toward her. "The jelly is valuable, rare stuff. It drives the whole Camp here, and two others, in the bottom. Still sopping cloths they are, though they shouldn't be."

"I don't understand," said Ginna.

"Never mind it," said Davik. "It's not something to talk about."

Steam rose from the pot on the grate. Ginna had finished adding vegetables to the soup and was kneading dough.

"Smells delectable, that." Davik said the word smoothly.

"I hope so," said Ginna. "Will Plietor and Janescz be along soon?"

"Yeh. They be soon enough," said Davik. "Pa-pa cleans up in the fob, the big shed, being super. Plietor stays around, moving gliders and wiping. But I...Ha! I got things better to do right here."

Ginna turned and smiled, a blush creeping up her neck. Davik was back straddling the bench, beaming back at her.

"Miss Ginna was at the glider sheds today." Davik had finished his soup and bread and was up and prowling the wall in the shadows, cradling his tea mug. The wavery light of the candle on the table made hills and hollows of the faces of Plietor and Janescz, sitting across from each other. Ginna sipped her own tea.

"We all know that," said Plietor.

"'Course you do," said Davik. "You told me yourself. 'She admired my costume,' you said." He said this in Plietor's voice, so truly Plietor's voice that Ginna looked up startled, to see Davik grinning at her. Plietor did not look up.

"I was just saying she came," Davik said. "First time off the Stack for her, and that worth saying." Ginna saw the white of Davik's teeth, smiling at her out of the shadows. Silence from Plietor and Janescz. "Did you make a good landing, brother, so she could see what a fine flyer you are?"

Ginna spoke up. "It was a beautiful landing, smooth and true," she said, "with a smart stop at the end."

"Ha!" said Davik. "There you go then, brother. You impressed the lady." Plietor bent over his bowl, spooning his soup.

"I do have a question, though," said Ginna, a little desperate to widen the conversation. "Where do you go after you...are flung up? I saw the glider disappear into the mist. How can you see to fly?"

"Those are good questions," said Davik from the wall. "It was you she saw, brother. Have a go to tell her."

Plietor put his spoon down into his empty bowl and sat back on the bench. He glanced at Janescz, who didn't look up. He inhaled, began as if a recitation.

"We need to get into the thickest of the mist to gather the chemical most efficiently in the net. The mist is thickest out over the Caldera, and closest to the bottom, to the pits."

"What is the bottom like? It is the floor of a volcano, isn't it?" Ginna interrupted before she thought about what she was doing. There was a moment of silence, then Davik spoke from the wall.

"It's a waste of rock," he said. "I tell you it is. All the rock blasted off this Shelf here, all boiled up from below, cracked and black, it's all down there. Blocks and flows big as the Stack, tumbled every way, and in among them all the bubbling pits of yellow muck. A fine place it is, and no fooling."

"Have you been there, to the bottom?" asked Ginna, glancing at Plietor, but filled with Davik's images.

"A bit," said Davik. "Not to work there, though, not at the pits. Neither Plietor." He paused. "But Janescz has."

Silence again. Plietor was staring at nothing, across Janescz's shoulder. Janescz pushed his empty bowl away and glanced up at Davik. Finally, he said, "We used to take the muck straight from the pits in the bottom, soaking cotton cloths heavy and carrying them up and over the Shelf to the pools on the outside, for the processing, to get the chemical out. Before the gliders. It was terrible work. I did it when we first came."

"And so they still do, at the T-One Camp, and at McCulloch," said Davik. "But not for ever, maybe."

Janescz and Plietor both looked at him then, looked quickly, and looked at each other.

"How do you fly down there, then, if it is so rugged?" said Ginna, desperate again.

"We don't go all the way down," said Plietor, in a determined way. "We only go so far, as we have learned from experience, then climb back out again above the mist to get our bearings, then down again, over and over, until the net is full, saturated."

"Thank you," said Ginna. "I am beginning to understand, I think."

"Tell her about the wind," said Davik. "She's a curious lady. She will want to know about the wind."

Plietor looked at Janescz, then at Ginna, who was looking hard at him, sitting very straight, her hands in her lap. Plietor cracked a smiled.

"We are able to do this, this over-and-over dive and climb, because of the wind. Our teacher explained this to us."

Ginna was dying to ask about "their teacher," to see what they would say about Horst, but knew she should not.

"The wind comes in strong from the north," said Plietor. "But the speed is different, at different levels, different altitudes above the bottom." He looked at Ginna, who nodded without thinking, then knew from Plietor's look that she shouldn't have. But no one said anything and after his look Plietor went on.

"The wind drags on the bottom, drags on all the rough rock and slows down, but a level above, it goes faster, and then rises up the ridge behind the Shelf, to go over." He looked at her again, appraising. "I could draw you a picture."

"She don't need a picture," said Davik from the corner. "She sees it fine in her head."

"Yes," said Ginna. "I think I do."

"So we start high and slow into the wind," said Plietor, raising his right arm over his head, the palm angled flat. He pointed to the palm with his left hand. "This is the glider, see." Ginna nodded. "Then we turn and dive with the wind, going faster and faster…" He tilted his palm thumb down and brought his hand down inward to his chest.

"Into the mist," said Ginna.

"That's so," said Plietor. "But the glider doesn't have a care about the mist. It only cares about the wind."

"And the wind is slow near the bottom," said Ginna.

"Ha!" said Davik from the wall. "I told you she was a quick one, I did."

"You said she was a 'curious' one," Plietor retorted, then

faltered, looked at Ginna, smiled an embarrassed smile, and said, "Yes. The wind is slow near the bottom. So there's so much energy, there is. The glider's fast, but the wind is slow." Ginna nodded again. "When we've gone down as far as we dare, we turn back into the wind and pull up…" He tilted his hand at his chest, small finger down, and raised it out and up over his head again. "And as we get higher, and the glider slows down—"

"I know. The wind speeds up," said Ginna, clapping her hands.

"Too right!" shouted Davik. Janescz looked up at him, and made a pushing, settling gesture with both hands. "Ha!" responded Davik.

"You see it then," said Plietor. "The energy is always the same. So we can keep going up and down like this as long as we want. And we do, until the net fills."

"Or the bloody wind quits," said Davik. "You don't want to be out over the Caldera with the wind quitting on you."

"Oh, my goodness, no," said Ginna. "But…how do you know when the net is full?"

"The glider flies all soggy," said Davik, coming back to the table to straddle the end of Plietor's bench.

"That makes Plietor's landing I saw all the more impressive," said Julia, looking from one to the other, smiling.

Davik slapped his palm on the table. "Ha! You should have seen Kemper, our teacher, with the landings. There was a slick one, every time. And no catchnet at the edge!"

"No heavy chemical net behind either," said Plietor.

Davik tossed his head. "We should tell you of this man Kemper, of how the gliders came to be here, for your curiosity." He smiled at Ginna with his mouth, but not his eyes.

"She does not need to know of Kemper," said Janescz. "He was just a man. And he is gone."

Davik slapped the table again. "He was more than a man, and you know this. He knew all about gliders, about the airs and the winds, about the wood and the cloth too. Where would you be, without Kemper, you tell me that, old man."

Davik, suddenly, was angry, Ginna realized. Just like that. What had happened? Janescz and Plietor were looking at nothing in particular, not at each other, not at Davik, not at her. Davik, though, was glaring across the table at Janescz. It was as though he had forgotten she was there.

"Kemper pulled you up from the pools to build sheds for gliders." Davik was half shouting. "He showed you to build gliders when they break." Slap on the table again. "Would you be glider super without Kemper? You would be back in the pools—"

"I was up from the pools before Kemper," Janescz said, in a hard voice.

"Ha!" Davik rode over him. "And where we would we be, Davik and Plietor, *eh?* In the dirt, among the stones, *eh?* Bartosz with his fist in our asses? Carnahan waving his pistol?"

Janescz slapped the table hard with both hands, standing up and pushing back on the bench, throwing Ginna off balance.

"Enough! You stop this now, Davik Boruski! This is a guest here, in our house." Janescz gestured to Ginna. "This talk goes nowhere. Nowhere. Bartosz is Bartosz. Carnahan is Carnahan. The Camp is the Camp. We are here—"

"And Kemper is Kemper." Davik interrupted in a soft, but deadly voice, paying no attention at all to Ginna, his gaze fixed on Janescz. "And Davik is Davik. And Kemper has shown Davik a better way. Kemper knows things, knows things about the world, the world bigger than the Camp. Gehlhausen knows things too…"

"Gehlhausen!" exploded Janescz. "How is Gehlhausen here? Do you go to the T-One Camp to talk to their Overseer now? To talk to Gehlhausen?"

"He is a German too," said Davik, "and he knows things, like Kemper does."

"*Acch!*" Janescz hacked. "Of course he is a German. What does this mean? Carnahan has cut off everything with the T-One Camp, the same with McCulloch. We do nothing with them. Carnahan is Carnahan. Carnahan is *always* Carnahan. Kemper is gone. And you..." he poked a long finger into Davik's chest, "are Davik, just Davik."

"Maybe not *always*," said Davik, even more quietly than before.

10.

Faolán Carnahan was pacing, half way down the long room and back, his hand pulling his chin.

The girl—more woman she looked now—sat in the small chair, erect, her hands in her lap, facing the table. The mist-diffused light from the east window formed her shadow indistinctly on the scarred floor.

She had just spoken the most outlandish bloody thing.

Carnahan had known he needed to have her in to him. What had it been? Nearly a month since the bloody Zeppelin had crashed and Davik had fetched her. Carnahan hadn't thought a great deal on her since. She had survived at the clinic, and he had sent her to the Boruskis. If Davik wanted her, he could have her, feed her from their ration, go hungry himself for all Carnahan cared, so long as he made his quotas in the glider. And the Boruskis had the room that could be freed, a room more than others had, from an agreement long ago with Dobbins. Carnahan had let Julia go to her, with Wetkin's permission. *It was a generous act of an Overseer,* Carnahan thought.

And it had kept Davik out of his hair. He had hardly seen Davik over the month. Bartosz said Davik was up the Terrace while the iron was still vibrating the out-ringing, leaving his pa and Plietor to clean up the gliders and the sheds. If that was the way they wanted it, so they had it, as long as the gliders were ready the next day. Janescz was a good super. Carnahan had never had a jot of trouble with him.

The Gatherings had been tame too. Davik came, as he must, and stood in the Yard and listened to the talk, but said not a word, his bloody mouth quiet for once. And then he was gone, back to the Stack and the girl. He didn't even stay for his nobbler. Karski had noted it. Now that was something.

But now the girl was out and about. Bartosz said she had come through the Terrace with Julia two days ago, disrupting the work, then out to the glider sheds and the same, jawing with Plietor on the Shelf, gliders coming and going. Then yesterday she had stopped Gilda coming up a terrace path after out-ringing and wanted to talk about pea plants. What the bloody hell was that? A girlie toff comes off the Zeppelin and wants to talk about sodding pea plants?

So today she sat before him. He figured to send her on her way with the camel train. The fall train was due the week next—good riddance to her. He had writ up a report on the Zeppelin crash: roster of the dead, as well as Wetkin could do it; items of the salvage; explanation of difficulties preventing earlier notice, etc. He was to send it with the drivers, telling the girl of it, so it was to be handed sure to authorities in Oodnadatta. He knew the bloody Mounted Constable would be out to see, and insurance blokes for the Zeppelin company would come some time. But that would be months away, likely not before the winter train. Who knew, between now and then?

"I must tell that you that I am Ginna MacReedy, daughter of Ian MacReedy, whose name you doubtless know."

That's what she had told him, just there, in the chair, looking at him steady over the table, in her Gathering dress—Julia's Gathering dress, Carnahan knew, Julia's boots too, and gloves; gloves on her hands, from the burns, and Julia's scarf lungee around her head.

"I must tell you that I am Ginna MacReedy."

What in the name of all the bloody, buggered saints in heaven was he going to do about that?

If it was even true. What more unlikely thing in the whole sodding world would it be that Ian MacReedy's daughter would be aflight the Zeppelin, and the only one to be saved? But it was not impossible. He had thought it of Ian MacReedy himself, when he first knew of the crash. "I'll be looking down on you," MacReedy had said to him once. And Carnahan knew MacReedy had a daughter. Couldn't talk to the man ten minutes before his daughter came into the conversation. That's the way it had been, back in Perth. And was this now sure and the very daughter, looking across at him?

The girl had turned on her seat, watching him down the room.

"You can ask me anything you like," she said, "to prove I'm who I say I am." She was reading his mind. But then, what else could he be thinking about, walking up and down as he was?

Carnahan moved back along the side of the table and sat down heavily in the armchair behind it. "You can answer me a question or two," he said. "You can indeed." He pulled sheets of paper to him from a sheaf on the table corner, a pen from a pen stand, though he had no plans to write.

"How came you to be on the Zeppelin then?"

The girl drew a breath. "I was on the Zeppelin cross country from Cairns to Perth, the regular scheduled route," she said firmly. "We have—my *father* has—a family house on the sea in Cairns. I was returning home to Perth with a friend from college…" She stopped. Tears sprang into her eyes. She tried to hold his gaze, but then looked down, wiped a finger across each eye. Carnahan sat, his face expressionless.

"How did the Zeppelin come to be in the wind and dust?"

The girl took another breath, looked up, breathed again. "It was a navigation error," she said. Carnahan worked to keep his face expressionless. "The Captain, a German trained in Friedrichshafen, mis-estimated the intensity of the wind, and was sucked in…into the vorticular flow."

Bastards in hell, thought Carnahan. With this girl it was just one bloody thing after another. A German Captain on the Zeppelin was it now? Another bloody Kemper? And what would a girlie toff like this know about places in Germany? 'Freeds-oven,' or wherever buggerall it was. She was looking at him steadily, but with her mouth open a little, uncertain. *I should bloody well think so,* he thought.

"The vorticular flow, was it?" he said.

"Yes…" she began. "The air—"

He waved a hand. "And did the 'vorticular flow' just happen to drive the Zeppelin down onto the Arltunga Caldera, not two miles from *your father's*"—he emphasized the words—"mining Camp?"

She hesitated, took a breath. "That was enormous good fortune…" she began, then stopped again suddenly, as she had before, this time looking stricken, with tears rushing into her eyes and her hand to her mouth.

"I mean…I mean…It was terrible. The most, most terrible thing." Her chest heaved. She did not know where to look. Carnahan felt a little sorry for her, but he just sat, not altering his gaze. And after a while, with great apparent effort and several deep breaths, she was able to face him again.

"You have to understand…" she said.

"I shall tell you what I understand." Carnahan spoke now in a stern voice. "I understand that I am Overseer of the Arltunga Mining Camp, a property of MacReedy Mining Limited, with a contract in that position to provide a minimum established quota by weight of threnium oxide powder three times in the year to the headquarters of MacReedy Mining in Perth. I understand that you, who have identified yourself as the daughter of the owner of MacReedy Mining, sits before me, the beneficiary of a bloody dangerous rescue from the crash of the Zeppelin not three miles from my Camp. You talk to me of German flyers and vorticular flow. But can I be excused for wondering at…matters of co-incidence here?"

Carnahan was proud of this speech even as his mouth was drawing down into its accustomed scowl.

Ginna looked stricken again. "What…what are you saying?"

Carnahan was not sure what he was saying. But he knew he felt that this girl had been sent by her father to spy on him. The Zeppelin crash had doubtless not been in the bargain, but now she sat, brought back to health by his generosity, in a perfect position to poke about and find things…things that no one, no one surely at MacReedy Mining Limited in Perth should be finding.

"Who else have you told this story to?" he asked.

"It is not a story," Ginna said, more firmly. "It is the positive truth."

Carnahan made his hand into a fist. "Truth or not. Who've you told?"

"No one," she said, still firm. "I've given no surname to anyone. I have no desire to take advantage. I am just Ginna."

Carnahan paused, spoke slowly now, in a steely voice. "And so shall you be. Miss Just-Ginna. For another week. You shall tell no one what you have told me. And as to your advantage…" He tilted his head forward, looked at her from under his eyebrows. "I say I cannot be responsible for your safety here if you do tell."

Ginna started. "What do you mean?"

"I will tell you this, Miss Just-Ginna. No one outside this Camp knows of the crash of the Zeppelin. No one knows of your rescue. No one knows you are alive. Do I make myself clear?"

"You mean you have sent no word?! How can you...? I don't understand."

Ginna sat rigid, her hands clenched in her lap. Carnahan sat still, his gaze steady, implacable.

Ginna took a breath, compressed her mouth into a hard line. "I do understand. You...you have made yourself clear."

Carnahan relaxed, sat back in his chair. "The summer camel train is due within the week, and you shall go out with it, back to Oodnadatta, and the steam railway, and wherever else you can talk your way to."

"I shall be going straight back to Perth," Ginna said, her eyes now as hard her mouth.

Carnahan didn't say that riding with her by camel and steam would be the sealed letter reciting the full report of the Zeppelin crash, and with it an account of all the generosity of the Camp in bringing this precious girl back from near-death and seeing to her welfare while she awaited transportation. Wetkin could put his oar in on that, and Janescz Boruski too. The girl could say whatever she liked in Perth, if to Perth she went. The letter would deny her.

"That's it, then," said Carnahan, shifting his sheets back to the corner of the table, the pen to the pen stand. "We shall extend our generosity of your lodging until the coming of the camel train. You may cavort with Boruskis as you like of the evenings in the Stack."

"Cavort!" said Ginna, sitting fully erect now, her eyes flashing. But Carnahan was going steadily on.

"I'm sure Davik is the most gracious host." Ginna started to rise from the chair, to face down the insult. *"But,"* said Carnahan, loudly, halting her rise, "You shall not go about on the Terrace or among any of the sheds. *Not,* you understand. We have our work here, every man…and woman. Everything we do supports production. We cannot have those who have work interrupted by one who does not."

"But…" Ginna began. Carnahan raised both hands, palms out, beside his shoulders, as if he wouldn't entertain any other comment, but Ginna was undeterred. "You are making me a prisoner!" she said.

Carnahan scowled more deeply than before.

"Far from it. You have, as I have said it, the full entertainment of—"

"Boruskis," Ginna shot back. "I know. Boruskis. And while we are speaking of Boruskis…." Carnahan gave her a warning look, but she continued.

"It is not fair, not just, that they should get no greater ration of food because of me. It is—"

Carnahan shot up from his chair, scraping it violently backward. Even across the wide table, he towered over Ginna. The sun behind him turned the girdle of ragged red hair above his ears to brazen copper. His pate gleamed.

"Do not speak to me of what is just. This is a working Camp. We are fifty-three souls, and we make for ourselves. Every one produces. Every one has work. There is no extra—for you, for me, for any one—no store of things to draw at convenience. The Boruskis have their ration. That is the end of it."

"But—" said Ginna.

"The *end!*" shouted Carnahan. He glared at her. "Do I have to send Karski with you, up the ladders?"

"No," said Ginna, softly, her head upright. "You do not."

11.

Ginna turned, walked firmly across the room and pulled the blue door open without looking back at Carnahan, closing it behind her, the latch dropping into place. She gathered her skirt and walked across the front of the Stack to the main ladder, mounted it hand and foot, her skirt now blowing in the wind, the mist swirling past. She stepped off the ladder at the first level and turned right, not pausing or hesitating until she came to the Boruskis' door. She didn't know if anyone was watching her. It seemed incredible that no one should know what had transpired between her and Carnahan. But who could know? And what would they think if they did? Was she surrounded by enemies here? Or only Carnahan? Or was it just that everyone was so desperately hard at work, driven remorselessly by their quotas, focused exclusively on "production."

Inside the Boruskis' door she leaned her forehead on the rough surface. How could Carnahan have sent no notice of the crash of the Zeppelin? Of course, he had not known who she was. But the whole world would be wondering at such a disappearance. *Did no one know? No one? Could the Outback simply swallow up a Zeppelin? How could my father not know that I'm alive? How could he think...?*

She should have told the doctor, Wetkin, who she was, told Julia, told someone, as soon as she could speak. But she was in such agony, in and out of awareness for days. And when she could have spoken something had held her back, some sensibility with Julia, and then with the Boruskis, some warning that the fragile comfort of their house would be irretrievably altered if she announced herself.

Now she must go, and no one must know. She opened the door and stood in the gap, the wind swirling her scarf, surveying the scene on the Shelf before her. She saw the lumps of stooped figures in the Terrace below, Bartosz striding out from the animal shed. Four men surrounded a newly-landed glider below the Terrace. She couldn't see the edge of the Shelf below that, nothing but the swirling yellow-white of the mist.

She knew that behind her, back of the Shelf and down the stony path to the desert floor outside the Caldera, men labored around pools, evaporating the hydrochloric acid solution, gathering the caked oxide to be crushed into powder, loaded into bags, hoisted to the backs of camels to be carried the many days to the rail head in Oodnadatta. She had never seen a camel train. But she would soon.

She drew in her breath at the suddenness of the image, saw herself in the next frame hoisted on the back of a camel beside bags of powder. Or...a thought more than an image...would she be expected to walk? Now a new frame: the blazing desert stretching out to the horizon. She had never been in the desert, only seen it from the Zeppelin. What was it like to walk there? She had no serious boots. Only this one dress, and it was not hers. Would she have to give it back? She had no hat, only the scarf for her head. What would she wear to leave this place? How could she not have thought of that before? How could she walk...walk...walk days in the desert, under the sun?

Tears welled in Ginna's eyes. She tried to think of the

camel train. The camel drivers were Pashtun tribesmen she knew, from the lands to the northwest of British India. "Afghans," her father called them, "toughest men on earth." Were they the ones with the great mustaches? She had seen pictures of Indian men with fierce eyes, turbans, wide black mustaches. Were they Afghans? "Best men with camels," her father said.

Her father. She thought of him in his office with the tall copper ceiling, his wide mahogany desk, his waistcoat and collar. He would have spoken of the Afghans through his own sandy mustache, pointing a finger for emphasis. What was he doing now, thinking of her...lost? What would he do if he knew of Carnahan's speech, his threat? But he did not know, could not know. And now she was to ride or walk across the desert with these camel men, alone, for days, many days, weeks. She shuddered, and her breath turned to a sob.

"NO!" shouted Davik. He brought his fist down hard on the table. Bowls and plates jumped. A mug bounced over, spreading a stain of tea despite Plietor's quick hand.

Ginna had been grateful that Davik had not come back to the Stack by himself just after out-ringing, as he usually did. She knew he would ask right away about her "talk-to" with Carnahan, and she had decided she must put him off if she could. She had no idea what he might know already about the conversation, but she did not want to speak alone with him about it, not without Janescz and Plietor. She had fretted about it all the day. There was not much else to do. Julia had not come back since the day they had gone out together.

When the three had arrived, their greeting had been strained, Davik speaking hardly at all, casting repeated quick looks at Janescz, Janescz returning them with warning eyebrows, *some kind of pact among them,* thought Ginna.

At the table Davik had drunk his soup from the pot without touching the spoon, ripped at his bread, then pivoted off the bench and moved to pace the wall, kicking at the corners as he turned. Janescz ate with studied care, Plietor with his head down, concentrating in his soup. Finally Janescz had pushed his bowl and mug away.

He had half-turned to Ginna on the bench beside him and nodded in his courtly way, held her eyes. "We will speak now of your interview with Mr. Carnahan," he had said. "It is time for that." Davik snorted loudly from the corner. Plietor looked up quickly, then back down.

Ginna was looking away from Janescz, smoothing her skirt in her lap, sitting up straight. What could she tell them?

"Mr. Carnahan has decided that I am to go out with the camel train next week when it comes, out and back to Oodnadatta," she said.

"NO!"

Davik had leaped back to the table, pounding his fist. "He cannot do this. He can not. I, Davik, say he can not." He glared at Janescz, glanced at Plietor. "It is impossible."

"Why is it impossible?" said Janescz evenly.

Davik stood, sucked in his breath. "No woman could walk the desert to Oodnadatta. You know this. You know what he wants. You know what must be done." He was puffing like a horse. The others were silent.

"You did," said Janescz.

"Did?" Davik stopped for a moment. "What is 'did' here?" What do you say?"

"You walked the desert from Oodnadatta," said Janescz, in the same even voice.

Davik was silent.

"You and Plietor," continued Janescz. "Barely eleven years you were. A small boy. You rode the camel, but the camel walked. Twenty-five days. Do you remember?"

"I was..." began Davik, still loud, but then, "Yes, I remember. It was hot, hotter than anything. I was thirsty, all the time thirsty. Sleeping on the ground with the camels... What are you saying?"

"I am saying," said Janescz, "that you rode the camel twenty-five days from Oodnadatta at eleven years. You were hot. You were thirsty. You slept on the ground with the camel. And yet you are here. It can be done."

"It will make a great difference to be able to ride a camel," said Ginna.

Davik turned on her. "How can you know?" he said, loud again. "How can you know? One month it is, I brought you from the Zeppelin, carried you across the rocks, so black-burned..." He bit his lower lip, inhaled and continued. "Your breath was...nothing, almost. I brought you to Carnahan in these arms..." He held out his arms before her, shaking them, fists clenched, "and you know what he said? Do you know?" He stared fiercely at her.

"Leave it!" said Janescz loudly.

"No!" shouted Davik. "It is Carnahan. It is what he is. He said..."

"We know what Carnahan said!" Plietor jerked up from the bench. "I was there too. We all stood before Carnahan, you, me, Rozum, Musil. Carnahan said what he said, but he sent her to the clinic. That's what he *did*. And Wetkin did his work. And here she is." Plietor stretched out his arm, his finger pointing at Ginna. "You see her here."

"We do not know what Carnahan wants," said Janescz. "We do not."

Davik stood, biting his lips, puffing in and out. Then he

took a step to the table, leaned over on his arms out straight
under him, looked at Janescz, at Plietor.

"This—I—do—know," he said. "I know what *Davik*
wants. If she goes, I go with her, with the camels. I go with
her to Oodnadatta. To see she is safe. This I *will* do." Finally,
he looked at Ginna, then away.

12.

Plietor pulled back on the control stick and felt the weight in his stomach, his chest. He could see nothing to tell him the nose of the glider was rising from the dive, only feel the weight. The sound of the wind was muted by the balaclava over his ears, the force of it diverted by the goggles. Only the vibration of the glider, like a tense string, told him how fast he was going, and the response to the gusts, a quick lurch left or right. He focused on holding steady, countering the lurches with instinctive motions of the stick, holding the pedals firm. He would be out of the mist in a few seconds. Above his head he sensed a brightening, and glanced up, relieved— every time, relieved.

Abruptly the mists dissipated and he could see, see that he was rising at a steep angle and banked to the right. You could never tell the orientation, in the mist. The tension in the glider relaxed as it slowed, and he pushed the stick forward and to the left, leveling the wings, bringing the nose down, feeling now the wind under him as an upwelling.

The surrounding mountain wrapped the horizon more than a mile on either side, still massive above his height. He was half way across, two miles from the Shelf, a safe distance, with the wind strong. Plietor rocked the stick and the pedals as he completed his rise into the wind, sensing the response of the glider, gauging the fullness of the net. Another dive was possible. Maybe two.

Floating for just a moment at the top of his climb, he thought of Davik. Davik had behaved as normal this morning, out to the sheds and the inspection of the gliders as any other day. No one had spoken of yesterday. Ginna had not come down for porridge. But some other days she did not.

What was in Davik's head? How could he think to leave the Camp, to go with Ginna and the camels? *Carnahan.* How could Davik confront Carnahan? Plietor drew a deep breath through the balaclava, the taste of the mist sour in his mouth. *Carnahan. Always Carnahan.* Plietor pushed the stick forward to the left, watched the nose drop, the right wing come up, the horizon rotate as he pressed the left pedal, felt the lightness in his chest. The mist rose, swirled around him, then blotted out everything.

Plietor saw the green dress from the corner of his eye. He was low over the Terrace in the final moments of the landing, his left and right hands moving on the airbrake handle and control stick, his feet busy on the pedals. Another glider sat canted on the east side. His own glider slewed with the gusts, dragged by the full net.

Ginna was standing at the corner of the sheds, looking up as he passed over. He forced his attention back forward, down, gauging the sink, the Shelf rising up, the edge with the catchnet approaching. His wheel hit and the stone rushed under him as he pushed the stick forward, driving the nose down on the skid, feeling the rasp of iron on stone. The glider slowed, the tail lifting for just a moment, then settling as the glider stopped, angling down on the right wingtip into the handler's hands. Plietor let out his breath.

"Davik's sheila's over to the sheds." Simcas, the handler, had walked down the wing to give him the news.

"Yeh," said Plietor, pulling at his goggles and balaclava. "I saw her as I passed over."

"Janescz is gone away back to the Stack," said Simcas.

Plietor glanced at him, then wrenched the belts apart, levered himself up on his elbows, keeping his voice matter-of-fact. "What's that about, then?"

"Nothing I know," said Simcas. "The sheila and him had a chat, then off he goes."

"What's that glider doing over there?"

"It's Davik's glider," said Simcas. "He's gone-like too."

"Bloody hell!" said Plietor. Simcas was smiling a twisted smile at him as Plietor turned and hurried to the shed.

"I didn't know what else to do," said Ginna. She and Plietor had moved far around the corner of the shed, away from any comings and goings in front. "He came in all of a sudden, just after the first midday ringing. He didn't have his oversuit on, only his ordinary clothes, and he hardly gave me a look. He went right up the ladder, I heard him throwing things around, then he came down in heavy boots. I thought the ladder would break."

Her hands were clenched high on her chest, her face raised. But Plietor was looking out to the Shelf. Another glider was coming in. There would be no room for a fourth to land.

He turned back to Ginna. "Did he say anything?"

"Only one thing. As he passed through the kitchen, he turned to me and said, 'I am doing this,' and made a fist. Just that. Do you know what it means?"

Plietor shook his head.

"So I came down here to the sheds. Carnahan told me not to go out, but I thought I must, to be sure you knew."

Plietor blinked. *Carnahan had told her not to go out?*

"You were in the air, so I told Janescz," said Ginna.

"And he went to the Stack to see for himself," said Plietor under his breath, "and now comes back again."

Janescz was hurrying down the main Terrace path to the launch area. He sailed into the handlers and men jumped, two breaking off and heading toward Davik's glider, two rolling Plietor's to clear a landing space.

"I must go," said Plietor, his voice urgent. "Go into the fob and stay there. Find a corner and sit. Don't go back to the Stack until I come." Ginna nodded, gathering her skirt to follow him.

"He is not here!" Janescz roared at Plietor, as Plietor approached his blue-tailed glider. Davik's red-tail had been rolled into their shed, Plietor's glider staged in its place for launch. A fourth glider had landed. Handlers bustled over the Shelf. "He is not! Where is the bloody *bachor*? Do you know?"

"No," returned Plietor. "Only what Ginna tells me." Janescz looked toward the sheds. "I told her to go sit in a corner in the fob. Carnahan told her not to be about."

"*Cholera!*" said Janescz. "Bloody Carnahan. We'll never make our quota today, and then what will it be with Davik and Carnahan."

"Maybe the rest of us can make up," said Plietor. Janescz looked at him. "Go deeper on the dives, fewer dives to a full net, faster on the Shelf."

"Going deeper is no good," said Janescz. "Too much risk."

"One second more," said Plietor. "We have a margin. Just for today. And you make the Shelf faster."

Janescz looked back at the sheds, at the gliders on the Shelf. He shook his head. "We will do it, just for today," he said. "Then the *bachor* comes back, or..." He pursed his lips. "Only one second more, you know?" Plietor was already pulling on his balaclava.

"Karolyi said he saw him go over the edge, down the old path to the pits."

Plietor and Janescz sat at the table, slumped on their elbows. Mustardy stains splotched Plietor's face below the eyes. Ginna was pouring water at the grate, dishes stacked beside her. She turned quickly. Plietor sat up. Janescz had spoken, the first words since they had sat down.

"When did you hear this?" said Plietor.

"In the sheds, after the gliders were all rolled in," said Janescz. "He saw it, during the midday, nobody about on the Terrace. Davik came down past the animal sheds, quick, and went over the edge on the path."

"Why did Karolyi wait the whole afternoon to tell you?"

"He was working too hard, he said." Janescz snorted, then sighed. "No matter. Nothing different, if I had known."

"Can I ask what this means?" said Ginna, coming back to the table.

"We do not know what it means," said Plietor, glancing at Janescz.

"Where does the path go?"

"Down to the pits, where the muck was gathered with cloths, before the gliders," said Plietor.

"I remember," said Ginna. "You said it was a bad place, great rocks and stench. Why would Davik go there?"

Plietor looked at Janescz. Neither spoke.

"Does the path go anywhere else?" asked Ginna.

Janescz looked away. "It winds the floor of the Caldera, through rocks...rocks and pits..." He paused. "It goes to the other camps."

Plietor was using the latrine behind the main room when he heard the tread of Davik's boots from the outside door. It was full night. Ginna had climbed the ladders to her room. Janescz sat at the table, his face craggy in the candle light, working blocks of wood with a knife and small saw, fittings for Fergus's glider. Plietor took up a cloth, wiping his face as he moved back into the kitchen. Janescz didn't look up as Davik came through the door.

"So," said Janescz.

"'So' to you," said Davik. "Is there food? I am hungry as the bear."

"What do you know of the bear?" said Janescz.

Davik pulled the outer bench and sat down. "So I am just hungry. Is there food, or has my ration gone to others?"

"There is food for you," said Janescz, 'but you must make it for yourself. We did not know to make it for you. No one told us."

Davik rolled his leg over the bench and moved to the shelf, returned with two circles of flat bread and a carrot. He bit the top off the carrot, not minding the peel. The wind whispered around the door, Davik's chewing audible over it. Janescz carved at the wood. Finally he said, "Are we to learn of your adventure?"

"*Acch*. My adventure," said Davik, snapping another bite of carrot. "I went to see a friend." He chewed. No one spoke.

"A friend," finally repeated Janescz "You walked to see a friend. From midday 'til night. How did you walk in the dark, in the bottom?"

"I followed the wires," said Davik, "the old wires for the electric talker, between the camps."

Janescz spat. "Yes. Between the camps. You walked to see Gehlhausen."

"What if I did?" said Davik.

"What if you did?" said Janescz, a note higher. He drove the knife blade into the table, the knife standing, quivering. "How many whats? What if Carnahan learns of this? What if he sends you to the pools again, a month this time? What if he locks you up? What is the gain here, *chłopiec,* in seeing Gehlhausen, against all this risk?"

Davik looked at Janescz, a dogged, determined expression. "I need his help, you know, against Carnahan, if Carnahan will send Ginna away."

"His *help?*" Janescz's voice was a bark. "What? The T-One Camp is to come and stand before Carnahan and tell him you must go with the camel train?"

"And what if they do?" Davik himself was near shouting now. Plietor raised both hands, then pushed them down, pointing to the ceiling.

"More whats," hissed Janescz. "This cannot happen, Davik. You know it cannot. Do you want camp against camp? Is that what you want?"

"We will rise up against Carnahan," said Davik, back to his dogged way.

Janescz sniffed loudly. "We will not," he said. "We will not rise up. Gehlhausen fills your head with this, like Kemper. This is the Arltunga Camp, not some post of Germany. Carnahan is the voice of MacReedy Mining. There is no rising up."

He looked hard at Davik, who looked back at him for a moment, then slumped over the table, gazing at the carrot. "Davik," Janescz said. "The girl goes with the camel train. She rides the camels for twenty days, and comes to Oodnadatta, where she goes back to her life. Davik, the girl came with the Zeppelin. She is a toff, to fly with the Zeppelin. She goes back to that. Carnahan cannot have harm come to her.

The Afghans will watch her, as they watched you, watched us, so long ago. She will come to Oodnadatta, and go back to her life. As you came here, to your life."

They sat, the wind whispering, the shutter creaking.

Davik suddenly jerked up, standing and hurling the carrot into the wall. "She is my life," he said fiercely. "My life is different. If she goes, I go. That is it. I go." He turned and heaved the door open, strode out into the night.

13.

In the days following, Ginna was left largely by herself, staying indoors, tortured by anxieties. The Boruskis were silent in the mornings, and no one came at midday. In the evening there was talk, but it was talk of production, of repairs to the gliders. The fuselage of the glider for Fergus was almost completed. Karpiak had made a hard landing, but nothing was broken. Musil had gone into the catchnet. Plietor tried to ask Ginna questions, where she would go from Oodnadatta, what she looked forward to. But she said only vague things in response, fluttering up and down from the table, and Davik snorted whenever Plietor asked.

During the long days her mind was all awhirl, full of confusions, unresolved memories, forebodings, no place of comfort for her thoughts to turn to. There was nothing for writing in the flat, no book anywhere to distract her.

She determined after two days that she must organize her thoughts, even if she could not write them down. She must go away from this place, this place she had so wanted to see and had come to at such a terrible price. And since she must go, and so soon, she needed to gather her thoughts, gather them for her father, and for the man from the Admiralty.

She would send a message to her father from Oodnadatta, a telegraph message, telling him she was alive and well.

She pushed thoughts of his reception of the message away. Too much emotion there. Would she say that *only* she was alive? Would her father contact the Zeppelin company? Eloise's family? She could not think about this either.

When she returned to Perth and made a report to her father she would speak of the efficiency of the mine operation, of the well-tended gardens, the clockwork drill of the glider manipulations on the Shelf. She would stress the role of Davik as the driving energy of the flyers, of Plietor as the refined technician, of Janescz as superintendent, craftsman, conscience of safety. She would recommend Julia for her medical skill and compassion, and the doctor Wetkin, she supposed, for his professionalism. She had hardly seen him, or remembered him anyway, from her first days. But her father took pride in the quality of his mining operations, in the competence of people he put into skilled positions, positions of authority. He would be glad to hear all these things.

Carnahan. What should she say of Carnahan, her father's chief man? Surely the operation reflected his hand throughout, his drive for efficiency, his focus on production as the highest value. But at what cost? Should she speak of that? And what of their conversation? What threat was she to him, that he should speak to her so? Still, he had presided over the rescue of an unknown invalid girl from a terrible crash and had supported her rehabilitation. And he was underwriting the expedient journey of this girl, now known to him as his employer's daughter, from the Camp to Oodnadatta. What more could be expected of him in that regard? Greater politeness? Carnahan was a brutal tyrant, to hear Davik talk, and she felt she had an impression of that side of him. But then Davik was...so...irrepressible? Was that the word for Davik? Or something stronger?

Davik. She owed her life to Davik. He was her great

champion. But she did not know his limits, the order of his thoughts and actions. And things he had said…comments about the other camps in the Caldera, a feeling of injustice for them. What he had said about Kemper too, when he had gone all angry, saying Kemper had shown him "a better way" of the world beyond the camp, calling up Gehlhausen, the Overseer of the T-One camp. She remembered something about Gehlhausen from her father. He was a German who had come as Overseer at T-One after Kemper left Arltunga, just before her father had ordered the cessation of relations between Arltunga and the other camps. *Germans.* Kemper and his passionate talk about the difficulties for Germany from the Treaty of Versailles, from extravagant reparations. Had he talked in the same way when he was here? Had Davik heard him, somewhere deep in his soul?

What should she say to the Admiralty man in Sydney when she returned? That Davik spoke well of Kemper? That he had contact with Gehlhausen? That he *still* had contact with Gehlhausen, even though her father had forbidden it? She knew that was what the row had been when Davik returned on the night of his absence. She had gone down the ladder to hear. *Poor Davik.* He was just trying to find help in standing up to Carnahan for her sake. What could he possibly have been thinking, saying she was his life, at the end? She thought he often spoke *without* thinking, acted too, though it would be wonderful if he could come with the camel train. But why go to Gehlhausen? Why would Gehlhausen help him?

On the fourth day after Ginna's conversation with Carnahan, Plietor arrived at the flat unexpectedly just after the first midday ring.

"*Hai!* Ginna!" he said, bounding in the door in his ordinary clothes, and stopped, seeing her sitting at the table.

She started up, with visions of Davik just three days ago coming like this, storming in the door at midday without his oversuit. But Davik had hardly spoken to her. Plietor stood now before her, all asmile. She sat back down.

"What do you do there, just sitting?" asked Plietor.

"I'm not 'just sitting'," she said. "I'm thinking."

"Ha!" said Plietor, "Deep thoughts, is it?"

"You sound like Davik," she said.

He looked down for a moment, then back up at her. "I suppose I do," he said. "I sometimes want to sound like Davik. He is everyone's favorite."

"Maybe not everyone's, not all the time," she said, smiling at him now. "But you? What do *you* do, here at midday? And no costume? Shouldn't you be flying? I hope you aren't—" She stopped.

"I am not doing what Davik did," said Plietor, a little carefully. But then he brightened again. "I have come to visit you. I am ahead on my quota for the day. Good flying. Exceptional flying!" He smiled more broadly, then, when she did not, he grew serious. "And you...are doing so much thinking. I see it in the evenings. You do not talk to us. I think you are worried about the camel train. It is natural for you to be worried. So I came, to worry with you." He tried another smile.

"I do have much to think about," she said. "My experience here has been so full of serious things, then new things, and new people. Now I am to leave it all, suddenly. And I am trying to find how to think about it." She looked down, and Plietor moved to sit on the bench across the table from her. "And I am worried about the camel train. I do admit that."

"What can I do for you?" Plietor said. "Is there anything?"

"It would help me in my thinking to be able to write,"

Ginna said.

Plietor shook his head. "We have nothing for writing here," he said. "Janescz has a notebook in the fob, for numbers and drawings, a pencil. But we have nothing here." He stopped for a moment, then, "Carnahan has paper, and pens."

"No!" she said quickly. "I cannot trouble Mr. Carnahan with my...thinking."

Plietor snorted. "Too right on that." He shrugged. "So...I don't know..."

"Is there any book?" Ginna said. "Do you have any book in the flat that I could read, to have someone thinking instead of me?" She smiled a wan smile.

"Yes!" Plietor sat up. "Janescz has a book. He has two books. I will get them."

Plietor pivoted over the bench and bounded up the ladder. She heard a trunk creak open, then he was down again, proudly holding two books.

One was a Bible, and Ginna smiled a little to herself when she saw it. If there was ever a book anywhere, it was a Bible. She thought idly that she had no idea whether there were services of any kind in the Camp. Surely some here were religious. People were religious everywhere. It was another thing about the camps she had never spoken about with her father.

The cover of the Bible was soft leather, once black, now worn, scarred. She took it from Plietor, opened it and saw it was in English. "This book I know," she said, giving him a smile.

"And this?" He held the second book out to her, a smaller book with a dark, hard cover. She turned it so she could see the spine and started back. *German Social Democracy* was printed in silver-colored letters, and below it, "Bertrand Russell." *Of all people. Bertrand Russell.* She knew of Lord Russell from Cambridge, knew he was thought an immensely intelligent man, and unbalanced. What should Janescz Boruski be doing with such a book?

"Do you know this book?" Plietor asked.

Ginna was not sure what to say but was relieved of saying anything as Plietor went on, saying the book came from Gehlhausen, who was Overseer of the T-One Camp down the Caldera, not knowing she knew very well who Gehlhausen was. There was a time, Plietor explained, when all the camps came together—T-One, McCulloch, and Arltunga—sharing Gatherings now and again. This book came from Gehlhausen during that time. Plietor didn't know that Janescz had ever studied at it. He himself certainly had not. Davik...Davik was not for reading.

Ginna thumbed the book, noting the 1896 imprimatur—well before the war—flipping pages absently. A letter, a single page folded into a square, fell from inside the back cover onto the table.

"It came with the book, from Gehlhausen," Plietor said, picking it up. "It is always in the book." He unfolded it freely, pointed to Gehlhausen's signature below a half-page of writing in a European hand. Her eye caught only a few phrases: "intuitive wisdom," "natural science," "Horst Kemper." *Horst Kemper.*

Plietor was speaking, "...can ask Janescz if you may read the book, for someone else's thinking, while you are...waiting?" he said, trailing off.

"No," she said, recovering. "I don't think...I would not ask Janescz for this book."

"And the Bible?" said Plietor. "Do you read the Bible? Some do here. My mother did..." he started, and stopped, a strange expression on his face.

Ginna looked at him.

"A letter is in the Bible," he said quickly. "A letter too, as in this one." He refolded and replaced the letter in the back of Lord Russell's book and placed that book on the table, taking up the Bible, opening the front cover. "This is an important letter," he said as he removed another square of paper. "It is from the earliest time for us of coming to the Camp."

Plietor unfolded the new letter as freely as he had the other, the creases deep, attesting to repeated folding and unfolding. Ginna saw the familiar letterhead of MacReedy Mining Ltd. above the typescript page. The letter was dated 11 August 1915.

"Here," said Plietor, pointing to the salutation: *Mr. Carleton Dobbins, Overseer, Arltunga Mine, Central Australia.* "Dobbins was Overseer before Carnahan," said Plietor, then pointed to the signature: *Angus McLoughlin, Vice President, MacReedy Mining Ltd.* "He was a big man, important in the mining company in Perth," said Plietor. "Janescz got the letter from him, from a stone building with marble floors in Perth. Janescz speaks of this, or he did. He spoke of it on the first day we came, spoke of it before Dobbins. Davik and I were there. I remember."

He sat, serious, holding the letter, not looking at Ginna.

Ginna certainly knew Angus McLoughlin. She knew his wife Beatrice, and their children Cian and Betsy. She had grown up with them. Strange, to see such a letter here. It was not a contract, nothing like the contracts she had seen, and not signed by Janescz. She hadn't known such letters accompanied workers as they journeyed to the mines. Ginna and Plietor sat, silent with their own thoughts.

The rings of the second midday iron made them both start. Plietor refolded the letter and placed it back in the Bible. "I must go," he said, with a quick smile to Ginna. He bounded up the ladder. She heard the creak of the trunk hinges. Then he was down and at the door.

"I hope your thinking is good in the afternoon," Plietor said.

"It will be better, for your coming to visit me," Ginna said. "Thank you."

"Plietor gave a bow, a full bow, of the sort Davik had given when he had come in the day she had first come down the ladder. She smiled, and Plietor was gone.

All afternoon, Ginna brooded. All evening, while the men talked of gliders and the actions and statements of other men. Plietor tried to catch her eye with puzzled looks, but she looked away, only to see Davik looking at her as well. That night she tossed on her bed, more unsettled than ever.

In the morning, she came down for porridge with the men, trying for lightness in her voice and eye. She wanted no more worries from Plietor or Davik, no more visits. She wanted the flat to herself.

When the men had gone, she sat at the table for half an hour. But she had decided. She would go and read the letters. After an interval she rose and went to the door, cracking it and looking out onto the Shelf. Then she turned and made her way up the ladder.

At the top of the ladder slot, the two beds for Davik and Plietor occupied the west side, the bed for Janescz by itself on the east. Plain wooden trunks stood at the base of each bed, Janescz's twice the size of Plietor's and Davik's, no locks, not even clasps on any of them. Ginna had never known what was in the trunks beyond Gathering clothes, which were removed and worn once a week. Now she approached Janescz's trunk, her heart thumping. The man at

Girton, Kingston, had told her she must be resourceful. She was being resourceful now.

The two books lay on top of the contents of the trunk, likely just where Plietor had dropped them the previous day. She saw clothes, boots, a closed cloth sack and a rolled-up swag. Ginna reached for the Bible first, permitting fleeting images of the McLoughlins to distract her as she unfolded the letter: their brick house on Eame's Hill, the arbor, with her and Betsy among the fragrant blossoms, so far way, so long ago. She scanned past the letterhead and salutation. The text of the letter directed that Mr. Carleton Dobbins, as Agent of MacReedy Mining Ltd. Arltunga Mine should grant fair employment to one Janescz Boruski with accompanying dependents Plietor Boruski and Davik Boruski in such a way as Dobbins saw fit. Such employment should be accompanied by provision of lodging in a separated dwelling and rations suitable to their needs. It *was* a strange letter, Ginna thought, quite generous-seeming, with the specified provision for lodging in a separated dwelling. That was because of the boys, she assumed. She had not known that her father employed boys at his mines. Of course, she had not known that he employed women either.

In Lord Russell's book Ginna glanced at the *Table of Contents* and *Preface*, scanned a few pages. Lord Russell appeared to be impressed with the German social framework and much concerned with the influence of Karl Marx. *Very dry reading,* she thought, *two hundred pages of it.* She couldn't imagine Janescz poring over the book. But it wasn't the book she wanted either. It was the letter.

The letter was written—a strong European hand—on ordinary stationary, without letterhead or identification of the writer by title or office. There was no date, only the signature, *Bernhard Gehlhausen.*

"My dear Janescz Boruski," Gehlhausen began. "I write in honor of our acquaintance." He spoke of his pleasure at discovering a comrade of such competence and "intuitive wisdom," one who understood the way of the world. He praised the Arltunga glider operation both for its efficiency and its "aesthetic quality." He was happy that German capability and natural science had been so effectively and creatively utilized through the knowledge and outstanding abilities of their mutual friend Horst Kemper.

Ginna paused, as the glimpse of Horst's name had made her pause the day before. She allowed a momentary image of Horst's smiling face, then tried to direct her mind. What to think of Horst in this place, working daily with Davik and Plietor, with Janescz? She tried to imagine the impact of Horst on these people, tried to imagine him, and them, the first time with the glider on the Shelf, Horst in his leather flyer's pullover hat, his goggles, up from the stony surface in the wind, flying into the mist. She tried to imagine Horst with them all, in one of their Gatherings, maybe with the other camps, Horst with his wit, his storytelling, his passion for all things German. She thought, as she had before, what seeds had he sown here? This letter was a seed, surely, nurtured by Gehlhausen

Ginna sighed and returned to the letter, thinking Gehlhausen's language so far quite erudite, even flowery. He knew, she read on, Janescz must be proud of his sons, of their natural vitality, their life force. *Life force, indeed,* thought Ginna.

A new paragraph. Gehlhausen, hoped, he said, for the "fruitfulness of their mutual aspiration." He hoped that "small minds with limited perspectives" would not "strangle their efforts," hoped for their "continued comradeship in noble pursuits." Ginna read the paragraph again. It was one long sentence, the only sentence in the whole flowery letter with a darker tone, the single sentence that looked to the future. Ginna put the letter down, letting the words sink in. What did it mean? What was Gehlhausen's and Janescz's "mutual aspiration?" What "efforts" of theirs might be strangled? What "noble pursuits?" There was no way of telling. But Gehlhausen's language echoed words, phrases, sentiments she had heard from Horst, echoed Horst's passion. She looked at the letter again. There was no more to it. Only that Gehlhausen was, *"Ihre lieber freund,"* Bernhard Gehlhausen.

Ginna closed the refolded letter inside the back cover of Lord Russell's book. *German Social Democracy.* Had Gehlhausen and Janescz talked of German social democracy? Or had they talked of more specific things? What did it signify that Plietor had not been concerned at all to show her the letter, or to suggest that she ask Janescz to have the book for her reading? Was she reading entirely too much into a few phrases? At least she would send a word about the letter to the Admiralty man in Sydney.

14.

The word came up from the processing pools in the early morning, before the shimmer of the horizon distorted all seeing. The camel train was coming, shapes moving far out on the desert. They would be there before nightfall.

When the word came to Carnahan, he ordered the iron rung. People stood up from their work all over the Shelf when they heard it. All knew what it meant. The day was week's Mid-day, only half a day of work. With the train arriving, the Gathering dance would be even more raucous than usual. Sometimes Carnahan even allowed an extra nobbler all around.

Plietor had landed from his second sortie of the morning and was pulling off his goggles in the cockpit when Simcas walked down the wing to tell him. *Camel train!* Plietor felt something in his chest drop. The camel train never stayed at the Camp more than a day. If it arrived late in the afternoon, that meant loading tomorrow, departure the day after at first light. And Ginna would be gone, gone with it.

Something else in Plietor's chest clenched. Where was Davik? Did Davik know? Plietor asked Simcas, who said Davik was in the air, likely landing second after Musil.

"Don't tell Davik," said Plietor, lifting himself over the cockpit side. "Tell the others not to tell him. I'll tell the same to Janescz, at the fob."

Simcas curled his mouth into a sneer. "He'll be all bloody over the sheila, eh?"

Plietor didn't like how fast Simcas had jumped to the point, though he knew Davik had been talking in the sheds, heads together with his mob.

"Maybe," said Plietor. "Davik will find out soon enough. But there's no reason for him to find out sooner than that. Let him fly his two more sorties without being distracted. Then it'll be midday and—"

"Oh!" snorted Simcas. "'Distracted' is what he'll be, is it? You been hanging about that sheila too much yourself. I can see it."

Plietor felt his blood in his ears. "You couldn't see shit on a plate," he hissed. Simcas took a step back. "Just do what's best for all, can you? And we'll come out the better for it. Can you see *that?*"

Simcas gave half a nod and moved back down the wing. "I won't say nothing for myself. I can't say about the others."

In the fob, Janescz and Walter Prokop were brushing the clear paint they called "dope" onto the tight linen covering Fergus's fuselage. The door was closed to reduce the mist, and the sickly-sweet smell of the dope was strong inside. Too much of it would make a man's head reel. Janescz looked up when Plietor walked in.

"Did you hear of the camel train?" said Janescz.

"Yeh. I heard," said Plietor, moving to a bucket in a corner to dunk his goggles. "Simcas was happy to tell me. I told him not to tell Davik when he lands, and to tell the others the same."

Prokop looked up quickly, then back down to his work.

"I wish I could go out and see to it myself, but we can't leave this work, now we've begun," said Janescz.

Plietor shrugged. He didn't want to talk more, with

Prokop there. He knew he and Janescz were thinking the same thing. If Davik could fly his two more sorties then the day's quota would be met, and they would have the midday and afternoon to try to keep him from doing anything wacker. And then the Gathering. Plietor didn't want to think about the Gathering. He couldn't think about it. They had to get through the rest of the day before that.

"I have to go to the glider," he said, wiping a stained cloth over his face.

Janescz looked up, nodded twice, his lips pressed, and went back to his brushing.

"And then what?" Janescz was shouting at Rozum outside the door of the fob. Musil and Karpiak stood by, and Simcas. Plietor stood behind Janescz. The rest had left with the midday ring.

"What should I know?" Rozum shouted back. "'Bloody hell!' he said. Just that. Then he stripped off his daks, left them lying, and took off for the old path over the edge. Right down the path he went. Right over. That's the last I saw Davik, the great bloody *idiotka*."

Janescz glared at him a moment, then looked away.

"*Cholera!*" said Rozum. "Nobody told me about saying to him. Karolyi says to me, handling the wing, 'Carnahan rung the iron for the camel train.' Davik comes by from his glider, going to the fob, and I says to him, 'Karolyi says Carnahan rung the iron.' What's the wrong in that? We was done for the day."

Janescz slumped. "Karolyi should have...oh... "He threw up his hands. "There's no wrong in it on you."

"Yeh," said Rozum. "Bloody well there's not. So watch who you're shouting, old man."

Janescz turned to the door of the fob, waving his hand

over his shoulder. Plietor gestured with his head that they should all go, then followed inside.

Janescz walked to the newly painted fuselage and stood over it, absently. "What do we do?" he asked, into the air.

"Do you think he'll come back with Gehlhausen?" Plietor asked, stripping his overdaks. "Or Gehlhausen at the head of an unruly regiment from the T-One?"

Janescz snorted. "A regiment. I don't see a regiment. But if Gehlhausen's his man…" He lifted his palms to his face and rubbed them down over this eyes. "We can't do anything, can we, not until he comes back."

Plietor shook his head. "I can't see going round, talking to men, trying to be ready…for something, when I don't know what."

"No," said Janescz. "You don't stir a hornet's nest." He looked at Plietor. "It's an old saying. A hornet is a great stinging fly."

Plietor trudged up the ladder to the flat. He had loaded the five buckets of jelly-sodden nets into the cart and rolled them down the path behind the Shelf to the processing site, making sure Helinski, the pool super, wrote them into his log. End of the day work. At the notch, he had scanned south over the desert, looking for the bobbing shapes of the camel train, but saw nothing save undulation. At the last vantage point back up on the path he had turned and looked again, with the benefit of height. Maybe there was a dark mass within the sandy red shimmer. Maybe not.

Ginna looked up at him as he entered the door. She was sitting at the table, her hands clasped in her lap. She must have been just sitting, staring into the rough grain of the wood. Now she lifted tired eyes in greeting.

Plietor smiled back. "You are thinking again?"

"All I do these days is think," she said.

He nodded, paused. "You heard the iron." A statement.

"You mean in the morning?" she said. "Yes, I heard it. I wasn't sure what it was for."

"Now you are sure?"

"Yes." She nodded. "Janescz told me." She glanced away. "Janescz was here. But he has gone to the bunkhouse, to wash his work clothes."

"I should do that too," said Plietor, not moving.

"Where…" she began. "Where is Davik?"

Plietor took a breath. "He went over the edge of the Shelf, down the path to the pits."

"You mean…like he did before, don't you?" she said.

Plietor shrugged.

She sat. He stood. The wind whistled in the shutter, but they didn't notice. Finally she drew a breath. "Carnahan will announce the camel train tonight at the Gathering?"

"Yes," said Plietor. "But everyone knows."

"And will he speak of me then too?"

"He must," said Plietor. "That will be the time. He will say some words. I can guess them. He will recall the Zeppelin, how you were rescued, how you have been nursed in the good household of the Boruskis." He gave a little bow. "How it is now time for you to return to your people, for you to tell the story of the Zeppelin, and the good work you have seen in the Arltunga Camp. How our thoughts go with you on the camel train." He gave a grimace. "I am sorry. I cannot do his voice, as Davik could."

Ginna's eyebrows were up. "Have you heard a speech like that before?"

"No," Plietor said, "not just like it. But I have heard Carnahan, many times."

Ginna looked down, then up at him again. "When will I

find out about…travelling clothes?" Now Plietor's eyebrows went up. "Or, am I to go just as I am?" She spread her hands. "I don't even know where this dress came from, you know, whom to thank for the use of it. Oh! I should wash it too, if I am to return it. And if not…"

Her eyes filled with tears. She looked down at the table.

Plietor felt tears come from behind his eyes too, a strange sensation. He wanted to go and touch Ginna, for her comfort. But he could not think how to do that, or what comfort it would be. So he stood, and in a few moments she took a deep breath and looked up at him again.

"Carnahan will not speak of traveling clothes at the Gathering speech," Plietor said. "He will call you in tomorrow, that's when, to settle things." Ginna looked at him a moment more, then turned her face away.

They were eating at the table when Davik burst in the door. He was breathing hard.

"Good!" he said, taking in the scene, closing the door quickly behind him, moving to his place at the table, where his soup and bread resided in the pot and the skillet.

"What is good?" said Janescz.

"Everything!" said Davik, lifting the soup pot to drink. Soup broth ran down his chin onto the table. "I am good. The day is good. The soup is good." He beamed at Ginna, his eyes bright.

"Do we ask—" began Janescz, but Davik cut him off.

"No. You do not ask. There is no reason to ask. It will all be shown. An hour and it will all be shown." He looked at Janescz, at Plietor, ripped a circle of bread in half and stuffed one piece in his mouth, smiled through heavy chewing.

An hour later they stood with the others in the Yard, the

whole Camp, waiting for Carnahan. Ginna stood between Janescz and Plietor, near the back of the congregation, Davik a step behind them, the half-dozen of his closest mob around him. Men and women both had turned to look at Ginna as she, Janescz, and Plietor had settled into their position. Julia had walked quickly past them in her work clothes, and Ginna smiled at her. But Julia had returned only a half-nod, with no change of expression.

The crowd murmured. A man, then a woman, then another man coughed, the ragged, raspy cough they all knew. The wind blew. The mist swirled around them, just beginning to turn salmon with the setting sun. Outside the Caldera, down in the yard before the grinding shed, sixteen camels and their four Afghan drivers sat in a circle.

The blue door opened and Carnahan emerged, khakis clean, broad hat, clipboard in hand. He advanced to the box beside the iron pole and took the step up, tall over the congregation. Karski rang the iron twice.

Plietor looked over his shoulder for Davik, found that he and his mob had stepped back so a gap was between them and the others. They were speaking low among themselves, heads in, now one then another glancing down to the Shelf and the path to the pits.

"I welcome you all to our Gathering," Carnahan said, in his large public voice. He surveyed the crowd. Plietor saw Carnahan's eyes linger just a moment in his direction, likely on Ginna, he thought. Carnahan had not provided word that Ginna was to come. But he had not provided word that she was not to come either. So they had brought her. Carnahan would surely give his opinion, if the choice was wrong.

Carnahan's glance now moved over Plietor's head, and Plietor knew he was looking at Davik and his mob. Plietor heard the murmur of their voices behind him cease. The ghost of an expression played over Carnahan's face, but Plietor could not read it.

"As always," said Carnahan, "we must enumerate our production, and celebrate it, if we have met our obligations." He consulted the clipboard. "In the matter of agriculture, Mr. Bartosz reports that cabbage, onion, sweet pepper, and carrot production all met quota, and bush bean exceeded quota by twelve percent." Carnahan nodded to someone in the front, likely Bartosz. Back to the clipboard. "Pole beans continue to suffer the malady of which we have spoken before, with consequent almost complete loss of production. Mr. Bartosz continues to investigate the source of this malady. Prospects are good for squash and zucchini as we approach the fall, and corn verges on maturity." Carnahan looked down, likely at Bartosz again, and adjusted a page on his clipboard. "Milk from the goats met quota, with consequent cheese as well. Egg production was fifteen percent over. Two hens were culled to stabilize the flock, with meat utilized for soup in the bunkhouse, as reported by Anna Drowicz, elsewise distributed to flats in accord with the schedule." He looked out over the crowd again. "Has anyone aught to add to Mr. Bartosz's report?"

Carnahan adjusted another page. "In the matter of health..." He read from Dr. Wetkin's report of work hours lost to various complaints: a crushed finger from miss-handing a heavy rock in a Terrace wall repair; stomach sickness in a couple living together in a flat, likely bad food preparation; an acid burn from a rake dropped and carelessly retrieved from a processing pool. "I do not have to say," said Carnahan, "how costly the loss of valuable work hours is to our overall production, and how costly those hours are to your wages awaiting you in Perth."

Plietor felt Ginna stir beside him when Carnahan said

this, and he looked down to meet her eyes. But Carnahan was going on.

"In the matter of the fundamental purpose of this Camp, the chemical recovery to which we are all dedicated…" Carnahan turned a page and read from Janescz's report of sorties flown and glider status. "We note the imminent return of the sixth glider to production," he said, then stopped and looked over the crowd until he found who he was looking for, raising an eyebrow and fixing a stare. "This return," he said, "is much to the benefit of he who caused the loss, to Eoghan Fergus here, who has sure and paid dearly in wages unearned and expenses deducted, as befits such a misadventure."

Plietor felt Ginna stir again and knew she was looking at him, another question in her eyes. But Carnahan had lifted his own eyes up from Fergus and was casting his gaze over the crowd. "Tis a lesson to you all," he said, "to be not a cost to yourself and a burden to your mates, vested responsible to make up your production when you falter, or else suffer likewise."

Plietor looked down at Ginna then, seeing her eyes wide. He compressed his lips, shook his head. Carnahan was reading now from Hilenski's report, pounds produced from the grinders only two percent below quota. "We acknowledge," said Carnahan, "the abilities of the other skilled lads who fly the gliders and Mr. Boruski, making quota despite the absence of the sixth glider, thereby experiencing no diminution." He gave a crooked smile, nodding over the heads of the crowd in the direction of Janescz and Plietor, then raising his gaze to Davik behind. "And we encourage them to maintain their close look to their affairs."

A few heads turned to look at Davik and his group, and Plietor turned with them. Davik stood up as tall as he was and tensed, and for a moment Plietor was afraid he would make a gesture or shout back at Carnahan. But he did not, and after a moment Carnahan's gaze moved back to his clipboard, and the crowd's attention moved back to Carnahan. Plietor heard murmurs begin again behind him and escalate to small explosions of exclamation. He turned to see the mob almost in a scrum, heads in, hands thrusting in tense gestures. Janescz and Ginna turned to look too, others nearby. Plietor caught Davik's eye, looking up from the scrum. It was wild, uncertain.

"We all know," Carnahan was saying from his box, "the fall camel train has come. We have in consequence our fresh supplies, food and materiel, all that we need from the world outside to supplement ourselves. In the morn the camel train will depart with the chemical harvest that justifies us all."

"Where?" Plietor heard in a hiss from Davik's group. "Where are the T-Ones!? Where the bloody hell—"

"*Shhh!*" several nearby hissed back in chorus. Plietor felt his heart speed up, felt Ginna's hand on his arm. A stir of agitation went through the crowd. Plietor looked to Carnahan, and found Carnahan looking back, a smile, a smirk on his face.

"Some may have heard," Carnahan said, in a louder voice, "that the camel train is to accommodate a passenger from the Camp."

Davik broke from his mob and began to stalk toward the front, a flank around the larger group's edge. Plietor pulled free from Ginna's grip and lunged after him, the other members of Davik's mob stringing behind. Faces turned toward them, a ripple of exclamation.

"Some may have heard!" Carnahan was saying, even louder than before. Plietor swung his attention from Davik to Carnahan. What was the man doing? He was still on his box, unmoving, his smirk broader than ever. Plietor caught one of Davik's arms and hauled backward, half spinning Davik around before Davik flung him off. The crowd was rumbling now, moving around Davik and Plietor, as Plietor caught Davik around the middle in a hug and dug in his heels.

"Shit!" shouted Davik. "Shit you!" as he tried to turn to get a grip.

"WHAT HAS BEEN HEARD IS NOT SO!" thundered Carnahan from the box.

Davik stopped. Plietor had his face against Davik's back, and felt the muscles release, felt Davik's breath coming in gasps, was suddenly aware that his was too, and that their two breaths were the loudest thing in his ears.

"I SAY," said Carnahan, before the now-hushed crowd, "that those who have spoken of a passenger from the Camp to go with the camel train have spoken falsely! They have spoken out of their own interest. They do not represent the interest of the Camp. They do not represent *my* interest!"

Plietor released his hold on Davik. Davik was looking around wildly, at his mob mates, toward the path to the pits, at Carnahan. And Carnahan was looking back, the same smirk of satisfaction on his face.

"If—I—may—have—attention," he said, "I will say what *is* my interest." Davik's breathing slowed. He stood stock still, as did everyone in the crowd.

"You all know of our guest, the young woman from the Zeppelin, so cruelly burned in the great fire of the crash. You all know she has been among us this month long, residing in the flat of the Boruskis." He smiled his smirk again at Davik. He did not look at Janescz and Ginna. "Some of you may have even seen her about of late, among the Terrace and the gliders." Now he did look at Ginna, and smiled a different smile.

"She is about, but who can say she has regained the full measure of her capacity?" Carnahan stretched out one arm, as if to invite contemplation of Ginna, and heads turned toward her. Eyes went to her gloves, her head scarf, saw her blush and look down. "By no means," intoned Carnahan, "could this young woman, brave may she be, be enjoined to the camel train to suffer the arduous trek to Oodnadatta, a trek every man and woman among you knows only too well."

There were mutterings in the crowd, shufflings. Plietor glanced at Davik, standing transfixed, only his eyes darting.

"*My* interest, and hers, is that she remain with us one further third of the year, until the coming of the winter train, whereupon her capacity and the mildness of the season will make for an assured return to her place, and the welcome of those who await her."

Plietor heard Davik inhale, and reached out to lay a hand on his arm to stop any remark. Davik flinched from the touch and darted a glance at Plietor, but he didn't open his mouth. Plietor looked up to see Carnahan regarding them, the smirk playing about his lips again.

"This is, above all things, a working camp. And though this young woman be our guest, yet must she join in the manufacture of our livelihood. To this end, I recommend her to Mr. Bartosz, for such work on the Terrace as he may find suitable." Carnahan nodded down to Bartosz, who lifted a hand in response. Then Carnahan looked back pointedly to Ginna and waited. Plietor saw that Ginna did not know what was required, but after a moment Janescz lifted his hand. Carnahan nodded.

"I give you thus the newest member of our working family. Her Christian name she has given as Ginna, a fine Irish name and no doubt. And for surname we shall call

her deBoruski"—he said it "dee-Brooski"—"as she is of the
house of Boruski." Carnahan smiled at his joke, *probably
chuckling to himself,* Plietor thought. What *was* Ginna's proper surname? There had never been a reason to ask. Proper
names were not something particular here. Some had left
their proper names far behind. Only Carnahan knew, from
their contracts. Had Ginna given her proper name to Carnahan?

Carnahan now spread both arms in a gesture of welcome and smiled a smile of benevolence that took in the
whole crowd. "We also offer Ginna deBoruski invitation to
the celebration customary to the evening." He turned and
gestured to the door. "May you all enter and be merry!"

Plietor heard a loud snort from one in Davik's mob,
echoed at lower levels throughout the crowd. "Be merrier if
he'd declared a twice nobbler," someone said nearby.

15.

Ginna bent her back to the rake, driving the two tines deep between the tall pole bean stakes, pulling the rake back to bring up the subsoil. Drimka had just passed by with his wheelbarrow of compost, forking a thick clump between each plant. Now it had to be worked in. Ginna barely noticed the smell, blending it into the background stench of the mist and the pungency of her own body.

She had been thinking hard about the pole beans, which really were in terrible shape, leaves yellowed and half-wilted, flowers falling off. There would be no production from this lot, as she understood there had been none from the last two. Soon the seed stock would be exhausted, and there would be no more of these beans at all. Would Bartosz blame her? Would the others? They would all suffer if the pole beans died. Some seemed eager to blame her for something.

It was two weeks since the camel train had left, since she was "taken in" at the Gathering, as Davik put it. What a night that had been; what a day before! Her own worry, all that day long. Janescz's and Plietor's worry about Davik's afternoon venture, then greater worry with his "all is to be shown" at dinner. Davik's terrible nervousness during Carnahan's speech, then his breaking out and marching up toward Carnahan when he thought Carnahan was going to announce her going, and Plietor's tackling him.

She herself had felt great relief when Carnahan had said she was not to go. Not because she didn't want to go. It was her greatest wish, to be back where she belonged in Perth, with her father and their friends. Though…

She worried the black compost into soil, pulling, pushing, punching with the rake, the muscles in her back and arms now far more capable than they were those first few days. Oh, how she had ached all over, an entirely different pain from the pain of the burns, but pain nonetheless. Only her gloves had saved her hands, though the gloves themselves were now sorely worn.

Perth. The way to Perth depended on the camel train, and she'd had less concern about her "capacity" than Carnahan had. Still, she *had* concern. And it *was* a relief when he had said she was not to go. "Ginna deBoruski" indeed. But what would he say? Not "Ginna MacReedy." Not after what he had said to her face.

But he also had said to her face that she was to go with the camel train. Why had he changed his mind about that? How was one to know what to expect of Carnahan?

Ginna moved to the other side of the plant and a new fork of compost. The Gathering dance had been torture for her. Everyone had stared, stared openly, and she had nowhere to turn. Davik had taken her into the long room and seated her on a bench beside the band, but then had left her to gather his drink and carouse with his mates. He came and went from her bench, still on edge, his eyes darting to the door at every movement there. And he was loud, calling out across the room, now in his own voice, now in the voices of others, even while music was being played. No one else had joined her on the bench, though there was space for four. Sitting by herself, she had for just one moment a powerful image: a jazz club in London—all her girl friends in pastel sleeveless chemises, their hair bobbed; the bright boys in tuxedos, slick hair and smiles; the Charleston. It was ridiculous. Ridiculous then, even more ridiculous to think of in that long room.

Plietor had come to speak with her once, and seemed about to sit, but Davik had rushed in and sat instead, calling out in the voice of one "Gwen" how much she missed dancing with Plietor. A woman down the room had turned at Davik's shout with a sour look at Davik—and her—and then turned away.

Into the soil went the compost. The physical quality of the soil seemed satisfactory: good texture and porosity, a dark, healthy color. Apparently no chemical analysis could be done. What was the problem with the bean plants? Standing up as they were, were they more susceptible to the mist than were the bush beans? Yet Tiska, the other woman on her row, had assured her they had grown for years without problem. What new thing had afflicted them?

There had been no question of her dancing. Davik had taken her hand once to pull her up but she had resisted and taken it back. She did not know these dances. And though they did not seem complex, she certainly had no desire to make herself an even greater object of study than she was already. The room had grown intolerably hot with all the bodies in motion, perspiring bodies, and though she thought she had become inured to odor, she found the body pungency that collected in the room deeply unpleasant.

The only other person to speak to her had been the man Karski, apparently assistant to Carnahan, the one who beat the iron triangle in the Yard. She remembered him as the man who had helped Davik carry her on the litter from the clinic to the Boruskis'. He sat at Carnahan's table at the end of the room during the dancing, with the whiskey and a clipboard, dispensing the drinks, presiding in Carnahan's absence. Janescz sat with him.

This Karski had journeyed down the room to her bench, after all the drinks had been dispensed. All eyes had followed him as he walked. He had for her a message: Mr. Carnahan would see her in the morn after the in-ringing. Just that. And her heart had fallen, though she was expecting the summons.

Ginna had done her best by the pole beans with the new compost. The bush beans crouched just by them, their foliage luxuriant by contrast, long pods hanging in bunches within their bowers. She harvested a double handful for her basket and moved on to the sweet peppers, marveling at the bulbous fruit, lustrous green despite the sallow cast of the leaves that came, she assumed there as always, from the constant bathing of the chemical mist.

The *whissh* of a glider passing low overhead caused her only a moment's glance. She had learned to ignore them. In her first days on the Terrace she had stood and looked every time one passed over, often holding her gaze through the landing and the next launch. She had quickly learned to recognize Davik's landings. He came in faster than any of the others and stood the glider right up on its nose to stop after it touched, sparks cascading from the front skid iron on the stone. Plietor she came to recognize too, his wheel touching at exactly the same distance down from the Terrace each time, his stops graceful, balletic. After two days Bartosz had spoken to her of her "gaping at the gliders" and threatened to increase her quota to keep her eyes and hands on her work.

She moved down her row from the sweet peppers to the tart ones, *paprikas* Tiska called them, destined to be dried and shredded for soup seasoning. And then to onions.

Carnahan's manner at their meeting had been positively

affable, despite Ginna's fears. He had welcomed her, hoped her experience of the dancing had been "appreciative." He had remarked on Davik's usual "energetic engagement" as a dancer and presumed she would join him when she felt more suitably inclined. He had asked, with a show of delicacy, if she should like to be included on the "nobbler roster," for a splash of whiskey at her wont.

She had not known what to say, finally fumbling out that perhaps that should wait for a future time. Carnahan had nodded, with a corner of the smirk she had noticed before, and then gone on to express his hopes that she had not been disconcerted by the rumors circulating in some quarters of the Camp that she was to depart with the camel train.

She had stared at him. *Rumors?* He had told her so, in that very room, three weeks before, in terms impossible to misunderstand! Surely he must have known the trajectory of such "rumors." And yet there he had sat, staring back at her with a bemused expression, that slightly twisted smile. Was he toying with her? The phrase, "a game of cat and mouse" popped into her head, an echo from some mystery novella. But she did not know how to play Carnahan's game.

"No," she had said, then as he had stared on, she had added that she had been "confident of an appropriate resolution."

Carnahan had snorted at that, then roused himself officiously, declaring that "an appropriate resolution" was for her to work on the Terrace, under the supervision of Mr. Bartosz. She would contribute her worthy labors to those others that produced their common harvest, such work to continue until the coming of the winter camel train, when, god willing, she would return to the life from which she had arrived there, "so unpropitiously." He had fixed her with another stare when he said the last words, a stare with no trace of a smile. Then, breaking off his look, he had declared that as she was to be "amongst them" she should have proper dress for work, which she could obtain by seeing Anna Drowicz, bunkhouse super. And that, Carnahan had said, was all there was to say. She could go, reporting to Mr. Bartosz after the second midday ring.

"The bastard," Davik had said at dinner that night, as she recounted the conversation. "Carnahan says just what he wants to, and no one dares say otherwise." There had been no discussion of Davik's thwarted hopes of the previous day, of what he had expected from Gehlhausen. Carnahan had made Davik look foolish, had turned his talk of Ginna's departure, wherever that talk had spread, into a false and destructive rumor. Ginna had no difficulty understanding why neither Janescz nor Plietor had wanted to bring up the day's events.

Ginna had been dressed at dinner in her new garment, the long-sleeved canvas shift all the rest of the women wore for work, undyed coarse cotton fabric tied with a leather thong about the waist. For an undergarment she wore the gown, just a shift, that Julia had given her for her convalescence. She didn't know what the other women wore.

She had gone to the "bunkhouse" straight from Carnahan's long room. The walk was not far, for the bunkhouse shared a wall with Carnahan's quarters, occupying almost the whole rest of the ground floor of the Stack, only the clinic's rooms at the very end. The long room symmetric to Carnahan's was the bedroom of the bunkhouse, two bedrooms actually, separated by a thick curtain, one for men, the other—much smaller—for women. Beds lined the walls on both sides of each, simple wooden platforms with mattresses, trunks at their feet, like those in the Boruskis' flat. Ginna had proceeded across that room to an inner doorway, and through that to a common room and kitchen, empty at this time of day. At her "Hallo," a severe squarish woman had emerged from another inner room and looked her up and down disapprovingly.

"So you're the Zeppelin lady," she said, "and you've come for suiting." She introduced herself as "Anna," and turned back through the doorway without further conversation, returning in a few moments with a shift, boots, and a clipboard. Ginna had taken the shift readily, less readily the boots, which were heavy and looked much too large. But Anna had been focused on notating her clipboard paper.

Ginna had hesitated, then asked about an undergarment. "No issue for that," said Anna, not looking up. "No need. Hot enough as it is."

"Might there be a hat?" Ginna had tried. Anna had looked up from her writing with a sour expression that changed to a squint as she peered at Ginna's scarf-wrapped head. Then, just as abruptly as before, she had gone back through the doorway, returning with an example of the loose-brimmed canvas hats Ginna had seen the other women and many of the men wearing. Anna had turned again to her clipboard.

"Might there be gloves as well?" Ginna had asked.

"Be damned!" Anna spat. "Gloves?!"

Ginna had held up her right hand, the glove stretched, frayed, thin at the fingertips.

"Julia, the nurse gave these to me," Ginna said. "Because of the burns."

"Ah," said Anna, her eyes lighting. "Let me see."

Ginna had blushed in spite of herself. She was terribly self-conscious of her hands, and wore the gloves whenever she was with people, even the Boruskis. But there seemed nothing for it, so she had removed the glove and held her hand out to Anna. The red of the skin when it was new had subsided to shades of yellowish pink, still nothing like her real skin, nor were the striations and cords of the scars. Anna had grasped Ginna's wrist and held the hand up, turning it around so she could see it from all angles.

"The other," Anna had said, and Ginna had removed the other glove, the inspection had been repeated, and repeated again when Anna pushed up the sleeves of Ginna's dress to view the scars on her forearms.

"Feet too, was it?" had said Anna.

"There's nothing distinctive about the feet," Ginna had said firmly. "Besides, I only asked for gloves."

"There's no issue for gloves," said Anna.

Ginna had felt her blood rush hot in her ears. *No issue for gloves.* Anna had looked her over like a laboratory specimen, merely to satisfy her curiosity.

"Thank you very *much*," Ginna had said.

Still, that night at dinner, she had been pleased with her new garment. And it was new. No strange odors about it, no stains. The green-checked gingham dress she had worn every day for more than a month she had folded and left in her room. She'd been able only to damp wash the dress before now. She had no other garment to wear in its place, no large container in the flat in which to wash, and water for drinking and such washing as was done had to be hauled from the common pool behind the Stack. Now with a work shift, Ginna had determined she would take the Gathering dress to the bunkhouse for a thorough washing, as the men did. She would then return the dress to Julia. Ginna had no need of a Gathering dress.

Onions. That's where she was on the row. There were many onions today, and then radishes. Ginna stood from her picking stoop. Her basket was heavy with vegetables, the day's production for her row. She hoped for quota. The afternoon would bring more working of soil, staking and pruning plants, transplanting seedlings from the sheds. Stooping, bending, thrusting, wrenching. Each day had been the same, from watering at first light to trudge to the Stack after out-ringing.

Davik, Janescz, and Plietor would come up from the glider sheds later than she, Davik and Plietor with mustard stains under their eyes and on their hands, Janescz hoarse from shouting on the Shelf. Ten sorties a day they flew when the bucket weights were as they should be, more when they were not. Soup and flat bread for dinner, now and again with cabbage and onions. To bed and sleep. Then up and to it again for another day. For Ginna it had been two weeks of days the same, except for Mid-Week. She had begged off the Gathering dancing after the first, citing exhaustion.

Two days later Ginna emerged from sleep with an idea about the pole beans. She slipped into her work shift and padded down the ladders, only to find the men already gone. Had she slept through the in-ringing? No. They had just left early, a bowl of porridge for her on the shelf, a mug of tea. She sat by herself at the table and marshaled her thoughts.

Beans "fixed" nitrogen from the air she knew, bacteria in nodules on the root of a plant transforming the nitrogen into ammonia, which the tissues of the plant took up. Special kinds of bacteria were required. She had thought of this when she first walked out from the Stack with Julia and saw beans growing. The soil must have been inoculated. Someone knew about beans. But when beans were stressed the activity of the bacteria in the root nodules was suppressed, and the plants faltered. Goodness knows the plants here were stressed, bathed in the chemical mists as they were, light obscured day after day. What if the pole beans were not fixing enough nitrogen for their own use? What if they had become more stress-susceptible over generations? Or the available nitrogen in the soil had been depleted beyond some critical limit? This could be corrected by supplemental fertilizer. But high-nitrogen fertilizer was required. Perhaps the compost available was not sufficiently high in nitrogen?

It was like a problem from the Botany *practicum* at Girton. She was excited to investigate. But how could she? Drimka distributed the compost, but he had never said a word to her. *What about Bartosz?* She sniffed to herself. She couldn't imagine approaching Bartosz for a discussion of the nitrogen content of Camp compost and a hypothesis about pole bean stress. *Who else? No one.* There was truly no one she could talk to. Well, save Davik, Plietor, and Janescz. Hadn't Davik said he and Plietor once worked on the Terrace, before the gliders? She would speak to them at dinner about her idea.

"Pole beans!?" exclaimed Davik from his corner. He had dashed down his soup as always, drinking straight from the pot. Now he was stalking the wall, pausing at the corners to tear off segments of flat bread to chew.

"Pole beans! *Polska* beans! We are all *polska* beans here."

"More like *zucchiniska*, you," said Plietor.

Janescz chuckled.

"Ha!" said Davik. "You—"

"No, no!" said Ginna. "I don't care about the name. I said I have a question about growing things on the Terrace, and it just happens to be about pole beans."

"*Zucchiniska…*" muttered Davik.

"Ask your question," said Janescz.

Ginna took a breath. "The poles beans are dying," she began, "dying for the third planting. Soon all the seed stock will be gone. I have a hypothesis about the difficulty."

Davik was quiet along the wall. Plietor looked at Janescz, cut his eyes across the table toward Ginna, then looked down. Ginna paused, then straightened herself and continued. She described the symptoms of the pole beans, the role of nitrogen, and her hypothesis about the relation. No one spoke. No one looked at her.

"If I had some high-nitrogen fertilizer, I could test my hypothesis," she said finally. "So far as I know, we have only compost. Here is my question: What is in the compost?"

"Ha!" said Davik, coming to life. Janescz looked up at him and raised a cautionary hand, to no avail. "Shit!" Davik said. "That's the compost. Shit!" Plietor was shaking his head, not looking at Ginna, but Davik careened on. "All the night pails from latrines in flats, in bunkhouse, pails from sheds—glider sheds, Terrace sheds, pools—pails from Gathering night, even the pail from Carnahan—foulest shit, that is—all this makes compost. No wonder *polska* beans are dying! That is *my* hypothesis." He fairly bounced in triumph.

"And yet you eat the vegetables that come from this shit," said Plietor.

"Ha!" said Davik.

"What he says is true," Plietor went on, before Davik could recover. He glanced at Ginna but did not hold her eyes. "Human shit is a component of the compost. We collect all the human shit and piss. And from animals too, the goats and the chickens, as much as we can. We collect all the scraps from eating, skins and peels, cores, seeds. There is the pail." He gestured under the shelf, glanced at Ginna again. "You use it every day."

"And Plietor takes it all to the Terrace shed," said Davik. "He is a good shit carrier."

"It all goes into a great bin behind the Terrace shed," said Plietor evenly. "Turning the compost is Drimka's work.

When it is ready, he takes it to the Terrace. And you..." he looked full face across the table at Ginna then, followed a shrug with a smile, "you work it in around the pole beans."

"Plietor knows all about this," said Davik coming to lean over the table between them, looking at one, then the other. "He was a great shit-compost worker, before he browned his nose in Bartosz's ass and got taken into the shed." He stood. "Ha!"

"Davik..." said Janescz, with a warning in his voice.

Ginna had sat, sat straight through all this, looking at the table top, her lips compressed.

Now she drew a breath. "I see," she said. Then quickly, "I see about the compost." She looked at Plietor, tilted her head. "Would it be possible to collect the waste from just the chickens?"

Plietor's eyebrows went up. "I don't know...I don't see," he began.

"Sure, sure," said Davik. "He'll go to the roost with a bloody trowel himself, scrape the shit up right off the floor-boards."

"Davik..." said Janescz.

"The reason is," said Ginna firmly, "chicken waste, and bird guano generally, is particularly high in nitrogen. If I had some, just enough for two or three plants, and permission of course, I could test my hypothesis."

"You know this?" said Plietor. "You know this about chicken...waste? And this 'nitrogen'?"

"I do," said Ginna. And closed her mouth. There was a long silence.

"*Zucchiniska*," snorted Davik from the wall. "I will tell you about the zucchiniska and the yellow squash. 'Oh, Mr. Zucchiniska,'" he said, in a high, female voice.

"No!" said Plietor, swinging his leg over the bench and

standing up. "It is late. I am for sleeping."

Davik looked at Ginna. She smiled back at him, shook her head, put her palms together under her tilted cheek. He smiled back, made the same gesture. Ginna rose to gather the dishes.

Ginna hurried up the ladder, out of breath. The last of the first midday beats of the iron were still ringing. This is what she did every day, breaking off her work as soon as she heard the iron, hurrying, hurrying back to the flat and twenty minutes to herself away from the sun, the wind, the mist, a round of flatbread, a carrot, a drink of clear water. The other women gathered in the Terrace shed, but no welcome had been offered to her.

Gloves off, she rinsed her hands at the shelf, casting an eye to the shredded tips of the first two fingers of the right glove. What would she do when the gloves fell apart? She rinsed the carrot in the same water and bit at the end. A year ago she would never have thought to eat a carrot without peeling. Now...She tore a piece of flatbread.

"Hai, Ginna!" Plietor burst in the door, as breathless as she had been.

Ginna felt a small flutter in her chest. "Hai, Plietor!" she said, turning with a quick smile. "What brings you here at midday?" A deeper smile. "Can I offer you a bite of carrot?"

Plietor shook his head. "We have tucker ration down at the sheds. I come to talk to you."

"Have you done more exceptional flying today?"

"I have," Plietor smiled, "but that's not the talk. The talk is of nitrogen."

Ginna cocked her head.

"What you said last dinner, about the chicken...chicken waste, and your hypothesis. I can help you with this." He looked at her intently. "What Davik said about Bartosz, me and Bartosz," he paused, pursed his lips, then went on, "It is true, partly true. Bartosz did take me from the dirt to the shed...to work with seeds, with the hybrid, for better production, you know." He paused. "You know? About the hybrid?"

"Yes, I do," said Ginna.

Plietor shook his head, a question in his eyes. But he continued. "If I ask Bartosz, he will listen to me. I can say we have talked about pole beans at our dinner." He gave a little smile. "That Miss Ginna deBoruski, who is a good *drtska,* is concerned about pole beans. And I have an idea. *My* idea." He shrugged. "But not about nitrogen!" The shrug turned to a smile. "I do not know about nitrogen. But my idea is for a special fertilizer, from chicken...chicken shit."

Ginna suppressed a giggle.

"I ask if I can collect special chicken shit for fertilizer, to try my idea. Bartosz will say yes. And it not so hard. Maybe we can use linen cloth from the glider stores to put in nest boxes and on the roost floor. Then, a week maybe, we pull up the cloth and scrape shit. Is chicken shit fertilizer, all by itself?"

"Yes it is," said Ginna. Her eyes were shining. "It does not need to be composted."

"So there!" exclaimed Plietor, spreading his arms. "You work chicken shit—now fertilizer—in the soil around pole beans and test your hypothesis."

Ginna's mouth twisted in on itself as she tried to smile but could not, overcome with a different emotion, tears springing to her eyes. She wanted to run to Plietor, but could not, knew she should not.

"Is it okay?" said Plietor from the doorway. "Is this a good help for you?"

"Oh, it is, Plietor," she said. "It is a great help."

16.

Plietor hovered into the wind. Five hundred feet below him the mist swirled and eddied, but up here the air was clear, the sun unwavering, the whole Caldera spread out around him. He took a deep breath, knowing the air a different substance from what he breathed all other hours of the day. Once, high like this, he had stripped off his goggles and mist-soaked balaclava just to breathe unencumbered. He had found the air like nothing at all: no smell, no taste, just pressure on his face, but somehow sweet all the same.

Now Plietor looked to the right and the top of the Caldera, searching for the deep cleft V in the rampart, then, finding it, turned his head west to locate the white gash of stone half way up the surrounding gray of the cliff face. He wanted to be exactly between them, and he was not. With the stick slightly forward, the glider made its way upwind, Plietor swiveling to gauge his landmarks, constructing an imaginary line across the Caldera between them, measuring his approach to the line. A few hundred feet further, fifty, then with a throb of his heartbeat and a deep breath Plietor pushed the stick all the way forward and right, stood on the right pedal. The left wing came up as the glider turned. The nose dropped. He dove downwind toward the mist.

The sound of the wind in his ears mounted with the quivering of the glider as the mist rose up to meet him, and

163

as the first light was blotted he began counting: "flying-one, flying-two, flying-three, flying-four…" Kemper had recommended a count of five before pulling up, speaking of "mist-top altitude uncertainty" and "margins of safety." But that was before Carnahan had got his teeth into their production efficiency and started to bite. For weeks Janescz had stood about on the Shelf with a clipboard, shouting seconds as handlers and flyers scrambled to re-stage between sorties. But the crucial time was the time of the nets in the mist, and the time deepest in the mist was the most productive. The very densest mist was right above the pits, but they couldn't fly down there, not anywhere close to the bottom of the Caldera, with its great ruined city of rock. But where *was* the bottom of the Caldera? There was no way to see it. So they counted, and each second was twenty feet down toward the rocks. After Kemper left they began holding their dives six seconds, then seven, until they began to sense shapes around them. Fergus reported jamming the stick back to his crotch to clear a looming block. Rozum bragged about a swift weaving S. Davik, never to be outdone, narrated standing his glider on a wingtip to pass between two walls of stone after an eight-second dive. So Janescz had declared six seconds the limit. Dive six seconds, pull and rise. That was the cycle.

They had pushed that cycle four weeks before, the day Davik first went down the pit path. One second more was all Janescz would permit, but it was enough for four flyers to meet the quota of six, at least for half a day. Now Fergus was back, and the pace was easier, five- and six-second dives again meeting more than quota. Not much more, though. They all knew, though Janescz never said: make over-quota too much and Carnahan would increase it. The man knew no limits, had never seen a rock rushing backward in the mist.

But Plietor had pushed the cycle too, and not for Carnahan. He had pushed it to talk to Ginna at midday, after Davik's explosion about the camel train. Three dives for two sorties he held to seven seconds and he was at quota. Only two sorties, instead of the usual morning three. With his time he went to Ginna, helping her bad thinking, showing Janescz's books. This was something he could do, to talk to Ginna by himself. With no Davik.

And so he studied it, searching for stations in the Caldera where he could hold a dive. They all knew the center was better, away from the walls and their rockfalls. But for days of sorties, on one dive in three he had taken a careful position and gone in for seven seconds. If he saw shapes the position was no good. But if he saw no shapes he went eight. On the day he had gone to Ginna at midday to speak of his idea for the pole beans he had made morning quota with two eight-second dives. She was very happy with his idea. He could tell, with her tears, she was happy inside. She made him happy too.

"Flying-five, flying-six, flying-seven..." Plietor's mouth clenched now. He squinted ahead through the streaking goggles, left and right. Was that a shape to the right? Was it his imagination that the glider was slowing? Could so much jelly be soaking into the net? "Flying-eight," he said to himself. It *was* slowing. "Flying-nine!" He let out his breath in a rush and pulled back and to the left, pushing the left pedal, feeling the familiar weight in his stomach. He started a new count to the top of the mist.

Eleven seconds moving up into the wind, slowing, slowing to the top. And the glider was wallowing, the full net dragging and drooping behind the tail. A single dive and a full net! It's true he was out a little further in the Caldera than the others flew, and he would have to fly a series of swoops to use the wind in getting back, so it would take more time.

But a nine-second dive! That was something. Who could he tell? *Ginna?* Would she understand?

"It's out of order you are," said Simcas, approaching down the wing with his wiping rag and bucket. "Musil went off after you, and he's already down. Janescz wants to know." He gestured with his head toward the fob.

"I'll see him," said Plietor. "Mind the net. It's soaked full, I think."

"That's Karolyi's lookout," said Simcas, stooping under the nose.

Plietor met Janescz at the door of the fob, the older man with a dark expression under his hat and raised his eyebrows.

"What?" said Plietor.

"What!?" returned Janescz. "I ask *you* 'what?' It's time and more you were back. You're a sortie behind. What's there to say about that?"

"Nothing to say about it, except what's in the net," said Plietor curtly. "Look to that before you jump me." He was working at the buttons on the side of his overdaks as he put his hand on the door.

Janescz stepped quickly in front of him. "What's this now? A sortie behind and you're taking yourself off?"

"You look to my net. I said it. It's sopping. I'm over quota for the morning, and I'm taking my midday tucker where I like."

"You're taking it with *who* you like, you mean. I know it. You can't be doing this, Plietor. A barney will come over it for sure."

"Who's to say about that," said Plietor, pushing past him and through the door.

"You know who's to say," said Janescz.

"Hai, Plietor!" Ginna greeted him gaily as he kicked through the doorway. He felt the blood rise in his neck. She was standing at the cooking shelf, her forearms wet from washing, gazing at her glove. "My poor glove," she said, holding the tattered fingertips for him to see. "Is there any cloth about, a needle and thread? I should have asked before this."

"No," he said. "None here. Anna down in the bunkhouse has sewing things, old cloths."

"Maybe I'll ask her," said Ginna dubiously, then brightened. "I saw Drimka today pulling the linen out of the nesting boxes. Will he be collecting the chicken...the chicken fertilizer from them himself? He didn't look very happy about it, but then he never does...look very happy." She smiled a little uncertainly at Plietor.

He raised an eyebrow. "Who is happy? Would you be happy, if you were Drimka?"

"You looked happy, when you came in the door," she said.

Plietor felt the blood in his neck again. "And you too," he said. "With all your torn fingers." Ginna began a smile with their eyes held, then looked down. Plietor thought he saw a flush in her neck too, as she turned back to the shelf and her gloves. Her fingertips showed pink through the right hand.

"Drimka will scrape the chicken shit and give it in a bowl to Bartosz," said Plietor.

"And then Bartosz will leave it for me, on the table by the door," finished Ginna. "That's what you said he would do."

Plietor nodded. "So, in two weeks maybe we will know if the hypothesis about the nitrogen is good?"

"About then," said Ginna. She bit her lower lip slightly. "I do...I do hope it works out, that the plants improve. It would be so good if it did."

Plietor smiled from the doorway. "Then Bartosz will

know that I am the famous...*botanist*. Is that the word?"

Ginna lifted her chin and smiled back. "Even that would be good," she said. "Even that."

Plietor's glider had barely stopped rolling when he heard Davik's voice booming behind him.

"So, brother. I come to tell you I am at morning quota."

Plietor wrenched his goggles and balaclava over his head, twisted the handle of his belts.

"Only two sorties and I am." Davik's voice was closer now. Simcas was advancing toward Plietor along the right wing, wiping and listening. "How is that to you?" said Davik.

Plietor concentrated on levering himself out of the cockpit. Davik was standing behind the wing now, smiling a challenging smile. "You have one sortie more to fly. Karolyi says it, for quota. But I..." Davik's smile broadened. "I will go up to the Stack for midday tucker."

Simcas was wiping away at the fuselage, almost under Plietor's nose. Plietor looked down at him, keeping his glance away from Davik's eyes.

"Take your tucker from the shed ration then," he said. "There's no extra in the flat, is there."

Davik held to his smile, patted the taut fabric at the back of the wing. "Out you go again then, eh? I'll see you at out-ringing. Maybe we can talk of the chicken shit."

Simcas snorted from under the fuselage.

Plietor knew there was trouble as soon as he saw the gliders on the Shelf. He was flying back with a full net, second-to-last sortie of the day. Coming in from the north over the mist a flyer only got glimpses through the eddies as he approached the south end of the Caldera. Only after the air-brakes were pulled out and the glider descended could the

Shelf and Camp be made out—the Stack, Terrace, sheds, and gliders. What was wrong now was three gliders pulled aside below the sheds. Maybe one flyer was finished for the day, but not three, not, so Plietor knew, with three gliders behind him in the order.

He made his turn and descended over the Terrace, spending just a glance to look for Ginna, then focusing on his touch-down spot. He had long ago ceased to be conscious of the coordination of his left and right hands on the air-brake handle and stick, the minor bucking and bumping of the glider in the gusts. Now he looked only for things out of place, a handler walking without looking, an uncollected net bucket. No problem this time, except for three gliders below the sheds.

"What is *this*, then!?"

Plietor heard Janescz's voice before he even got to the corner of the sheds, heard the hard note in it. Coming around the corner he saw Davik, Musil, and Karpiak lounging against the side of the building, their overdaks in a heap against the wall. So it was *their* gliders pulled aside, askew below them on the Shelf.

Janescz had just emerged from the fob. He had been working inside the last two times Plietor had been in between sorties. He obviously did not know before this that the three had quit flying.

"We three are done for the day, pa-pa," said Davik, with a smirky smile.

"Done?" said Janescz. "What is 'done'? How many sorties?"

"Six, pa-pa," said Davik, "But—"

"Six? Six!? Seven we fly, *chłopców*. Every day we fly seven after—"

"No!" Davik broke back in. "We fly to quota. That is

why we fly, how we fly. Seven sorties, many days. But today, we"—he spread his hands to indicate Musil and Karpiak— "we fly to quota in six sorties. That is that. Ask Karolyi with the buckets. He will tell you." Musil and Karpiak nodded vigorously, Karpiak's nod transforming into his insistent cough.

Plietor drew up to the group and Davik gestured at him.

"He does this too. Two sorties in a morning and he is off to the Stack. You know this." Janescz looked at Plietor and tightened his lips. "I only follow Plietor," said Davik with a shrug and his squinty smile.

"Morning and after midday *both,* you follow him today," said Janescz. Davik shrugged again, larger, gesturing with both hands, Musil making the same gesture, as Janescz moved his eyes to him. Karpiak was coughing, turned away to the wall.

There was no conversation at dinner. Davik prowled the wall in the flickering shadows from the candle, talking in voices as if to himself, an improvised conversation between two old women *drtskas* about who was to use a rake and who a shovel. Every so often he would look at Ginna and smile, letting her know the conversation was for her. Plietor ate in silence, only glancing up to see the glances of Davik and Ginna. Janescz finished his soup and bread and arose to the shelf, returning with two radishes. He removed his folding knife from his pocket and carved unpeeled slices, chewing them deliberately, one by one. Two or three times Ginna drew breath as though to speak, but then did not. Finally she stood and collected the dishes to take to the shelf for washing. Plietor and Janescz sat. Davik paced, whistling now under his breath.

When Ginna was finished, she came to the table and stood for a moment, then, when no one looked, said she would go up to sleep. She retired to the wash room, came out after an interval, and stepped onto the ladder.

"Happy dreams, my Miss Ginna," called Davik. She half-turned and smiled, then stepped up into the darkness.

"So," said Janescz, closing his knife and returning it to his pocket, but not looking up. "We must talk of flying."

"What is to say?" said Davik. "Did we make quota?"

"Yes, we made quota," said Janescz. "Today we made quota. But the way we fly…we must make quota tomorrow, and the day after, and the day after that."

"Who says we can not?" said Davik.

Janescz looked up at him. "We all know the cycle and the production. Five-second dive. Six gliders. Three sorties before midday, seven after, makes quota. Carnahan is happy. We are safe. Three years we do this. Until now."

Davik came to the table and pointed a finger at Plietor, his voice rising. "Plietor, he is the one. He makes the long dive for two sorties so to come to the Stack for midday, back here for Ginna—"

Plietor felt the blood in his ears. He stood up in front of Davik, the sound of the bench rasping back loud in the room. "Who is the one!? Who? Who made us first go away from five seconds? You! You did."

"What!?"

"Sit!" ordered Janescz. "Sit. Both." He thrust his hands toward the benches. They sat, slowly, glaring at each other across the table. "Plietor means," said Janescz, "the day you went over the Shelf at midday, the first time. Four flyers then; only four we had. They had to fly deeper dives to make quota. Without quota, Carnahan wants to know why. And then…Did you not wonder why there was nothing against you, from that day?"

Davik chewed his lower lip and looked away. "It was important."

"It was important that you not be sent a month to the pools!" said Plietor.

Janescz raised both hands over his head. "I will talk this out," he said. "I. To you both." He looked at one, then the other.

"We cannot go away from five seconds. Not for Ginna. Not for Carnahan. With five seconds we are safe. The gliders are safe. We make quota. It is simple. We do not change it."

"It is not simple," said Davik.

"Why is it not?" said Janescz.

Davik looked at Plietor, started to say something, checked himself, and stood. He drew a breath and snorted it out. Finally he burst.

"It is boring!" Plietor looked up. "It is boring!" Davik said. "It is the same, time on time, day on day. Fly to station, dive five seconds, pull up, dive again, three times, five seconds, then back, and off again for the same, the same, the same."

"And seven seconds is not the same?" said Janescz.

Davik looked at Plietor, then back at Janescz.

"Seven seconds is not. Seven, eight seconds, there come the rocks in the mist." Davik stared intently at Janescz, raised his left hand, palm under, swooped it up, over, down. "*Whaaa*," he breathed, his right fist at his waist moving back and forth, as with the control stick. "*Whoaaa*." His palm banked out and left, reversing to right, his fist moving with it, his eyes shining, following images in his head.

"It is me and the glider, one thing only, through the mist like a snake." His left hand traced a sinuous curve. "This is excitement! This is life! Five seconds...five seconds is nothing." He shrugged, looked at Plietor. Janescz looked at Plietor too, who realized he had been sitting up very straight, tense, watching not Davik, but his own images. He nodded, shrugged too.

"So," said Janescz. "You both fly this way. Not for Ginna, but for excitement?" Two shrugs again. "Sometimes for Ginna, but always for excitement?" Davik and Plietor were both looking down.

"How long? How long is it that you do this?" Janescz looked from one to the other. "Always? From the beginning? Three years?" Neither looked up.

"Not always," said Plietor quietly. "More in the last—"

"What if we do?" broke in Davik. "We fly the gliders. We make quota. Who is to say how we fly the gliders? No one is there with us."

Janescz was rolling his eyes, raising his hand, but Davik plowed on.

"No one can see how we fly. Why can we not be excited? What is the rest of all this!?"

He made a sweeping gesture with his whole right arm across his body, backhand from the left side to the right. "The rest of everything in this place is shit. It is compost. In the gliders we can be excited. Where else? Tell me that? Where else?"

Plietor wanted to say, "At the dances," but he did not. Davik was in no mood for fine points. Plietor wanted to say, "With Ginna." But a bucket of reasons stopped him there.

"So. So. So," said Janescz, standing up. "Do the others fly this way too?"

Plietor shrugged. "Not all. Some do. Some times. Davik knows better what they do."

"Some and some," said Davik. "As he says."

Janescz shook his head. Plietor thought he suddenly looked old in the wavering candle light, his face haggard, lines deep, skin sagging.

"You are right," Janescz said. "No one is there with you,

in the glider. No one can make you fly any way. What I know…maybe it makes no difference to you. You know it too, and it makes no difference, you have said. But what we both know…" He shook his head again, looking not at them, but down at the table. "What we both know is that rocks are there, in the bottom where you cannot see, in the mist. And if you dive for excitement, you will find rocks. Not today. Not tomorrow, maybe. Not the day after. Not the day after that. But we fly every day, every day, every day for quota. And if you fly for excitement—or any reason besides quota—you will find rocks one day. For the rest of us it will be the lost wage for production, expense for a new glider, new-training another flyer, big monies away from us. But for who finds the rocks, it will be the end."

The room was silent, the wind sighing in the shutter. Janescz looked at them, each in turn, then stepped over the bench, moving toward the wash room. He stopped in the doorway.

"One thing more. However you fly, fly your sorties. Gliders pulled aside, flyers standing about with no overdaks, these things will be noticed. Bartosz watches us, as I watch Bartosz. Maybe our handlers even…" He gestured with his hand. "I don't know. But if word gets to Carnahan, our quotas will go…" He made a sour face. "They will go to the moon. We will be diving eight seconds, every flyer, every dive." Janescz took in his breath, let it out in a great sigh. "Until the rocks take us."

17.

The moat around the last pole bean plant was almost complete. Ginna knelt on the high side of the terrace wall, bent far over, wielding the trowel. She had finished the low side first, moving the scoops of soil into berms on the outside of the troughs. Two inches for the moats was deep enough, she had decided. Now just a bit more and she would be all the way around the last plant.

After the last scoop she rocked back, gathered her legs under her and stood, her back complaining bitterly from the stress. She arched to relieve the strain and surveyed her work: a chain of three joined moats around three adjacent plants. Very neat, though the plants themselves were certainly pitiful, as were the other seven in the row. She looked to the pottery bowl, with its mound of speckled chicken droppings. Drimka had been not at all happy to scrape the linen laid in the nesting boxes and roost floor, less happy than usual even, but under Bartosz's orders he had done it. She was just as glad he had blamed Plietor.

Was this one cup of droppings sufficient to make a difference for three plants? She was wholly guessing. If there was no result, was her hypothesis wrong? Or had she underestimated the amount of fertilizer needed? She would never know. But if it *did* make a difference…She tried not to think about that, tried not to let her hopes run away.

A glider passed low overhead. She was already standing so she looked, thinking it too low, and slow in the bargain. She thought the airbrakes must be out, but they shouldn't be, not with the glider so low already. Somebody was not paying attention. Even as she looked, the glider dropped its nose and picked up speed, salvaging the landing, but only at the last minute. *Bad flying,* she thought.

Something was wrong at the glider sheds. She understood that, though no Boruski had spoken about it at the flat. Well, except that one time, and then....

She should have understood earlier, understood when Plietor came to the flat that midday before the first Gathering, when she was so despondent. "Good flying," he had said. "Exceptional flying." It had put him ahead on his quota, so he could come. They had looked at the letters that day. More "good flying" the next time, when he had come to say he would speak to Bartosz about the chicken fertilizer for the pole beans. And the very next day Davik himself at midday, full of enthusiasm about sopping nets, with his own story of pole beans: a speech given by the chicken...she couldn't say the word...by the chicken fertilizer itself, running through the soil like a blind mole, a low, raspy voice seeking the roots of a bean plant. It was so funny! How did Davik compose these stories? How did he fashion the voices?

But she should have known it was not right, that it was not "exceptional flying" that gave them the luxury of a midday respite. She had noticed gliders pulled aside before the end of a day, when other gliders were still flying sorties. She had wondered why. Why were gliders suddenly out of order, after all the previous weeks of clockwork regularity?

The dinner after Davik had visited her at midday had been strange, tense, nobody speaking except Davik with his imaginary conversation. When she had gone up the ladder she had halted at the second level, listening in the shadow. "We must talk of flying," Janescz had said. And then they had argued about *her*, about Plietor and Davik coming to see her at midday, and she had understood: they were endangering themselves to do this. She had gone up then to her room. What could she do, to keep this from happening? What could she do…about Davik and Plietor?

She used her left hand to take pinches of fertilizer and spread it around the moats. It was clumsy using her left hand, but three fingers of her right glove were shredded to the first knuckle, and she thought it best not to handle the fertilizer with her bare, pink fingers, even caked with soil as they were already.

She stood up a moment, resting her back and looking over the thin circular lines of fertilizer. It was neat enough, if that was any benefit. She said something like a prayer before kneeling back down to trowel the bermed soil into the troughs.

At first Ginna thought it was just her imagination, wishful thinking. But two days more and she was almost sure, and when she came down from the Stack after in-ringing the next morning to find Tiska standing before the three plants there could be no doubt. They were unquestionably greener than the others, up and erect from the stakes. Tiska nodded at her as she approached, then put out her hand to a plant to part its leaves and reveal two delicate white flowers.

"This is good," said Tiska. "You have done good here."

"Oh…"said Ginna. She was about to say it had all been Plietor's idea, that they had to wait to see if the plants went all the way through bearing, and that before the weather changed. But she said neither thing.

"I hope so," she said.

"It is wonderful, those beans!" Plietor said, barely in the door in the evening. Ginna was setting out soup and bread. She looked up and smiled a closed, pleased smile.

"I have been looking, looking, every morning on the way to the gliders, and not saying," Plietor said, smiling a wide smile. He shook a finger at her. "You have been not saying either."

Ginna held his eyes for a moment with her own smile, then turned back to the shelf.

"Ha!" said Davik in the door behind Plietor. "It is beans again, is it? "Polska beans again?"

"It is!" Plietor said, stepping past the table to Davik's wall. "The polska beans with the chicken fertilizer are greening, greening and standing up. The others are…*pfft*." He gestured with his hand.

Davik took his place at the table and studied his pot of soup a moment before looking up, beaming. "So," he said. "Chicken shit is better than Carnahan shit. That is hypothesis."

Janescz emerged from the wash room just then, started to shake his head at Davik, then lapsed into a chuckle as he seated himself. Ginna, approaching the table with bowls in both hands, suppressed a giggle.

"Does Bartosz know?" asked Plietor from the wall.

"He has not come by to look, that I know of," said Ginna.

"He will then," said Plietor. "He will."

And Bartosz did, first thing the next morning. The irrigation water was still running down the paths and through the troughs when Ginna saw him stride from the sheds and head towards her and Tiska's row. They were working on the low side of the terrace and shared a glance before returning to their trowels. Bartosz went straight to the pole bean plants, walked the few steps down the row of ten, then returned and stopped before the three. He ruffled the foliage, then stepped back and looked down the row to Ginna and Tiska. They looked up, but he waved off their looks with a hand, turned, and moved across the central path to another row. Ginna and Tiska looked at each other and shrugged. What was there to say?

"Bartosz wants you, in the main shed, after out-ringing." Ginna looked up to see Tina, a woman who worked two rows below her, on the west side. Tina was returning to her row after a walk up to the sheds, probably to use the latrine, Ginna thought. Tina had never spoken to her before. Her voice was high, girlish, like one of the voices Davik used. She had turned before Ginna could read her face, to see what she might be saying about Bartosz's summons. Surely there could be no problem. Surely Bartosz was happy with the bean plants. But she had never been summoned by Bartosz before.

"So." said Bartosz as he turned in his chair. His work desk was a square table with a nest of pigeonholes at the rear edge. He had been writing with a pencil on a paper clamped to a clipboard. Small spectacles covered half his eyes. Ginna had never been so close to him before. His shoulders were round and full like Davik's but he was much taller, half a foot maybe, with black hair surrounding a dish of pale scalp in the center.

'So. I have seen the bean plants." Bartosz pushed back his chair and snorted. "Everyone has seen the bean plants. They are royalty of the garden."

Ginna widened her eyes.

Bartosz looked up at her, his head cocked over. "What do you say about this?"

"I..." Ginna began, "I suppose...they have perked up." She bit her tongue. What a ridiculous thing to say.

Bartosz snorted again, looked at her over his spectacles. "'Perked up.' You say they have 'perked up'?"

"Well..." Ginna drew a breath. "They have clearly improved a great deal over the way they were, over the way the others are."

"And this is from fertilizer, pure chicken shit fertilizer?"

"I...think it is," said Ginna. "I don't know what else to attribute...what else it could be. Everything else, for all the plants, has been the same."

Bartosz leaned back.

"That is what Plietor says to me. Chicken shit fertilizer on three plants, everything else the same. To find out if pole beans need special fertilizer."

Ginna gave a small shrug.

"And this is Plietor's idea?"

"Of course," said Ginna. Then, going on quickly, "He worked with you here in the plant shed. He told me that. He worked on hybrids. And..." Bartosz was looking at her, one eyebrow up, over his glasses. "And he still cares about the garden. I mean, everyone cares about the garden, but Plietor particularly."

A smile played around Bartosz's lips. "So. This idea of Plietor's. I say it is a good idea. The bean plants have life. We will get beans from them, to make up the seed stock, then we will replant in the spring, with many months to collect chicken shit fertilizer." His smile moved into his eyes. "Drimka will be most happy."

Ginna permitted herself a smile too.

"So. Your work is good. Your row is for production…" he reached for the clipboard, moved the glasses up on his nose, "…twenty percent above quota."

"It is Tiska's row too," Ginna broke in. "Her work is good too."

Bartosz's eyebrow went up again. "Yes it is. It is Tiska's row too. But that is the same…like seven bean plants without fertilizer." He was suddenly not smiling.

Ginna felt a wrench in her stomach. "Surely you…what are you…?" She drew a deeper breath then, squared her shoulders. "We all can make each other better."

Bartosz's expression softened again. "So. Each one makes the other better. It is a good thought. But some are better than others."

He turned back to the desk, reached into a pigeonhole and drew something out, held it up to Ginna. "This is for you," he said, "for good work, and good idea."

Ginna took the gloves from him, new gloves of sturdy canvas, too large, but…*new gloves!* She felt tears come into her eyes.

The garden shed room was lined on three sides with wooden counters, waist high, two feet deep. Covering the counters were narrow trays, also of wood, filled with dirt and fragile green sprouts. All the sprouts in each tray were the same, and Ginna moved among them, trying to identify them. Here sweet peppers, there radishes, potatoes, onions, tiny frothy greens of carrots. A dozen women and a few men clustered at the far end of the room, foraging among two wide sets of shelves and producing vegetables they spread upon a scarred table. A tall stack of flat bread rounds stood in the center, two fat jugs of water, many mugs.

"Hai, Ginna!" called a woman's voice. "It is to eat now.

Much time to work with those when they are due."

A second woman moved toward her, holding out a mug of water, eating a sweet pepper cut in half.

"Here's a mug for you. Look to it and use it regular. We all have our own." She stood beside Ginna before a tray bristling with diminutive stalks of onion. "Three weeks," she said. "In the earth three weeks, these are. Four weeks more and they go in the terraces. Always new coming, to replace those harvested. Bless the sun here, even through the mist. These…" she gestured to the trays, "nothing is more fresh in this place."

Ginna selected from the pile on the table a carrot, a segment of sweet pepper, a radish, a round of bread. A man sitting nearby gestured and pulled a folding knife from his pocket. Ginna hesitated, then handed him the radish, which he peeled deftly and handed back with a nod. Two women slid together on a bench to make a place for her. They smiled; she smiled back and sat. She smoothed her shift at the lap, set the bread on it, the mug atop that, took a hard bite of radish, and surveyed her fellow *drtskas*.

The talk was of mostly of vegetables: a potato that looked like it had stubs of arms, an eighteen-inch zucchini, a green worm no one had ever seen before. Some women sat or stood with men. One woman standing by herself in a corner was looking hard at Ginna but looked away when Ginna caught her eye.

All the women wore the same issue work shift, but Ginna noticed that some shifts had worn spots low on the fronts, some not. After a moment she realized the wear was from kneeling. She had seen some women kneeling on their shifts, while others pulled their shifts up to kneel on their bare knees. She looked at her own garment, worn spots just beginning to show, and caught the eyes of her seat companion on her hands, her gloves. The woman smiled uncertainly and looked away.

"I think I will go to the Gathering dance tonight," said Ginna. She had waited at the flat for the men, sitting at the table in the kitchen after the midday out-ringing, to make the announcement.

The men were shuffling around in the room, Davik eating at vegetables he had brought in his pockets from the shed ration. Janescz glanced from Davik to Plietor and moved to the ladder. He always washed his work clothes on midweek day, changing into his Gathering clothes for the trip down to the bunkhouse and the wash tubs there.

Plietor looked at Davik, and Davik returned a shrug. It was less than the enthusiasm Ginna had expected. But almost immediately Davik brightened. "This is good. I think it is. This is what should be. Miss Ginna with Davik for the dance." He moved to sit across from her at the table.

Plietor brushed past to the ladder, two steps up before Davik called to him. "Gwen is all for you tonight then, brother. She will be the happy lady." He winked at Ginna.

They sat for a moment in slightly awkward silence before Ginna stood up. "I must wash my work shift," she said, more in the way of another announcement than a comment to Davik. "And then I want to return the green dress to Julia, so that it may go back to its owner."

Ginna's work shift was still damp under her arms, though it had dried rapidly in the hot wind as she stood outside the bunkhouse a moment before walking next door to the clinic. She hadn't been back to the clinic since Davik and Karski had carried her up the ladder to the Boruskis'. And even her memories of the room there were unclear, dazed as she was by pain, sleeplessness, dreadful thoughts. Some of those thoughts, pushed away over the past four months, returned as she stepped into the door. Julia was not there, not in this front room where people were seen who were only slightly injured or ill. A table used for a desk, with a rack of pigeon-holes and a chair, stood in one corner. A tall cabinet with doors filled the opposite wall. In the center a long low table was covered with a pad for lying down.

Ginna passed through this room to the doorway on the back wall, parted the curtain and looked into the room beyond. This was where she had lain for three weeks, lain between life and death for...how many days? And then death in life with the pain for...Oh!...Eloise! The images rushed in on Ginna. Eloise was dead, and the German captain who had not wanted to go into the dust storm and...all the others, and her father didn't know...

"Julia!" she called, a little desperately. "Hai, Julia!"

"*Hai!*" Julia called from the room beyond.

What was in that room? *Another treatment bed?* thought Ginna.

Then Julia was coming through the doorway in her white apron, wiping her hands on a clean cloth. Her eyes lighted when she first saw it was Ginna, then faded into a frown.

"What?" said Julia.

Ginna tried her own smile. "I have come to return this dress," she said. She had taken extra care with the folding, and now held it out, speaking quickly. "It was wonderful for you to get it for me. I don't know what I should have done without it. But now I have my own working shift..." she did a small step "...and it should go back—"

"No!" said Julia. "It does not come back to me. The dress is for you. You have worn it. Everyone has seen you."

"But I don't need it," protested Ginna. "I don't need a Gathering dress. And whose dress it is will surely have missed it. I need to thank someone for the use of it. I am so grateful…and for the gloves and the boots, though…"

"No. No," said Julia, shaking her head strongly. "It is all for you. For you! It does not come back…" She clamped her lips tightly together.

Ginna's eyes widened suddenly. "These are *your* things, aren't they! Oh. Oh! They all came from you and…and…I am so sorry about the gloves." Tears welled into her eyes, and without thinking she stepped forward and put her arms out and then she and Julia were clasped in a hug and stood there, both crying, for a long moment.

Finally they stepped back a pace and stood, Julia lifting her apron to dry her eyes and then offering the cloth, held unnoticed in her hand, to Ginna.

"I do thank you so," said Ginna. "I don't know how I can ever repay you. You were so kind to me, so comforting through all the days here, and after, coming every day. I have so missed you…"

They were both crying again, but after a moment controlled themselves and redried their eyes. "Can we meet again?" asked Ginna. "On midweek days, in the afternoon, after I have washed? Can I come here, to talk?"

Julia smiled. "Yes. I would like that if you come…if your men will see you go."

Ginna looked to see if Julia was making a joke. But Julia's face was serious, questioning.

"I am sure they will have nothing to say about it—" began Ginna.

"Julia!" A man's voice called from beyond the inner doorway. "Julia! Where the bloody hell are you? Is somebody out there?"

"No! Yes! Someone is here. But I come..."

Dr. Wetkin appeared in the inner doorway, holding onto the side, coatless, his hair lank and disheveled. The tail of his shirt hung outside his trousers along one side.

"Who is this then?" he asked, peering at Ginna. His eyes were odd, she thought, almost no black at the center at all.

"It is Ginna," said Julia quickly, looking from the doctor to Ginna and back again. "From the Zeppelin."

'Ah," said Wetkin, nodding loosely. "From the Zeppelin. Yes. With the Boruskis. And is she well?"

Julia looked back and forth again. "Yes, she is well. She has just come...to return some clothes."

"Very good," nodded Wetkin again. "Well, if she is well she has no need of us. Come back here then."

"I will, in just a moment," said Julia, with a grimace. "You go to lie down, to rest. I will come."

Wetkin nodded and turned back into the dimness of the inner room. Julia looked at Ginna, her lips compressed, then looked down.

"I will go," said Ginna. "I will keep the dress, with the greatest gratitude." She reached out to touch Julia on the arm. Julia put her hand over Ginna's glove and pressed it, then looked up into Ginna's eyes.

"He needs the morphine," she said, "For the pain. His back, at the base, it is very bad. He cannot stand, you see, cannot sleep, without the morphine."

"I understand," said Ginna, just beginning to, tears in her eyes again. "Shall I come back, next midweek?"

"Please," said Julia.

"As always," Carnahan was saying, "we must enumerate our production, and celebrate it, if we have met our obligations." Ginna was only half listening. She had heard these words several times now. Everyone had to come to hear Carnahan's Gathering speech, whether or not they were going to stay for dancing. Julia and Dr. Wetkin never stayed, for instance. Julia always wore her work shift and apron, and Ginna had always assumed this was because Julia would not be dancing or needed to be dressed for a possible medical emergency. Now she knew another reason. Ginna herself had worn her own shift tonight. She did not feel she could wear the green dress.

Ginna looked for Julia but could not see her over the heads of the others. Julia and the doctor always stood near the front of the crowd, the Boruskis near the rear, Davik and his mob behind everyone else. But not tonight. Davik stood solid beside her, Janescz and Plietor on her other side.

"...a triumph over the malady of the pole beans," Ginna heard, and her attention fastened on Carnahan.

"Mr. Bartosz reports that the malady has been overcome by the application of a special fertilizer—"

"Special to chickens," said Davik beside her, in a loud stage whisper that carried around them, eliciting snorts from his mob and backward glances from others.

Ginna saw Carnahan look over the crowd to them and pause before going on.

"...the idea for such treatment arising from Plietor Boruski, who maintains his interest in food production even in his present work as a flyer for our aerial collection." Faces in the crowd turned to them, appraising looks. But Carnahan wasn't finished.

"The application of this idea was carried out by Ginna deBoruski, our newest worker on the Terrace and an example to us all." Ginna felt the blood come up in her neck and looked down, but not before she saw other faces turning, some she recognized from the Terrace. She only vaguely heard Carnahan going on with "thanks to the Boruski household" and a statement about resumption of pole bean production to occur with the fall planting. Davik shifted beside her.

"...chemical recovery," Carnahan was now saying, "twenty-two percent over quota..." "outstanding production from our full complement of flyers..." Ginna felt Janescz shift on her other side at this and glanced over to see him looking hard at Plietor, who looked back, his lips tight.

"In light of this outstanding production," Carnahan said, and Ginna now felt both Janescz and Davik tense, "I am happy to say I am able to raise the production quota for our aerial collection by ten percent, with the attendant opportunity that sure and provides for enhancement of wages for all." Ginna heard someone begin clapping in the front.

"Bloody Karski," muttered Davik, as ragged clapping swept over the crowd and Carnahan nodded from his box.

"*Cholera!*" Janescz whispered fiercely, but so soft only Ginna and Plietor heard.

"Dance now!" said Davik, stepping back into his deep bow before her.

Davik had brought Ginna into Carnahan's long room and installed her on the bench by the band, as he had at her first Gathering dance. Then, as before, he had taken himself off to secure his nobbler. There was quite a queue at Karski's table, and the band players noodled to themselves while the crowd milled. Ginna recognized some of the couples standing together from the Terrace middays. Other women and men moved separately up and down the room, conversing, feeling the warmth of their drinks. Some smiled at her as they passed, but no one sat.

After an interval, the band organized itself and the clarinet led into a slow dance tune. Couples emerged from the flux and formed into a circle, men on the outside, women on the inside, swaying to the rhythm.

And then there was Davik, suddenly before her with his bow. "Dance now!" She was up without thinking, then standing before Davik on the inside of the circle. She did give a thought as she reached her gloved hands to the women on her either sides. But they took her hands freely, a shrug from one and a smile from the other. And soon the music rose and the circles moved, men as the clock, women counter, with a slide and a slide and a step forward and back until she was once again before Davik, who beamed at her from under his blond mop, sweat already beading his forehead. A chord from the concertina, the music changed, and they were off, Davik's firm grip directing her through hops and skips, ins and outs, twirls and cross-overs. To move thus to music was something she had not done in a long time, and Ginna gave herself over to it, Davik coming and going before her, she conscious of their arms wrapped this way and that, her hands clasped with his. Once or twice over the course of the dances she found herself in partnership with Plietor, as couples exchanged with the steps. But he only just met her eyes with an even expression, and his grip was tentative.

Davik began every dance with her, his Gathering shirt soaked with perspiration, the back of her shift as well, if truth be known. They were no different in this from any of the other dancers, but where the pungency of bodies had assaulted her at her first Gathering dance, it did not at all on this night, adding only a certain tang to the thickness of the background. Here and there a man or a woman coughed, but no one took any notice

When the band stopped for the interval, Davik sat her on her bench and announced he would take himself off but be back "sooner than a wink." Sooner than that, though, a woman was beside her, fanning herself with her hands, her ample flesh above her bodice a rosy flush. Ginna knew who she was, knew her from the Terrace as the one who watched her, day after day, from a corner of the shed room when they took their midday ration. Ginna thought she worked a terrace above her, on the west side.

"Ooh! It is sure and the very heat of Hades here."

Ginna recognized the voice immediately. It was "Gwen," the woman whose voice Davik did to annoy Plietor, though now Ginna heard the voice from its source, she thought Davik did not precisely catch the Irish of it.

"And we poor creatures, we frolic in the very midst of it. What's that make us then?"

Gwen looked sideways at Ginna, continuing her fanning.

Ginna smiled a small smile. "That's an interesting sentiment," she said. "Do you wish an answer to your question?"

"*Ohh,* the question comes with its own answer, I think," said Gwen, interrupting her fanning with one hand to wave it in the air. "Yet we *are* poor creatures, who take our comfort where and when we can." She smiled back at Ginna, an odd smile. "And do you take your comfort with Davik, Miss Ginna deBoruski?"

Ginna started back, then stopped herself. What was this woman saying? "I…I'm sorry not to know you, as you know me," she said.

Gwen sniffed. "Oh, you know me well enough, I should think. It's a simple question, coming, it does, from my interest in the Boruski household, which is no secret."

"Well…" began Ginna. "I am certainly enjoying myself with the dancing tonight, with Davik, and with all."

Gwen sniffed again, smiled her odd smile deeper this time. "As I am, with Plietor, and with all. But not with Plietor as you are with Davik. Though..." she paused to raise an eyebrow, "I well wish it were so." Ginna felt herself beginning to blush. "Do you know," Gwen had ceased her fanning now, "I never thought the two as brothers so much as when I saw them with you, you and Plietor so much the same about the mouth, Davik and you about the eyes. Maybe that's the advantage you have with them." Ginna's blush had turned to a rush of blood in her face. What *was* the woman saying? Gwen smiled on at her, smiled, smiled..."Or maybe it's just the advantage of the third level bed in the Boruski household."

Ginna started up from her seat, the blood roaring in her ears, Gwen reaching a hand out to her, her smile now a cool smirk stretched across her broad face. Ginna jerked from a hand on her waist.

"Hold up now," Davik said from behind her. "It is only me, your dancing partner." He looked down at Gwen on the bench, with his own half smile. "And I see you make the acquaintance of the late Gwendolyn O'Shanahan, who herself is only happy to make acquaintance of brother Plietor, whenever she is able." Ginna saw that Davik's smile had twisted into what she could only call a leer, and Gwen was leering right back at him.

"And don't we all wish to make acquaintance whenever we are able?" said Gwen, rising from the bench as the clarinet sounded a rising sequence. "I leave you to your...dancing."

Davik still had his hand on Ginna's waist. He shook his head at Gwen's departing as the concertina played an introductory chord. Couples were forming a circle in the center of the room. "The Lady Gwen," Davik said. "She is the hot one."

"Can I ask you something?" said Ginna. The dancing had

ended and she was standing with Plietor in the Yard beyond Carnahan's standing box. Janescz had already climbed
the ladder up to their flat. Davik was trying out a new Cos-
sack-style step inside with a few others. Other couples and
groups stood around the Yard cooling off before retiring, but
none within earshot.

"Yes. Of course," said Plietor.

"Gwen…" began Ginna.

"*Acch*, Gwen!" Plietor kicked a stone with his boot toe.
"I saw, when she came to you on the bench, Davik not five
steps gone." He snorted. "She talked, and you jumped up,
jumped again when Davik came behind you." He kicked another stone, swinging his leg back and forth. "What is about
Gwen?"

"Well…" began Ginna again. "The question is not about
Gwen, specifically. It's about…how men and women are…
together here."

Plietor stopped swinging. "Ah," he said.

"I mean," Ginna went on hurriedly, "I see men and wom-
en together, standing together at midday among the *drtskas,*
at the Gathering speech too, and at the dancing. And Julia
said once that some men and women are…they stay together, in the Stack. How is this done?"

"It is an ordinary question," said Plietor, looking out into
the night. "There is no mystery. When a man and woman
want to be together, to stay with each other, they apply to
Carnahan. When a flat comes open in the Stack, he thinks
of them."

"How does a flat come open?" Ginna asked.

"One dies. One is too sick. One is angry. Or…" Plietor
shrugged, "Carnahan just decides."

Ginna was silent a moment. "What do they do while
they are waiting?"

Plietor turned and looked at her, then looked away again. "They go to the root flat."

Ginna was silent. The moment extended, both standing in the dark, until Plietor suddenly stepped around to stand squarely before her.

"You want to know, do you? You are for sure about it? We're all close here, you know. Every one knows every one's business. It's men and women, and men and women do what men and women do. The root flat is just a flat, one room with a bed, at the end of our level, above the clinic rooms." Plietor paused, and she realized he was angry, or terribly impatient with her.

"The clinic, you know it. Do you know your friend Julia is together with the doctor? Do you know *that*, eh? They stay in the clinic flat, behind the sick rooms. She keeps him upright, is what she does, as much as he is. And she goes to Carnahan too, when he wants her."

Ginna looked away.

"What else do you want to know? Oh, yeh, the root flat. There's a schedule. Anna keeps it in the bunkhouse, on a clipboard. Can't have rooting in the bunkhouse, can we? You sign up and you get your hour. Great demand on Mid-Week afternoon, I tell you, and now, and after now. I can say for sure and there's a couple—man and woman most likely— rooting away in there right at this minute."

Ginna was looking at the ground, staring dry eyed, feeling Plietor's anger wash over her. Plietor reached down to pick up a stone and flung it out over the Shelf. "Shit!" he rasped, under his breath. Then he turned on her again.

"Oh, yeh. One last thing. The Lady Gwendolyn you asked about. The Lady Gwendolyn would have me up in the flat rooting her twice a day if she could. But she can't, so she roots whoever'll go with her, including..." He broke off, turned away. *"Cholera."*

"I…" Ginna caught her breath. "I'm…going up now. I'm going…please tell Davik." She turned without looking at Plietor and started back to the Stack ladder.

"Everyone expects, you know," he called after her. "Everyone expects…" Ginna gathered her shift in both hands and broke into a run.

18.

Plietor hurried from his glider across the Shelf to the glider sheds, his balaclava and goggles dangling from his hand. Janescz was out from the fob with his watch and clipboard, as he was almost always these days, just now shouting at the handlers for Karpiak's glider. Karpiak was already belted in the cockpit from the look of him, with a handler yet wiping at the tail, others just beginning to attach the stretching rope. Too slow.

"*Szybciej!*" Janescz was shouting. "Make faster! Faster!"

This was the way since Carnahan's last pronouncement of more quota for them. The first increase of ten percent was nothing. Janescz was not happy, because it was the thing he feared: make over-quota too much and Carnahan would raise it. But more quota for chemical production was a higher wage for everyone in the Camp, so everyone but Janescz was happy.

The flyers, though, were not so much concerned with quota. Davik had said it, in the night after the midday he came to see Ginna. Flying was the only time they were free men, away from the Camp, where they could make their own excitement. They made it with the dives. If deeper dives made more production, that was as it was. If Janescz wanted ten sorties a day, production was going up. More excitement was more production. And once excitement was into the open, all the flyers wanted more, even Plietor himself.

And so Carnahan had raised quota again, fifteen percent, with great praise for "industrious flyers" and more talk of wages for all. Everyone in Camp was happier but Janescz, and he was less happy, in equal proportion.

What Janescz could do he did, make the time less on the Shelf for a glider between sorties. More time in the air meant a flyer could fly more dives to a full net, and so dive only six seconds, maybe seven. Plietor had used this time Janescz made, but not the others, at least to hear the talk in the sheds. More dives was not excitement. Deeper dives, rocks in the mist, that was excitement. And Davik, with his stories, was most excited of any.

Plietor dunked his goggles into the water bucket in the corner of the fob and wiped over his face with a cloth. He heard a call from outside, knew it meant Musil landing, behind Plietor in the sequence. Three gliders on the Shelf, if Karpiak was not off yet. Plietor needed to get back and be off himself, but piss first.

Szybciej! Faster! Faster! So it was on the Shelf. But this made time in the air more precious, to fly above the mist in the clear air, to dive deep. How could Janescz offer anything for that?

"We have our first hybrid peppers!"

They were at the table, eating soup and bread. Plietor could tell that Ginna had a secret. Her eyes were alive and she smiled for nothing. But Janescz only frowned into his soup—he frowned all the time now—and Davik drank his pot down and stood to the wall tearing pieces of bread, talking to himself in his throat.

Finally Plietor had said into the silence, "How is the dirt?" And that was when Ginna had said it: "We have our first hybrid peppers!" as excited as Davik after a deep-dive flight. Bartosz had taken her into the shed, as he had taken Plietor himself six years before. Since the gliders had come and Plietor had been taken as a flyer—four years nearly now—Bartosz had found no other *drtski* good for the work in the shed. Until Ginna. Ginna had found the problem of the pole beans and Bartosz saw what she was and brought her into the shed. And now she had hybrid peppers.

Plietor remembered the night Ginna had tried to tell them about the cross, a *paprika* with a green sweet-type, big and fast growing. Davik had asked about the *paprika*, all interest, and Ginna, poor Ginna, had explained the small round thing with the bite to its taste. And Davik...Davik had gone off into a loud story about a small round red breast and a big green one and the taste of each from a big naked gardener. And Ginna had turned red into her hair, and Janescz had to make Davik stop.

Now Ginna was excited because you could never tell before you tried if the cross would go. If she had peppers on the plants then this cross was okay, and now she could wait for a month to see what the fruit was.

Davik muttered from the wall, then came to the table and squatted at the end, his elbows lying out.

"I remember the hybrid," he said. Janescz with his frown looked over at him, but Davik smiled a child's smile. "The one too small and red. The one too big and green. So you put them together to make one better by itself." He smiled the child's smile again at Janescz. "I remember a story, from my mother."

When he said this everybody looked. Plietor looked at Janescz, Janescz at Davik, and Ginna looked at them all with an odd expression. But Davik was smiling, and saying in his own voice, "In this story there is a girl, and her name is Złotowłosa."

"Goldilocks," said Janescz.

Davik smiled at him. "Goldy-loks, then. And she goes to the house of the three women."

"Three bears," said Janescz.

"Three bare women," said Davik. Janescz looked at him, one eyebrow up. Davik smiled the child's smile at him a moment more, then said "Ha!" standing and putting his two hands to his chest, on either side.

"And Złotowłosa looks at one bare woman and says—"

"No!" said Janescz.

Plietor looked down at the table, shaking his head. Ginna looked at Davik, her eyes wide. But Davik would not stop for Janescz, and he said in a little-girl voice, "Those breasts are too small and red."

"No!" said Janescz again and began to stand.

"At the other bare one Złotowłosa says, 'Those breasts are too big and green.'"

Janescz lunged toward him, but Davik retreated to the corner, falling over himself with laughing.

"But at the third woman," Davik gasped, barely able to speak with laughing, "Złotowłosa says, 'Those are just right,' and she takes a big bite!"

Janescz reached Davik and tried to hold his arms, but Davik put his hands up to his face and Janescz could not move them, even though Davik was laughing silly. Janescz was so angry at him laughing. He shouted, "Why can we not have a conversation at this table? Why can we not talk without a bawdry story every time any one speaks of a vegetable?"

And suddenly Davik was not laughing. His face was red and he was shouting too.

"Who wants to talk of vegetables? Who? Only Plietor. Plietor! So can Plietor talk of vegetables with Ginna, but

Davik, what can Davik talk with Ginna? Does Ginna know flying? The deep dives? Does she know Germany? Davik thinks." He hit the heel of his hand against his head. "Davik thinks too. Not just Plietor, Plietor, Plietor."

Plietor felt his heart thudding. Ginna was sitting rigid, her fists pressed against her throat. They were like this a long moment, Davik breathing like a horse. Then he pushed past Janescz, threw open the door to bang against the wall, and thrashed out into the night.

"Did you see Rozum?!"

Plietor was hurrying from his glider across the Shelf to the fob. Janescz was out with his clipboard, called to him as he passed by Karpiak's glider.

"No," called back Plietor. "He is after Davik, before Fergus. I would not see him. Ask them."

Janescz raised a hand and Plietor stopped while Janescz moved over to him. "I did ask Davik and Fergus. They have not seen him since the last launch. He is half an hour behind. Now I am asking everybody."

"Half an hour!" said Plietor.

Janescz gestured with his head toward the fob. "Go. Stay in the sequence. Two more sorties."

The whole of the glider crew were gathered at the door of the fob. The flyers stood together—Davik and Plietor, Fergus, Musil, Karpiak on the edge, coughing into his sleeve. The handlers stood too—Simcas, Karolyi, six others. Walter Prokup stood with Janescz. But no Rozum. Rozum was not there.

The gliders were in: checked over, wiped, pushed into the sheds. The iron had beaten out-ringing. But they all stood. And Janescz was speaking.

"The last to see him was Fergus. Fergus launched right behind and followed him to his station, continuing beyond and west to his own." Janescz looked at Fergus. "It is sure you saw nothing strange in the flying to station?" Fergus shrugged, shook his head. "Did you see him go in on the first dive?"

"Aye. I half-seen, you know, back over my shoulder," said Fergus. "I wasn't looking for nothing, now was I?"

"No," said Janescz, "no reason for looking. But maybe even half-looking...anything...did you see anything at all? Any strangeness in the way of flying for the glider?"

"Nothing I saw." Fergus said, beginning to scowl. "What's to see? The glider turns, noses over, down into the mist. *Poof!* It's gone. Nothing for anyone to see after that."

"You saw no flutter, no strange movement?"

Fergus shook his head, scowling more, his neck reddening.

"And did you see him come up again, out of the mist?"

"Sweet Jesus, old man! No! I didn't see him nothing after he is into the mist. I never look for him on sortie after I turn to my station. I sure and got my own business to attend to in my own bloody glider."

"But this time you were the last to see him—"

"So!?" Fergus was looking hard at Janescz now. "He does what he always does. I do what I do. There's nil to remark on."

"Except that he didn't come back," said Janescz.

Men shuffled. Plietor saw Simcas and Karolyi exchange a look.

"Aye, he didn't," said Fergus. "And we bloody well know what that's about, don't we? You've sure and told us enough."

More shuffling, and a murmur growing through the group.

Davik broke in. "We *don't* know, do we! It's what we try to figure here."

"Oh, piss off, Davik," Fergus said. "You know more than buggerall anybody—"

Davik and Fergus sprang towards each other almost at the same instant, but they were steps apart, and Plietor and Janescz were at once between them, while other men filled in around.

"This is not the way we will know about Rozum!" shouted Janescz, pushing Davik backward, while Plietor pushed Fergus. "We must know about Rozum."

"You'll never know about Rozum," growled Musil, on the edge of the scuffling. And as men stood once more, eyes turned to him.

"He's bloody down in the rocks somewhere, is all you'll know. But you *must* know that, if you know anything! And tomorrow—" Musil stabbed a finger at Davik, at Plietor, at Karpiak in turn, "it is one of us."

Men stood, the flyers looking every way but at each other, the handlers gaping from the edges.

Finally Janescz spoke, his head up. "It is true what Fergus says, about my telling. I have warned and warned about the deep dives. I know about the high flying, about the freedom, about the excitement." He passed his eyes over the flyers. "It is what you have, and I understand that. But the danger...the danger is too great, as Musil has just told. Rozum will not come back, and we cannot find him, and...a glider is gone too."

The murmur rose in the group again, and Janescz scanned over them.

"There will be much wage lost to that, for all of us here." The murmur swelled, and Janescz raised his voice to speak above it. "You know it will be so. A new glider from Perth. A new man trained to fly. A flyer off production to train him. We will all lose wage and have penalties, every one."

The others were moving around the flyers, the murmur with a new tone.

"Gott damn production!" growled Musil. "Every one is a slave to the bloody quota."

"And who do we have to thank for the bloody new quota? Tell me that," called a voice from the edge of the group, and the murmur swelled louder.

Janescz raised his hand. "The quota is here," he said. "Carnahan will not change the quota. And if we do not make quota, the wage is lost to the whole Camp, and none will be pleased."

"Bloody gottdamn Carnahan," said Davik under his breath, but Janescz ignored him.

"But we can make quota, the new quota, if we work together all, if we…" Janescz paused, continued in a lower voice, "if we fly for production, and for no reason other."

Plietor was not looking up. But he felt the eyes of all the men on him and the other flyers.

"And then no one will be not pleased," Janescz said, "not any, and not Carnahan."

19.

Bugger the whole bloody bunch of them. Carnahan stood behind his table, his hands clasped behind him, looking through the window at the mist swirling up over the edge of the Shelf. Just when things were skating so right, such a sodding misery as this had to fall on him.

He had understood it could come at any time. Kemper had said it. "Aerial collection is inherently uncertain." Kemper had writ it so in the report he had sent back to Mr. Ian MacReedy, when he declared flying with the nets a success. "Inherently uncertain." So many things to go buggered. A glider to break all by itself from bad materials. Or from being knocked, a bad gust at an ill time. The trailing net to snag from flying too close. A flyer nackered, or just careless. *Daredevil?* Kemper had not had that in his list.

Gliders had broken and flyers had sagged, as Kemper said they would. A broken glider was out a day or two, rarely a week. Janescz was good for fixing them. Flyers got the grippe or the trots like everyone, but it was only days there too. Fergus...Fergus had broken his glider bad, and it was four weeks for Janescz putting it back to go. But production had stayed up, even then. He had said it must be so, said it clear to Janescz, and Janescz had kept the bit in all his lads' teeth. No drop in production. The others made up.

Sure and that made him think. How much could they

make up, if they were hard pushed? How much quota could they meet? It was a business choice, is what it was. Leave the quota below what they could make and have it stay up when the "inherently uncertain" came by? Or raise quota and bear the fruits in the best times, to see production fall below in the ill? How close to walk the horse to the edge of the cliff, yet have a care it did not step over?

He had decided on stability. That's what the toffs in Perth wanted to see. "Dependable production," as Mr. MacReedy himself had said, "a sign of a well-oiled operation." Not so good for his own side-bet, though.

And then, with no push at all from himself, production started to go up. He saw it first in Janescz's dailies, and then from the pools. No drop in purity, just more of the same. *And why?* He had no idea. Bartosz had told him flyers were standing around, voices up gay. Bartosz had production up too, but he knew the why of that. It was the girl, pushing them all with naught more than her ways. The pole beans, then production from her whole sector, then the other *drtskas* up too. Bartosz had her in the sheds now, "making better plants," whatever that was about. Bartosz knew what he was doing.

But Janescz. When he asked Janescz the why of production going up Janescz had said "efficiency and morale." *Morale.* Not bloody likely. Something was going with the gliders. Well, he would go with it. So up quota ten percent. Now talk of morale! More production pushed higher wages. He told all of them at the Gathering when he announced the new quota, and he could make the wages so, with the right word to Perth. He would make the bloody morale in his Camp!

As to production from the gliders, though, it went up still. Janescz would not speak on it frankly. The flyers were "excited," he said, warning "flying begets daredeviltry."

What the bloody hell was that? It was not safe, said Janescz. He would control it. But Carnahan did not want Janescz's control. Carnahan could have the stability they expected in Perth and put the overage in his side bet. The more he ran the sums on that, the better he liked it. That was the true stability he wanted, with the pounds dancing in his head, and he made *that* so. Up quota fifteen percent.

And it was met and stable for weeks. Until now. Now Janescz had lost a flyer and a glider. Rozum, dead in the Caldera—or dead to them anyway—and a glider gone. A buggered misery for sure.

Janescz had no more than spoken him the news yesterday evening than he was asking that the fifteen percent up on the quota be taken back. *Taken back!* How would that be then. Every sodding soul in the Camp would want something taken back. Except wages. Tell all to speak to Janescz about loss of wages from lower production from the gliders, and Janescz would learn soon enough about bloody morale. Janescz would have his hands full with the flyers and handlers anyway. The loss and penalty from Rozum would fall big on them. But the biggest loss if Carnahan took back the quota would be to himself. He would not have that. He would not.

Was the horse stepping over the cliff? He was sure it was not. Janescz could make the quota. Rozum had gone the way of the "inherently uncertain," but that was just one glider in five years, a hundred thousand sorties. Carnahan had done those sums too. To keep the quota was a business decision. That's what it was.

"We gather at this special time in sorrow, at the loss of one of our own."

It was not midweek, but Carnahan knew there must be a Gathering to deal with Rozum. He had always done this for any death, after out-ringing the day after, so there'd be no loss of production. But especially this, the loss of a flyer and glider. All would want to know what followed from it.

Carnahan swept his eye over the assemblage, seeing faces in their usual places. Wetkin and Julia in the front, Wetkin swaying as usual, Julia's two hands on his arm. Carnahan would have to do something about Wetkin somewise, but he didn't know what. Bartosz behind to the left, head above the rest, a strong man, a good super. Where was Helinski? Should be in the center halfway back, in his acid-stained hat. Yes. He was just bent over talking. Janescz was at the back, Plietor and the girl, and Davik with his mob behind all, at least looking to the front now they were. Davik had been standing with the girl for the regular midweek Gatherings, but there was no dance tonight. Where was Gwen? He liked to look at her, when he could. He would like to do a right lot more than that, and she would be for it, no doubt. But he knew he could not.

"Vol Rozum was a brave man, as all our flyers." Carnahan let the words drop, then spoke on the perils of the Caldera, on the vitalness of chemical production, their-all dedication to it. He wanted to hold up Rozum just a proper degree, but no more. The bloody flyers went their own way enough as it was. Janescz said flying begat "daredeviltry." Well, the devil take Rozum, then. Carnahan for sure didn't want anyone speaking for a party to go looking for him.

"So though we shall not have him to lay with those who have gone before to the stony ground, yet will he live for us in our memories as one who gave the best he could to our mutual effort."

Carnahan removed his hat and held it over his chest, bowed his head, though not more than that he could see the other men did the same. He nodded over to Karski, who laid the hammer on the iron five great strokes for an out-ringing. A moment more, then just as people began to shift Carnahan restored his hat and spoke again.

"Now must we all, who are not yet at our appointed time, go back to our work. I will send for a new glider from Perth. MacReedy Mining is well aware of the vitalness of our gliders in the quota of production we must meet, and I have every confidence at their response...as well as their sympathy at our loss." He added this phrase at the last moment, and was glad he had thought of it, though he was not too sure of the word.

"But my sending cannot go out before the next camel train, and the response from MacReedy Mining cannot come before the one after. So we can not expect the new glider before winter, and possibly the spring next, as much as half the year."

Carnahan was prepared for the shifting among them. Eyes were upon him sure.

"You will all be thinking, 'What is the consequence of this loss to chemical production, and thus to my wage, increased generously twice the last fortnight?'"

"Too right on that," Carnahan heard from the left side, with a murmur after it. Carnahan nodded in the direction of the voice. "I have given this much thought, and spoken with Janescz Boruski upon it, as to production capacity of the remaining aerial collection." He looked over the assemblage, not pausing at Janescz. "My word is that the quota will remain as it is, with the wage increased retained all round."

"*Yah!*" he heard from several throats, and a murmur swept the group, with heads turning, eyes meeting eyes in agreement. Carnahan permitted himself a small smile, keeping his eyes from the Boruskis. He would speak at least a token for them, though.

"The burden falls on the flyers, as well those who handle the gliders, Janescz's men in the shed and on the Shelf. They must bear the load of their lost comrade, and we owe them for their fortitude in this difficult time. Speak to them of your appreciation, when you see them." Now he looked at Janescz and nodded. He could not see Janescz's expression, under his hat. But Janescz did not nod back.

20.

"He has the soul of a snake!" said Plietor.

He had barely been able to contain himself, climbing the ladder to the flat. They had not spoken among themselves as the assemblage had filed from the Yard into the Stack. No one had spoken to them either, though many had glanced from the corners of their eyes.

Davik spoke from behind Plietor, closing the door behind them. "*Psshht!* We can fly his bloody quota and see him in hell. We are men, we are."

Plietor turned on him. "Oh gag it, Davik! We were barely flying it before with six. Now with five—"

"Let us wash and eat," interrupted Janescz wearily. "We can speak with better calm after food."

Ginna lighted the candle on the table and went silently into the wash room. Plietor pulled at the bench, half bent over to sit, following Ginna with his eyes without thinking. A sharp kick from the other end of the bench, and he jerked up to see Davik scowling at him. Plietor set his lips and turned away.

Janescz pushed his empty soup bowl forward, pulled his knife from his pocket and unfolded it. He chose a turnip from vegetables Ginna had brought to the table and began to peel, a long purple ribbon. "Here is what it is," he said.

Plietor looked up from his own soup. Davik stopped his pacing in the shadows along the wall.

"We can fly for Carnahan's quota—" began Janescz.

"With only five?" broke in Plietor.

Janescz put down the knife and lifted his hand for him to be quiet. "Even with five, I say we can. I said it yesterday, when we all stood at the fob, *men* of the air and Shelf." He emphasized the word, glancing up at Davik in the corner, then resumed his peeling. "If the flyers fly *only* for production, only that, and we are quick with the gliders between sorties, we can fly the quota." He looked pointedly at Davik, then met Plietor's eyes. "And Carnahan cannot turn the whole rest of the Camp against us."

Plietor felt the blood rush up his neck. "Bloody shit, that," he said before he thought, then looked quickly at Ginna, who was sitting straight, her hands in her lap, looking at him. He looked away, stood from the bench, and spoke.

"Carnahan says, 'The whole Camp.' It boils my blood to hear him! 'They must bear the load of their lost comrade.' The 'must' is all Carnahan's 'must.' For two years we flew the same quota, and there was no problem, no problem with Perth that Carnahan ever said, no problem with the Camp. Now in just weeks the quota is up and up and 'must' stay up. And the whole Camp is against us if it is not? Because of the wage? I don't believe that. It's a bloody damn lie is what it is." He looked at Ginna again, but she was looking at Janescz. "Half the Camp will never see their wage. They will die here and—"

Plietor's head was already hot, but when he said this the blood roared in his ears, and he stopped. Janescz and Ginna were both looking at him sharply.

"They must bear the load of their lost comrade," crooned Davik from the shadows, soft, in Carnahan's voice.

Janescz looked away for a moment and then breathed a deep sigh. "What you say is true, likely true, though you say it here, and nowhere other." He glanced into the shadows. "Davik, do you hear this?"

"Yes, pa-pa," said Davik.

"But we cannot know what Carnahan thinks," continued Janescz. "We say it and we say it because it is true. We can know only what Carnahan says. He says we will fly the new quota, and we will. And we will be safe, if we fly with discipline. Horst Kemper was the big one for discipline in flying, and we have gone away from his words. We must go back. Do you hear this too, my Davik?"

"*Achtung!* Attention you all," said Davik. Ginna started and stared, because it was Horst's voice coming from the wall, as real as if he were standing right there. Davik smiled at her from the gloom.

Janescz sighed again. "So now we have said it and now we will sleep. Tomorrow will be all discipline. We will speak these things on the Shelf, with everyone. We will not argue…with Fergus, with Simcas. We will all be for one thing. You both will show the way." He nodded at Plietor, at Davik.

On the table the peel from the turnip Janescz was carving curled in a purple and white ringlet. Janescz quartered the meat into four wedges. Ginna took a wedge and carried it with bowls to the basin. Janescz stood stiffly and moved to the wash room. Plietor went to the ladder. Davik sat himself down, taking two wedges, biting one in half, watching Ginna at the shelf.

"Karpiak coughed blood today." Davik spoke from the corner of another dinner.

Plietor felt a skip in his heart. Janescz looked up quickly, and they stared at Davik, bowls and the plate of bread before them. Ginna followed their motions, her spoon poised, her eyes going from one to the other.

"Tell us," said Janescz.

"I came quick to the fob in the afternoon," said Davik. "After the third sortie, to clean and to piss." Plietor saw him glance quickly at Ginna, back to Janescz. "And Karpiak was still there, with a cloth for his face, coughing, you know."

Janescz nodded. "We have all heard Karpiak with the cough."

"Yeh," said Davik, coming from the corner over to the table, into the light from the candle. "He coughed so." Davik raised his hands near his mouth. "And when the cloth came away, it was dots and streaks, brown to see."

"*Pan Bóg,*" said Janescz. "I knew it was coming, but when...Did he know you saw?"

"Yeh. I saw his eyes."

Plietor slumped over his bowl, his mind dark. No one spoke, Davik in the corner again, Ginna erect, her eyes on Janescz.

"Can you tell me what this means?" she said. "I think I know, but..."

"It means he is a dead man," said Davik.

Janescz raised his hand, then dropped it. "It is so. Weeks, maybe. But he will die. We have seen it with others, many others, in our years. The dry cough, more and more. Then the blood. Then they cannot breathe, and they die."

"It's the mist, isn't it?" said Ginna.

"Yeh," said Davik. "The devil's own breath. But some cough and some don't, not every one. So who's to say."

Silence again.

"What about...what about the flying?" Ginna asked.

Plietor felt his mind go darker.

"*Acch.* Now there's the crook of it." Davik moved back to

the table. "That's what all's thinking and none's saying, it is."

"We are thinking about *Karpiak!*" said Janescz. "A man is facing his dying. That's what there is to think about."

Silence another moment. Then Plietor burst out. "D'you think that's what Carnahan'll be thinking about? Do you? Bloody not. He'll be thinking about production, about quota, all he ever thinks. How to make quota with four flyers only, that's what he'll be thinking. He would drive us all into the rocks, every one. That's what he'd do for quota." Plietor could not sit. He bolted up, stalked to the ladder, leaned on his arms.

"But then no quota at all, not with no flyers," said Davik.

Plietor wanted to smash him. "Bugger off, Davik! Maybe it's back to sheets in the pits then. How do I know! Gott bloody damn Carnahan. Gott damn him to hell."

"Hey here, hey," said Janescz. "Stop this. We don't know what Carnahan will do. But he can't keep up the quota, not with only four flyers. He will have to back off, at least to the time another glider comes, and we can train another…two other flyers."

Plietor shook his head like a dog. "And what, for now? Will we take Karpiak's glider down to the desert to train another flyer? Who will do it? Which of us will go from production to this training? *Three* flyers working? What will Carnahan say to that? And who will we take to train? Who? Who will decide? Carnahan? Ho! Maybe we will train Carnahan himself. He flew the glider, one day, with Kemper. Maybe *Davik* will train Carnahan. That would be a show." He beat his fist on the ladder. "Shit. Shit. Shit." He almost sobbed. "Everything is buggered to hell."

"I…" Ginna began, halted, began again. "I can…" She glanced around at them all, then looked down. "I can…fly a glider."

21.

No one spoke. The shutter creaked with the wind. Ginna was conscious of Davik breathing through his mouth in the corner.

"What is this?" said Janescz after a long moment. "What have you said?"

"I said…" Ginna took a deep breath, conscious of the flush of blood in her neck, her heart thudding. "I can fly a glider. I know how to fly a glider."

Davik came to the table, into the light, loomed over the end. Ginna felt Plietor staring at her from the ladder.

"How could you know this?" said Janescz.

Ginna held herself erect, her hands together tight in her lap. She looked down, focusing on the table.

"It doesn't matter how I know," she said. "But I do. I have flown gliders."

"*Ho!*" said Davik, throwing his head back and wheeling in a circle. "Now that's ace, it is. Miss bloody Ginna the bloody flyer. I don't—" Ginna felt the blood flood past her ears, but Janescz reacted too.

"Davik!" he barked. "You watch your talk!"

Davik had turned and was stalking the wall again. "My bloody fuken talk!?" he said, throwing his hands in the air. "Plietor's for sending us all back to the pits. Our household sheila here up and says she's a flyer. And *I'm* the one who's to watch my talk?! There's no sense being made here, no bloody sense at all."

"Davik!" Janescz raised a rigid arm, pointing his finger.

"Oh bugger off, old man," said Davik.

Janescz lunged toward Davik, stumbling over the bench, Plietor two swift steps behind him.

Ginna, recoiled, half standing, not sure what to do.

Davik moved to meet Janescz, grappled with him a moment, then gave him a mighty shove backwards, toppling him into Plietor, who threw his arms around him, staggering.

"STOP!" Ginna found herself shouting. "Stop it, you all!" Her voice reverberated on the walls.

"*Heh!*" voices came in from outside. "What's it about?" "Stuff it!"

Davik moved back into the shadows of the corner, breathing hard. Plietor released Janescz, who stood glaring, panting and swaying.

Ginna was speaking again. "Can we not sit, and at least understand each other?"

The men relaxed their tension, but Janescz kept his eyes on Davik as he moved back onto the bench. Plietor retreated to the ladder.

Ginna sat again, hands clasped hard at her waist, looking from one to the other. She took a deep breath, began slowly.

"I know it may seem strange to you, for a woman to know about gliders. But I do." She took time to look at each man. "You don't know…I think you don't know what women do in…outside, in other places. But woman do many things. Some drive motorcars. Some fly aeroplanes with motors. Some fly gliders. I know how to fly a glider, and you need someone to do so. You need it very badly."

"I don't bloody see—" began Davik.

"What?" said Janescz. "What don't you see?"

"A bloody...a sheila in a glider."

"Gott damn you—" began Plietor, but Ginna spoke over him.

"Can you see *me*! Not just some sheila? I can tell you things...*Fuselage! Vertical stabilizer! Wingspan! Airbrake!* Do you know the glider you fly is called the *"Baby?"* It was designed by a German named Edmund Schneider at his factory in Grunau, in the eastern part of Germany. I *know* this. Do you?"

She would so much have liked to say that she knew of this factory from Horst Kemper, Davik's idol, who himself had met Edmund Schneider, seen *Baby*s being made. But she knew she could not say this. Had she already said too much?

"Acch!" said Davik. "What do I see? I *do* see you! Maybe more than I want. You know things. I know this too. But you can know things from books, names of things. What *I* know"—he thumped his hand against his chest—"what I see from my own eyes, is the feel of the control stick in my hand, the pedals, the gust of the wind, the force of the dive. These things you cannot know from books. How can *you* know these things? How can *any* sheila know?"

Ginna compressed her lips hard, fresh anger surging. "I already said—"

Janescz stood, waving his arms, crossing them over his head. "This talk goes in a circle. There is only one way, and you know what it must be, *chłopiec*. You know. You say it to me."

"I will not say it," said Davik. "You say it, if you are so sure."

"I will say this and I am sure: she speaks the truth about our need for some one to fly Karpiak's glider. If one can come forth and do that, it is a big problem we do not have.

So. She has come forth. And how can we know what she knows? How can we?" He stared into the gloom at Davik, but it was Plietor who spoke from the ladder.

"We put her in Karpiak's glider to fly it. I'll say it."

"And what if she crashes it?" said Davik, in one stride back at the table, looking past Ginna to Plietor. "What if she lands hard and breaks everything?"

"Then we are no worse than we are now," said Janescz. "Four gliders flying."

Davik threw back his head. "*Acch!* You sound like Carnahan." He pointed a finger at Ginna. "Where is *she* then? Where is *she* if she crashes the glider?"

"I won't crash—" Ginna began, but now Plietor was at the table too.

"Where is she if she *doesn't* crash? Where is she if she is what she says, flies the glider and takes over for Karpiak, flies production every day like the four of us, with the high quota?" Davik stood, uncertain. Janescz and Ginna looked up at him, questions on their faces as well.

"Will she be the next Rozum?" Plietor whispered, looking straight at Davik. "Will she disappear into the mist, and be gone?"

22.

Speak, now," said Carnahan. "Speak for yourself."

The girl stood before him, this girl-woman who said she was Ginna MacReedy. He knew what she was about. Janescz had told him yesterday, when he came after out-ringing to speak of Karpiak and his bloody cough. *Ha!* Bloody cough it was and sure. But no joke in that. Another flyer gone, so soon after Rozum. Sodding Beelzebub was looking over his shoulder, he was. Could this girl be the way to get round his gaze? Carnahan had thought about it all the night.

Of course he had sent Karpiak straight around to Wetkin, for whatever Wetkin would say. Wetkin himself was sure to be steeped, as he was nearly every day Carnahan saw him, reeling and swaying, only Julia holding him up. But Karpiak's breathing had been listened to by one of them with a stethoscope and Wetkin himself brought the word: lungs obstructed, function severely diminished. He didn't have to say the rest.

"She knows things about gliders," Janescz had said to him. She knew the names of parts of the glider, names Kemper had told them. She said she knew the design of this glider itself, the name from a town in Germany.

Freeds-oven, Carnahan had thought, the German town she had named for him, talking of the Zeppelin.

"She says she can fly gliders," said Janescz. "She talks

of women who drive motorcars, fly aeroplanes where she comes from. She says she can fly this glider, this one."

Where she comes from. It was easy for Carnahan to forget where this Ginna came from. It had been a long time since he had seen Perth, six years and more. Where men went about in the evening in long coats and cravats, women in shapely dresses, hats. Where motorcars drove on macadam roads and the sun was clean, no infernal mist. It was not impossible this Ginna MacReedy from Perth could fly a glider. The gliders and Kemper had come from Ian MacReedy's idea of aerial collection. MacReedy had said it when he had talked to Carnahan man-to-man. Kemper had never said otherwise. Ian MacReedy knew about gliders, no doubt. And if this was his daughter she might know too. Even know to fly one. Was MacReedy the sort of toff to do that, put his daughter in a glider?

Janescz was for it, putting this girl in Karpiak's glider on the Shelf. She had convinced Janescz. Could she convince Carnahan?

She stood before him now. He had invited her to sit, and the chair was there. But she had said she would stand. And so she stood, straight, looking at him directly, hands together at her waist with the gloves, always the gloves. The scarf wrapped her head. Always the scarf too. *What underneath?* He did not know, did not care to think.

"I can fly Karpiak's glider," she said, in a firm voice. "It is a simple proposition. You have need of another flyer for the central work of the Camp, as you have distinguished it many times. I can take over Karpiak's flying, and there will be no loss of production."

"You speak with great confidence, Miss Ginna deBoruski," Carnahan said, "on a matter of which until now you have not uttered a single word."

He saw the trace of a frown flit over her face when he called the name, but she continued the same. "There was no need for me to speak of it until now. But there is a need now, and I can fulfill it."

Carnahan looked at her for a moment. "Why should I believe this of you?"

"Why should I offer myself, if I were not able?" she said. "What good would it do me to crash the glider, and myself in it?"

Carnahan raised an eyebrow. *What, indeed?* He leaned forward. "And what's the good to you if you be able?"

Carnahan was happy to see a shadow of doubt pass across her face, a flicker of frown deeper than before. He thought she started to say something, then did not. Finally she took a breath.

"I am Ian MacReedy's daughter, after all. I hope for nothing more than the success of this mining operation. If I can do aught to contribute to that success—while I am here—I will, I must. I have done so on the Terrace. I offer the same now. My father would expect nothing less of me."

Carnahan sat back in his chair. *Ah yes.* Mr. Ian Mac-Reedy's daughter. He smiled a dark smile. "And do you feel any similar obligation to the Boruski household?"

"The Boruskis have not pressed me in any way. In fact, Davik—" She stopped.

Carnahan smiled more. "I'm sure Davik takes this all with...mixed emotion, strongly expressed, as I hear of it."

She did not speak, just stood looking at him, her lips pressed together. Carnahan touched his fingertips together under his chin.

"I will share my thoughts with you, Miss Ginna deBoruski. Let me say that I too hope for nothing more than the success of the Arltunga Mine. So my judgment must be to that end." He held her eyes for a moment, then looked away.

"Perhaps you can do what you say. Perhaps you are indeed possessed of this mysterious ability of flying, which you have just now seen fit to share with us. If you can fly Karpiak's glider off the Shelf like Karpiak himself, then we may resume production with five gliders, thereby meeting the current quota without serious difficulty. Janescz assures me of this, and it will be well so, for the whole Camp. A happy outcome for all."

The girl drew breath to interrupt but did not. He put his palms together, looked down, then up again at her.

"But perhaps you cannot do what you say. Perhaps you misrepresent yourself, from some motive which you have also not seen fit to share with us—"

"You can't—" The girl now did interrupt, but he raised his voice over hers.

"Or from simple bravado."

She glared. But he went on.

"In this case the glider is crashed, and we…" He pulled his mouth up into the grimace of a smile. "We have lost the production of a valuable Terrace worker." He pulled the smile down. "And also the glider. So we must now apply to Perth for two more gliders, and account for the loss of the second."

"My father," the girl broke in now, "my father will understand what I did. He—"

"Your father," Carnahan rode over her, "will never know of what you did, what you have done these many weeks in this case."

Now she stared, her eyes wide.

"But it will not come to that, will it," said Carnahan, with his crooked smile again. "For I shall simply say it shall not be so."

"No!" she cried, her hands in fists now. "No! I didn't mean that. I *can* fly the glider. I can. It will not be crashed. How can I make you see…"

"Yes. How?" said Carnahan, sitting up now. "That is the question, isn't it? How am I to know?"

He locked his eyes on hers, held, and waited for her to look away. She did not, and he finally sighed, looked away himself, and spoke wearily.

"I see three choices. I can put you in the glider. What follows will be either the best…or the worst. Or, I can say not. What follows there is neither best nor worst, but the sacrifice is in production, and that makes no one happy. Or…"

He turned his head to the window, the mist swirling by, reaching for the cliff face behind the Stack. He spoke without turning back.

"I can have Karpiak's glider taken to pieces and hauled down past the pools, put back together like Humpty Dumpty, to try you out in bits." He turned to face her again. "That's the way the others got to the flying."

The girl was finally at a loss. This was something she appeared not to have thought of. She just stood now, an uncertain look. He gave her half an honest smile.

"That's the compromise it is, my Miss Ginna. Loss of production sure, bad for a while. But likely not loss of the glider, or the flyer."

"I…" she began.

"I don't need to know what you think, now do I?" he said. "You spoke and I've spoke. It's for me to decide." He looked away, made a gesture toward the door. "Back to Bartosz."

23.

Ginna sat belted into the glider cockpit, her heart thudding. The goggles pressed against her cheekbones, and she moved both hands up to shift them, searching for a better position. They were Karpiak's goggles, the leather molded to his face from use.

"They will seat better in time," Janescz had said, as he tightened the strap. Surely he was thinking, as she was, *if there is time.*

She had no one to blame but herself. She had spoken up at the flat on impulse. The situation called desperately for a pilot, and she was a pilot, of sorts. She had flown a glider. But not this glider. Not any glider by herself.

She should have been more careful, more cautious in exploring possibilities. Maybe the possibility Carnahan had mentioned would have been suggested by Janescz. But Davik had made her so angry with his "Miss...oh! bloody Ginna the bloody flier" and his "household sheila up and saying" that she had not been cautious. After Janescz had fought with Davik and been so eager to believe the best of her, she didn't feel she could...retract, when Plietor spoke Janescz's wish: "Put her in Karpiak's glider."

And then Carnahan! She was determined not to appear weak and undecided before Carnahan. The man was surely.... What he had said about not telling her father that she had been rescued from the fiery crash of the Zeppelin! He had implied as much before. But to say it so baldly. He had not asked for details of her flying. Neither he nor the Boruskis. But she knew he had believed her when he put forward the idea of trying out the glider in stages on the desert. She thought that "compromise" might be a reprieve from her own impulsiveness. But then Karski came down after in-ringing to get Janescz from the fob and Bartosz from the Terrace, and when they returned from Carnahan, Janescz took her. And here she was.

At least Plietor had come with a new balaclava from Anna. It would have been dreadful to have to use Karpiak's. She had slipped into the shed latrine to unwrap the scarf and pull the new cloth tight over her head. She had no overdaks and needed to pull her shifts far up to be able to move the control stick freely. Janescz said she should have overdaks if she were "successful." *A strange word. But what better?* If she "survived?"

Janescz's instructions were those from Kemper for all the flyers their first time on the Shelf. Simply climb above the mist, fly out over the Caldera, turn back toward the Shelf, turn again. Repeat three times, getting the feel of the glider in the wind. *It wasn't so different,* she had thought, *from flying back and forth across the face of the Wasserkuppe.* But…after the third time, Janescz had said, pull the airbrakes, descend into the wind, land. *That would be different.* Horst had his hands and feet on the controls when they landed the glider. There would be no hands now but hers.

"Flyin's a piece o' cake," had said Fergus with a sneer, after Janescz's instructions. Davik had started to lunge toward him but pulled up. That had been at the meeting. But she didn't have time to think of the meeting.

"Just don't stall out at the top," Plietor had said, catching her aside for just a moment. "Push over. Better too early than too late."

Janescz had made everyone stay back but the necessary handlers. He had helped her with the belts himself, providing a cushion for the unpadded seat to raise her so she could see over the sides, casting only the briefest of looks at her bare, burn-welted legs.

And now she was belted in, the wind and mist in her face, the goggles pressing in, and the handlers were straightening the elastic rope. She tightened her right fist on the control stick, then released it, hearing Horst in her head. "Keep a light touch, *liebchen*, to feel the glider." *Liebchen*. She looked to the release—the red ball to pull in the center of the bulkhead; checked the airbrakes one last time—handle all the way forward, locked into the notch; pressed her boots against the pedals—the soles too thick; none of the flyers wore boots, but nothing to be done.

"*Fort!*" she heard Janescz shout behind her, saw the handlers on either end begin to stretch the rope, moving forward with it across their shoulders, heads going down against the strain. Her heart thudded harder. She was panting, trembling.

"Push over. Better too early than too late." She would not fail to push over. She would not.

"*Halt!*" cried Janescz. She saw the handlers bent double against the strain. Her heart...

"*Weg!*"

The acceleration drove her against the back of the seat and all sight disappeared to gray. For a second she could not breathe and felt a wave of panic before she realized her mouth was open under the balaclava. Simply closing it gave her a measure of control.

Push over! Push over! she thought, and did, pushing the

stick forward, feeling the glider nose go down, then go down much too fast. She lunged with her left hand for the red ball, pulled it hard, felt the glider lift instantly, pulled it again without thinking. The speed...the speed was dropping, and she could see, see the blue sky above. She turned her head, glimpsed the walls of the Caldera, saw she was in a right bank, a turn. She moved the stick left, pushed the left pedal, was comforted by the ready response of the glider. *Straight and level.* She was straight and level, under control. Somewhere behind her was the Shelf, but for now she was above the mist, out over the Caldera, and she was under control. She took a deep breath and smiled to herself under the balaclava.

She pulled the stick back ever so slightly and the nose of the glide rose, slightly more, and again, and the glider began to shudder and she knew she was close to a stall. Stick forward and the shudder went away, the glider still climbing slightly, her eyes told her. *Time to turn back. Left or right?* It didn't matter. She was in the center of the Caldera.

She pushed the stick left, followed with the pedal. The glider banked left, then overbanked as though pushed by a great hand. *The wind!* She had turned down the wind, and it was pushing her over. She pulled right to control the bank and brought the glider around the full turn, *ein-hundert acht-sig* Horst would have said. The Caldera was fleeing past now with all her new speed, the high stone of the south end rushing toward her. She caught glimpses of the Shelf through the mist, but she didn't need to find it now, just go a respectable distance in towards it and turn around. *Now.* Stick and pedal to the right, the glider banking, turning sluggish into the wind, stick forward to drop the nose and make way over the ground, over the rock down there, beneath the mist.

The second circle was easier. Her heart was down enough

for her to feel the residual clutch in her stomach, there because she still had to land, set the glider down on the narrow edge of the Shelf below the Terrace. But not this time. This time she could see the view, take in the full expanse of the Caldera, the sky clear and blue...*how many months since...?* She thought of touring the glider toward the far end of the Caldera, to see where the other mining camps were. *But no. Nothing extra. Time to turn again downwind.*

On the third circle, cruising upwind, she tried out the airbrakes. Left hand to the handle, out of its locking notch and back, not far, but she felt the force of the wind in it, the glider slowing, mushing down. Glancing left and right, she saw the panels up in the wings, rectangular blades breaking the smooth top surfaces. She pulled the handle all the way back, felt the glider drop and quiver, pushed back full forward into the notch. The airbrakes were what would bring her down, keep her forward speed low enough to stop on the Shelf. She took a deep breath through the balaclava and banked back with the wind, feeling her heartbeat start to rise.

She had the airbrakes out again before she even reached the turnaround point near the high stone. The Camp was directly below, though she could see it only intermittently. She seemed very high before the turn back upwind, and then, as she lowered the nose to make the glider bite into the wind, suddenly low. She rammed the airbrake lever forward and the glider jumped up, far too much. Back then with the lever, and now she was in the mist and seeing ahead was suddenly impossible. She swallowed a moment of panic before she realized that seeing ahead was not necessary. It was seeing down she needed, and after a second or two the dull gray of the organized stone structures of the Camp materialized, the Stack backed against the rising wall, the Terrace out below, the arc of the Shelf below that. No other gliders were out, as Janescz had promised. She had the width of the Shelf to herself, but it was the depth that frightened her: so narrow, so narrow it looked from where she sat. She thought fleetingly of the catch-net. If she could just get down…

But she was too high, so high! as she swooped over the Terrace, pulling the airbrake handle desperately back to its furthest travel, pushing the stick forward to lower the nose, to sink. *Oh!* Now she was too fast! And the ground was rushing toward her, and the edge of the Shelf was so close…

She felt the jolt all through her back as the glider banged down on the rock surface. *Push!* Push the nose over to the skid! With the stick jammed forward the tail of the glider came up and she could feel the skid grinding below her feet, feel the rasp in her boot soles. Yet still the edge was coming, and she knew she would go over, and…

And then she stopped. In slow motion the tail of the glider came down and hit with a *whump* she felt up through her neck. And then there was just the wind and the mist in her face, and the thudding of her heart.

"It's all right! It's all right, Miss!" came a voice from her right. She looked to see one of the handlers holding the wing and waving a cloth. She looked to the fob, saw Janescz trotting toward her, Davik and Plietor standing at the corner, men behind them. She released the stick and waved, and Davik waved back, put his hands to his mouth and gave a piercing whistle. She smiled wide under the balaclava.

"It was fantastic, Julia!" Ginna said.

They were sitting together in the front room of the clinic, Julia in the desk chair, Ginna on a stool Julia had brought from the patient-bed room behind.

"I was so happy. Happy to be down again on the ground! Happy to have done it."

Julia gave her a smile. "Do you remember the first time we walked out, when you could?"

"I remember it well," Ginna said.

"When a glider first went over us, you looked up and said 'aerial collection.' And I knew right then myself *you* knew things you weren't telling."

"I do remember that," said Ginna. "It was surely not the time for me to be speaking of flying gliders. I could hardly walk."

Julia gave her a sidelong look. "And now is the time?"

"Well, certainly. The flyers were in a desperate situation, with the high quota and the loss of the one flyer and glider and then Karpiak."

Julia gave a shallow nod. "And you can make it right for them."

"Well, I don't know about 'right.'" Ginna looked back at Julia. "I can help get them back to where they were with five gliders flying."

"Like you did with the pole beans," said Julia.

Ginna looked at her sharply. "What are you saying, Julia?"

Julia stood and went over to the window, folded back the shutter an inch to look out.

"We saved you, and now you will save us. People talk. They say things about you, what you must be, where you came from. Many have secrets here, but not your secrets. People talk of you and Davik too. You must know that."

"What about me and Davik?"

Julia came back from the window, pulled her chair closer to Ginna's stool, reached out to pat Ginna on the knee. "Tell me about the rest of the flying," she said.

Ginna hesitated for a moment, but was soon animated again, speaking quickly. Janescz had led her back to the fob, where the whole group of them had clapped for her. *Clapped!* It was such a difference from before, when Janescz had first told them, "Mr. Carnahan has said this lady is to fly Karpiak's glider." First there was only silence and stares, then voices were raised, but Janescz had said, "Who shall I send to speak 'No' to Mr. Carnahan on what he has said?" and no one had been willing to look him in the eye. But now they had clapped, and most were smiling, and Fergus had said, "I told you it was a piece o' cake," something he'd said before the flight that had made Davik angry then, but not now. Janescz had talked to her, all of them standing and listening, the other flyers putting in remarks: her waiting too long to go off the rope, flying too fast at the last; how she should have brought the tail down with the stick before the glider stopped. "The Davik-school of landing," one of the other flyers had said, *Musil,* she thought. "Sparks and all."

Then it was back in the glider for another flight, three diving cycles into the mist. "Four seconds only," Janescz had warned. She now knew what they had been talking about, the Boruskis, about the seconds in the dive, and holding too long. It was so impossible, not being able to see at all in the dive, just to count and then to pull up and turn. How lovely the sky looked when it appeared through the mist again!

"What is the 'holding too long' with the Boruskis?" Julia asked. Ginna had stopped for breath.

"Oh, it was an argument they had, about how long to hold the dive." Ginna wanted to talk about flying, not the argument, besides...She waved her hand. "They argue all the time," she said. "Davik..." She didn't want to talk about Davik either.

"Do they argue about you?" said Julia.

Ginna looked at her, compressed her lips. "Sometimes," she said. Then, "Yes, they do. Sometimes quite...forcefully."

She looked harder at Julia, reading her expression. "But not *against* me!" She lifted her hands, pushing them away. "Never against me." She took a breath. "This time they were arguing about the dive. And now I understand that."

She went on to tell about the next flight, with the short net behind, three circles above the mist, as on the first flight, then three dive cycles, four seconds only, feeling the drag on the glider, and a better landing, better than the second, even with the net. Karolyi had come to take the net from the glider. Her first aerial collection! First production. First contribution to quota, a line on Janescz's clipboard.

Julia smiled, nodded.

It was now a week, Ginna said. She was number five in the rotation: Davik, Plietor, Fergus, Musil, her. Two gliders on the Shelf when she landed, sometimes three. She was landing more like Plietor now, a consistent distance past the Terrace, no sparks from the skid. Ten sorties a day. They sent her back to the flat after out-ringing, while they did the final wiping, pushed the gliders into the sheds. They sent her back so she could have food for them on the table when they came in! Some things were always the same.

Julia smiled a half smile, *a smile of understanding,* Ginna thought, not of joy.

"So," Julia said. "Tonight is Gathering. And Carnahan will speak of you. And you will dance with Davik."

Ginna looked down. "I hope he—Carnahan—doesn't say anything...anything too..."

"He will say what he will say," said Julia. "Everyone has heard Carnahan's speeches, in good times and in bad."

Ginna looked up at her. "How are...How are *your* times?" she asked.

Julia looked away a moment, looked back, shrugged. "The same," she said. "Karpiak—"

"Oh!" said Ginna. "Karpiak. Poor Karpiak. I have been so full of myself I have not said a word about Karpiak. Janescz made a nice speech about him at the meeting. He said Karpiak had been a good flyer, careful, dependable. They would all miss him. But Carnahan—and the doctor—they had determined that he could not fly safely, not safe for him, nor for the glider. Then Janescz said I was to fly, and...I have told you that already."

"That is true enough about Karpiak," said Julia. "With the lungs, at this stage of disease, he could go into spasm at a moment and...A man could not fly in spasm."

Ginna sat for a moment, looking down at her hands. She spoke quietly without looking up. "You see this disease often, don't you?"

"Yes," said Julia.

"I hear people, at the Gatherings, coughing the same cough. Do they all have the disease?"

There was a moment before Julia spoke, and when she did Ginna heard a new tone.

"People cough for many reasons."

Ginna looked up at her. "How many people here have died from this disease?"

Julia turned away and rose from the chair to go back to the window. She spoke looking out. "If you wish to know such things you will have to ask Mr. Carnahan."

They were both silent. Ginna stood.

"I need to be going," she said. "Thank you...thank you for listening to me. I am sure I have been tedious."

Julia turned. "No," she said. "I enjoy our talk."

"If I may..." Ginna said, "How is the doctor? Dr. Wetkin? How is his back?"

Julia drew a deep breath and looked out the slot in the shutter again, a bar of light now falling on her face.

"He is the same," she said. "No worse. No better." She turned back to Ginna, gave her a smile, a tired smile, Ginna thought. "You enjoy your dancing tonight. You and Davik."

24.

By the middle of the second week, Ginna had become confident of herself, able to take joy from all the details of the day. She awoke alert and got straight into the overdaks. They were Karpiak's overdaks, too big, stained at the neck like all the others' and filled with his smell when she got them. But she had washed them thoroughly, three soapings in the bunkhouse tub, and they were clean enough now. She had made her undershift into bloomers, cutting the fabric up the center front and back and stitching the edges together for legs, a needle and thread from a suspicious Anna.

The first few mornings, walking down the Terrace path with the three men, she was conscious of looks from the *drtskis*. But then she wasn't. Maybe they quit looking. Maybe she did.

She helped with the pulling out of the gliders, went over Karpiak's glider—her glider—as carefully as any of the men, more carefully than some. Janescz had showed her what to look for on the fabric: unwiped jelly dried to a hard crust, a puncture, tear, a soft, stretched place where a hand had pushed too hard. Under the fabric she looked and felt for hairline cracks in wood. She moved surfaces with the lightest touch, feeling for loose, bent, binding hinges.

No sooner was the wind up than Davik's glider was ready on the open Shelf, Davik in, the handlers stretching the rope, the glider leaping up and away. Then Plietor, Fergus. She would pull her balaclava over her head in the latrine, hang the scarf from her hook, out the door with her goggles, her heart up, yes, but nothing like the first day. Musil next. Then her turn, hurrying over the rock to the glider, into the cockpit, belt tight, goggles up. *Fort!* to the men on the rope. *Halt!* Then *Weg!* and the colossal jerk, the dizzying rise, pushing over and pulling the red knob, straight and level and off down the Caldera to her station and the first dive cycle.

She had thought in the evenings they would be able all to talk together, now of mutual things. She remembered every dive, every landing. "How were your dives?" "How were your landings?" she would say, to provoke conversation. But after the first days neither Davik nor Plietor wanted to talk. When Davik would say something about a dive, Janescz's eyes would be on him. When Plietor would say something about a landing, Davik stopped his pacing. One day Fergus had been very fast on a landing and gone into the catch net. She had tried to ask about "coordination"—airbrakes and stick moving together in response to gusts. Plietor had begun to explain.

"Bugger it!" Davik broke in. "A flyer doesn't think when he flies, no more than walking. You just fly the bloody glider, like you put one foot in front of the other. Fergus is an idiot, is what he is." And he broke into a long train of excuses in a mewling version of Fergus's voice. Plietor looked at her and clamped his lips. But the look…Davik had seen the look. He broke off his Fergus voice.

"What's that bloody look about?"

"What look?" said Plietor.

"You looked at her, then, when I was speaking as Fergus."

"Who am I to look at? She sits right here before me."

Ginna kept her eyes down.

"Yeh. So she does. But that was a special look." Davik had come to the end of the table, was leaning forward, toward Plietor. Ginna glanced toward Janescz, who was tearing bread, the tendons in his hands standing out.

Plietor rolled his eyes.

"Ha!" said Davik. "I'll tell you what *that* look said. That look said, 'Davik is—'"

"Enough!" said Janescz, pointing with one tensed hand to Davik, the other to Plietor. "Can we speak without looks and challenges? We will talk of coordination, of airbrakes, and control sticks, or we will talk of nothing."

Davik wheeled back to the wall. Plietor looked down to the table. They were silent.

"Fergus said he saw you coming back from far down the Caldera, coming back high and fast."

Janescz had finished his soup, was peeling his turnip. Ginna saw him look up briefly at Davik, leaned back in the dark corner.

"What is Fergus doing looking for other gliders down the Caldera?" said Davik. "He was behind Plietor. What did Plietor see?"

Janescz looked under his brows at Plietor.

"I saw no other gliders," said Plietor. I was flying cycles, up and down with the mist, flying with discipline."

Ginna waited for Janescz's look to come to her, but it did not. He turned instead back to the turnip before speaking again to Davik.

"So," Janescz said, "were you? Down the Caldera?"

"Did I make quota?" Davik said. "Does Fergus tell you that?"

"Karolyi tells me that. You made quota."

"Then why are we talking?"

Janescz finished his peeling, cut the turnip in half, half again, making four neat pieces. He raised his eyes to Davik in the corner.

"We are talking about discipline. We agreed to fly with discipline, agreed at this table after Rozum, and then all together, in the air and on the Shelf, together at the fob. For safety, as Kemper told us."

Ginna tensed for an outburst, but Davik only took a great breath.

"Kemper," Davik said. "He did not fly five cycles a sortie, ten sorties a day, six days and one half every week, all the weeks of the year, every year. I would like to talk to Kemper about discipline, with the blue sky above, the land spread out all around…"

"And Carnahan at his heels," said Plietor.

"Bugger Carnahan!" Davik came out of the corner. "We give him his bloody quota. What else does he want to take from us? What do you have, that he has not taken?"

He was at the table then, leaning in from the end, on his heavy arms. He looked through Ginna to Janescz, across to Plietor. "Do you have anything left, with your *discipline?*" He spat the word. "Do you have anything that makes you a man?" He looked at Ginna then, turned back to the wall.

Ginna heard Plietor's sharp intake of breath and glanced at him. His mouth was clenched, a vein throbbing in his jaw. But he sat, unmoving, staring at nothing.

"Davik, Davik," said Janescz wearily beside her. "Was Rozum a man, because he is dead?"

"Karolyi has told me," said Janescz in a loud voice. He was talking after out-ringing. He had summoned the flyers to stay, Ginna with them, and Karolyi. Some of the other handlers had stayed too.

"Karolyi has told me that twice today gliders, different gliders, returned from sortie with jelly in the nets dried and crusted, cracking off. This he has not seen before today."

Ginna saw looks exchanged, questions in eyes. Few looked at Janescz, though his eyes swept the group.

"What does this mean?" said Janescz. "I will say it. For quota: Quota is by weight, and weight is for wet jelly. Dried jelly is less. Did we make quota today, on the scale? No. No! Not by weight. We are less. I must report that we did not make quota. Report to Carnahan."

More eyes, and a muttering from the group of handlers.

"I do not know if in the processing, the same quantity of chemical comes out pure from dried jelly as from wet jelly." Janescz gave a snort. "Ha! I am sure I can have a conversation with Helinski at the pools, to determine the production from the dried jelly, and then go speak to Carnahan of the result." He paused. "And I am sure I will not!"

Janescz looked now just at the flyers, standing together. Ginna caught his eye as it swept past her. Some others were looking up. Davik and Musil were looking down.

"I will not because we will have no more dried jelly in the nets. No more! I know how this jelly becomes dried, the flying that makes it so...the temptation of the blue sky above, the land spread out all around." He pointedly did not look at Davik. "We will not have it, I say. We will not. You all stand and hear my words."

He looked around the whole group now, slowly, man by man, waiting for eyes to meet, for nods. He waited for Musil, who finally raised his head and nodded. Last was Davik, who had his head up, but did not nod. He locked eyes with Janescz for a long second, before Janescz gave a half nod himself, and looked away.

And then there was the eagle.

Ginna had just reached her station on an afternoon sortie, the glider clean, or as clean as it was with a twenty-foot streamer of net behind it. She was hovering in the clear air above the mist, about to turn back down the wind for her first dive, when a shadow crossed over her head. *A shadow!* Something between her and the sun. *What could it be?* She looked up...to see the silhouette of a great bird. A hundred feet above her head, broad wings extended, a strange square-pointed tail, a huge bird flying overhead, parallel.

She had hesitated, then pulled back to try and rise to the bird's level, having no idea what it would do. It rose as she did, maintaining its height over her, a great blackish-brown bird, unmistakably a bird of prey. She saw its head turning, now toward her, now away, a long-hooked beak, yellow talons folded back under its belly. Feathers riffled along its wings.

Ginna felt the glider shudder. Looking up at the bird, she had held the control stick back too long, slowing the glider to the edge of a stall. She pushed forward, focusing on the glider for a moment, and saw the shadow change shape. A quick glance up and she froze. The bird had partially folded its wings and was diving toward her. She was about to dive away herself when it extended again and soared upward, resuming its position. Its head turned, toward her and away. She was fascinated. The dive was repeated, twice more, each time coming down farther. *This is a display,* she thought, a male bird warning off a perceived intruder. The concept was familiar from biology. How wonderful to see this up close. She saw the wings fold again, but this time the trajectory was different. The bird was sinking rather than diving, and Ginna saw the talons, talons now held out and below, talons spread a man's hand width. The bird's head was riveted on her.

Without thinking Ginna threw the control stick forward and to the left, stood on the left pedal. The right wing came up and over, the nose dropped, and the glider twisted into a spiral dive, the wind whistling against her balaclava. No sooner in, then out: stick and pedal right, then stick back. The glider strained back to straight and level and rose, bleeding off its speed. Ginna looked up for the bird. It was far above her, and as she watched she saw it bank away and rise swiftly.

Eine thermal! Horst's voice resonated in her head. She had not encountered a thermal before over the Caldera, a mass of warmed, rising air. She was always too low, down just above the mist. But the bird was unmistakably climbing in a thermal, higher and higher. Her fear left her and was replaced by a sudden yearning to see what it saw, the huge land outside, the red desert extending in all directions for miles and miles, and her above it, flying to the horizon. For just an instant she had a thought to follow the bird.

Then thought took over from wish and impression. She couldn't follow the bird. Even if she could, it wouldn't be wise. Hadn't it done its best to warn her off? And where was she even now? Off-station, off-altitude. If anyone saw her... She turned, reaching for the airbrake handle, pulled it back hard to the stop, felt the glider shudder as it dropped.

She was out of sequence when she got back to the Shelf with her full net. Musil had come and gone. Davik was on the Shelf, Plietor expected any moment. Davik in his glider gave her a shout as she hurried to the fob, but she only waved. Would Janescz roar up at her before the others after out-ringing?

Janescz asked in private, coming beside her in the fob as she dunked her goggles and wiped under her eyes. She said she had been "distracted" for a bit in flying to her station but had no problem beyond that. He held her eyes for a moment and shook his head, but there was no time to linger.

She worried the rest of the afternoon, but Janescz did not speak to her after her last sortie, and she went quickly up to their flat. She didn't know if she should be grateful to be ignored or not. All the others would want some kind of an explanation. But she would talk at least to the three of them at dinner. Maybe Davik or Plietor had an experience of the bird.

Davik asked her as soon as he was through the door, but Janescz waved talk away. "We will talk after we eat," he said.

Davik stayed at the table after he drank his soup, peeling a turnip with the knife from the shelf. He cut it into four neat sections, as Janescz did, reaching out to place one before each. Finally Janescz pushed his empty bowl forward. He took up his slice of turnip and nodded to Davik.

"Now we will hear of Miss Ginna's distraction in her flying," he said.

She told them of the shadow, of seeing the bird, its attack and flight away high in the thermal. They listened.

"It was so fierce in its last attack, and then so high. What must it be to see so far out over the desert, to feel so strong and free?"

She was sorry as soon as she said the last, to have opened the word.

"*Acch,*" Davik breathed out and stood, looked at her for just a second, then retreated into the shadows of the wall.

"We have seen this bird," said Plietor, his voice quiet. "All the flyers. It has dived on us, every one, and every one given way. No one wants to hold, to see what it…" He shook his head. "And when the bird flies away, on the thermal, we have felt…I have felt…as you felt." He looked at Davik, but Davik was silent. "Kemper saw the bird. He named it an eagle, but he didn't know the kind. The tail was distinctive to him."

"Where does it live?" Ginna asked. Plietor shrugged. "Does it have a mate?" He gave her just a glance before shrugging again.

"Does it go out over the desert? It must. It could find nothing to eat in the Caldera."

Plietor glanced toward Davik, lifted his hands to shrug again, but Davik spoke out of the shadows.

"I will tell you what it eats," he said, in a hoarse voice. "I will tell you." He moved toward the table, into the wavering light. Ginna looked at Janescz but saw no warning in his face.

"I have flown with this bird. It flies high. It goes and goes. But if you wait, over the animal sheds you will see it too. Not so high. Not so high at all. Looking at goats! *Baa-aa-aa!*"

The goat sound was so sudden, so loud. Gina started back. Davik snorted, leaned over the table.

"We used to go look at this bird, Plietor and me, when we were young, before the gliders, sitting by the shed-yard fence, watching it over our heads, the great wings, the square tail, the head looking and looking. So free, as you say. So *free!* Ha!"

"So free it was one day when it dived down out of the sky onto the back of a goat in the shed-yard, a young goat. We jumped up, Plietor and me, but what could we do? The bird was a giant thing in the yard, with its wings. It bit the goat on the neck and the goat sagged, and it clenched the goat..." Davik spread his hands before him, making them into talons, and snapped them down into fists. "It pulled the goat up, flapping great wings over the sheds, out over the Shelf. Women ran and screamed, and Dobbins came out with his gun. But it was too far." Davik was breathing deep, his face flushed, Ginna staring at him, rapt. He looked in her eyes, curled his mouth, snorted again.

"Now, when the bird comes over the Camp someone runs to tell Carnahan, and he comes out with his long gun and shoots, and the bird knows the threat and glides away. But!"

Davik shook his pointing finger over the table, shaking it at Ginna. She looked at the hand, back at Davik's face.

"Why does this great *free* bird come back to this Camp? With the whole of the desert to fly in?" He stood up tall, swept his hands in arcs over his head. "With all this out there we see when we are high in the gliders, why does this great eagle bird come back to this stench and mist and rock of the Camp, to a gun shooting for him?"

"The goats," breathed Ginna.

"Too *right!*" said Davik. "The bird is *not* free. It can go wherever it wants, but it must eat. It is not free. And we..." His face twisted. Ginna could not read the emotion. "Even when we fly, we are not...Ah, bugger it." He turned away, speaking toward the wall. "Maybe the bird would be better if Carnahan shot it with his gun. Maybe it would be better at the bottom of the compost." Ginna looked at Plietor, at Janescz, but they were looking down, stony. Davik kicked the wall.

"You could stay with me now. Now, you could."

Ginna stood at the window of the clinic's front room. Julia sat in the desk chair. Her face was turned toward Ginna, the offer open on it.

"I don't know," said Ginna. "Would it be wrong to take advantage...? And I don't know how they would feel, the Boruskis. And even so, I don't know if Carnahan would allow it."

"Who else would come here? Who? A new doctor, in

time. But that will be long."

"I'm sure there would be many who would be very happy…" Julia's face fell, and Ginna saw what she was thinking.

"I will speak to Janescz, by himself if I can. And if he says…well, then I will speak to Carnahan."

Carnahan was leaning back in his chair, which he had turned at an angle behind the table to accommodate his crossed legs. He held a pen in his right hand. Standing before him, Ginna could see him running two fingers along its length, up and down.

"What do the Boruskis think of this idea?" he said.

"I spoke with Janescz about it, yesterday evening," she said. "He thought it would…not be harmful to them."

Carnahan snorted. "Oh, come now. Something better than that must be said. My intuition is of an increase in, shall we say it, dissatisfaction within the household if you depart. The extreme dedication shown by our good Davik on your behalf…I would be irresponsible to ignore that. And there might be twenty men who would appreciate a bed in the clinic."

"No!" said Ginna. "I mean…"

"What *do* you mean?" said Carnahan sharply. "'No' is not said in this room. Not before me."

Ginna straightened her shoulders, took a breath. "I mean to say, with respect to Janescz's opinion, that my departure from the Boruski household would produce a reduction in tension there." Carnahan's raised eyebrows demanded she continue. "Tension between Davik and Plietor."

A smile played about Carnahan's lips. "Tension over you?"

"I fear so. Yes," she said. Carnahan sat, his smile moving toward a smirk, and Ginna found herself rushing into the silence. "They are under such stress, with the high quota and only five flyers and—"

Carnahan's smile disappeared. He snapped the pen down onto the table. "Do not speak to me of stress. We all live with stress here. We live with high quota because our central purpose is chemical production. We have no other purpose, as I say at all Gatherings, as you should sure and well know yourself, my Miss Ginna MacReedy."

Ginna felt the blood rise up in her neck. She clenched her hands. Carnahan narrowed his eyes. "This tension…you are sure Janescz speaks of this. It is not your opinion only."

She shook her head.

"I can have Janescz before me. I *will* have Janescz before me. So if you mislead me…"

"I am not misleading you," said Ginna. "Janescz and I both know it to be true."

Carnahan relaxed again, his smile returning. "So. You give me one reason for departure from the Boruski household. What is your reason to go to the clinic? Why should you not go to the bunkhouse, to a bed among the women there?"

No! The word formed in Ginna's mind. But she did not say it. She tightened her mouth, took a breath before she spoke.

"I can help Julia. We have no doctor now and—"

"*Ohhh!*" interrupted Carnahan, spreading his arms wide. "Now you will be telling me you are a bloody doctor too." His smile was a sneer now. "A botanist. A flyer. And now a doctor. What else can we need here?"

"I am *not* a doctor," said Ginna, through tight lips. "But…I do have some personal experience in medical treatment." She held his gaze hard. "I can help Julia. In the evenings. In the nights. In the mornings before in-ringing. I can help her with cooking, with antisepsis—"

"*Anti-sepsis* is it?" broke in Carnahan. "Vorticular flow. Antisepsis. So many long words."

"Dis-infecting," said Ginna, drawing out the syllables, willing herself not to react. "I know the operation of the clinic. Who knows it better than I?"

Carnahan's eyes were locked with hers for a long moment. Then he reached for the pen, sat back stroking it again, turned to look out the window behind him.

"I have heard you. Now I will hear Janescz. And then Julia. And then you will know my words."

Ginna stood a moment more, then walked across to the blue door. Carnahan did not turn.

25.

The dog was howling. Plietor knew the dream, knew he was dreaming, but dreamed on. He went to the window, pressed his nose against the lowest pane. In the pool of light from the lamppost the shiny black dog lifted his muzzle.

"What does that bloody *psia* want?" called the woman's voice from the next room. "What do you see?"

He was drawing breath to answer. He always drew breath, but never answered. The front door of the flat rattled.

Plietor opened his eyes, tense, his heart thudding. The door of the flat. The door of *their* flat. Had the door of their flat rattled? Or was it only the dream? Davik breathed in his bed beside him. Plietor lay, waiting for his heart to subside, listening for a wind outside that would rattle their door, listening for the creak of shutters.

When the door of the flat rattled again, it was not from wind. The floor vibrated. A deep gnashing sounded through the walls.

Plietor threw off the blanket, reached for his daks, stepped into his boots.

"Eh?" said Davik, sitting up.

"Something bloody outside. Something big. Pa-pa! Ja-nescz! Up. Up." Then louder, "Ginna! Ginna!" before he remembered she was not above them up the ladder, not in the flat.

"Ho…" began Davik.

"Belt up, Davik! This is real."

Plietor slid down the ladder, across the kitchen room in two steps, threw open the door. He looked right first, east, into the light from the rising full moon just above the ridge, the long shadows across the Shelf. Nothing there. Motion caught the edge of his sight to the left, a shower of bouncing rock caroming and crackling down the cliff behind the Shelf, larger pieces arcing up, bouncing onto the Shelf with clearer cracks, some propelling themselves over the edge, some lying where they rolled.

"It's a bloody rockslide, is all it is." Davik was behind him.

"Where?" Janescz was behind Davik. "What's it taking?"

Davik pushed Plietor out the door, moved past him onto the ledge. "It's not taking nothing. Just a bloody rockslide making a mess for itself."

Another shower kicked down the cliff. Plietor looked left and right on the ledge and below, saw in the moonlight others out, underdaks and less. He winced as a larger boulder hit the Shelf, then turned his head to a new sound, a deeper boom from high up the cliff. A sudden cloud rose against the moonlit sky and a slab of the cliff face seemed to slip down all at once, releasing another shower of smaller rocks at its base before separating at its top edge and beginning a slow-motion tumble. A woman screamed below them; a man shouted a hoarse curse. Plietor stood transfixed as the great slab fell free for a hundred feet, fell impossibly slowly, turning, turning, before crumpling into a jutting ledge…and exploding.

The roar was a pressure wave in his ears. The slab fragmented into a thousand shards, a thousand trajectories out from the cliff face and over the Shelf. Now women screamed in earnest, and everyone was moving.

"Bloody fuken hell," said Davik, bounding past Plietor to the ladder and down. A chunk of rock the size of a melon cracked into the ledge ten feet away, the sound of others beginning a staccato tattoo on the Stack and the rock of the Yard. Janescz gripped the ladder and began to descend.

"Where are you going?" shouted Plietor.

Janescz looked up from the ladder. "I don't bloody know. East side. Garden sheds maybe. Can't stay here." Another rock hit down the ledge, spattering them both with debris.

"Why not?" said Plietor. "At least there's three levels over us inside."

Janescz hesitated. They both ducked as a shard hit the wall, bounced onto the ledge and over. They were standing irresolute when the ground shook under them, the ladder dancing against the wall. Their eyes turned together. A boulder the size of a shed had been dislodged from behind the Stack, high up the cliff, away from the main slide. It was rolling now, an indistinct shadow through a field of scree, slowly, but picking up inexorable speed, volleyed bluntly from one ledge to the next.

"*Jezus!*" said Janescz.

Plietor flicked his eye from the boulder down to the west side of the Stack, up again, and his stomach dropped. *Ginna. Ginna!* Ginna was in the clinic room, the far west end. Was she out? Did she know the danger?

"Go!" he shouted, grabbing the top of the ladder. "Go! Go!"

Janescz scrambled down, Plietor sliding behind him. But when Plietor turned at the bottom, Janescz seized his arm.

"Where? Where do you go? This way. Run!"

" No! Ginna is in the clinic…" He tried to tear himself

Roger Jones

away, but Janescz's grip was too strong.

"You will not get there. You will not. We have to save ourselves if we can!"

Janescz was jerking him, jerking him off his feet, toward the east side. A terrific crack echoed over the Shelf. The boulder had hit a ledge and split, the two pieces careening crazily down now, rolling, sliding, tumbling, loosing a sky-filling cloud of pulverized rock.

"Come!" shouted Janescz desperately. "Come!" And then they were running toward the sheds, gravel nicking their backs and heads, larger chunks falling and bouncing all around, the background roar punctuated by louder cracks and bursts. They were still twenty feet away from the garden shed door when Plietor could stand it no longer and skidded to a stop, turned…and threw his arms in the air, his shout lost under the colossal crack of stone on stone.

One of the boulder pieces hit a garden terrace half way out on the Shelf and rolled, slewing sideways to the edge and over. But the other…the other dropped the last two hundred feet free from a ledge, down, straight down onto the west edge of the Stack, crushing it in a cloud of brick dust like the mud house it was.

Plietor put his hands on his head, suddenly oblivious to the rock falling all around him. He felt darkness coming into his eyes, his legs giving way, and he would have fallen, but Janescz was there, supporting him, half-carrying him the final feet into the shed. Plietor understood dimly that others were there, crouched under the long wooden counters along the walls and the wide table in the center. Room was made for him and Janescz and they crouched themselves, Plietor's ears filled with the cracks and thwocks of rocks on the stone outside and the wooden roof over their heads.

The time seemed long, but Plietor knew it was not, and

the percussion had hardly abated before they heard the ring of the iron from the Yard. People scrambled from beneath the tables and crowded to the door, only to stop and gape at the rock-littered Shelf, the dust rising and filtering out from the base of the cliffs.

"*Pan Bóg,*" said Janescz at Plietor's elbow.

Then the iron rang again and people began to move, clutching what clothes they had around them, bare feet stepping with care among the rocks. But Plietor did not move with them. He moved out and past, his jaw set, toward the smashed west end of the Stack. Janescz caught up and pulled at his shirt from behind.

"*Chłopiec. Chłopiec!* We must go to the Yard. We must hear what Carnahan says."

"You go," said Plietor. "You hear. You know where I am."

Carnahan's voice itself now rose over the Shelf, echoing against the cliff. "Come! Come! Gather here. Gather you all. I say it." Plietor hesitated, looked again, then turned with Janescz toward the Yard.

People were milling about in the Yard, searching for others in the moonlight shadows, bare heads and underdaks, coughing here and there in the filtering rock dust. Carnahan was on his box in his hat, his long coat over his shoulders. Plietor looked hard for Davik as he and Janescz moved into the crowd. He allowed himself to look for Ginna or Julia too, though he had steeled himself inside not to see them. A voice called a name, then another.

"Do not call out," shouted Carnahan, "or we will have confusion. We will construct a census at the soonest."

An abrupt clattering of rocks from the far end of the Stack drew all eyes. But there was no fall from above, and a moment later a group emerged from the rubble, four or five, and moved toward the rest of them. Carnahan waited, and in a few steps Plietor could see it was Davik at the head of the group. Janescz moved to meet him at the edge of the crowd, grasped his arm, but they did not speak.

Carnahan swept his eyes over all, then raised his voice.

"We have this night experienced a great tragedy. By this act of God through the forces of unstable geology we are sure and sorely afflicted. How afflicted we have yet to determine. But we will determine, and we will recover, and we will go on. We are a firm people. This is a hard land, but we are firmer, and we will recover."

People shuffled and murmured.

"We must be orderly in our recovery. We will at the next moment take census to see who is not…with us, and of you all, who may have suffered injury."

"Yeh, and where shall we go for our injury?" a man's voice called. "Me arm here…"

"All will be tended to," Carnahan overrode him. "We have resources."

Davik stirred about next to Plietor, muttering under his breath.

"After our census, we will organize parties to search for any that are missing."

Davik drew breath to speak, but Janescz laid a quick hand on his arm, and Davik let out the breath in a rush. A few heads turned.

"Then we must determine the extent of damage to our materiel, our structures, gardens, equipment."

"Bloody hell," said Davik, in a stage whisper that carried in the still air all around them.

Did Carnahan hear? After the slightest of pauses, Carnahan went on.

"We must, even in this time of crisis, feed ourselves. And

we must, as soon as we are able, return to production."

"Fuken sod that," said Davik, no stage whisper this time, and he turned and took a step out from the crowd. Janescz moved after him, but Davik shrugged him off.

"For the census, you must report to Mr. Karski here, who has the roll of our numbers," Carnahan was saying, before he caught sight of Davik.

"Davik Boruski, have you heard me?"

A ripple of murmur swept over the group. Heads turned. Janescz stood, not knowing what to do. Davik walked on.

"Davik Boruski. You are to stand yourself there." Davik lifted his arm, his two fingers in forked salute. A woman gasped. The murmur swelled.

Plietor was torn only for an instant. Then he stepped out too, after Davik, and heard the steps of others behind him. The murmur swelled to a sullen roar.

"There will be consequences," shouted Carnahan from his box. "You have heard me."

The great boulder had smashed down squarely in the middle of the west end Stack rooms and rolled forward fifty feet, leaving a trail of crushed rock and brick for a path. No traces of the outside walls were left, and only the foundation stones in the front stood to the east of the boulder path. Fragments of the inside walls of clinic rooms still stood, but the ceilings and the roof and walls of the root flat above had been driven down, filling the separated spaces with brick debris.

At the front Plietor saw fragments of furniture: half the splintered front desk of the clinic, the cabinet toppled over, crushed, cloth from the lying-table pad. The men—four of them who had come away—stood, not knowing where to begin.

"What were you doing before you came back to the

group?" Plietor asked Davik.

"Just flinging out, to try to get to the back," Davik said, catching Plietor's eye for the briefest second before looking away.

"That's as good an idea as any," said Plietor. He spoke to the group. "Mind you look before you fling, and don't pull on anything that might fall on you. It's hard-seeing in the dark." He glanced back along the front of the Stack to Carnahan's door. Many had gone inside, but a queue still extended out into the Yard. Light wavered from the front window.

The six men worked, flinging or carrying stones from the front rooms into the Yard, placing more carefully in a separate pile pieces of furniture, medicine pots, cloth. Davik was deepest into the rubble, hoisting large stones and sections of mortared brick by himself. Plietor worked a few steps off, leaving a clear route out for Davik. Musil was there, Karolyi, Walter Prokup, Gregor Natov from the Terrace, and then Tiska. Tiska had come while they worked. She approached Plietor.

"I walked away after my name was called," she said. "No one watched me. They…" she hesitated. "They are not there."

"We didn't need a bloody census to know that," said Plietor, then softer, "It's good you came. Have a care for your hands."

Over the next hour the space outside the walls filled with debris as the space inside was cleared. Bricks slipped from sweaty fingers. The moon was high, shadows working beneath the moving figures. Two men or three carried out fallen sections of wall, except for Davik, who worked alone, his shirt torn and soaked dark with sweat in the darker shadows. Plietor spoke to him once, warning again of unstable walls, but Davik only looked at him and moved for another stone.

"Hai!" It was Musil, near the east wall of the second room. "There is a hand here! It is a man." Then, "Do not hurry. It is cold."

The others gathered around. Davik took a look and moved away, back to where he was before, the collapsed doorway of the interior flat. The rest began carefully moving and heaving bricks, revealing the forearm, the arm to the shoulder, then below in the debris a foot, a bare leg, six people not speaking, only breathing. Then the face was cleared, and they could all see it was Simcas.

"Bloody hell," Plietor said.

"Who is it?" called Davik across the floor.

"Simcas," said Musil.

"Well at least he died hap—"

"Davik!" said Plietor sharply.

Davik didn't speak back, only threw a fist-sized rock he was holding far out onto the Shelf, where it cracked onto the stone.

"Here," said Tiska quietly from the corner. She was stooped, scraping at the edges of another mounded pile with a length of board. "Here is the other."

Gwen lay face down, one arm under her, her undershift high over her buttocks. Tiska pulled it down as the rock was cleared.

Careful hands moved around the bodies, clearing enough so they could be pulled free and carried out, laid side-by-side, partially covered with the lying-table pad. The group stood a circle around them, Plietor wondering what to say. Across the two rooms Davik grunted with the effort of a broken section of wall.

The rasp of shifting stone jerked them all away from their thoughts. Davik leaped out from within the doorway as the wall twisted, then broke apart and collapsed, a sheet of dust pluming out from beneath it.

"Gott damn it!"

They all stood frozen, waiting for more, but nothing more fell, and after a moment Plietor said, "The walls—"

"Gott damn it, I know the walls are bad!" shouted Davik, his chest heaving. "But the walls have to come out, if we are to go in. They have to…to…" He stared at Plietor, his mouth contorted, then moved his hands to his face, covered his eyes, bowed his head, and slowly collapsed onto his knees, his breath coming in great sobs.

Plietor moved uncertainly toward him, but Tiska was there before, wrapping her arms about Davik's head, bending over him.

Down the Stack, Carnahan's door smacked against the wall, and Plietor turned to see two figures silhouetted against the light from within. Carnahan was one, in his hat and long coat. The other was as tall, almost as thick. Bartosz. What were they saying? The moon was past the zenith, descending in the west. In another hour it would sink behind the Caldera ridge and the Shelf would be dark. First light would be two hours after that. And then the work day. What would be the work day tomorrow? What would Carnahan do?

"I think…" Walter Prokop's high voice came over Davik's still-uneven breaths. He was standing by the place where the door to the inner room had been, on the bricks of the collapsed wall. "I think…I don't want to say, but I think I heard…something, from inside. Something…"

"What?" said Davik, on his feet in an instant. "What did you hear?"

"I don't know," said Prokop, squeezing his hands. "A voice, a calling voice, maybe? I'm not sure…but I thought…"

Davik leaped at the collapsed wall and began tearing at it, grasping bricks and hurling them out onto the Shelf.

"Davik! No!" Plietor sprang across the floor. "You can't do this by yourself. There are seven of us. We can do it so much faster all together. We will make…a brigade. Like the passing of water for a fire."

The others understood immediately. Musil, Karolyi, and Gregor Natov joined Plietor in a line, Davik at the inside, and began passing two, three at a time mortared bricks out, man to man. Walter Prokop and Tiska worked by themselves off to the side, ferrying smaller pieces. Twice they all had to jump as a new collapse overtook an overburdened section. But they worked steadily, even as the moon dropped and the Shelf descended into shadow, working by feel as much as by sight, no sound but the grating of brick on brick, and their panting breaths.

When the human sound came again they all heard it. A cry, a moan, a whimper, all in one.

"*Aye!*" shouted Davik, deepest into the rubble. "Are you there? We hear. We hear! We are coming."

A frenzy overtook them all and they redoubled their efforts, bricks flying from hand to hand and out onto the Shelf, the cleared space of the floor expanding, expanding…until another collapse sent them all scurrying. They gathered in the second room, panting raggedly, their clothes torn and sweated through and through, cuts and scrapes all along their arms, over their hands.

"We must…go slow now," panted Plietor, "much as we want to hurry. We must be close to the back wall. Wherever…" he swallowed with effort, "wherever they are, they must be close. After all this, we don't want to make a collapse, a collapse that…" He swallowed again, looked at Davik. "You must test every brick, every stone, before you pull it from where others may lie on it. If it binds, we must remove from above it. Do we understand this?"

Davik nodded, rubbing his bleeding hands across his chest.

The first to see something was Tiska, working ten steps to the side in her careful way.

"*Hai!* There is wood here, upright wood." She was kneeling, her arms reaching behind a standing section of collapsed ceiling. "Come and feel. I cannot see it."

The others clustered around. "Karolyi has the longest arms," said Plietor. "Let him reach."

Tiska backed away as Karolyi crouched and reached into the space, shifted his feet, moving his arms up and down within, his face pressed against the jagged edge.

"It is…a wood frame, turned so." He pulled back, holding his hands out, fingers up, parallel before him, then turned them, still parallel, at an angle.

"A bed platform," said Musil, "standing up, on its side."

Karolyi shrugged. "It may be."

Tiska leaned into the space again. "Is anyone there?" she called, in a soft voice. "Ginna? Julia?"

Plietor winced at the names, but there was not time for emotion. Davik was eying the tall section of fallen ceiling.

"We must be the most careful here," Plietor said. "If this is a bed frame propped up, creating a space, it may fall at the slightest push of anything standing against it. But it must not fall. It *must* not. Do we all understand this?"

The men nodded. Tiska crouched at the space, listening.

Brick by careful brick they cleared the loose rubble from the area, walking carefully as though the floor was made of glass, until there was nothing but three standing sections of the collapsed ceiling, the wood behind the largest. They stood and looked.

Plietor drew a breath in and let it out. "This one first," he said, pointing to the rightmost, a roughly triangular piece, its point up. "We need to tip it back and over, to get to the one standing under it."

"If we could pull from the top with a rope…" said Musil.

"*Acch!*" growled Davik. "We have no rope. We have no time. We must push, like men, from the edge. You push high, Musil. I push low. We must do it."

Plietor shook his head, but he could think of nothing better. Davik took a stance, one leg forward, one leg back, both hands against the brick. Musil leaned above him. Karolyi reached in from the side, with no leverage but the strength of his arms. Davik took a deep breath, and then brought the full pressure of his legs, a grunting groan with effort. Musil closed his eyes and clenched his mouth. Tendons stood out in Karolyi's arms. For two seconds nothing happened, then in the shadow Plietor saw the high tip of the triangle move. A stone clattered down, pebbles sifted, and as Plietor watched the tip went up to vertical, then past. Davik shifted his feet. Karolyi backed away, then Musil, and finally Davik too as the section tilted backward, backward, and crashed to the floor, breaking apart in a rising cloud of dust.

Plietor held his breath, watching the other two sections for movement. But they stood immobile. Tiska was stooping in the dust into the space the section had covered.

"It is a bed frame," she cried. "Two frames, standing in a steeple. But there is so much rock…" Walter Prokop rushed beside her and they began digging like dogs, flinging debris behind them as they knelt. The men moved to confront the two sections remaining.

"Davik, is it you?" Ginna's voice. And they all froze. "Davik, can you hear?" Ginna's voice, weak, from within the cavity, behind the mound of debris.

"Yeh! Yeh! Ginna! It's Davik here. I am here. Only a bit away. You stay. Just stay."

He looked at Plietor, wild eyed. Plietor knew nothing to do but move.

They all attacked the mound of debris before the second section, taking no care for careful walking now, scooping armloads of rock shards and broken bricks to their chests with both arms, carrying them but a few steps back before dropping them to the newly cleared floor.

Then Davik was inside the cavity, but he could not push into the steeple of the bed frames, not with the debris still there and the obstruction of the two remaining sections.

"I will push this section away," he called out. "Stand you all back."

"No!" said Plietor. "You cannot do this alone. Think of the other one. We can bring more small pieces out, then someone can get in with you to push, and—"

"Stand you back!" shouted Davik, already pushing, his legs quivering, veins standing out in his neck. His breath exploded from his lungs. The rest jumped backward, as the whole section tilted out from the wall behind and smashed onto the floor with an apron of flying stone and dust.

"Here. Here! Help me now," cried Davik. And then they were all crouched and stooped under the one remaining section. The air was filled again with flung and scooped stone and brick and panting breaths.

"She is here. She is!" shouted Davik from deep within. "Tiska, come. Tiska!" The rest of them backed out and made way for Tiska, who gathered her shift around her and crawled into the space. Small sounds of excavation came around Davik's breath, whispered words, then silence, until Davik's backside came into view, his back, his arms out before him, and in his arms Ginna's shoulders, and her head, and as he backed her body, and then Tiska, holding her feet. And when they were clear Davik stood up and gathered

Gina in his arms as he had the day of the Zeppelin crash and walked with her out over the rubble to the Shelf.

Tiska looked up from the mouth of the space, where she had released Ginna's feet. "Julia," she said. "Julia is there." And Musil, who was standing closest crouched and crawled after her, to emerge in a few moments as Davik had, with Julia's head and shoulders under his arms, Tiska at her feet.

'We must go to the bunkhouse," said Tiska, looking up at Plietor. "You bring Davik there."

Davik was standing alone, out from the piles of ruin, his head bowed. Ginna lay in his arms, her own arms around his neck, sobbing, sobbing.

26.

The flat was quiet, Mid-Week Day afternoon. Plietor sat at the table, alone in body and thought, looking at his bare arms. The scabs were well-formed, pecks and stripes, no rings of infection anywhere. That was important to watch for, Anna had said, particularly where she had sewed three stitches to close the deep rip. He pressed fingers against his chest, feeling the bruises under his shirt, the soreness of muscle.

Musil's left wrist was wrenched and Natov's ankle too, where he had taken a bad step on a brick and fallen. Davik had stitches in two places, one in his hair on the back. Anna had to shave around the place. "Now you will lose all your strength, like Samson," Ginna had joked. Janescz had said later that Samson was a man in the Bible.

From outside Plietor could hear the chinks of hammers, the rasp of pallets dragged on stone, men's voices of conversation. Work on the west end was going, wall base stones mortared in place already, new bricks drying on racks. Carts went down and up the steep pit path continuously, bringing clay from the quarry.

Janescz was below in the bunkhouse, washing his work clothes. Davik, too, with Ginna. Plietor sat, peelings of turnip and beet before him and the knife from the shelf, staring at his arms.

Three days since the slide. Yesterday they flew. The two

days before everyone had worked to clear the Shelf, carts and carts of rocks and broken bricks over the edge, what was not saved to rebuild broken terraces. Almost everyone. Food must be harvested, vegetables, eggs, and milk. As Carnahan said, they must eat. And they must return to production.

So yesterday they flew. Eight sorties only, four flyers. Far below the high quota, but still they flew, and it was good to fly, though not so good to look at the south cliff face, to see the exposure of new surface from the rock that had fallen.

Before the in-ringing and after the out, Davik went to Ginna, in the bunkhouse. Her bed was against the east wall, the woman's section. Gwen's bed it was, though no one made anything over it. Julia was beside her. Tiska had given her bed for Julia and moved to the second bed in the super's flat, with Anna. Carnahan must have said yes to all this.

Anna had taken over nursing, stitching rips, pouring medicines she had herself against infections, wrapping what needed to be wrapped. Julia's left arm was wrapped and tied across her chest. Anna helped her eat. Tiska sat with her after out-ringing.

And Davik sat with Ginna. Plietor had come after their dinner each day, and Ginna was glad he came. But there could be no talk between them, not with Davik hovering.

This evening would be the Gathering. Carnahan would speak about the slide, in his own way. What would he say about production? Ginna would be able to fly in a day. She was bruised, had breathed dust, but had not been cut or wrenched. It was so smart of her—her and Julia, because she would not claim the plan alone—to stand the bed platforms up in the "steeple" as Tiska said, to make a roof for them to lie under. They had surely been crushed without it.

What would Carnahan say about quota? Would he leave it high? Take a man from the pools or the Terrace to replace

Simcas?

And what would he say about the night of the slide, about them going off to the west end, against his order? "There will be consequences," he had said. But there had been no consequences yet. If they had not gone then—Davik had not gone—if they had waited for Carnahan's order, Ginna would have…been dead. And Julia. Carnahan must know this. Everyone knew. But to go against his order, for Davik to do it—Davik, that everyone knew was so against…What would Carnahan do?

"Hai, Plietor." A woman's voice outside the door, not Ginna. Tiska. Tiska was there.

"I have come from Ginna, for the green dress," she said, when Plietor opened the door and stood before her. "She will go to the Gathering dance tonight and wants the green dress, the dress from Julia."

"I know the dress." Plietor spoke more sharply than he intended and smiled to fix it. "Will you come inside?"

Tiska glanced past him, then moved through the doorway. Plietor stood aside, closing the door against the wind.

"How is Ginna today?"

"Good," said Tiska. She was looking about. Plietor knew she had never been in their flat before. Maybe she had never been in any separate flat, except for Anna's now.

"She is good, I think. She does not cough, and she is walking. She and Davik walked about the Yard. Did you see them?"

"No," said Plietor. "I have been here since tucker."

Tiska glanced at the peelings and knife. "At this table? All by yourself then?"

"Yeh," said Plietor. "Just trying to get straight."

Tiska looked at him, and after a moment he said, "Well… the dress, eh? It's up top level, where she sleeps." He gave a quick shrug. "Or where she was sleeping, when she was here."

He felt the blood rising in his neck. "I suppose I should get it…" But he made no move to do so.

"Oh, I could," Tiska said.

"I might like that," said Plietor. "It's just in the trunk."

Tiska gave him a smile and moved to the ladder, mounting it quickly. He watched her step off at the slot, side step to the second ladder and disappear up it. In a moment she was back down at the slot.

"Got it well enough," she said. Plietor watched her back down the ladder, holding the neatly folded dress gently with one hand.

"Well," she said, smiling at him again. "I'll be going then. Will you be dancing tonight?"

"I don't know," said Plietor. "It may depend."

Tiska cocked an eyebrow at him.

"It may depend on what Carnahan says."

"Ah," Tiska said. "Carnahan. Yeh. There is that."

Plietor stood at the rear wall of the big room next to the inner door, feeling the warmth of the whiskey in his stomach. It hadn't gone to his head yet. He was waiting for that, before having his second glass. Carnahan had declared double nobblers tonight, a rare enough event and for sure. Even Ginna had tried a glass. Davik had presented it to her with his bow, and she had downed it with her eyes locked with Davik's, before almost falling over, gasping and sputtering. There had been a rip around the room at it, men clapping and whistling.

Barely a half hour and the band was going strong, Anton raking on his washboard at a fearsome rate, his face the color of beet juice. The dancers moved in and out and promenaded, kicking toes and heels, Davik spinning Ginna twice around for every once of the others when he had her, the green dress twirling. Tiska had walked by Plietor three times, but he was not for dancing, at least not yet.

Carnahan. The man had outdone himself with fancy speech, though not so much as he had at the laying out of Gwen and Simcas the day after the slide. There it was will-of-God-this and will-of-God-that and people's appointed time, the price of work in a hard land. Davik had been dark beyond any feeling for Gwen and Simcas, but only Plietor and Janescz knew of it, and Davik had not spoke, even to them.

This day when Carnahan began on the will of God, Davik could hardly stand settled, shifting on his feet like he was on coals until Ginna, who had hold of his arm, pulled hard on it. Simcas and Gwen were praised again, invaluable workers on the Terrace and in the glider sheds. And then it was on to Ginna and Julia. Plietor tensed to hear what was coming, feeling Janescz and Davik tense on either side. Julia had come back from her usual place to stand by Ginna, all of them at the back. Ginna was on Davik's arm, in her new gloves. Anna had found gloves in Gwen's chest and passed them to Ginna, in full confidence of Gwen's wishes, so Plietor had heard.

Ginna and Julia were declared models of resourcefulness and fortitude, spared, however, only by the unfathomable Will which…to go on with their important work…Plietor drew breath, tried to focus. Now. But Carnahan was speaking on the power of the Camp's recovery, and then into a schedule for rebuilding the clinic rooms and garden terraces. Was there to be nothing? Not a word of Davik and them walking away, of digging and carrying through the night, of finding Gwen and Simcas, Ginna and Julia? Plietor looked at Janescz, who shrugged. Davik was shifting, his head up, a half smile. *Nothing.* Carnahan would say nothing. Plietor shook his head to no one but himself. Maybe it was best, after all. *Carnahan*. No one could ever think what he would say.

No one could think of double nobblers either, but when Carnahan said his word for them, "to slough off the woes of this hard land," there was a whoop from all.

Plietor looked now about the room—the swirl of dancers in the light of the lamps, the shuffle and stamp of feet, the drive of the music, faces of men and women along the walls shouting conversation. The round of whiskey had settled, with now two more bottles on the table with Karski. Plietor thought he was ready for more.

At the table was Tiska, for her second as well. They clinked and poured down. It watered Plietor's eyes, but Tiska's eyes were on him, and soon they were in the dance, his arm around her waist, on promenade. Three exchanges later Ginna was before him, her eyes too bright, her cheeks flushed, and her chest above the lace edge of the bodice of the green dress. Plietor tried to push away thought but could not. Three dark nights before she had lain under a death's weight of fallen rock and masonry, and here she danced as gay as gay, an open smile on her face for Plietor as she passed away from him on the next exchange.

At the interval, Davik left Ginna on the bench. Julia was there already. She wore her work shift, her arm tied across in its white wrapping. But a red ribbon bound her waist, with a bow at the back. Plietor supposed it too had come from Gwen's chest. Karolyi had come to sit with her while Ginna danced, and Musil, with a tight wrap on his wrist. Plietor would sit too, after the interval. Tiska had gone out into the Yard.

Davik came in the door with three mates behind: Karolyi, Gregor Natov limping from his ankle, another man from the pools. Davik didn't go to Ginna, but to Hilenski with his *dorma,* heads down together, then a slap on Hilenski's back. Plietor knew the prospect as Hilenski gave a nod to the others with their instruments and flailed the strings in an opening chord.

The four Cossacks linked their shoulders and began, most of the others crowding back into the room to watch the familiar show, hooting and whistling encouragement. The dancers turned their radial line, stomping and kicking with the rhythm of the music, which settled in for two choruses before beginning its steady advance. Stomping gave way to bouncing, and then, as the music swelled and bounded, to the leg-flying, twisting jumps and squatting kicks. Natov was not much for this with his ankle, despite the encouragement of whiskey, but the others made up for it. The crowd along the walls whooped their appreciation. Plietor looked to Ginna, saw her face aglow, her eyes fixed on Davik, who at that same moment, facing her at the finish of a leap, gave a salute before descending for another round of kicks. She waved back, turned the wave into a blown kiss. Julia, Plietor saw, was not so comfortable, sitting with a frozen smile, twisting her free hand in her lap.

Plietor felt his own discomfort. He leaned on the back wall, impatient for the climax, the others to miss their steps and fall over one then another, Davik to go on and on, besting the most frantic efforts of the music with kick after kick, balancing on his forefeet at the end, toppling backward to lie in his hair. Plietor wondered if Davik would fall on the shaved and stitched place, would feel the pain of the blow.

But the other dancers did not fall over. At Davik's shout they all stood in one motion and surged out separately into the room. Davik came to Ginna, almost lifting her up by the hand. Karolyi found Tiska. Gregor Natov dragged Anna in, and almost within the rhythm the four couples were whirling in the center of the room, hands on waists and shoulders as the music swept on and the rest roared and whistled from the walls. Another shout from Davik and high hands led the women in fast stepping twirls, hair falling and swinging out behind. Almost as if time itself slowed, Plietor saw the scarf lungee that had wrapped Ginna's head all the months loosen, unwind, and fling out before she caught it and tossed it high. Davik reached, but at that moment no eyes were on Davik.

Ginna's hair was to her shoulders, a cascade of glistening red-brown like a wind-blown waterfall. If time had slowed before for Plietor, at this moment it stopped. Ginna's face was ecstatic, and the effect...the dress, the hair, her face, even the new gloves...Plietor's heart stopped too, and it was a moment before he was aware that the roaring and whistling from around the walls had stopped as well. There was only the frantic music, as with one last shout from Davik the men all reached for the women and lofted them high overhead to turn, turn, turn, the women's arms out, stretched as though...as though they were flying.

And then the women were down, the music collapsed into a final drawn chord, and the roar from all shook the room. Tiska was suddenly before Plietor, her eyes shining, reaching for his hand. But Plietor had no eyes or hand for her. He made a gesture, he did not know what, and brushed past, out across the surging room of shouts and slaps, pushing past and past until he was out the door, across the Yard, and into the night.

27.

Plietor passed quickly through the Yard and a dozen paces further before he stopped and turned back to the west end. The moon was not yet over the Caldera ridge and the whole Shelf was shrouded, shreds of thicker mist ghosting up over the edge in the remainder of the day's wind.

On the newly mortared wall Plietor sat, trying to empty his head. Light poured out of Carnahan's door, tags of conversation, a long coughing by a woman who stood along the wall. People came from the door, turned to shapes as they moved out into the Yard, fading away into shadows as they stepped beyond. A lightening of the sky above the ridge showed where the moon would be.

A woman's voice, and then a couple were out the door with a gay step, past the coughing woman, slowing, arms linked into one shape in silhouette. Plietor felt the pace of his heart pick up. Then the couple were at the ladder, the woman mounting, behind her the man close, the ladder creaking with the weight. Plietor stood, a sound as of the wind beginning in his ears, his thoughts too, blown and ragged. He moved along the wall.

Above him he heard the door of their own flat scrape open and close. He waited a beat, then put his foot on the ladder. What would he do? What could he do? No answers came. But he put his weight on the foot and brought up the next.

At the top of the ledge he stepped to the door. Lamplight came in strips through the shuttered window, and he moved along the wall to it, hearing murmurs, a rumbling chuckle, a sound...lips on lips. He closed his eyes hard, pressing them up with his cheeks, working to control his breathing.

The creak of the ladder inside came, then again, and as the light went out of the window he moved back to the door, pushing the latch down gently, gently, the door inch by inch, until he could glimpse the dark room and the slot at the top of the ladder, where the light now came, and the murmuring, and the wet sound of lips.

Plietor stood in the dark, but with the creak of the second ladder he felt something rise within him, a force, a compulsion. Before he could think his heart and his breathing exploded. And then Davik's face was looking down on him from the slot, a wild expression, a contortion.

"Bugger the fuck off!" Davik hissed. Their eyes locked for a long second, then Plietor was blind, and up the ladder somehow, and drawing back and throwing a long fist into Davik's amazed face, the recoil of bone on gristle. Davik shouted, and Ginna was screaming, and then everything was kicks and punches and beds overturned and Davik's strong hands around his throat, and twisting, and butting and...

Plietor didn't realize at first he was over the edge. He bounced on the ladder once and then onto the absolute hardness of the floor. Davik leaned through the slot above him, his face smeared with blood.

"You bloody fuken bastard!" he was shouting. "You gottdamn bloody fucken bastard!" Then up and calling, "Ginna! Ginna!" Plietor tried to stand while Davik disappeared up the second ladder, still calling, then down again, his face in the slot.

"She's bloody gone. Is she there? Is she?" Davik leaped down the ladder, but Plietor was out the door and then down the Stack ladder and out onto the Shelf, one leg dragging.

"Ginna! Ginna!" Davik called from the ledge. But she did not answer.

Plietor kept moving until he was twenty paces down the path to the pools. There the pain in his knee overcame him, and he slumped down against a rock. For a few moments he knew nothing but his breath and his heart, but as these subsided other pains rose up. The taste of blood was in his mouth. One eye was swelling. His fist, his right fist where he landed the first blow was throbbing. And his knee...his weight must have come on it when he fell. Faint from the Stack he heard a sudden swell of voices, shouts, a woman's scream. But they were no concern of his. He slumped further against the rock. Tears came from behind his eyes and welled over. His breath sagged again. Alone in the shadows of the path, he put his head down and sobbed.

In the bunkhouse, next morning, Anna wielded her needle.

"*Acch!*" Plietor jerked back from the pain.

"Does it hurt, love?" Anna said, not looking into his eyes, focused on her work. "It should. Your tooth came right through the lip. Lucky the tooth is not gone as well. But the lip's got to be closed up, it does." She looked at Julia, who was holding the lamp with her good arm, peering over Anna's shoulder into Plietor's mouth. Julia nodded as Anna pulled the needle through, the black thread following.

"Very cool we was about it, us folks left in the long room," Anna said. "Considering one minute we was all happy with dancing, and the next we was looking at ten strange men at the door, and one of them with an ugly pistol. Then comes Davik with his nose and all...Aye, we was very cool."

"*Acch!*" Plietor jerked again.

"Two more, love. Hold still." The needle was in and out.

"None of us had the least of an idea what was to happen. But when Musil at the window saw the torch down by the glider sheds and called out about it…well, it was all for nothing then. There…how is it?"

She held his lip turned back, shifted on her stool so Julia could get a clear look. "It'll do for a ragged man who has spent the night on the stone," said Julia.

"Ragged he is, him and Davik both," said Anna. "I can't tell about your knee. My fingers can't feel the insides as Julia's could."

"If it was broken, he'd never walked across the Shelf with it," said Julia. Then, "See there," pointing a finger at Plietor's mouth, "don't be running your tongue to it. It needs to lie still as you can let it, to close up."

Anna stood. "Go then," she said. "Get to the gliders. The day's work's going."

Plietor tried to speak, grimaced, then started again. "What of Ginna? It's everything but Ginna with you both, since I walked in the door."

Anna and Julia exchanged a look. "We don't know," said Anna.

"What?!" said Plietor, then squeezed his eyes in pain, recovered. "What can you mean?"

Anna took a breath. "I'll say it to you as I know. You might as well hear it from me as another." She looked at Julia again and shrugged.

"I said it as after Musil saw the torch. Davik moved so fast then and kicked the pistol right away, then our men was on the others and the rest of us scurried. Carnahan disappeared inside his door, but by the time he was back with his own pistol the fight was out the blue door and in the dark and he weren't to go out himself, said he would stand for protecting us women." She snorted.

"I don't know what then, outside. But after a bit our men came back, saying they drove the others off. Eoghan Fergus had his nose all bloodied, but none of the others was the worse for it. And then Davik came back, asking all of Ginna. And no one knew. The last anyone knew…" She stopped and looked at Plietor.

"She has not been seen, all the night and this day?" Plietor's face was twisted.

Anna shook her head. "Karolyi told me Davik expected her in the glider sheds. But they looked over all, and she was not. The ten strange men went over the edge at the pit path and away, Karolyi said, every one. Guess that tells us who they were, if we needed more to know."

"Tells us what?" said Plietor. His brain was spinning. He was dark, dizzy.

"Tells us they come from the other camp."

"What? Come to raid us? That is craziness. But Ginna? What of Ginna?" The tears were behind his eyes again.

Anna looked at Julia. They both shrugged, looked away.

28.

It was a cave. It had taken Ginna a bit to understand that. But that's what it was, a storage cave. Along one in-curving wall were three stuffed burlap bags, flour from the feel and smell of it. Other collapsed and empty bags lay in a stack. Against the wall across were wooden crates, two full of identical tins, various sizes of tins in another, five other crates empty. Two empty pallets were stacked at the back. *Supplies running low,* she thought.

She had done all the counting after the first half hour, after it became clear nothing was to be done with her right away. The cave was entirely dark. It was not the dark of night. That was the dark she was in when she had been taken up, more dark with the lungee scarf tied around her eyes. But nothing like the absolute dark of the cave, where a blink or a hand before one's eye gave nothing at all.

She had stood for a moment after the door was closed and she heard the lock fitted, awaiting some form of vision to come from acclimation. In what she thought would be temporary darkness her attention had inevitably moved to smell. Her first moments down among the pits as she was being taken had been almost unbearable, the stench suffocating, worse ever than her first response on the Shelf. But more quickly than she would have imagined the stench faded into the background, as it had finally above. Now she had to make an effort to distinguish it.

No amount of effort had produced any visual response to her surroundings, though, and she had known by then that nothing would come. Yet still she stood. She was not in fear of her life. Maybe she should have been, but she was not. She had just stood, there in the absolute dark, letting events play through her head, trying to make order, waiting for another step at the door.

When none came, and she finally tired of standing, she had undertaken the reconnoiter by careful touch, finding the bags and the crates and the pallets, and above them, low to her head, unworked stone. Then she had known she was in a cave. And she had sat down on the pallets, pulling the green dress around her, and...wept. She wept from exhaustion, from fear—for she was afraid, if not mortally—but most from confusion.

Four nights ago she had truly thought she would die, lying under the fragile balance of the propped bed frames. First had come the sudden awakening, the roar. She had no idea at first. But Julia had screamed "Rockslide!" even before her feet touched the stone floor, and all Ginna could think was for a cover. So they had erected the bed frames, ridiculous as it seemed at first, and lay under that triangular space as the booms and roars shook the stone, until finally the world crashed down upon them, and the ends of their shelter filled with rubble, and they were sealed in. They could not see, not breathe from the dust, and Julia had lapsed. She herself had faded into a stupor, her only thought that she would die.

She did not know how long they had lain, but then there was Davik's voice, and she called back, and then Davik's hands, and she was lifted and in his arms in the open air and she could breathe and the night was around her and she was glad, so deeply glad. And then Julia was alive as well and it was perfect.

The two days they lay in the bunkhouse beds Davik had come early and late when he could. He sat and sat beside her bed like a great blond puppy, telling silly stories of rocks and bricks and mountains, sending the nightmare away with laughter, even for Anna, who cast off her severity and looked to the both of them with the greatest of care. Anna gave her the gloves from Gwen's chest, gave to Julia the ribbon, and even spoke of Gwen's Gathering dress for Julia, though much reshaping must be done.

When the Gathering day came, the first day she could go about with her full breath, she and Davik walked the Shelf. She had felt tender toward him, very tender before the eyes of all. At the dance her tenderness swelled with exertion. She knew it came from the whiskey in part, but only in part, and she did not resist. The feeling was so large, so filled her, and then after the dancing when it turned to want...when they kissed...

But then Plietor. *Oh, Plietor! Poor Plietor.* He had been steady too, there in the night when Davik drew her out of the rubble, in the bunkhouse every day. He did not sit long as Davik did, but why should he? He could not speak around Davik. She knew this, but still...*Poor Plietor.* So wise, so yearning to know, so droll in his way. *But Davik, Davik...*

When Plietor came at Davik in the flat it was terrible, and then Davik was terrible too, and she had gone down the ladder while they wrestled, and out the door, and down the Stack ladder, and out onto the Shelf, running, running... *Where? To the glider sheds.* They seemed in that moment the only sanctuary.

But they were not. There were men there, men she could not see to know in the shadows. She had barely spoken when strong hands were laid on her. She screamed once, but a hand was over her mouth.

"Can this be the one?" she heard.

"Gloves she has, 's truth, and a long scarf in her hand."

"Bloody ace if it was."

"Take her. Send two back."

That was when the scarf was wrapped around her eyes and tied, and though she kicked and thrashed her wrists and ankles were bound and she was taken up and over a shoulder like a bag of flour. She knew from the incline her carrier was over the edge, and when the stench increased almost beyond bearing she knew she was among the pits. And then it was all twists and jogs. *How could the men know such a path in the dark?* she had leisure to wonder. And then they did not, for they stopped and argued, and turned back and after awhile she was exchanged to the shoulder of the other man.

When she was finally stood upright it was in a lighter place, and men muttered around her until a strong voice came, a voice in German tones, and she had two thoughts only: *Horst!* was first, but it was not Horst. And then she thought of the letter, Janescz's letter in the volume of Lord Russell's, the letter and the German Overseer of the T-One Camp.

"I am known to Horst Kemper!" she had shouted into the darkness of the blindfolding scarf. "He will hear of this!" And then she had shuddered because of the stupidity of the utterance.

Surely it could cause her as ill as good if these men knew who she was. And when, and how, could Horst Kemper ever hear of her abduction in any way to intervene? It was appalling that she had spoken thus, desperate. But the German voice was not repeated, and it was almost a relief when she was lifted up again and carried to this place, her wrists and ankles unbound, thrust in and locked away, left to untie the scarf herself from around her eyes and bind up her hair with it once more.

She was no longer weeping after this rumination, but she was no less beset by confusion. Where was she, and why was she here? The men who had taken her had spoken as though they were looking for her, her particularly. "The gloves," they had said. "The scarf." Who could have identified her to…others? What others? And why? *Why?*

It would settle her to think systematically. Sitting on the pallets, she squared her shoulders. First, what others? There were the two other mining camps in the Caldera, north along the east wall she thought, though she had never seen them. McCulloch was one, T-One the other, Australian partnerships, Sydney and Brisbane offices. So strange, to think of these mute facts she had from her father. "T-One" was really "Threnium-One," the camp with the German Overseer. Gehlhausen was his name, installed after her father had pulled Horst back to Perth and sent him on to Germany. Some difficulty between her father and Horst; she had never known what.

The camps had cooperated before the gliders came. She knew that, and Plietor had reminded her the day they had looked at Janescz's letters. But when her father brought Horst back he had ended cooperation. *Why?* She had never asked in a serious way, always thought just of the gliders. Aerial collection gave her father a competitive advantage. Why offer his advantage to others? She had never thought of actual men flying gliders, others still sopping threnium jelly from steaming pits with cloths. Davik had said once, "It will not always be so." She had never thought what that might mean either.

Davik had a connection with Gehlhausen. She knew

this, though in thinking who might have identified her to another camp she would first think of Carnahan. Carnahan was Overseer when there was still cooperation between the camps. He would know Gehlhausen.

But Davik had spoken of Gehlhausen too. When? Once was the night after the day she had first gone walking on the Shelf with Julia, when she had first seen the gliders. Davik had been angry, talking of Horst, and then Gehlhausen. "Gehlhausen knows things," he had said, "things about the world bigger than the Camp." Had he really said that? She wasn't sure. She had known so little then. The other time: when she had thought she must go with the camel train, when she came down from her room to listen after going up after dinner. Davik had walked that day to the T-One camp to talk to Gehlhausen. Janescz had accused him of it, and Davik had not denied it. "Do you want camp against camp?" Janescz had said. "We will rise up against Carnahan," had returned Davik. But that was the night Davik had also said she was his life. He was extreme, always so extreme.

Janescz had the letter from Gehlhausen, folded in the book by Lord Russell. She remembered Gehlhausen in the letter speaking of their "mutual aspiration." There was no knowing what that was, had been.

She had considered the "others," and those who might have identified her, who had some connection to Gehlhausen. Now: *Why?*

Carnahan was the only one who knew she was Ginna MacReedy. The only one. Could he have arranged with Gehlhausen to abduct her for ransom from her father? How could he have arranged it? There was no communication between the camps. *And why?* Carnahan did so badly want to be rid of her...except sometimes it seemed he didn't. He had kept her on after the first camel train. Now he needed her to fly a glider, for production. And how would any ransom work? Carnahan would have to send word to her father via the telegraph in Stuart. And what would he say in such a message? That she had been in the Arltunga Camp for four months and had now been abducted for ransom by T-One? Please send funds for exchange? Not bloody likely. *Oh!* What words now in her head.

Maybe it would not be about simple money. She knew the T-One camp wanted gliders for themselves. Maybe they would hold her against the exchange of a glider, or a glider and a pilot. Maybe the matter was of the "world bigger than the camp," Davik had spoken of. The Admiralty, after all, was hungry to be apprised of German efforts to obtain threnium for themselves. Was Gehlhausen's Overseer's position a sign of German influence among the owners of the T-One Mine? Was it conceivable that she be held against the exchange of threnium powder, pure and simple? A one-time exchange? That was absurd, when the T-One was collecting threnium daily, even if more slowly than Arltunga.

She could make no hypothesis that went very far. One certainty only: no one could know her for herself, know her in hope of ransom, without Carnahan's telling them.

But what if not for ransom? Davik had spoken of camp against camp, of rising up against Carnahan. Could Davik be planning an uprising with Gehlhausen? He had visited the T-One once at least, that she knew. Could Davik have arranged then for Gehlhausen to take her, to keep her out of harm's way during an abetted insurrection? Davik was extreme and chafed miserably, fiercely, under Carnahan's ways, but insurrection could never succeed for long. Her father would come in force. Surely Gehlhausen and the T-One's owners would know this, even if Davik did not. They could lose their own mine to the Law. The Law had made no appearance that she had seen in the deep Outback but moved much more powerfully in the courts of Perth, Sydney, and Brisbane. The owners of T-One would not risk this.

What of Janescz? Janescz had spoken strongly against Davik's connection to Gehlhausen on at least two occasions. But there was the letter. Was it solely a remnant of the former time of cooperation before the gliders? Or was there still some connection of ideals, if not more, between Janescz and Gehlhausen? Ginna did not know Janescz. He was strange to her.

She sighed a deep sigh, and shifted painfully on the pallet, aware of her need for a latrine. Hours had passed surely. She had been taken before the middle of the night, three hours at least in transit, an hour to settle and reconnoiter, now more than that to turn over and over these speculations, her poor brain upside down with possibilities, every one leading to a wall or a gap of ignorance. It was too impossible.

Davik. Could she think about Davik? Davik and Plietor? There in the dark, all alone, she shook her head. There was no need for confusion with Davik and Plietor at least. She simply must distance herself. There was no other course. That had been her intent when she went to stay with Julia in the clinic. But then had come the dreadful night, and her rescue in Davik's arms, and the days in the bunkhouse, and Davik...and Davik. She must deny the part of herself that wanted him. She must. There was no other way for them all to live together...if they were to live together again.

She must have slept, because she was lying back on the pallets when the door latch rattled. A bar of light appeared underneath, then with it one on the side, then she was blinded and put her hands over her eyes.

"I hope you were not too uncomfortable in your accommodation." The German was older than Horst, or maybe only looked older. He was dressed in clean khakis, dark hair slicked back, blue eyes, half spectacles like Bartosz's. He sat behind a small table, another man standing behind him to his right at a kind of attention, hands crossed behind his back. There was no other furniture in the room, no chair for Ginna. She stood, conscious of the green dress, clasping her hands in their gloves at her waist. The man behind the German was staring openly at her, his mouth slightly open. She gave a slight nod to the German.

"We wanted to be sure you were quite safe in the case of any…ah…reactive attempt at intervention from the Arltunga Camp." Ginna looked at him steadily. His eyes turned up the least bit, *a mocking look,* Ginna thought.

"But, as you may have seen, it is midday, and no one has come. So…We will see fit to place you in a more comfortable room for yourself. You will want to eat, and…do other things. You will of course be permitted this. We have no wish to harm you."

"What *is* your wish for me?" Gina said.

His mocking look was more pronounced. "You have no need to trouble yourself with inter-camp…diplomacy. I will say that we will make certain requests of the Arltunga Camp. Your presence with us will encourage them to hear our requests in a favorable light. If our requests are accommodated, then you shall be returned, and we shall all go on."

This man is not going to tell you anything, Ginna said to herself, though he had told her she was a hostage. She thought he spoke from the assumption of a mutual understanding of who she was, but she would not ask him, would not try to point out the difficulties for Carnahan of agreeing to any "accommodation" that required communication with her father, not ask the obvious question of the outcome if requests were not accommodated. She had no desire to serve as an occasion for his high-blown mocking sarcasm, a game for him, worse than a conversation with Carnahan. But, perhaps…

"May I know with whom I have the honor of speaking?" she said, on the impulse.

His mouth twitched up. "I am Bernhard Gehlhausen, Overseer here, at your service." He gave a nod. "And you, to return the favor?"

"I am Miss Ginna deBoruski," she said, "guest at the Arltunga Camp."

Gehlhausen sat back slightly, a man expressing his comfort, his mouth twitching up more. "Ah, yes. Miss Ginna *deBoruski. Now*…guest at the T-One Camp."

Ginna nodded, keeping her expression bland. "May I say I have seen your name before, Herr Gehlhausen, attached to a letter which I noticed…" Gehlhausen's mocking smile vanished, but Ginna continued. "…associated with a volume of social commentary by Lord Bertrand Russell. Perhaps…" Gehlhausen's hands were on the table, pushing as though he were about to stand. The man behind him moved forward, uncertain. "Perhaps we might sit together of an evening and discuss Lord Russell's position on German social democracy." Gehlhausen was standing now, his jaw clenched, his man looking from him to Ginna and back. Ginna smiled.

Gehlhausen gestured with his head to the man, now beside him. "Take her," he said.

"This room's a deal better than where you was before," the man said. He was a small man, holding his hat at his waist in both hands, round faced and almost completely bald, his pate leathery, mottled with irregular spots. There was on odd smell about him. *Garlic?* It seemed unlikely.

He had led her out into a deeply mist-shrouded yard and down a row of rooms rather like the garden sheds at the Arltunga Camp, clay bricks plastered just as she knew, gray on gray. She could see no more than twenty feet in the mist, the perpetual condition in the heart of the Caldera she supposed, marveling again that her acclimation to the stench was so complete. To come here for the first time straight from the desert...how could sense survive it?

The room they had turned into was perhaps ten-feet square, a mattress on a low platform with a rug beside it, a chair, a shelf with a pottery pitcher, mug, and bowl, a lidded metal pail on the floor in a corner. The window opening was barred, covered on the inside with a heavy shutter.

"I heard you say you was a Miss Ginna," said the man, his eyes on her. "I am Albert, here to do Mr. Gehlhausen's bidding."

"Hello then, Albert," said Ginna, and nodded to him.

He smiled and nodded in return. "You see the place. It's a room we keep for the owner, when he comes. That's a rare thing, so here it sits. And now you are to be here. There's water in the pitcher. And the pail for..." He flushed over his whole head. "For...business. I'll deal with the pail once a day. I'll bring your food. Mr. Gehlhausen says you are not to go out, that I am to lock the door, with you in it." He looked at her uncertainly and shrugged.

"If that's what Mr. Gehlhausen says, then that is the way it shall be," said Ginna. Albert smiled and shrugged again.

"I don't know what you'll do, all the day here, by yourself."

"Perhaps you can come and talk to me," said Ginna.

"Oh, I would," said Albert. "I will. I mean, if I can, when Mr. Gehlhausen is about and doesn't need me."

"I would like that very much," said Ginna. Albert flushed

again. He stood for a moment, looking at her in glances, turned to the door, then turned back.

"We don't get guests here," he said.

"No?" said Ginna, raising her eyebrows.

"No, we don't. Only the owner, with the camel train once in the year." Ginna held her look. "I heard you say you was a guest at Arltunga."

"Yes, I was," she said, now more serious.

"Do they get guests there?"

"Sometimes," she said.

"Women guests…like you?"

"Yes," said Ginna. "Women, sometimes." Albert took a step back to her.

"I heard," he said in a more tentative voice, "I heard… from the men talking, the men who went up there, that you came back with…" Ginna nodded encouragement, wondering what was coming. "I heard that when they went in, there was women standing around a big room, in clothes…like yours there." He flushed furiously again. "Like in the city, like Brisbane."

Ginna smiled. "Do you know Brisbane?" she asked.

"Aye. I was there. That's where I came in."

Ginna thought to ask him where he had come in from. He was Irish by heritage; that much was clear. But that was not where she wanted the conversation to go, this unexpected conversation.

"Well," she said instead, "There are women at the Arltunga Camp. Quite a few women."

"All as guests?" said Albert, a step closer.

"Not all," said Ginna. "Some work there all the time."

"Lor'," breathed Albert. "Women all the time. Imagine it!"

"Have you no women here?"

Albert stepped back, shook his head. "No. No women. Ever. Though some of the men..." He flushed deeply again and turned quickly to the door.

"Wait!" said Ginna. "Can I ask you...a favor?"

Albert eyed her now, a wary look. "Now what would that be then?"

"Some of the women at the Arltunga Camp have become my friends. Some of the men too." Albert's look deepened. Ginna went on quickly, a little desperately. "Mr. Carnahan, for instance, the Overseer there. He and I have conversations..."

Albert brightened. "*Ogh*. Like you said to Mr. Gehlhausen, about the book. That was to his interest, I could tell. I have heard of Mr. Carnahan too, I have."

Ginna smiled her best smile. "Exactly that kind of conversation," she said. "I should so like to hear news of my friends, while I...am a guest here. Could you tell me, if you hear other men talking, as you said before? Could you remember the names you hear? Could you do that? It would give us something to talk about...when you visit me."

Albert smiled back at her from the door. "Aye. I can do that. I can remember things I hear. I have an ear for names, I do."

"I'm sure you do," said Ginna.

"'Deboruski,'" said Albert. "That is your name you said to Mr. Gehlhausen. "Miss Ginna Deboruski."

"You are remarkable," said Ginna. "And what is your whole name, Albert?"

"Albert McCutcheon, I am," said Albert, drawing himself up.

Ginna gave a small curtsy. "I am happy to meet you, Mr. Albert McCutcheon. I am sure we shall have much to say to each other."

Albert flushed a last time, then was out the door. Ginna heard him placing the padlock.

29.

"This is an extraordinary meeting to deal with extraordinary circumstances."

Karski had gone around to the supers in the afternoon. Carnahan wanted a meeting after out-ringing.

Now Carnahan stood behind his long table, leaning forward on his arms, running his eyes over the five of them. They had moved two benches from along the wall to make a line before the table. Plietor sat on the far side of the bench away from the door, with Davik and Janescz.

Bartosz and Helinski sat with their hats beside them on the other. Only Anna of the supers had not been summoned. Karski had stood by as they gathered but had disappeared out the door.

Carnahan's eyes lingered on Davik, who was looking down, his nose stuffed by rolled cloth plugs, bruises under his eyes. Plietor could imagine what his own mouth looked like, swollen and throbbing where Anna had put the stitches. He stretched out his leg to change the pain in his knee, reminding him of every time he had pressed the pedal of the glider during the day. Davik shifted on the bench, now knocking his fists together. Plietor didn't think Davik had ever sat in Carnahan's presence before.

"The Overseer of the T-One Camp has contacted me..." Carnahan began.

"Eh?" interrupted Hilenski before thinking, then raised his hands and shrugged. Carnahan looked at him with a cold eye.

"It was just to wonder," said Hilenksi. "T-One was it? That's one thing. But...How did he do so? I didn't hear of any coming back."

Carnahan tightened his lips. "No one came back," he said.

"The electric talker," said Davik, not looking up.

Carnahan slammed his palm against the table. "I am to speak here," he said. "Only I, unless I say." The others looked at the floor.

"As it happens, Davik is in this case correct," said Carnahan. "The T-One Overseer contacted me on the field telephonic machine." He paused. Plietor knew of this machine. They all did, though Plietor was sure no one had thought of it in a long while. Well, except Davik.

Plietor and Davik had been part of the crew that laid the connector, miles of two wires tight twisted that came to them wrapped and wrapped around huge spindles on the camel train. The wire started in the Overseer's back room, out through a hole in the brick of the wall then across the Shelf to the pit path. Once over the edge it was down and down the broken track through all the miles' misery of rock, boiling pits, and stench mist to the T-One. Plietor knew wire had been laid beyond that too, to the McCulloch Camp. But he had never seen that stretch. That had been T-One and McCulloch crews. Plietor had never seen the talking machine itself either. There was a crank to turn to create electricity he had heard, horns to speak into and hear from. Overseers had talked on the machine when the Camps were friendly, before the gliders. But Carnahan had not spoken of any talk in a long while, until now.

Now, except for Davik, they were all looking at Carnahan. He scowled at them.

"The T-One Overseer wishes certain…accommodations," Carnahan said. They waited. "He wishes a share of our production."

No one spoke. Plietor darted his eyes down the row of them, all still looking at Carnahan, a little blankly now. Carnahan looked back, his eyebrows up. They all waited longer.

Bartosz finally let his breath out in a rush. "Is that all there is now? Is there not more to it?"

Carnahan scowled deeper. "What more did you expect?"

"I expect…I expected nothing," said Bartosz, flustered. "Only…a glider maybe, to go with the girl."

"What good would that be for them then?" said Carnahan. "They have no shelf to launch from, no elastic rope."

"Yah. Yah. I see it," said Bartosz, more flustered. "I was not thinking."

"I will do the thinking," said Carnahan. He paused again, while they all sat, tense. "And I think I cannot do this."

"What?!" Davik started up. Janescz put a strong hand onto his arm, to keep him from standing. "You won't trade some bloody powder for Ginna?"

Carnahan stood erect now behind the table, as Janescz pulled harder on Davik's arm.

"I might have expected you to see so narrow," he said coldly, "and not to listen to my words. I did not say I *won't* do. I said I *can* not. And the bloody powder you name is nothing more than our life's blood, the flesh of our bodies here."

Plietor saw that Davik's neck was red, the muscles of his jaw clenched. But he did not speak.

"I can not do this because I do not represent myself here, as Overseer. I represent the interests of MacReedy Mining Limited. I am sworn to those interests by contract and oath.

I must consult before I could ever take any step which would threaten our own production quotas."

"Bloody—" started Davik, but Janescz overrode him. "And how do you consult, sir?"

Carnahan looked from him to Davik and back again, always with his scowl. "My plan is this, and I bring you here to hear it." He nodded to Bartosz and Hilenski, brought his eyes back to the Boruskis.

"The camel train is due in the second week from now. It is my thought that correspondence will come with it from Perth, from MacReedy Mining, some directive. It is not in my mind that Gehlhausen has acted on his own idea, with the raid, and the abduction."

"*Gehlhausen?*" said Bartosz, then, hurriedly, "pardoning myself, sir."

"Gehlhausen is Overseer at T-One," said Carnahan. "Bernhard Gelhausen. We have known him, known of him, since the early days after I came myself."

Plietor glanced from the corner of his eye at Janescz. He was looking at Carnahan with no expression at all on his face.

"*Ach,* now I remember the name, I do," said Bartosz. Hilenski nodded beside him. Carnahan turned his head and brought his hand to his chin, as though he were thinking.

"The raid was for the abduction, by my thought. I cannot think what else, and the fighting was not very great."

"More for some than others," mumbled Davik under his breath.

"What about the torch, at the glider sheds?" said Hilenski.

Carnahan gave him a sour look but did not scold. "A signal, perhaps, that the girl was taken."

How can he know that? Plietor thought. *How can he know*

where Ginna was found? How can he know that the torch was not to burn the gliders? Plietor had not spoken to Davik since their own fight, did not know what Davik judged of the fighting with the other men, of the torch. But Carnahan did not want more talk.

"I was speaking of the camel train," he said, his voice up, "of a directive, of Gehlhausen's ideas." Bartosz and Hilenski clamped their lips and nodded. "Maybe Gehlhausen's ideas are not his own. Maybe they come from higher levels of ownership of the T-One. And if higher levels of T-One ownership have planned against us, they may have spoken with MacReedy Mining ownership in Perth. And thereby may come a directive with the camel train. That is my thinking."

Plietor gave an inward grimace. Carnahan's thinking was full of questions. But who could ask them? Janescz was still expressionless. Davik was leaned over again, his elbows on his knees, his eyes on the floor, twisting his hands. Carnahan had looked away, stroking his chin. Bartosz and Hilenski sat. The seconds dragged.

Bartosz finally let out his breath, as he had before. "Pardoning myself again, sir. What if there is none? No directive, you know?"

Carnahan looked back at them, his face mild now. "There is no need to consider a circumstance before its time. But…" He said this as he looked at their faces, at Davik now twisting his feet on the floor. "If there is no directive I will send a delegation to Stuart-town, to communicate over the telegraph. Or perhaps…" he gave a tight smile, "I may and sure go myself."

Bartosz and Hilenksi sat back, nodded then. Even Janescz.

"So," said Carnahan. "On tomorrow after in-ringing you will tell your people my words. I had no wish for a special

Gathering, so soon after Mid-Week. And I wanted to lay out my thinking, so you can take it for yourself." He looked toward Davik, but Davik was still leaned over, looking at the floor. "When you tell them, all will know my plan, and we can go about our work, which is first and always our production." He looked at Janescz, to Plietor, swept across Davik and back to Janescz.

"In the gliders you will continue with your daily quota on a *pro-rata* basis, reduced by a fifth that is. Is there any question about that, Boruskis?" Janescz and Plietor shook their heads. Davik did not look up.

"So that's all then. I will use the telephonic machine to send my words to Gehlhausen. You're to your boards and beds. The morrow, the Lord and geology willing, is a full production day."

"Bugger Carnahan's sodding thinking."
Davik spoke from the dark corner, his voice strange with the plugs in his nose. Plietor stood at the shelf favoring his knee, soapy water in the large bowl, washing the soup bowls and mugs. Janescz was peeling a turnip at the table. They had all been silent from Carnahan's room to the flat, tense—Plietor knew his own tension, could read Davik's in his hands—but silent nonetheless. Their silence had continued as Plietor boiled potatoes, beets, and leeks into soup, continued as he mixed water, flour, salt to make the flat bread, and on as they ate. Plietor was slow in eating, taking care with the spoon and the chewing of bread, with the placement of his tongue, but still his puffed mouth throbbed. No one had spoken at all, the sounds of eating just over the sighing of the wind. Plietor had stood a last time, his knee tortured, to collect dishes and wash. When Davik finally spoke, Janescz gave a deep sigh.

"*Tak,*" he said. "It is the time to talk." Plietor turned from the shelf and sat, sighing himself.

"I have said what I think," said Davik.

"*Psshh,*" said Plietor. "There must be more than that. There *is* much more, to say and to ask." He looked toward Davik in the dark corner. "How did you know about the electric talker?"

Davik didn't speak for a moment. "How else could Overseers talk?" he said finally. "No one came back from T-One." He paused. "And I know the wires."

"That you do," said Plietor.

"*Acchh,*" said Janescz. "What does it matter how Davik thought?"

"It…" Plietor began, stopped, began again. "Too right, then. What did Bartosz mean when he said the T-One might want a glider to go with the girl?"

Davik snorted.

"Come, *chłopiec,*" Janescz said quickly. "Bartosz only meant that if T-One had taken a flyer, they might want a glider for the flyer to fly."

"But it makes no sense," said Plietor. "They took a hostage. If they wanted a glider, and Carnahan gave them a glider, they would give the hostage back. Then who would there be to fly? Did Bartosz think they would teach themselves?"

"*Chłopiec, chłopiec,*" said Janescz. "Bartosz was not thinking. He said so."

"But Carnahan," said Plietor. "Was Carnahan thinking? When Bartosz said T-One might want a glider to go with the girl, he made sense only if T-One knew the girl was flyer. But how could T-One know this, you tell me?"

Davik moved out of the shadows. Janescz looked at Plietor for a moment, then said, "Bartosz did not know what T-One knew, only what Bartosz knows. And he knows the girl is a flyer. This is all. He was not thinking."

"Then why did not Carnahan say this?" Plietor was looking hard at him. "Why did Carnahan speak only of a shelf
and rope T-One did not have? Why did he not say, 'T-One
can not know the girl is a flyer.' How could they? How could
anyone think a sheila is a flyer?"

Janescz looked down, brought his hands up and put
them together on the back of his head.

"I do not know what Carnahan knows, what Bartosz
knows, what T-One knows. I only know Bartosz was not
thinking. That is what he said, and it is what I know."

Plietor made a sound in his throat. "Leave that, then,"
he said. "Think of Carnahan's other words. When Hilenski
spoke of the torch at the glider sheds, Carnahan said it was a
signal that the girl was taken. How did he know Ginna was
taken at the glider sheds? Do you know this?" He looked at
Janescz, over to Davik, who was now standing at the end of
the table. Janescz shrugged.

"I did not know," said Davik, in his strange voice. "After we landed some blows these men ran down the Shelf
to the pit path and over. I did not know they were T-One
men. We chased only to the edge. The torch...it went over
the edge too, I think. I did not see it. Nothing was with fire.
I looked for Ginna then. But she was not in the sheds with
the gliders. I called...and I looked in the dark..." He leaned
slowly down, his hands gripping the end of the table, staring
at Plietor. "And you," he said. "Where is it you were, in the
fighting, and the calling, and the long night?"

"*Ehhh,*" said Janescz, in a warning voice.

Plietor stared back at him. "I went off by myself," he said
evenly. "I thought there was no place for me here."

"There is a place," said Janescz quickly. "This is where
we are. This is where we must be."

"*Acchh,*" said Davik, standing up, turning away into the dark of the corner. They were all silent until Plietor spoke again.

"Carnahan knows more than he says, or his saying so makes no sense."

Janescz snorted. "Of course Carnahan knows. He always knows more. And he talked through the electric machine with Gehlhausen."

Plietor shook his head. "Gehlhausen said that he wanted production. Bloody powder. But what else did he say on the electric machine? What did Carnahan say?"

"Oh come, *chłopiec,*" said Janescz. "We cannot know what they said. What is this knowing good for? We know what Carnahan will do, what he wants. What more?"

"Let me ask you, but once more," said Plietor.

Janescz shrugged. Davik was silent.

"Carnahan will wait for the camel train. He expects a letter from MacReedy Mining. I ask, what could this letter be?"

Janescz rolled his eyes, but Plietor continued.

"Think yourself to MacReedy Mining in Perth, and to T-One, wherever they are."

"Brisbane," said Janescz, then raised his hands, surprised at his own speech. Plietor's eyebrows were up.

Janescz shrugged. "I know this from years ago, when the camps came together. It is no matter. Nothing."

"Listen to me then," said Plietor. "T-One wants Arltunga's production. So what do they do? They ask for it! Ha! And MacReedy says 'No.' Why should they say 'Yes'?"

Davik snorted from the corner.

"So T-One tells MacReedy they will take a hostage if MacReedy does not give them production. Is MacReedy to send a directive to Carnahan just then to give up production *in the case* T-One takes a hostage?"

Davik snorted again. "This is a story of fairies," he said. "You need to give MacReedy and T-One voices so we can hear this story."

"I don't need voices," said Plietor. "This is what must be if Carnahan is to speak any sense."

"Say your story," said Janescz.

"Davik is right that for MacReedy to send a directive like this is a fairy story. But what if T-One says they will take a *special* hostage? Maybe MacReedy will care about this special hostage. But why…" Plietor leaned forward toward Janescz, raised his finger to point. "Why would T-One in Brisbane know there is a special hostage to be taken? And why would Ginna be special?"

"Oh *chłopiec*," said Janescz. "We have never known anything of Ginna. She has never told. We have never asked. *I* have never asked, I know." He looked at Plietor, into the shadows toward Davik.

"We know she came with the Zeppelin," said Plietor. "We know she knows botany. We know she flies a glider. This is nothing?"

"We do not know why she would be special in Perth, or in Brisbane."

"Perth," said Plietor. "She would have to be special to MacReedy Mining if they would trade production for her."

Janescz threw his hands in the air. "This is a crazy fairy story. How can we be here, two thousand miles away from business toffs in Perth we have never seen, asking why a girl would be special to them?"

"But it is what Carnahan *said*," protested Plietor. "He waits for a directive from Perth telling him to exchange life's blood, flesh of our bodies—"

Davik snorted loudly from the corner.

"…to exchange for Ginna to come back to us. Carnahan

must think she is very special to MacReedy Mining, or how could he expect such a directive?"

Janescz was silent. Davik came back to the end of the table. Plietor looked from one to the other.

"Here is the thing," he said. "How would T-One in Brisbane, or Gehlhausen down the Caldera, know a special hostage is here to be taken?" He looked back and forth again. "Carnahan has sent no word about Ginna out. No one has left the Camp to go to the telegraph in Stuart-town. If Gehlhausen knew about her, he could have sent word out to Brisbane from Stuart-town himself. But how could Gehlhausen know?" He looked back and forth again, opened his mouth to continue.

"I know how," said Davik, thickly, from the end of the table.

Plietor stopped, his mouth still open. Janescz looked at Davik.

"I know how bloody Gehlhausen knew about Ginna. I told him." Davik pulled the bench out and sat, looked at Plietor and Janescz.

"*Ahhh,*" said Janescz. "When you went over the pit path."

"That was it," said Davik.

"I knew you talked," said Janescz. "I knew it. You talked of rising up against Carnahan with men from the T-One. But I didn't—"

"Carnahan said Ginna was to go with the camel train," said Davik. "He said it to her. She told us. He wanted her to die in the desert. I knew it, but there was no one to understand this." Davik looked at Janescz, moved his eyes to Plietor's, back to Janescz. "No one but Gehlhausen. We once talked, Kemper, Gehlhausen, me, when Kemper was here, before Carnahan cut it all off." Davik looked even harder at Janescz. "You talked too. I know it. I watched you."

Plietor thought of the book, the letter, but he said nothing.

"What did Gehlhausen say to you, when you went to him?" Janescz said.

Davik shrugged. "I told him of Ginna, how she came with the Zeppelin, how I saved her, how she was…different." He looked quickly at Plietor. "I told him Carnahan was to send her on the camel train, what I told you, to die."

"And what did Gehlhausen say?"

"I told him I would go with her, I must go with her, to see she did not die, to protect her from the desert, from Afghans. But I knew Carnahan would not say it. I could not make him say it. Not by myself, not with a few from the camp, even if they would." He started to look at Plietor, then stopped himself.

Janescz nodded.

"I told him if he would come with some men on Mid-Week Day, then Carnahan would not fight for it, for me to stay and Ginna go."

"And Gehlhausen said…" Janescz was still nodding.

"He said he would. He would come with some men. Not to fight, but to stand beside me, so Carnahan could see us." Davik pursed his mouth, wincing from the pain in his nose.

"I told him. I told him about Ginna. That is how he knew." Davik shook his head, his hair moving in the lamplight. There was silence.

"But he did not come," said Janescz after a moment. "Gehlhausen did not come to the Gathering with his men."

"No. He did not." Davik shook his head again, with more energy. "I thought there was some reason, but Gehlhausen could not send some one to tell me. And then Carnahan said that Ginna was to stay, so it was no matter, no matter." Davik's eyes changed, *a wary look,* Plietor thought.

"We had some other talk, Gehlhausen and me," Davik said, and pursed his lips again. "But after he did not come, and did not send some one, and Ginna could stay, it was no matter. I did not think of it. It was no matter, because of what Carnahan said."

"But it was…it did matter," said Plietor. "And you shouldn't blame yourself for telling Gehlhausen—"

"Who is to blame?! I do not blame myself!" Davik stood up, his brows together, a glare at Plietor.

Plietor put up his hands. "I only meant that what you said to Gehlhausen was not enough…" Davik glared harder. Plietor rolled his eyes up, then back down. "What you said to Gehlhausen did not tell him that Ginna was special to Mac-Reedy Mining."

Davik's look eased.

"I will think of this in a moment," said Plietor. "For now, think that Gehlhausen knows Ginna is special, and tells this with the Stuart-town telegraph to T-One in Brisbane, and T-One wants Arltunga powder production. Now do they say to MacReedy in Perth that they will take special-Ginna hostage if MacReedy does not give them production? What directive does MacReedy send to Carnahan? It is the same problem as before. Do they say, 'If the special hostage is taken, give up production. If not, guard the special hostage close?'"

"This is the same fairy story as before," said Davik. "Gehlhausen takes Ginna. We give up production to them. Gehlhausen gives Ginna back. What will we do? We raid T-One and take a hostage for ourselves, to get our production. It's a bloody fairy circle, round and round."

"Which says to me it can't be right," said Plietor. "Carnahan can't think to get a directive like that."

"So what then?" said Davik. "Bloody what? I'm fagged

with this talk."

"Just a bit," said Plietor. "I'm getting clear with it, talking it out."

"The normal thing," said Janescz, "is to take the hostage and then make the demand."

Plietor looked at him. "I can see that," he said. "But there's no time for that here. The camel train left Oodnadatta when? More than a week ago, due here two weeks yet. The directive from MacReedy would have to be with it. But Ginna was taken only *one day* before this. It does not work out."

Davik slapped his palms on the table. Janescz's long-forgotten turnip jumped. "You can go with this all the bloody night if you want. But I'm fagged. I said it. I ask you one thing. The camel train comes. The bloody direct-ed comes with it. It says, 'No powder for T-One.' What then? What does Carnahan do? What does Gehlhausen do?" He looked at Plietor, Janescz, back to Plietor, a hard look.

Janescz and Plietor both sat.

"That's a nub of it, it is," said Janescz.

"Yeh," said Davik. "So. Until you tell me that, you may go with your fairy stories—"

"Just stuff it one second," said Plietor. "I'll tell you what I think, about everything. I've been thinking and now I'll say it." Davik looked at him, his palms still on the table.

"I think Carnahan and Gehlhausen have been together with the electric talker all along. I don't think one has gone to Stuart-town, to telegraph to Perth or Brisbane. I think it's all Carnahan and Gehlhausen."

Davik pushed himself up. "More fairy stories," he said.

"Hear this!" Plietor said. "I think that's why Gehlhausen did not come with his men to the Gathering. He knew what Carnahan was to say on Ginna and the camel train, and he knew it would be enough for you." Davik stood, his arms tense.

"I think the rock slide was not geology. I think it was dynamite."

Davik jerked like someone stuck him with a sharp thing. His eyes were big. Plietor looked at him but went on in a rush.

"After we all went out to the ledge, just before the great slab slipped, the sound I heard was not a rock sound. It was deep, and I saw dust against the sky, a cloud going up. This is not what rocks do. This is what dynamite does. I have seen dynamite, making blocks for the walls of the Terrace."

"No!" said Davik. "He would not do this!" He shook his head, his hair flying.

"What are you saying?!" said Janescz.

Davik looked from one to the other, wild and uncertain.

"I don't know. But he would not. He would not."

"Who, Davik? Who?" said Janescz.

"Gehlhausen!" said Davik.

"What would he not?" said Janescz. "Talk to me! Tell me this."

"The thing Gehlhausen talked with me about," said Davik. "It *was* a rock slide with dynamite. We talked about rising up against Carnahan, with men from the T-One. And Gehlhausen said he could make us soft—*soften*, he said—with a rockslide. Not to do damage, but to make confusion, so when he came with men Carnahan would not be looking." Davik looked back and forth again, his eyes still big, his face working, hurting with his winces.

"It was Gehlhausen's idea. I never said yes to this idea. I thought it was wacker. And after he did not come and did not send some one—I said this before—Ginna was staying, and I thought it was no matter. I did not think of it after that."

"Maybe not before," said Janescz. "But did you think that night? You ran away from us, down the ladder, with the rocks falling."

Davik pursed his lips again, winced and nodded. "I did. In that moment, I did. But then the rocks were falling at the end of the Stack, and I thought, *This can not be any plan.* Not with rocks falling on Ginna."

He turned to Plietor, his eyes growing harder. "Here is for your fairy story. If Gehlhausen knows Ginna is special and wants her hostage, why does he try to kill her with rocks and dynamite?"

Plietor shrugged, stood, shrugged again. "Maybe Gehlhausen didn't know she was no longer with us, with Boruskis. It was only two days before she had gone to stay with Julia, at the west end. Maybe he didn't know she was there."

"Ha!" said Davik, his voice up. "If Carnahan and Gehlhausen talk on the electric machine, Carnahan would have told this."

"I don't know what they talk about," said Plietor, his voice up too. "Maybe this is Gehlhausen's plan only, like you said, and not Carnahan's."

"Then why take Ginna in three days? Why not come in force the same night?"

"I don't know," said Plietor.

"*Chłopiec, chłopiec,*" said Janescz. "This is how it is. You cannot know these things—"

"Enough with your *chłopiec!*" Plietor said. "I do not know. I say it. I do not know if it is Gehlhausen, or Carnahan, or the two together. "

"Carnahan!" said Janescz. "You say now the rockslide is Carnahan!?"

"*I do not know!*" said Plietor. "Was it Carnahan wanting

Ginna to die in the desert, as Davik says? Did Carnahan send Karski to the cliff top with dynamite, to kill her in her new bed? *I do not know!* But a directive from MacReedy Mining makes no sense. No sense! Waiting two weeks for the camel train, for a directive that makes no sense—"

"I will not do it!" said Davik, on his feet now too, his eyes fierce. "I will not. I will not wait. I will not leave Ginna there, at T-One. I want her here. That is the only way she is safe. With me."

Plietor looked away. But Davik reached for him. "Will you come, with me, to take her back?"

Plietor drew away a step, but stopped, and set his lips over the pain. He nodded, whispered, "I will."

30.

Albert McCutcheon had brought Ginna's noon meal, a sort of gruel made with salted meat, with flat bread. It was the same as yesterday evening, apparently a staple of the T-One camp. Ginna had thought yearningly of the vegetables at Arltunga.

Albert had not lingered in delivering her food in the evening yesterday. He had removed his hat, but kept his eyes from her, setting the tray on the shelf, padlocking the door behind him, not to reappear until the morning. He had come then well after she had opened the shutter to first light, silent again with a plate of flat bread and some nuts, new water for her pitcher. He had departed with her chamber pot, returning with it in twenty minutes to collect her two plates.

But now he waited, his hat in his hands, stood by her as she arranged the tray on her lap, took a sip of the acrid water before spooning the soup. His smell enveloped her. It was garlic, of all things. She had glanced at him several times, always his eyes averted, until she finally caught him looking. Now he stepped back from her and took a breath.

"Aye, and I have news for you, Miss Ginna."

"Do you now?" she said, putting down the spoon and looking up with an encouraging smile.

"Aye. I do. But first...I might ask you..." He was blushing already. "You see and I've been thinking all the night...

about the women at Arltunga…" He blushed deeper, the color spreading over his head, but went on in a determined way. "I have a question for you, if I may."

"Certainly," said Ginna, still smiling, though not at all sure what was to come.

"With your dresses and all…begging your pardon…" He gestured to her, resolved the gesture into a pointing finger. "Is it gloves you all wear, there, with your dresses?"

Ginna felt a sudden blush too. She looked down at her hands, her poor hands, held them up with their gloves, Gwen's gloves, unworked-in cotton gloves. Was she to tell of her hands? What could this man be thinking?

"Women do wear gloves," she said simply. "Our hands… are more delicate than men's strong hands, and our fingernails too."

Albert's eyebrows went up, then he nodded and smiled, his blush receding. "Aye, I thought so. From what I seen in Brisbane. But your fingernails! Why, I never thought of that."

Ginna smiled back. "As to your news, Albert. What news do you have for me?"

"Oh," said Albert, more sure of himself now. "I have a name for you, I do."

"Oh, good," Ginna said. "Who is it then?"

"I'm not so sure you'll think it good when I tell you."

"I shall withhold my opinion then, until you do," she said.

"Do you know of one called Davik?"

Something turned over in Ginna's stomach. She kept her smile, decided there was no value in probing Arthur's face for a preview. "Yes, I know of Davik," she said.

"Mr. Gehlhausen has spoken his name before. A troublemaker he is. Does he make trouble for you?"

Ginna smiled her smile, said that she had found Davik

sometimes had strong opinions.

"Aye," said Arthur. "Well, Mr. Gehlhausen said he was happy to hear that Davik had been *neutralized*. That was his word. I'm not sure what it means, but it was his word. I heard it."

Ginna's stomach turned again. What else could Arthur tell her?

"How did Mr. Gehlhausen hear this about Davik?" she said.

"Oh," said Arthur. "He talks on the electric voice telegraph. He talks with Mr. Carnahan. He was talking to Mr. Carnahan about this Davik, and he said he was extremely happy to hear that Davik was *neutralized*." He beamed at her. "Is this good news for you...if his strong opinions are too strong for you?"

"Well, I'm not sure," said Ginna, with her smile. "It depends on what of Davik's strong opinions Mr. Gehlhausen was talking about. Do you know that?"

Albert shook his head. *No.* There was nothing more about Davik. His face twisted into an impish smile. He had another piece of news.

Ginna raised her eyebrows, took another sip of water to still her nervousness, suppressing her grimace at the taste. Arthur stood and smiled. "Well," she said, "are you going to tell me?"

Arthur smiled more broadly. "It's about you!" he said.

Ginna drew back and widened her eyes, only half-acting an expression of surprise. "Really!" she said. "Well, you have my full attention."

Arthur shuffled his feet. "You will be going out with the camel train," he said.

Ginna's pulse quickened.

"I heard him say it," said Albert. "The camel train is late, it is. It's usually here earlier than this, with supplies, and to pick up the threnium ore bags. We are almost out of flour and meat. I heard Henderson, who cooks for us, tell Mr. Gehlhausen this, the day before you came."

Ginna looked down at her soup, back at Arthur.

"But when it does come, you will go out with it," said Arthur, still smiling, though now in a wistful way. "You will go back to Oodnadatta. You will not be our guest any more."

"Goodness…" said Ginna, not sure what else to say. "Such a short time here…"

"Well," said Arthur, looking serious now, "You never know that. You never know when the camel train will come." Then, brightening. "Did you ride on a camel when you came in, to Arltunga? Our owner rides when he comes in, once a year, far up on a saddle behind the hump, sure and stirrups and everything, just like a horse." His smile turned shy. "I didn't ride when I came in. I walked the way, with the Afghan pullers."

"Well…" began Ginna, wondering if she should ask about Afghan pullers. But she was saved from replying by a shout and a kick against the door.

"McCutcheon! Get your bloody arse out here. Gehlhausen wants you."

Arthur turned quickly to the door, hat on, reaching for the padlock. "I'll see you with dinner," he said. Ginna sighed and waved.

She stalked the room all afternoon, like Davik along his wall at the Boruskis'. Gehlhausen and Carnahan were in collusion. There was no doubt about that now. Gehlhausen and Carnahan talked on a sort of bush telephone. They had planned her abduction together. *But why?* Her mind returned to her speculations in the cave, to Gehlhausen's statement about "accommodations," though she had no idea that was the whole truth of the matter, and maybe no truth at all. Still…might there be money for Gehlhausen in the plot? A glider and a pilot for the T-One camp? Threnium powder? Was this to be an arrangement between the two of them, with no communication at all to her father or the Wonthaggi owners? What could be Carnahan's interest? *Carnahan!* So inscrutable to her.

One thing seemed certain: Davik was not part of this plot. *Neutralized.* What did it mean that Davik had been "neutralized?" That he wouldn't act? Or…couldn't? Her stomach roiled again. Surely he would be straining to act… to save her. Had the risk to her safety been held up to him by Carnahan, to keep him from acting while she was a hostage? Or…

The camel train. She was to leave with the camel train. Arthur had overheard Gehlhausen say it to Carnahan, or re-peat it from Carnahan, she couldn't tell which from Arthur's pronouncement. But they had agreed to it. She didn't think Arthur would dissemble.

The bare fact that she would leave with the camel train was not in itself overwhelming. After all, Carnahan had spo-ken of it before. That was when Davik had thought Carna-han was sending her to die in the desert, when Davik was talking insurrection. But Carnahan had changed his mind then, for reasons she had never understood. He had project-ed this next train. But that was before she had become a fly-er, an integral part of production. Was her leaving now more important to Carnahan than her capability as a flyer? *Why?*

And why was she to go out from the T-One mine? That circumstance and Davik might be the key. For what would Davik have done at Arltunga when Carnahan said she was to go with the camel train? Would he have made a terrific row…or worse? Maybe Carnahan had feared the row Davik would make, feared an insurrection, and had colluded with Gehlhausen in her abduction to "neutralize" Davik. The camel train repaired at the Arltunga mine first in its journey, before going round to T-One and then McCulloch. If Davik could be "neutralized" for fear of her safety at T-One, only to be informed, after the fact, that she was with the train back to Oodnadatta, then maybe he would…subside, and Carnahan would have controlled him in her leaving. At least that might be what Carnahan was thinking. She wouldn't die in the desert now, not from her own weakness, anyway.

And what if Davik did not subside when he learned that she was gone? What if he went truly…berserk? Could Janescz and Plietor control him?

Ginna stalked the afternoon quite away, barely conscious of the waning of sickly light through the window. Voices and footsteps came and went outside, pausing sometime as they passed. But she did not look up. Hypotheses roiled in her mind, roiled and collided in uncertainty, doubt, or threat. By the time she heard Arthur at the lock on her door, she was hectic and frazzled.

Salt meat gruel and flat bread again, this time with a dollop of tinned beans, kidney beans they appeared. She felt like dashing the plate to the floor, but she forced herself to smile, and to sit tidily with the tray on her lap. Arthur stood with his hat in his hands, apparently prepared to watch her eat, and she obliged by taking a spoonful of beans.

"Aye, and it's news again I have," he said, as she chewed.

"You had such interesting news before," she said, swallowing with some difficulty.

"Aye," he said, smiling back. "And I'll ask before I tell, again. Did you have a bit of rockslide at Arltunga days ago?"

Ginna started slightly, recovered and cut a piece of salted

meat. "Indeed, we did," she said. What else should she say? "It was quite terrifying." That would do.

Arthur nodded. "I thought you did," he said, with his impish smile. "Mr. Gehlhausen and Mr. Carnahan had a bit of a carry-on over the voice telegraph this afternoon, you see. 'Forces of nature,' was what Mr. Gehlhausen kept saying. But Mr. Carnahan…why, what do you think he said?"

"I'm sure I have no idea," said Ginna. "Could you hear him, over the telephone?"

"Oh no," said Arthur. "I never hear, only what Mr. Gehlhausen says. I just thought you might know. Mr. Gehlhausen was very excited by it. He was saying *Scheisse*, which is what he says when he is excited, angry, you know."

"Oh dear," said Ginna.

"I'm sure it's not a nice word," said Arthur. He blushed, smiled at her, was silent for a moment, apparently waiting for her to eat something else. She tore a piece of flat bread.

"'There will be no paying,' Mr. Gehlhausen was saying, and 'Forces of nature' again. He was very excited."

"My goodness," said Ginna, chewing on the bread. Arthur watched her.

"Some men from here went to Arltunga, you know, before the night they…brought you back," he said. "Four days ago they went."

Ginna widened her eyes. "What did they do at Arltunga?"

Arthur shrugged. "I'm sure and I don't know myself. I just wondered…'Our men did not bungle anything,' was something Mr. Gehlhausen said on the telegraph. 'Bungle' is not a word he says. I thought it might be something Mr. Carnahan said. And the men…I thought it might be the men who went there before."

Ginna felt her heart speed up. T-One men at Arltunga

the night of the rockslide. Something bungled. Forces of nature. She turned her gaze to cutting another piece of meat, her mind racing, while Arthur waited. When she looked up, it was with a big smile. "You are very good at reading between the lines of a conversation, Arthur."

Arthur smiled, and blushed again. "I don't know what you're saying quite, but it's a good thing, is it?"

"It's a *very* good thing," said Ginna, "to be able to understand what you can't hear."

Arthur smiled and nodded his head. "I guess I can do that, I can."

They smiled back and forth, but Ginna's mind was racing on. Had Gehlhausen's men been associated with the rockslide? Had Gehlhausen and Carnahan colluded to…bring it about? It was a monstrous thought. But she had no time for another round of hypothesizing. She made a decision, tightened her lips, looked down at her plate.

"Albert," she said, without looking up, "would you be so kind as to give me a moment of privacy?" She glanced up at him. He stood, puzzled.

"But you've not finished your dinner," he said.

"I know," she said, looking down again. "And I shall. But just for the moment, could you…?" She looked up, acting an uncertain smile.

Albert stood a moment longer, then ducked as a furious blush overtook his head.

"Oh, yes ma'am, my…lady," he stammered. "Begging your pardon, ma'am. Of course I'll step outside. Of course. You just…strike the door when you want me."

"I will, thank you," said Ginna, her smile thankful, she hoped.

Albert slipped hatless out the door, pushing it solidly closed behind him. Ginna went to the window and closed the shutter, then straight to the pitcher on the shelf. She seized it and poured the water into the bowl, then swung the pitcher from side to side. She shook her head, returned it to the shelf, and cast irresolutely around the room. Her glance swept once past the pail in the corner, then returned, more slowly. She walked to the corner, lifted the pail by the swinging handle, swung it left and right, gingerly. The contents slid and sloshed inside. She grimaced, swung the pail again, harder, shook her head again. At the shelf she removed the pail's lid, poured in the water from the bowl, replaced the lid and swung the pail a third time. She hesitated, then nodded and placed it on the floor. Now she reached to her hair for the lungee, unwinding it, shaking her head so her hair fell around her shoulders. She looked at the long scarf for a moment, then wrenched at the end, starting a tear that she followed the whole length. Two pieces now, and each piece she tore again across the middle, placing the four pieces on the bed beside the hat Albert had left there. Then she set her lips, took up the pail, and walked to the door.

The door was hinged on the left to open inward. She stood against the wall on the hinged side, the pail hanging in her right hand, trying to control her breathing. After a moment she shut her eyes tightly, then opened them, took a breath, then reached with her left hand to knock against the door. The blows were muted by the glove, but the door opened instantly, and Albert stepped partially in. Standing behind the door, Ginna couldn't see him. He was evidently looking around the room, hesitating before coming fully in.

Ginna clenched her teeth. *Come in! Please come in!* On the other side of the door Albert took a step.

"Miss Ginna?" he said. "Are you…?"

Ginna could see his shoulder, leaning forward, his head turning. *One more step.*

"Miss Ginna?"

Ginna swung the pail in a wide, stiff-armed arc, stepping forward into the swing. Albert half-turned at the sound of her step and took the blow on his right temple, the pail clattering out of Ginna's hand, the lid departing, the contents spattering. Albert gave a groan and toppled left, sideways. Ginna spared barely a glance at the spatter, pushing frantically at the door. Albert's legs blocked the opening and he lay, his breath harsh, making feeble crawling motions. *Please let no one come!* Ginna grasped his legs and pulled them to her, now on her knees, her own breath coming fast.

Then the door was closed and she was away to the bed and the strips of scarf. Down on her knees again, she wadded one strip of scarf into a tight ball and thrust it deep into Albert's mouth. She started to roll him fully onto his stomach, then stopped, thought, then rolled him onto his back instead. She grimaced, and began wrenching off his overshirt, pulling it over his arms and head. *The garlic!* She yanked at braces, buttons, and boots, pulling down his trousers, leaving him in stained and baggy undershorts, socks that reeked up at her. Back over on his stomach, and now he was mewling and gagging, kicking feebly. She pulled his hands together on his back, laying one on the other and crisscrossing the second strip of the scarf between and around his wrists, tying a double knot. She did the same for his ankles with the third strip, stood over him for a moment, then tugged him by the feet into the far corner of the room.

He was kicking harder, an undulating motion of his stubby body that succeeded in turning him on his side. She saw that his eyes were open, turned him so that he was facing the wall, and went to the bed. There she stripped off the green dress, wrapped and tied it around her waist over her bloomered undershift, and slipped on the trousers and shirt. The trousers were an acceptable length with the braces tightened as far as they would go, but huge in the waist. *Clown's trousers,* she thought, but plenty of room at least in which to tuck the overshirt, which hung down off her shoulders. It would have to suffice. In the dim light…it had to.

Albert was twisting and kicking in the corner, but his sock feet made little sound that would pass outside. Ginna went to the door and eased it open, heard voices not too far off, moving away. The light was very dim, barely enough to see. The padlock hung from the doorway hasp outside. Ginna reached into the pocket of Albert's pants and found the key. She moved back into the room, pulling the door behind her. Albert had twisted around to look out again. She could just make out his eyes, a contorted expression. *He would have a bad opinion of Arltunga women,* she thought dryly.

"I'm sorry, Albert," she whispered. "I'm sorry to repay your kindness in this way."

She took the last strip of lungee from the bed and tied her hair up behind as well as she could. Albert's hat fit over it. Out the door, she affixed the padlock and shut it with a snap, then ducked her head and moved left, south, toward the Arltunga Camp.

31.

There was no question in Ginna's mind of the direction. She knew the T-One camp to be at the east wall of the Caldera, and though she could not see the wall rising up behind the row of rooms, she was certain it must. Besides, the afternoon sun had lighted the sky outside her window. The room faced west. The path south to Arltunga surely lay to the left. If she could keep on the path.

In the dimming light and mist she dared not move away from the row of rooms out into the yard. Voices came from inside one room as she passed, its shutter only partially closed. In another she saw clearly two men by oil-light at a table with food. She prayed no one would look out or emerge from a room to accost her.

Just beyond the row of rooms she found the yard edge, and turned right along it, walking twenty yards in uncertainty before she came to a wide path again to the left, which she took gratefully. At intervals as she hurried along, smaller paths came in from the right at angles, and she heard pits bubbling and gurgling, *the working pits,* she presumed, that were sopped with cloths for T-One production.

All at once a figure emerged from the mist along one such path and almost barreled into her, only saved from doing so by her jerking aside at the last instant.

"*Heh,* McCutcheon!" said the man. "What bloody business you on at such an hour?"

Ginna's heart pounded in her ears, but she kept her head down, gurgling as deep a sound as she could make in her throat, touching her hat brim as she moved past, only then thinking of her gloved hand. The man did not notice, though, or made no sign that he did, moving off with a grumble of his own. "Bloody Gehlhausen" is what she heard.

It was a bit before she registered that no path had come in from the right for some tens of yards. Then her foot struck a stone, she stumbled, and she knew that the path had dwindled to a track. She was past the T-One site then, and the danger of coming upon a T-One man by accident. But now the difficulty of following the path truly presented itself.

She cast around, the light almost too dim for her to see even her feet, no star-shine through the mist, though that was some less than it had been. She still knew the direction but did not know how long she could keep to it. And if she came to wandering in circles in the heart of the Caldera...

When would Albert be discovered? Surely Gehlhausen would send another to fetch him when he did not appear. And then...How long would the lock deter them? *Not long,* she thought. She had perhaps a half-hour start at most. And they would have torches—electric and fire—and had traversed before the way in the dark.

Ginna felt hopelessness welling up within her. Should she just go off the path into the Caldera, find a rock by touch and sit under it, hoping not to be discovered until daylight? That seemed a poor chance. But what was the chance otherwise?

As she reasoned she had wandered, letting her feet pick their own way while her mind was occupied. But now her shin ran against something angular and sharp, and she stopped, groped with her hand, and felt a small constructed framework, a kind of low wooden trestle. What would such a thing be doing here along the path? Then her groping fingers touched twisted wire, and she knew.

The wires! The wires for the bush telephone. She remembered Davik saying that he had followed the wires between the camps, when he had come back in the night from visiting the T-One camp. He had followed the wires in the dark. Here were the wires, lying clipped to this trestle. If Davik could follow them, she could too.

She moved her hands carefully down the twisted spiral, away from the trestle, cautiously side-stepping, but she found no impediment. The wires must truly mark the track. She moved faster, stooped over in the dark, the spiral slipping through her fingers, grateful, so grateful for the gloves, though wishing she had her more sturdy canvas workers. The wires dipped to the stony surface and her hands dipped with them, her back announcing a complaint already, her feet sliding across small rocks and gravel, but nothing to stumble over, until after a bit the wires made their way up again and onto another trestle. She released her grip and stood. How far had she gone? Two hundred paces? She looked back north into the dark. Was there light from the direction of the T-One? *Oh, let there not be.* But she shouldn't stand.

Her feet told her the wire was to the left of the track. She would grip it with her left hand alone; that way she could walk facing forward. And she didn't have to follow the arc of the wire as it sagged between trestles. She could simply carry it along at waist height. That way she wouldn't have to bend over. It would be much faster. She had to be fast as she could be.

So she walked, gaining confidence with every step. Her heart came up with the exertion and she felt perspiration under her arms with the heavy drape of Arthur's overshirt.

Now and again a sharp edge of the sliding wire did pene-trate her glove, pricking her hand painfully. She could not help crying out, knowing she was bleeding and the glove was torn. But she dared not stop, not to adjust Arthur's clothes, not to examine her glove or hand. A third trestle passed. Should she count them? How many were there? She had no idea. She also had no clear idea of how long she had been carried when the T-One men had brought her from Arltun-ga. They had argued about the path, she remembered. Had they been following the wire?

A fourth trestle. She took a bad step on a round stone and fell, releasing her grip, experiencing a moment of pan-ic until she had recovered the wire, crawling with groping hands. Then it was forward again. A fifth trestle.

A sudden bend in the wire to the left carried her with it, but not before her right shoulder had struck a great rock the bend went around, quite invisible to her in the dark. She rubbed at the pain as she proceeded, acknowledging that the path was twisting more, snaking its way among larger rocks. She must be deep into the Caldera floor, must go with more care, more slowly. A sixth trestle passed. A seventh, or had she passed one without counting?

She became aware dimly, then forcefully with a deep prick of the wire that its sliding had worn through the glove. She stopped then and twisted the glove on her hand, try-ing for a fresh aspect, but it twisted back as she went on. Eight trestles. Or nine? She tried the glove backwards, but it was shredding, and fell apart completely in five minutes. She could use the right one. *Would it last until…? Was it nine trestles now, or ten?*

The shout was faint but unmistakable behind her. She stood frozen, the right glove half-pulled onto her left hand. She turned but saw nothing. *How far?* How far behind her were they? Should she try to find a rock to climb to see? Could she even see their torches through the mist? *No.* She must go on. She must go as fast as she was able.

She took up the cable and set off, quickening her step, quickening more, until she skipped every fourth or fifth. She rebounded sideways from a waist-high rock, barely saved herself from falling forward when her toe kicked another. The guiding wires coursed through her hand, the pricks coming more often, dragging at the glove. *Another shout!* She turned and saw muted glows wavering behind her, fire torches moving through the rocks.

Her pulse raced, and her breath came in a sob. She turned forward again, straining her eyes through the mist. Was there any light there? Any at all? It would be high, up on the Shelf. Would she even be able to see it? *Where, oh where was the Camp!?* Was she close? She had come so far. To be taken now…Should she shout? Scream? Would they hear her at the Camp? They would hear her behind, that was certain. She knew only one thing: to go forward.

So she did, in desperation now, half-running, stumbling, her breath rasping in her throat, tripping, caroming off rocks, the sliding wire shredding her glove, lacerating her hand, but what could she do…but run, run.

She ran full into him. Her head was down. She had no warning before the impact and only one thought after the shock: *It is not a rock.* What she had struck gave before her with a grunt, and then she was down in a tumble of arms and legs, and one strong arm was around her waist.

"Eh! One's here already," a voice nearby hissed.

"Stop his mouth. Don't let him shout," from another voice, as a hand in a coarse glove pressed hard across her mouth and other hands pinioned her arms. "Shall I knock him?" said a voice at her ear.

She squirmed and tried to speak but could only emit a kind of groan.

"No. Truss him quick and leave him." A firm voice.

Ginna's brain flared. *Davik!* It was Davik's voice! Or like Davik's voice, but pinched. Could it possibly be? She squirmed harder, groaning fiercely, as the arms tightened around her.

Suddenly a light, an electric torch shone in her face.

"What's this?" said another voice. *Plietor's voice!* She stared into the light, squinting, her eyes dazzled. He *had* to see her, to know her! She blinked wildly, twisting her head to free the grip on her mouth, tears from the light and frustration starting down her face. Her hat was jerked to the side.

"Wait!" said Plietor. "Let me look at him."

Her hat was tugged free, the light full in her face again.

"Bloody what!" said Plietor. "It's Ginna. It's her!"

Then men were pushed aside, and Davik's face was behind the light saying, "Ginna, Ginna!" as his hands took her and stood her up, she crying full out now with relief.

"Now we know why this lot's out here, the bastards," said one of the earlier voices. *Was that Fergus?* And then, "Her hand's bleeding there, it is." *That was surely Walter Prokup,* and while Davik held her Plietor looked at her hand with the torch, sucking in his breath. She was aware now of a press of men around her. Plietor stepped away. She heard whispered words exchanged, then he was back, binding her hand in a cloth and asking her if she could stand and be by herself.

"Yeh," said Davik, in his pinched voice. "It's true we've got business to do with the lot coming up."

Ginna turned and saw, not fifty yards distant, the dull glow of torchlight, heard the muted scurry of boots, kicked gravel.

"Let me take her up into the rocks," said Plietor, gesturing quickly with the torch. "She'll be away from it there, until we're done."

"I don't like that," said Davik.

"Don't wuss it, Davik," said Fergus. "We'll be done soon enough."

Davik growled in his throat, but he handed Ginna to Plietor. "Keep the torch down," said a voice from the dark. *Karolyi,* thought Ginna. There were five of them, at least. How many were pursuing her?

Then Plietor was pulling her by the right wrist, up off the path, climbing toward the wall of the Caldera, the torch down low, close to the ground, moving carefully through the rocks.

"Not too far," said Ginna.

"Far enough, though," said Plietor. "Now you stay here, sit low. When I'm coming for you I'll give a hoot…and you hoot back to guide me."

"What will you do with them, the T-One men?"

"Thrash them bloody well, I think," said Plietor, turning away with the torch.

Ginna clutched at him. "It's a game, Plietor! You must know it's a game between Carnahan and Gehlhausen. They plan it all out on the telephone, though sometimes it doesn't work out—"

"We know. Or we guess it," said Plietor.

"But then the T-One men are just doing what Gehlhausen tells them to do." Ginna held his sleeve. "There's no reason for a great thrashing in which…people could be badly hurt."

"We will not be badly hurt," Plietor said, pulling away. "I must go. You sit. Sit quiet. I will come for you. Do not move until I do."

The pale circle of the torch light vanished behind a rock.

The dark and the mist enfolded her. She heard only the muffled sound of approaching boots, felt only the pulsing of pain in her left hand.

32.

Plietor had no time to pass on Ginna's words to Davik. The T-One men were almost upon them, and the others had arranged themselves behind rocks beside the path. Karolyi was there, and Musil, and Fergus, insistent even with his bad leg, going on about paying back for his smashed nose. Gergor Natov would have come, but could not, his ankle gone worse. And Walter Prokup. This was not the place for Walter Prokup, but he came with the others quiet from the bunkhouse, and Plietor had thought they could not deny him.

Someone had a spade and someone a rake, taken from the garden sheds. Fergus had wanted to take the ax, but Plietor said *No* and Davik agreed, said too much blood would come with an ax. Fergus was about to be loud about it but shut his mouth when he found a long-handled hammer instead. Plietor himself had a stick of wood from the glider fob, two-by-two ash. And Davik...four-feet of two-by-four white oak. Janescz would be unhappy they had taken his wood.

Plietor could see individual flames from torches now, three torches, black smoke streaking up into the mist. How many men? Four at least; from the sound of boots and the torches, probably at least one more. *Five men to track one girl, by herself.* Plietor shook his head. He had turned off the light of his torch, which now hung on his back from its lanyard. He stretched his leg, feeling the pain in his knee. The sound of approaching boots was loud. Then a shout from Davik, and Plietor leaped from his place, his stick raised high.

The first man Plietor saw was looking around wildly, waving his torch. Plietor came at him when he was looking away, but he was turning back when Plietor's blow struck, and the stick glanced off his raised arm. The man shouted in pain but didn't drop the torch, thrusting it at Plietor and circling. All around, Plietor heard the sounds of other blows, of curses and grunts and harsh breathing, the metallic sound of a spade on stone. Plietor circled with his man, both feinting, until two grappling men crashed out of the dark into his man's back and he lurched forward. Then Plietor struck once, twice on the arm holding the torch until it was dropped, and the man rolled on the stone, covering himself against further blows. Plietor reached down, grabbed his arm, pulled him up, cowering.

"Get up and away. Go. Go!" Plietor hissed. The man gave him one look, then turned and bolted into the dark.

Plietor stood erect then and swung around. The two grappling figures were against a rock. Plietor couldn't tell who was who. A torch waved five yards away and in its light he saw Davik's great club raised, then brought down to a sharp cry that faded instantly. Out of the corner of his eye he saw two more figures scrambling back up the path. Then two cries came almost at the same time. From across the path a high voice called frantically, *A knife! He has a knife!* And from one of the men against the rock, a harsh croak: *Plietor. Plietor!* Plietor sprang to the rock and saw that one man was pinned, the other man's forearm against his throat. Plietor took his stick back and swung it against the outer man's back. It hit solidly and the man gave a grunt of breath. Before he had turned, Plietor had struck him again, and then the other was off the rock and had his own hands around his opponent's throat. In such close quarters Plietor could see it was Fergus, and from his grip he knew Fergus was bent on murder.

"Fergus!" he shouted, thrusting the stick under his wrists and twisting hard. "Let him be! He will go. He will go back."

"Shit!" exploded Fergus, as his hands were wrenched apart. But he stepped back, stumbling on his leg, and the man gasped.

"Go! Get out!" said Plietor, giving him a strong push with the end of his stick as the man turned and staggered away, holding his neck.

"Plietor! The torch! Bring the torch!" The call was from across the path, where Plietor had seen Davik. Plietor pulled the electric torch around from his back and turned on its light, making his way across the path, moving among rocks to where Davik and another were standing over a third man kneeling, that man's hands under a fourth lying curled on the ground.

"Here," said Davik, his hair gleaming in the light, "Show the light for Karolyi to see."

Plietor stooped beside the kneeling Karolyi, directed the beam down Karolyi's arms.

"I am trying…" Karolyi said, in a muffled voice, reaching as though for a better grip, "I am trying to stop…"

The figure on the ground gave a slight gasp, a long shudder, then was still.

"*Accch,*" said Karolyi in a drawn-out way, then pulled his hands back. By the light of the torch Plietor could see that Karolyi's hands and forearms were covered in blood.

"Walter Prokup," said Plietor.

"*Ach,* but I got one of the bastards in exchange," snorted Davik. "Show over here."

Plietor moved the light. A T-One man was lying face up, one arm out, his forehead crushed, his head at an unnatural angle.

"An eye for an eye," said Davik.

But your eye came first, brother, thought Plietor, and it was not the man with the knife. They stood in silence, until a high-pitched hoot came from up the Caldera wall.

"Ginna!" said Plietor, springing back toward the path, giving his own hoot.

"Is that you, Plietor? I need help," Ginna called, her voice far off. Davik pressed behind Plietor, as well as Fergus.

"Keep hooting, so we can find you," called Plietor.

"Are they all gone?" Ginna called back. "Are you sure?"

"Yes, we are," roared Davik. "They've all gone bloody back to bloody Gehlhausen."

"Just the same…" called Ginna.

They scrambled, depending on Plietor's torch, clambering and slipping among the boulders.

"She must have moved," said Plietor. "I didn't take her this high."

"Ginna!" called Davik. "Ginna, where are you?"

A soft hoot sounded just five yards off. Plietor shined his light toward the sound, but they saw nothing.

"Ginna!" whispered Davik.

"Eh? What's bloody this?" said Fergus. "I've stepped on something."

Plietor shined his torch. A man laid unmoving, twisted among the rocks. A T-One man, hatless. Fergus reached down, feeling under his neck.

"Sure and he's dead," said Fergus. "Show me the light here."

Plietor moved the light to the side of the man's head. Even through his tangled hair they could see an indentation.

"Fell and smacked his head, is what it looks," said Fergus. "That's what did him."

"He didn't fall," said Ginna behind them. Plietor started, turned the light around. Davik reached for Ginna's hand, holding it as he looked her over.

"Quite the fashion, you are," he said, snorting. "And you're bloody rank."

"The clothes served," Ginna said curtly. She looked at the downed man. "I don't know how he came up here. I heard a cry from where you all were below, then a voice calling about a knife, then quiet, except…except for this scrabbling, coming up toward me, hard breathing I knew was a man. And he had an electric torch. He would turn it on an instant, then off again. I thought…I thought he was going to find me, so I moved. I dared not call out. I moved, and he moved behind me. I don't know how he knew I was here."

"He may have guessed," Plietor said. "He may have guessed you had to be here, to have come to us before the T-One men did, and to be hiding up the wall, away from any pits."

"And then the smell," said Fergus. "The clothes you have…they do…they have a nose all their own."

Davik snorted again.

Ginna took a breath. "Anyway. I couldn't just keep going up. I got a good rock…" She shaped her hands as though around a melon. "And when a cry came from below for Plietor and a torch the man turned and stood, and I came from behind him and hit him on the back with the rock, and he fell forward and…and…is dead." She took in another breath, a catch in it.

Plietor shone the light around. "Here's the torch," he said, reaching between two rocks and emerging with a torch like his own. He pushed the switch, but no light came.

Fergus was feeling over the body. "Show me here," he said, and Plietor shone the light on the man's right leg, where

Fergus had pushed the trouser leg up past the boot. From the boot top projected a handle, and Fergus withdraw it to show a knife with a blade of eight inches.

"Two knives they had at least, the bastards," he said. "And how many men? To track a girl? Had more on their minds than her, I say."

"Coming again to our camp, *I* say," said Davik. "Bastards, too right. Bloody bastards."

33.

Janescz was sitting in the dark when they returned. They pushed through the doorway, Plietor first, then Ginna and Davik, to find him there, as they left him. Davik pulled the door behind them. No one spoke as they arranged themselves around the table. No one spoke for a time thereafter.

Finally Davik said, in a low voice, "We are returned. You see Ginna here."

"I see you all," said Janescz. "Her, I barely know."

"It is a disguise," said Plietor. "She left the T-One camp by herself, an escape. She has things to tell."

"And she walked to here, walked the pit path, in the full of the dark?" said Janescz.

"Not all the way, but much," said Plietor. "Her hand is terribly cut, from following the wire."

They could not see Janescz's face, to read his eyes, but they knew he did not move. "And men from the T-One. Did they follow after her?" Janescz said.

There was another silence. "Yes. Yes they did," said Plietor. "And…and we met them."

Janescz made a clucking sound with his tongue. "Come, Plietor, tell me," he said.

"*Acch,*" broke in Davik. "We met them and we thrashed them, and they have gone back to their bloody camp and bloody Gehlhausen. And we have Ginna back with us. What more is to say?"

Janescz snorted. "Oh, there is more. More for you to say now, and I will hear it. More to be said after by others. You know that."

"There is more," said Plietor.

He told of Walter Prokup, of the knife, and how Karolyi had tried to save Prokup from bleeding, but could not. How Davik had laid out a man, but it was not the man with the knife, who had gone away. How another man with a knife had pursued Ginna hiding in the rocks, and Ginna had struck him so that he had fallen, and killed himself.

Janescz sat in the dark. "Who else will speak?" he said.

"I will," said Ginna. She told of what Gehlhausen had said to her, and what she had learned from Albert McCutcheon, at least what he had said about the rockslide and her leaving with the camel train. Davik got up from the table to walk the wall when she spoke of the rockslide, came back when she told of the camel train. He muttered hard under his breath, barely holding himself in.

Plietor whispered. "I see it. I do. Carnahan sent her, he *sent* her to T-One to keep us from acting when the time came for her to go with the camel train, to keep us from upsetting his plans, whatever they were, his plans with Gehlhausen."

"But we *did* act," growled Davik. "Here is Ginna. And where is his plans?"

There was silence. Finally Janescz sighed. "Soon we shall know what Carnahan will do. We shall know it and…" He clucked again with his tongue.

Plietor's head was up before the third stroke of Karski's iron. He was still at the table, though his head was down on his hands. He supposed he had slept. It was not yet first light. Davik's snoring came from above, ragged through his broken nose. Ginna had gone up after him, to her own room. The outside door opened and Janescz pushed in.

"We are to be in Carnahan's room at first light," he said. "Me, you, Davik. Ginna stays here. She does not go out."

"What about her hand?" said Plietor.

Janescz had shrugged in the dark.

"You bastards!!" spit Carnahan. His long coat draped his shoulders, red hair tangled over his ears, setting off the red-blotched scalp above it. His face was blotched too, ruddier even than usual.

They were before him, as they had been the evening past: Plietor and Davik and the three supers. Carnahan stood big behind the long table, his arms away from his sides, fists clenched, glaring. Plietor and Davik stood just across the table in the full face of his anger, Bartosz and Hilenski on one bench behind them, Janescz by himself on the other bench, head down. Plietor's mouth and knee still throbbed; Davik's nose still swelled with plugs; but they stood with heads up, lips tight.

"My clear words," said Carnahan, "sure and just hours ago, meant nothing to you. Clear words with a clear plan. Could you not wait for the camel train? Was that such a hard thing? *No!* You must go on your own, with your own plan. And now!" He threw his hands into the air, looked skyward. "Now! One of our men is dead, two from T-One, and the T-One Overseer is our enemy forever."

Davik drew breath as though to speak, but Plietor twisted his leg into Davik's and Davik breathed out silently. Carnahan rolled his eyes. "Can you two have had two thoughts between you? Did you understand you threaten our very effort here, the only reason we are in this place? Can you have even passed by consequences in your thought? What am I to do with men who will not hear my words, who will not think of consequences? *What am I to do?* I ask all of you."

No one spoke. None of the supers met Carnahan's eyes.

"Ginna—" began Davik before Plietor could stop him.

"Ginna!" Carnahan stopped him instead. "Sure and our Miss Ginna." His voice dripped.

"You did it all for the rescue of our Miss Ginna. What can I say to that? That our contract, our work, the lives of fifty-three souls in this place and those in the T-One do not revolve around the place of our Miss Ginna? A plan, my men! A plan was in place for her to be restored to us. In good time, with no men dead and no mortal enemy. What is a plan if I, who am charged by oath and contract to look over the fortunes of all and justify us here, can be *ignored by those of* my charge for their own purposes and schedules?" Carnahan shrugged large, shook his head, turned it away.

What a bloody actor, Plietor thought. He exchanged a quick look with Davik, then half-turned to meet Janescz's eyes.

Carnahan pulled his chair around, sat heavily in it. He steepled his fingers, put them joined under his chin, and looked down onto the table. Plietor and Davik stood. The others sat, still. The silence lengthened.

A show, thought Plietor. *It is all a show.* Carnahan and Gehlhausen had worked out what to do on the electric telephone. But Carnahan would go through this theatric. The justification of the Camp. Oath and contract. The good of fifty-three souls. Plietor had heard it all so many times. What about the rockslide? Was that part of the oath and contract? Was that for the good of fifty-three souls? Walter Prokup was dead, yes. But so were Gwen and Simcas. And Rozum, the doctor Wetkin, soon Karpiak. Was it forty-seven souls now? Carnahan was shaking his head at him and Davik.

What was their "good" anyway? Ask Karpiak that, before he died. What was Carnahan's good? What was Gehlhausen's?

Finally Carnahan drew a breath, sat back in his chair, laced his fingers across his chest.

"This is what I say," he said. 'You *will* hear me. *All* of you." He looked around the room, waiting for eyes and a nod from every man. Plietor nodded in his turn, his lips still tight. Davik beside him tilted his head barely to the side.

"This is sure and a huge transgression. I am in my rights for any response. *Any*. I do not consider in the same way the acts of Karolyi, Musil, Fergus, and the sad Prokup. They do not act by themselves, but only with you two." He glared at Plietor and Davik. "You act with no other consultation. This must be true."

Carnahan tilted his head to look around Plietor to Janescz, but Janescz made no sound or motion. Carnahan went on.

"Still, even against my words as you two have acted, my response must bear the burden of my obligation. I have just said it; I will say it again. My obligation is to the good of this Camp and its value to those who furnish our livelihood, to MacReedy Mining. To remove you two transgressors from production would run against that obligation. You must do your work to justify yourselves here, as must we all. You must fly the gliders and gather our lifeblood ore. You must and you will."

He stared at them from deep under his eye brows. They stared back.

"But!" Carnahan raised a hand, a hard finger pointing at them. "The injury you have done us all must be repaid. A man is dead, one of our good men, because of you. A new man there must be to work with Janescz in the shop, and for that a man must come to us from the outside, either to be that man for Janescz, or to take the place of one that is moved over, from the work of Mr. Hilenski or Mr. Bartosz." Carnahan's finger moved to each in turn. *Bringing them both in,* thought Plietor, *both in against us.*

"Now," said Carnahan, "where shall this man's wage come from? By justice, from only one place, from the wages of them whose actions brought the need for him. You two here." His finger waved back and forth between Davik and Plietor. "None other than them that went against my plan with their own and brought this need. So." He slapped the table with both hands, "So I tell it to you, and so shall I tell it to MacReedy Mining in Perth, that this new man shall take his wages from those of you two, for one year. And that is as it shall be."

Plietor sensed a stirring in the men behind him, a lightening of tension. Wages? Was it only to be wages? Carnahan had talked much of wages the past weeks, but who knew of wages? Clouds in a bank in Perth. There must be something else.

"How shall I tell this to MacReedy Mining in Perth?" said Carnahan, standing up again, pacing behind his table, half turned away from them. "I have much to tell MacReedy Mining. Rozum and his glider down in the mist. Our doctor gone, other…" he paused just a beat, "…other comrades. We have had sore tribulation. We have many needs. But production! Brave production through all our troubles. Increased wages for the whole Camp. My report will be long." He stopped, still half-turned away.

"But this with the T-One. It is different. It is not a matter for writing in reports. It is a matter for men to confer. There *was* a plan, but now…" He turned, a shrug with both hands, turned back. "Now I must confer directly with MacReedy Mining."

He faced them, leaned forward on both his arms, looked past Davik and Plietor to the supers. "I will go with the camel train."

Plietor felt Davik jerk beside him, heard Bartosz begin to say "Wha...?!"

Carnahan's mouth was a tight smile. "I will go with the camel train. But not to Oodnadatta. Only a ways, then split off to Stuart-town, and its telegraph. There I will confer, electric messages across the country to Perth, talking man to man."

"Ginna—" began Davik again.

"Yes, *Ginna!*" said Carnahan. "Now *Ginna!* Always *Ginna* with you, Davik. Ginna goes with this camel train. I said it four months past and I have not unsaid it. I say it again now. Ginna goes with this train." He riveted Davik with his eyes.

"She goes back to her people, whoever they are, as she should have long since. I will go with her, to keep her safe from camels and Afghans, until she knows them." His voice dripped again, then hardened, as Davik twisted, hesitating to speak.

"There is nothing more to say on this," said Carnahan. "It was said long ago." He looked past Davik. "Bartosz, Hilenski, I want one man from each of you, a man who can go in the bush. For five days. Two days of travel to Stuart-town, a day of messages, two days back here. We leave with the camel train, when it comes. One more thing. Janescz is to be Overseer for my time away, for the five days. You will answer to him as you answer to me. Until I return. Then *he* will answer to me."

He smiled his twisted smile, then unsmiled it, looked under his brows at Bartosz and Hilenski until he was satisfied with what he saw in their eyes, looked at Janescz, who was staring back at him, his mouth slightly open.

"I will say all this to the Camp, when we gather after out-ringing this evening to speak of Walter Prokup. Until then it is a day like all days, a day of production."

Hilenski had his hand raised, like a schoolboy. "Sir, I need a word. It is a question of supplies, with the camel train so late."

Carnahan nodded. "Janescz, you two..." he nodded toward Davik and Plietor, "you will wait for me here. Karski will wait with you."

Carnahan walked out the door into the blowing mist with Hilenski and Bartosz. Karski went out with them, looked back in, then shut the door.

"Ginna—" began Davik.

"A moment, brother," said Plietor. "It is important we see what Carnahan has done." He balled his fist against his mouth as he stood and thought. Then he nodded to himself.

"Carnahan knows wages are nothing," Plietor said. Janescz put up his hand in protest, but Plietor shook his head. "Nothing to us," he said, gesturing to Davik. Davik looked at him, waiting. "Nothing to the Camp either, not as consequence for...what we did. And for consequences: no consequences for Karolyi, Musil, Fergus, for you either, our father."

Janescz's mouth hardened. He waited too.

"So to the Camp, in this evening when he speaks, it will be Carnahan the generous one, as after the rockslide. 'The good of the Camp,' he will say. 'The oath and contract.' You have heard these words many times." Plietor looked from Davik to Janescz.

"Now all of us who went to get Ginna must be grateful that some great consequence does not fall on us. The rest of the Camp will be grateful things can go on. How and to who could we speak dark words about this generous Carnahan and be heard?"

"And why should you speak dark words?" said Janescz. "What do you want from him? Why can you not simply hear *his* words and do them? Why must it all be a great plot that you must show to all?"

"But it *is* a plot!" said Plietor. "With him and Gehlhausen. We are sure of it. Ginna told us."

"What is the difference if it is?" said Janescz. "You can do your work. It *is* what you are here for. Is Carnahan wrong to say that? Carnahan will let you do your work, in spite of everything. So do it. Fly the gliders. Leave the plotting to others."

"But Ginna—" Davik again.

"Don't you see how Carnahan has used Ginna?" said Plietor, swinging around to him. "Of course she must go with the camel train. Now Carnahan must go with the camel train too. He is so generous again, the man of obligation and concern. By saying and doing this he turns everyone's mind to him and Ginna with Afghans and camels, and away from Ginna and the T-One, and Gehlhausen's 'accommodations,' and what we did, and what is the real reason for him to go."

"What 'real reason?'" said Janescz, standing up from the bench, his voice rising. "What can you know of 'real reasons?' Is it so cracked that he would go to telegraph to Perth? He should have done this when the Zeppelin came down. You said yourself. Now he goes and you are all suspicions."

"Oh, Janescz." Plietor shook his head, his eyes pleading. "How do we even know he goes to telegraph to Perth? When he comes back with a 'directive,' how do we know it comes from Perth? Maybe it comes from himself? Maybe from Gehlhausen? And now you are to be Overseer. Don't you see how he plots? With you as Overseer our hands are tied..." He held his arms out toward Davik, his wrists crossed above

---

Roger Jones

his fisted hands.

"*Cholera!*" Janescz swept his own arms before him as though clearing a table. "It is all plots with you two. Plots and Ginna! Why can we not just do our work?"

"Until what?" thundered Davik now. "Until we are all Karpiak? Is that what you want? Ginna goes back and we go to lie under a mound of stones?"

"*Acch!* I cannot speak to you," said Janescz. He strode to the door, jerked it open, slammed it behind him. After a moment Karski opened it again, looked in at each of them, shut it quietly.

They stood a moment, chests heaving with breath and emotion. Then Davik threw himself down on the left bench, Plietor taking the other. They sat.

Plietor didn't know how much time passed. Five minutes, maybe. Ten. His brain roiled with anger and frustration and images: Karolyi's bloody hands emerging from under Walter Prokup, Ginna's strange clothes, her smell, her torn hand, the great boulder falling to the edge of the Stack, the cloud of stone and brick dust. Davik stood and walked the length of the room and back, then stopped.

"What?" he said. "What is that? Plietor?"

Ringing. It was a ringing, behind the inside door, back in Carnahan's rooms. Davik went to put his ear against the door, looked back at Plietor. "The electric talker," he said. "Bloody Gehlhausen."

"Carnahan—" began Plietor.

"Carnahan is not here," said Davik, pushing at the door, which opened wide, without a lock.

They both stared into the dark hallway. The ringing was louder, insistent. Davik stepped over the threshold. "Janescz—" said Plietor. He looked toward the outside door.

348

"Karski—" No sound came from outside but the wind around the edges of the door. Davik was out of sight down the hall. Plietor followed.

Ten feet down the hall candlelight guttered from a partially-opened doorway. Davik was past it. Plietor glanced into Carnahan's bedroom, saw a bed with a blanket tossed, a tall closed cabinet like the one in the outside room, a small desk with papers in pigeonholes, a chair against the wall beside it. Across from Carnahan's doorway another, a closed door. Plietor pushed and it opened into dark, with dim shapes—another bed, another cabinet, a closed door on the far side. Did it connect to the clinic?

Still the ringing. "Plietor. This way," called Davik from down the hall.

The room was no larger than Ginna's in their flat. Plietor's glance took in a table with a stub of flickering candle in a dish, a stool. Two papers with numbers written on them lay on one corner of the table. On the other stood the electric telephone: a closed wooden box half a foot square and a foot high braced with brass corners, a battery beside it, as for an electric torch. Davik stood over it, unsure, listening to its ringing. Plietor stepped forward and tilted back the lid. Inside stood up a black handle with bulbs on both ends, a wire from one down into the box where more wires crawled, a battery, a bell that vibrated and rang as they watched. Plietor looked at Davik, then lifted the black handle. The ringing stopped abruptly, and in a moment came a voice from one of the bulbs, a tinny sound, as from a long pipe.

"Carnahan! So long I am waiting here."

Davik looked at Plietor, his eyebrows up. "Gehlhausen," he said. "It is Gehlhausen's voice."

Plietor held the bulb with the sound of the voice to his ear.

"*Also*, you are there now, yes?" said Gehlhausen.

Plietor looked at Davik. The other end of the handle was near his mouth. "Yes," he said into the bulb.

"*Gut*," said Gehlhausen. So, the meeting has gone as you said, no problems?"

Plietor thrust the handle at Davik. "Use Carnahan's voice," he whispered. "Say, 'Yes. No problems.'"

Davik said it.

"*Sehr gut*," said Gehlhausen. "Then you come here on the camel train, with the girl. And the two brothers—Davik and the other—they make no trouble for the Camp, or for us."

"No. They make no trouble," whispered Plietor.

Davik said it.

"When you come, we talk man-to-man. But I tell you again it is two more ore bags for T-One to pay for my two dead men. I will have to send more men to gather those back from the long path, make a hard speech about the girl to settle things. This was a bad plan to take her."

Plietor felt a surge of excitement. "Say, 'It was sure and a *good* plan to take her. You don't know these brothers like I do. What was bad was to have her escape.'"

Davik spoke.

"*Sheisse*," returned Gehlhausen. "My men would have caught her soon enough. The bad was to have your mob come down the path and attack us."

"Ha," whispered Plietor.

"Say, 'What of your men with fire torches and knives?'" Davik spoke Carnahan's voice.

"What do you say!?" They could tell even over the wire that Gehlhausen was shouting. "What do you know of torches and knives? What have you spoken in your meeting that was no trouble?!"

Plietor rolled his eyes, exchanged half a smile with Davik, whispered, "No trouble. Just a report. The brothers stay here. I come to you, and then to Stuart-town."

There was a moment's pause. Then Gehlhausen said in a normal voice, "*Ja wohl*. And you tell MacReedy Mining there what you need, for your Camp and for Wonthaggi, to make up for the girl and for spilled blood. The overage comes back to you, as always, and we are all happy, *gemütlich*, as we say."

"Yes. As you say."

"You ring me when the camel train comes to you, so we are ready for you in turn, and for the girl."

"I will sure."

"Out, then."

"Out," spoke Davik, handing the black handle to Plietor, who replaced it in the box, closed the lid. They looked at one another.

"*Bloody 'Out' is right.*" Carnahan's voice spoke with cold menace from the door. Plietor jerked and froze, with just a glance at Davik, who had whirled around, then frozen too.

Carnahan stood in the doorway, dark behind him, dark in his face, his long revolver in his hand, sweeping it from side to side. "I'm coming to think there's nothing you two won't do. And your father on the doorstep." He clucked his tongue, shook his head, while Plietor's heart thudded in his chest.

"Such as you can't be about," said Carnahan. "It's too dangerous for all." He stood a little aside, nodded his head toward the hall behind him. "Come out, with space between you. I have no wish to shoot you down where you stand, but I will, you may believe it. Put your hands behind your head like, like proper prisoners. Davik first."

He herded them into the dark room across the hall, shut the door behind them. Plietor heard him fiddling with the hasp, the snick of a padlock, then Carnahan's steps fading, the shut of another door. That would be the inside door to the big room. What would Carnahan tell Janescz? Plietor felt his way to the bed and sat down.

"Well, I guess it's buggered good and proper now," he said into the dark.

"He's the one will be buggered in the end," growled Davik, off against the wall.

"What will he tell the Camp?" said Plietor.

"Oh, he'll make a story," said Davik. "'Davik and Plietor, dingoes on the chase, dangerous to themselves and all others.' He said it already."

"And what of Ginna?" said Plietor.

"You are the man with hypothesis," said Davik. "But I say Ginna will not see light before the camel train comes. Carnahan will give over production, for once."

They remained in silence for a time. Then Plietor said, "And what of us?"

Davik snorted. "Are all your ideas gone away? You should ask, 'Can Carnahan have us among the others, after this?' He will not think he can, and he will be right. Maybe he thinks of the camel train for us, Carnahan up in a saddle with his pistol, our own feet in chains to walk twenty days. But that will not happen. I say it will not."

Plietor did not respond. He heard Davik move along the far wall to try the door there. It was locked from the other side, as they knew it would be. Davik rattled it hard.

"Maybe Julia will hear," said Plietor. Davik snorted.

After a while Davik came to the bed. "You sit where you like, or stand," he said. "I will sleep." Plietor moved off the bed and sat on the stone floor at its base. In three minutes Davik was snoring.

34.

It was hours and hours. Davik had slept, waked to piss in the corner, then stalked the wall. Plietor lay down after Davik and slept too. He didn't know how long. They heard the faint thud of a door slam, once, twice—the blue door probably, Carnahan coming and going. They heard voices faint too, Carnahan's voice. The Gathering. Carnahan with his story, announcing their fates, his walkabout to Stuart-town. Then silence for a long time. Plietor lay on the bed, staring into the dark, listening to Davik along the wall, his boots back and forth.

The hasp of the lock moved on the outside of the door. Plietor stopped his breath, heard Davik's boots stop too. The movement at the lock was cautious, quiet. Plietor heard the snick of the padlock releasing, the slide of the lock shaft through the steel loop. Then a creak at the door's edge, a breath of cooler air.

"*Shhh,*" a voice whispered. "I am coming in. It's me, Karski. I am for you, and I have news."

Davik growled from the corner. "What kind of bloody trick is it?"

"Quiet, quiet," whispered Karski. "Listen to me and decide." He pulled the door shut behind him, all three in the dark.

"What is the hour?" said Plietor.

"It is onto the night's middle," said Karski. "But let me speak first, before you ask."

Plietor heard him draw a breath. "I have seen something...something...I can not be part of this. I can not know it and only stand aside."

"What?" said Plietor. "What have you seen?"

"This day...I will tell about the day if you will. But after...after I tell this other." He drew another breath.

"After the Gathering, after Carnahan went in here, I went in to the bunkhouse, all of us, in to the bunkhouse and up to the flats, Hilenski, Bartosz...Janescz...all. I went in to my bed but I could not sleep. I came out, walked the Shelf, took seat on a terrace among tall plants. I sat. It was a long while. And then sitting I saw someone moving against the Stack. I looked, and I saw Carnahan himself, come quiet from the blue door in his long coat, with an electric torch in his hand, on-off, very quick. He walked soft across the Yard, down the Terrace beside the garden sheds, turned to the glider sheds along the edge. I got up then and came behind him, even softer, wondering. He went past the fob to the first glider stall and went in, through the curtain. I saw the light from the torch go on and stay, so I came behind him, to the corner of the fob, then the corner of the stall, where I knelt low."

"Such a burglar you are," growled Davik.

"And you're bloody to the good I am," said Karpiak, his whisper harsh.

"Let him tell it," said Plietor.

"Yah, so Carnahan is bending over the body of the front glider—Davik's, is it? With the red tail? Light from Carnahan's torch is inside the body, inside the hole where Davik sits. Carnahan is bending far over, his head and arms down inside, and he's moving his arm, I see the shoulder, fore and back, and I hear a scrape, a rasp on metal, *bzz, bzz, bzz* when he moves. He does this for a bit, then stands up with the torch and I move back behind the fob, so that's all I see of that. But there's not much more. Carnahan goes out and back up the Shelf to the Stack the same way he came down. He goes in the blue door and that's that."

"We didn't hear him go and come," said Plietor.

"What I say is true," said Karski, a note in his whispered voice. "Believe me. You must."

"What do you think Carnahan was doing with the glider?" said Plietor to Karski.

"I don't know this," said Karski. "How would I? You know the gliders. I think it can not be good, though. I think Carnahan makes a plan...this is what I can not stand aside for. I think he makes a plan for death for Davik in the glider. I can not stand aside for this, no matter what."

They were all silent for a moment.

"He was filing a control cable," said Plietor, speaking now to Davik. "He knows enough to do that. Rudder...elevator. Elevator probably. You go up, push over, the cable separates, you stall and go in."

"No more Davik," said Davik.

"I can not stand aside for this," said Karski again. He made a sound in his throat. "I have stood aside long. The rockslide...it was not to go so. They took Ginna, but there was to be no harm. It was just to keep you...And I know ore goes to T-One, our ore, and Carnahan gets wages from Wonthaggi Coal for it. All this..."

"You listen to Carnahan on the electric telephone," said Plietor, a flat statement.

"What if I do?" said Karski. "I look out for myself. It is good to know things."

Davik snorted.

"So what now?" said Plietor.

"This is how it will be," said Karski. "The lock on this door is down. It will stay down two hours. Then you must be back here. What you do in two hours, I do not know. But you must be back. The lock goes up then. You must be inside here, you understand."

"At least we can piss and eat," said Davik. Karski gave a grunt.

"We will be back," said Plietor. "We owe you that. And we are grateful."

"We are, if you're not on a trick," said Davik.

"I am not," said Karski. "What do I gain from a trick? Go see the glider. Then you will know."

Plietor looked at Carnahan across the table. *Three times in three days,* he thought. Three times for him and Davik before Carnahan. They had been marched in from the dark room by Karski, him holding Carnahan's rifle, not meeting their eyes at all. All the rest were standing in the long room, Carnahan behind the table in his long coat, Bartosz and Hilenski before one bench to Carnahan's right, Janescz before another to his left. Plietor saw that Janescz's bench was in front of Bartosz and Hilenski's, halfway between Davik and Plietor and the others. *A statement from Carnahan about responsibility,* Plietor thought grimly. Karski had marched them in front of the table and moved toward the door.

Carnahan stood with his arms across his chest, a stern face under his eyebrows. His long revolver lay on the table before him, the barrel toward them. Beside the pistol was a thick book, Carnahan's Bible, Plietor saw. Karski now stood by the door with the rifle.

"This is sure and a crossroads in our lives," Carnahan began, in his deepest voice. "I say it, come to it pondering all the night. I see one way that goes forward from this crossway. I see another too. That other way is a way of dissolution and scatter, but it is a way, and we must choose. We will make the choice here, in this room, here and now. I will lay it before you." He spread his arms. "Let us all sit, so we may reason together. Mr. Karski, a bench for these men."

Karski stood the rifle against the door and moved quickly to the inner wall for a bench for Davik and Plietor. They stood, awkward, not knowing if they should move to help, while Karski dragged a bench beside Janescz's, left it, went back to the rifle and the door. Carnahan sat down then and they all followed, except Karski.

Carnahan half turned his chair, looking out his window, the mist blowing up and over, shades of dark in the half-light. He spoke without looking around.

"Mr. Bartosz, Mr. Hilenski, Mr. Boruski—the elder Mr. Boruski—you heard me speak at the Gathering yesterday. How I was prepared to balance the initial grave transgression against my vested authority by these two and its tragic outcome, balance it against the obligation of our work here. And how that balance was then over-weighted by their after act of...*espionage*." He turned his head suddenly to Davik and Plietor and fixed them with a fierce eye, then turned away again. Plietor didn't know the word, doubted the others did either. He knew it meant their secret listening, though.

"I have to say that when I spoke at the Gathering I was dark in my mind. In the face of such willful transgression, such and total disregard for the orderly conduct of our business here, I saw no course other than..."

Carnahan turned his head, then his whole chair around. He leaned forward at the table on his arms, looking past Davik and Plietor at the supers.

"I did not say this at the Gathering. But in my mind I thought the only course was to take these two..." he tilted his head toward the two of them "…with me and your men, take them with the camel train under my armed arrest, take them to Stuart-town and remand them there to the Constable, with a full bill of particulars of their transgressions. *Let the force of the Law rule them,* I thought, since they consider themselves beyond my authority."

Plietor felt Davik tense beside him but subside at Plietor's soft snort. Carnahan was still looking beyond them. "This was the way of dissolution, of the scatter of our community here, the only way I saw yesterday."

He paused, looked down at the table, staring at the revolver, then slowly moved his eyes to the Bible, lifting his hand and placing it on it. "As I tossed through the night, sleepless on these dark thoughts, I turned to the Holy Bible for solace." He looked up at them.

Plietor was watching Carnahan's face. When he raised it his eyes had a look, a sharp look but veiled, *a secret challenge,* Plietor thought, a look that almost made him shiver.

"In this Bible," said Carnahan, "guided by a higher power I'm sure, I came to the story of the Prodigal Son. Now may it be"—Carnahan said this so smooth—"that you all remember the story of the Prodigal Son, the boy who goes away from the good order of his father's home, goes away leaving his father and brother to do his work, goes out beyond their home with plans of his own. The father and brother are sore bitter at all this son's plans and his leaving, at him making harder work for the all of them left. When after years away this son comes back, his plans gone all to ashes…Oh, and sure you all remember the upshot." Carnahan scanned them all, still with his secret look.

"At first the father is not inclined to take the son back, to make him pay instead for the hardness he left them with. But then this father, he has a change of heart, and he welcomes this son as being all the more precious for coming back, more precious even than the brother who never left."

Plietor heard Janescz shifting on his bench beside them. Davik was looking at the floor.

"In the heart of the night," said Carnahan, "I said to myself...am I not like that father? And mayn't these boys"—he nodded toward Plietor and Davik, but looked back at the supers—"be like prodigal sons? After a dark night of thinking on themselves, mayn't they come back to us, and we welcome them as the Bible father did? Can we not go back to the order of our lives, with lessons learned? Can we not understand the passing of our Ginna from us, her who came so unbidden...can we not understand her passing from us as the natural order of things, as a thing that must happen now as its right time? Is this not a better way at the crossroads than that other?"

No one spoke. The wind whispered at the corners of the window and the blue door, which creaked behind Karski. Plietor realized that Carnahan was looking straight at him.

"What say you to this, my lads? Can I welcome you back into the order of our home here, as the Bible says, or—" His words hung.

Plietor looked out of the side of his eye at Davik. Davik was still looking at the floor. He seemed to be in a daze.

"Can you lay it out for us?" said Plietor. "The crossroads and the son?"

Carnahan rolled his eyes but kept his scowl in check. "Sure and I can. I can lay it out plain as day, for any as needs that."

Plietor kicked the side of his foot against Davik's. Davik sat up.

"The one road takes you two boys with me and the camel train to Stuart-town. That road goes to the Constable, who will do with you as he likes, according to your transgressions against my legal and contractual authority that led to the death of one of our men and two from the T-One mine. That's one road. Do you understand that?"

"Ginna goes with the camel train too," said Davik.

Carnahan looked at him. "Yes, she does. But she'll be no lookout of yours. You will be under my arrest and bound for a different place when we split off for Stuart-town, and the good Lord only knows what place after that in the hands of the Law."

"And the son," said Plietor.

Carnahan turned his eyes to him, shook his head. "The other road keeps you here, in spite of your transgressions, keeps you here to do your lawful work, support your father, and earn your honest wage. We let bygones be bygones for the sake of our work here, with you walking the straight and narrow with my authority like all the rest."

He paused, looked hard from Plietor to Davik and back again.

"This is the choice, boys. You make it now and you make it forever. One road and you're criminals under the Law. The other and you're valuable flyers for the MacReedy Mining Company's Arltunga Mine. What's it to be?"

"If we take the second road, what then?" said Davik.

Carnahan scowled. "I've said it," he said. "Today's a day of production, like every day of our lives here. We have quota to make. You go out there and fly the glider, making your part of the quota. You and Plietor. And Janescz."

"Fly the glider," said Davik.

A new look came into Carnahan's eyes, the beginnings of a hard, wary look. His lips tightened.

Bartosz stood up from his bench, clearing his throat loudly. Plietor felt his heart whack against his chest. "Beg pardon, Mr. Carnahan," he said, "but there's a third road to this crossing."

Carnahan's wary look deepened. Plietor saw him take his hand off the Bible, where it had rested all this time, and place it on the table. "Mr. Bartosz," he said.

"Yes sir, there's a third road," said Bartosz. "We're thinking not all transgressions here are Davik's and Plietor's. We've heard things...about the rockslide, about how Ginna came to be taken, about the fight with the T-One men on the pit path, about..." He glanced beside him at Hilenski, forward to Janescz. "...about the German Overseer at the T-One, how you talk to him."

Carnahan slapped his hand hard on the table. Bartosz flinched, but stood his ground as Carnahan leaned forward.

"How have you heard these things, Mr. Bartosz?" Carnahan's voice was soft with menace.

"I think you can know that," said Bartosz. "I think you know who knows what around here, whether they be free to tell for themselves or not."

Carnahan didn't move his head, but his eyes darted to Plietor, to Janescz, to Karski by the door, then back. "What third road is it you see, Mr. Bartosz?"

Plietor felt Davik's arms tense beside him, heard Janescz's bench creak as Janescz moved on it. For himself, over the thudding of his heart and the burn high in his neck, Plietor was watching Carnahan's hand.

"We think..." started Bartosz, then stronger. "We think it should be you under arrest, going to Stuart-town, you going...with Hilenski it would be, and with Plietor, for them to bring particulars to the Constable, and to talk in telegrams to MacReedy Mining in Perth. That's what we think here. And we have talked it over the whole Camp in the night. We are all in agreement."

Carnahan glared, his face dark with blood. "You have talked it over the whole Camp."

"You can not take on the whole Camp," said Bartosz.

Carnahan's hand moved, and Plietor moved with it up from the bench, but Carnahan's hand was faster. He gestured with the barrel of the revolver, and Plietor resumed his seat.

"Karski," said Carnahan without looking at him, "you may bring that rifle to me. I don't know your mind, but in case you have ideas, you should know it has no bullets in it."

Karski looked down at the rifle in his hands, then moved from the door toward Carnahan, his face confused. "I'll advise you not to come between my revolver and any of these other gentlemen," said Carnahan, taking a step back as Karski approached and placed the rifle on the table. Then, "You might stand there, between the Boruskis young and old. And you, Mr. Bartosz, you may and sit yourself down too, as having delivered your speech."

Carnahan moved the barrel of the gun across the room, taking them all in. "So," he said, "we have here mutiny. That's what we have, mutiny, pure and simple. The laws for mutiny are plain as the crime, and it's glad I am you have laid your cards on the table, for now I can have the pleasure of looking forward to you all hanging, as the Law requires." He smiled a terrible smile. Plietor thought he saw in it a trace of desperation, but it was mostly dark determination.

"No, Mr. Bartosz, I don't think I'll be marching to Stuart-town under the arrest of Mr. Hilenski and Mr. Plietor Boruski here. Since you have laid the game out as you have, I think I'll be taking myself off to more convivial surroundings...or at least to more convivial companionship." He twisted his smile. "As was my plan before, I leave the Camp in the capable hands of Mr. Janescz Boruski"—he gestured toward Janescz with the revolver barrel—"who can tend it to his pleasure until the constabulary, or the army, or even Mr. Ian MacReedy himself comes from Perth to lead you all to the gallows. There is no place for anyone to go in this great desert, so I am sure you will all be here to make a proper greeting, having ample time to consider your folly."

Carnahan stood, then bent over, reaching under the table and emerging with a flat wooden box with a leather handle. "I had taken the precaution of gathering all the Camp ledgers and keeping them about me. It is good I have done so, and I will carry them along with me, always the dutiful Overseer I am." He smiled deeper, as much to himself as to them. Then his smile vanished.

"Up!" He gestured with the pistol. They rose in ragged unison. "Make you a line from the door now, well spaced. Mark I have six bullets in this pistol and six of you to shoot. Don't doubt that I will do so. Now march very orderly out to the Yard, Karski, you last." Carnahan moved hatless toward the doorway, the box in one hand, his revolver in the other never wavering.

Bartosz went first, then Hilenski. They exchanged looks as they walked, but nothing more. Then went Janescz, *looking pale*, Plietor thought, and uncomposed. Davik tromped through, Plietor at his back, Karski behind him. They stood in their rough line in the Yard. Then Carnahan emerged, squinting into the thickening light, pulling the blue door behind him. "Move now," he said, gesturing with the pistol down the Shelf. The line of them moved, Carnahan moving up alongside, and as he did so Karski bolted back toward the door.

"No!" shouted Plietor, possessed in an instant of the sure idea that Karski was making a break for the rifle, that Karski knew, or thought he knew, where bullets were for it. But Plietor knew Karski would never make it, and he didn't.

Carnahan whirled, and the gun roared in his hand. Karski pitched forward into the door, which caromed open as he fell against it, slammed into the wall inside and bounced back, hitting him on the head as he lay face-down on the threshold.

They all stood frozen for a moment. Then Carnahan said, "Plietor Boruski, step out."

Plietor's heart lurched. He took a deep breath and stepped. "I send you on an errand," Carnahan said. "Go bring to us our Miss Ginna. We rest go to the glider sheds. If you are not there when we are I will shoot your brother like Karski, shoot him down. Do you hear me? Go now."

Plietor glanced at Davik. Davik's face was working. Dark arcs of sweat stained his shirt under his arms, beads on his temples too. He stood, focused on Carnahan, clenching and unclenching his fists.

Plietor gave him a final look and bolted for the ladder.

35.

Ginna saw the line of men from the window. She had been at the table when she heard the gunshot from just below in the Yard. She had dashed to the window, looked out the crack in the shutter. Carnahan was there alongside the line, hatless, things in his hands. Bartosz stood, Hilenski, Janescz, then Davik, finally Plietor. Plietor stepped forward. What was in Carnahan's right hand? His pistol! Was he going to shoot Plietor!? Who had he shot before?

Ginna was frantically opening the door when she saw Plietor turn and run toward their ladder. *What, oh what! What was happening!?*

Yesterday...yesterday had been so horrible. It had been more than an hour before Janescz had returned, more than an hour after he and Davik and Plietor had gone to Carnahan's room on Karski's summons. Janescz had looked old, pale; his hands shook. Davik and Plietor had talked on Carnahan's electric telephone he had said, stammering the story. When Carnahan and Hilenski went out, they had talked to Gehlhausen, the T-One Overseer. He—Janescz—and Karski had been outside the blue door, waiting for Carnahan's return.

Wait! Ginna had said. *Wait!* What had Carnahan said about her escape? About the fight with the T-One men? What about Walter Prokup? What was to happen—?

365

But Janescz could not wait. He stammered on. Carnahan had returned, found him and Karski at the blue door, pushed in…Davik and Plietor were not in the long room. Janescz could see it. His blood had frozen. Carnahan had told him and Karski to stand and had gone in the inner door. There was nothing, nothing to see, nothing to hear except Carnahan's voice, low. They couldn't understand the words. Then Carnahan had come out, his face stony. Davik and Plietor were locked away, he said. They had gone where they shouldn't, and now they could stay there until he decided what to do with them. He could have shot them on the spot. That's what Carnahan said.

Ginna's hands pressed her cheeks, her fingertips white. Janescz was seeing Carnahan in his head, hearing his voice shouting, *Where were you, Karski and Janescz, when the boys were prowling? Idiots! Idiots! All Boruskis are idiots.*

Then Carnahan said Janescz should go and fly the gliders, make production with Fergus, with Musil and Karolyi, if they were fit to fly. Not with Ginna. She should stay in. Not go out for anything. It was all terrible, Janescz had said. *Okropne! Okropne!*

Then Janescz was gone. And Ginna had sat, sat the long day, sat with her worry dark inside her, and her hand, her poor hand, throbbing and oozing. She had washed the hand the night before, crushed some parsley and bound it up against her skin. But she daren't go down to Julia in the clinic. Carnahan…Carnahan was a deadly man. She was sure of it. He had Davik and Plietor locked somewhere in his rooms. He could do anything.

Janescz had not spoken to her when he came from the gliders after out-ringing. He had eaten silently, gone up to his bed. She had too, after a long while. But she couldn't sleep, with her worry and her hand.

And then Davik and Plietor had been there, in the darkest of the night, come back with no light. Plietor had come up to her. Karski had let them out, Plietor said, unlocked the door, told them...They had two hours. *What could they do in two hours?* They could rouse the Camp against Carnahan, that's what. They could tell everyone what they had heard, what Ginna had heard, what Karski had seen that their own hands had confirmed. The people of the Camp would understand that Carnahan was only for himself, that he would risk them all for himself, that he stood with Gehlhausen and the T-One. And so Davik and Plietor had gone out into the night, to the other flats and down to the bunkhouse, waking people in the dark and telling them, whispers everywhere, one telling another over the whole Camp, while Carnahan slept, and she waited. She could not go out. None...or hardly any one...would listen to her.

Janescz sat in the main room, talking to those who came to their flat. Ginna was up the two ladders, away from everything, with her worry and her throbbing hand, through all the rest of the night.

When she came down—did she sleep, finally, before the first light?—Janescz was gone. She looked out the window onto the empty Yard, nothing but mist swirling over the Shelf until...

Now Plietor was jerking up the ladder to their door. And Davik...Davik, Janescz, and the others were marching in a line down the Shelf, with Carnahan and his pistol, a wooden case in Carnahan's other hand. She saw a few people creeping out cautiously from the Stack to the Yard. It was time for in-ringing. But there was no in-ringing. Just Carnahan and the line of men.

"Ginna! Come quick! Carnahan..." Plietor was gasping, fear on his face. Ginna gathered her workshift at the knee and raced behind him to the ladder.

"Ah," said Carnahan, as Plietor and Ginna flailed to a stop before him. Carnahan had marched the line of other men to just below the last terrace, at the top of the staging area for the gliders. Davik stood out from the line, under the shadow of the revolver. Knots of people were trickling now down the Terrace walks, but Carnahan paid them no attention.

"Miss Ginna deBoruski has sure and given us the pleasure of her company this morning, so you, Davik, may step back into line, and I will have her before me in your place."

"Wait!" shouted Plietor. "What do you want from us?" But Ginna pulled away from him and stood to face Carnahan. Davik's features were contorted, his hands and arms flexing, his eyes bouncing from Carnahan to Ginna.

"Go," she whispered fiercely to him. "Go!" Davik hesitated, but finally backed toward the line. Ginna moved two paces in front of Carnahan, turning her head to watch Davik, and as she did Carnahan dropped his wooden case, stepped forward reaching, and grasped her arm, pulled her back to him, raising the revolver to point toward her head.

"Now, gentlemen," Carnahan said, "we must be very calm here. Janescz, I'll be needing a glider to speed me on my way from among you mutinous lot. I'll thank you to stand one out here for me." He glanced up at the Terrace, now filling with people. "I'm sure your handler lads have arrived by now among this crowd of gawkers to our little drama. So call them down and be quick about it. I shall keep Miss Ginna here close at hand to encourage all your cooperation." He looked over the line of men, jerked his head at Janescz. "Move."

Carnahan's grip on Ginna's arm was painful. She could feel the tension in him. But more than that was her wonder.

Carnahan planned to fly a glider away from the Camp?! This was no idea she had ever heard. Carnahan had almost no experience of flying a glider. *What had Plietor said?* Only a few low flights in the desert when he and Davik were first learning. *How could Carnahan possibly think with only that to fly off the Shelf?* Though…even as she thought this, she thought of herself, of her own minimal experience when she flew there for the first time. Carnahan had seen thousands of launches. Had he been practicing in his head all that time? Where would he go, if he got off? The T-One camp? There was no Shelf there, no place to land. Could he be thinking of going over the Caldera wall to the desert? No one of them had ever done that. How could Carnahan *possibly* be thinking this? Were there depths to his planning they had no idea of?

"*Move,* Janescz," said Carnahan again, and Janescz stepped forward from his place, uncertain, then turned and raised his eyes to the Terrace. "Karolyi, Musil, five more, come down," he shouted.

"Take my glider," said Davik, in a loud voice.

Carnahan pulled Ginna tighter to him, smiled his twisted smile at Davik. "I think as not," he said. "I think it'll be Plietor's glider, now you mention it." He called out, "Janescz, tell your lads to stand out Plietor's glider."

"It'll be a tight fit," said Plietor. "Davik's cockpit is bigger."

"I'm sure it can be managed," said Carnahan, with his smile.

They all stood, the line of men fidgeting, Davik fidgeting most of all, while Musil and the handlers worked, pulling out Davik's and Plietor's gliders together, then three bringing Plietor's and backing it up to the Terrace, two carrying the great coils of elastic rope. Ginna stood stoic, her mouth tight, her eyes moving from Davik to Plietor, up to the knots of people along the Terrace edges. Julia was there, her face white.

Carnahan adjusted his grip on Ginna's arm. He had picked up his case, run his arm through the handle. She could feel the jerk of his body as he swiveled his head from the line of men to Janescz and the handlers. But the pistol didn't jerk. She could see in the corner of her eye the barrel slanting up toward her head.

"Get a move there, old man," Carnahan shouted to Janescz, who was peering into the cockpit of the glider.

"You don't want an unsafe glider," shouted Janescz back.

"I think I know where safety lies," shouted Carnahan. "See to your ropes."

He turned, pulling Ginna roughly. She stumbled, heard a sound behind, then felt the cold barrel of the pistol hard against her jaw, Carnahan's face close beside.

"Move you back, Davik." She could feel Carnahan's voice in his body, tight pressed to hers. "Move back I say, or the first bullet goes through the sheila's brain. You have no chance. Don't waste her and yourself."

"You bloody bastard." Davik's voice was behind them, moving away.

Carnahan pulled her to the glider until they stood beside the cockpit. Before them was the edge of the Shelf, the wind in their faces, the mist curling over. The V of the rope stretched to the two trios of men holding the ends, expectant. Karolyi crouched at the tail of the glider over the tie-rope, his knife ready. Janescz stood to the side.

"Now, Miss Ginna MacReedy," growled Carnahan in her ear, "now it's just you and me. All you have to do is be a good father's girl and this Arltunga Mine's done with Faolán Carnahan and I with it. You can go and tell the world whatever you like. Your daddy can rattle his moneybags in Perth and send someone to put things together again. But I'll be well and beyond the reach of all of you." He gave her his twisted smile as he released her arm and climbed over the side of the glider, the wooden case knocking, but the pistol barrel never wavering. He wormed his way down into the seat, sitting right on the belt, making no move to secure it, wedging the case by his left side. The control surfaces of the glider bounced from stop to stop as he pushed the pedals and waggled the stick with his left hand, all the while never taking his eyes off her.

"Now you move off, dearie, so the tail doesn't smack you, but not a step further. I can sure and shoot you just as well there as here beside me, so don't be planning any drama."

Ginna stepped back, one step, two, three, keeping her own eyes on Carnahan, ready for anything. She glanced to see that she was clear of the empennage, then stopped.

"*Aye*, Janescz!" Carnahan shouted. "I'm ready for your *Fort-en'* and *Hal-ten'*." Janescz made gestures, to his eyes and the crown of his head, but Carnahan only glanced at him and shook his own head.

"No stalling, old man. It's off I'm going, and now. *Fort* and *Halt*. Let's go."

Janescz gave a shrug, drew in his breath. "*Fort!*" he shouted, and the men on the rope ends raised them to their shoulders and walked, leaning forward into the strain. Carnahan's eyes moved continuously, to Ginna, Janescz, the men on the ropes, the edge of the Shelf, but his arm was outside the cockpit, the pistol pointed at her. The men on the rope were slowing, doubled over.

"*Halt!*" shouted Janescz, his arm raised, rigid.

"Bloody GO!" roared Carnahan, giving one last glance at Ginna before he jerked in the pistol as Janescz shouted

"*Weg!*" and the glider leaped forward, Carnahan's tangled red hair twisting in the slipstream, the empennage rushing past her.

The glider lifted. *Too soon!* thought Ginna. The nose came down almost at her thought then rose again, a bobbing, weaving course into the air. *Drunken seagull,* Ginna thought. *He can never do this.* But then the glider was up, the rope was vertical, and she was thinking without thinking, *Push over! Push over!* just before the nose came down, the rope dropped away, and the glider was flying, free into the mist.

Plietor and Davik were at her sides. "Are you fine?" said Plietor. Davik's hand was on her waist. But they were looking at the departing glider. She was looking toward the sheds.

"I must follow him," she said. "I must see where he goes, what he does."

"Who is to care?" said Davik. "He will kill himself. He is gone from us and we are good for it."

"It might be important to know," said Plietor. "I will go. Janescz!" he called, moving away, but Ginna pulled his arm and spun him around.

"He has taken your glider," she said. "And Davik's is sabotaged. I will go in my glider. I can see as well as you, and my father…" She stopped, looked at them both fiercely, her mouth set. "I will go," she said. "It is right that I do."

36.

She was ten full minutes behind Carnahan, and for her own first minutes in the air she despaired of finding him. It was trouble enough staying up. The sun was barely above the Caldera wall, had not heated the Caldera air, so there were no upwellings to rise with in the center. She had to hug the walls, rising and falling with the undulations of the wind over the rock face. How could Carnahan have done this? How would he know to fly in this way? Davik was right. Carnahan had almost certainly crashed by now, the glider lying shattered among the bottom rocks, deep in the mist. She would never find him.

But he *had* launched the glider. With no goggles, no balaclava, the frothy mist on his face, in his eyes. He had launched the glider and disappeared into the mist. So she flew on, crisscrossing the Caldera when she gained enough altitude to do so, her eyes straining into the mist below, probing the clearer air above. She passed over the T-One camp, glimpsed the structures dim below her in a momentary clearing. No one could land there. She looked east at the walls of the Caldera five hundred feet above her. It would be almost impossible to climb over them at this time of day. She thought then she was truly wasting her time. Carnahan could never have gotten this far. And she would never find him if he had. She turned back.

She was in the middle of her turn when the shadow passed across her glider. Her first thought was of the eagle, and she looked up. But there was no eagle, and the sun was still low above the eastern Caldera ridge. She changed her turn to look toward the sun and saw, first in silhouette, then in full detail with its blue tail, the other glider, Plietor's glider. *Carnahan!*

So he had gotten this far. Ginna shook her head. He must be the luckiest man in the world, or the quickest study in a glider. He was higher than she was, close to the wall, flying away from her. Was he trying to gain enough altitude to go over? Would the wind let him do that? Ginna flew toward him, trying to gain altitude herself in what upwellings there were.

The other glider turned, coming back steadily along the wall, gaining altitude slowly. Ginna was closing on it, still below, when the other glider turned out, toward her. Carnahan had seen her, and he was coming. She could see his head in the cockpit, his wild hair flying about his scalp, red in the sun. What should she do? What could *he* do? She flew on.

She saw the burst of red flame before she heard the report of the pistol. Carnahan was almost on her, two hundred feet above, and he had shot the pistol at her. She had heard nothing of the bullet, but she knew she must get away. She threw the stick forward and to the left, pressed the left pedal. The nose swung, the right wing came up, and she dove away, one second, two, three, before she straightened and pulled up, swiveling her head, coming around in a tight right turn to see where the other glider had gone.

She was relieved to see it back alongside the Caldera wall, now well above her. The shot had been a warning. She thought now that Carnahan was trying to surmount the wall. What if he could? Were T-One men waiting in the desert on the other side, waiting to take him in? Did he have some idea of flying all the way to Stuart? That was sixty miles away. Could he possibly do that? She was not at all as certain of his limitations as she had been before.

At least she could follow him. She gauged his progress along the wall and fell in behind him, behind and necessarily below. He could not possibly shoot at her in this position, and if he turned to attack, she could be away. But she did not think he would do that.

They flew a stately ballet along the east wall for three cycles: north for five minutes, turn away, then back in and south along the same path. Carnahan was gaining altitude, but she was gaining faster, and by the fourth cycle she was level with him, two hundred yards behind. The wall of the Caldera still loomed beside them but now only two hundred feet. What would she do when Carnahan went over? Would she follow? Could she get back if she did?

The eagle dropped out of the sun when Ginna was turning back into the wall to begin the fifth cycle, an elongated dark shape over Carnahan's glider, a hundred feet over it, flying parallel. She knew immediately that it was the eagle, and that Carnahan had not seen it. It would cast no shadow on his glider.

Ginna knew what the eagle would do. She waited.

After thirty seconds the eagle dove. From Ginna's perspective it did not look like a serious dive, just a dip in its flight. She remembered how it had looked from the cockpit, though, the wings folding, the bird plummeting toward her, even if just for a few seconds. She remembered her fascination after, and Davik's speech.

The eagle dove again, farther down, a V in its flight this time. Still Carnahan's glider flew steady, northward along the wall, banking out and in to match the undulations of rock, trying to find the rising air. Carnahan still did not know what was above him.

The third time he knew. At the base of the eagle's dive the glider rocked violently from side to side. Carnahan had seen it and flailed the stick. She could imagine him craning up, his hair flying behind him, wondering what to do, what the eagle would do next. She pushed her own stick forward to gain speed, close the gap, curved to the side to gain perspective, to see what was to be seen.

She saw the eagle partially fold and twist its wings to brake its flight, saw the great talons go forward, saw the eagle drop toward the glider, drop and drop. Then Carnahan's arm was above his head, and the pistol flashed and boomed, once, twice. The eagle staggered in the air, then folded tighter, dropped faster, dropped and fell straight into the cockpit of the glider in a mass of flailing wings, feathers, and arms. The glider slewed, stalled, rolled lazily over to the right and tucked the wing, spiraled, spiraled down, down towards the rocks of the wall. The right wing hit halfway down and broke away. The fuselage crumpled and exploded, a shower of debris down the wall.

Then a fold of mist rose and covered it all.

Eight hundred feet above, Ginna circled and stared. It had been a matter of only two minutes. All Carnahan's scheming and machinations with Gehlhausen, his bombast, cleverness, skill, his bravery—yes, some bravery, she would admit—had been brought to nothing by an eagle, an eagle guarding its range and its goats. Was this some form of justice, or nature red in tooth and claw? She shook her head. She had seen Carnahan's end. That's what she had come for. But she felt no satisfaction.

She was moving out over the Caldera's center when she

felt the thermal, the giddy sink in her stomach of the upward acceleration. She had not accepted the air's invitation when she was here before, driven back into the mist by the eagle and her quota. Now the eagle was gone, and the quota too. Why should she not accept the thermal today?

The glider circled up, pivoting on its left wing, its tip pointed down toward the mist. Above, the sky was blue, clear and achingly blue, true color she understood she was starved for. The Caldera wall dropped below her. A few more turns and she saw the notch that gave access to the T-One Camp. Dark shapes were milling at the desert throat, ants on the surface, circling round shapes. Were these T-One men simply at work around their pools? Or were they waiting for Carnahan, who would not come?

More climbing circles and she could see the Caldera itself as a whole thing, a whole for the first time, as she had so wanted…so wanted from the Zeppelin. And it looked…It looked like nothing so much as a great rough pox in the hide of the red desert, a spewing carbuncle against the surface. She grimaced. Was this what she would have thought, those long seven months ago?

The air was cool. Surely it would be delicious to breathe, without the balaclava. She could pull it off, thrust her face into the wind. But no. To do that she would have to release the control stick, and she would not do that. She realized she was tense, not from seeing Carnahan die, but from the extent of altitude, the entirely unaccustomed distance below her. The glider seemed tiny, frail within the immeasurably great expanse of earth and air. It was time to descend.

She pulled the airbrake handle back to the stop and turned south, looking down the length of the Caldera, searching for signs of the Arltunga Camp. So far away below it was, so very far. The desert seemed much closer by its immensity, detail irrelevant in the sheer size of it. But there was detail even so. A spurt of ridge here and there, the sinuous track of washes from former ages. And…a thread, a dark segmented thread, not so far southwest. A close-packed double line of dark shapes aiming to the Caldera, like nothing else in the whole expanse. What could that be?

The camel train! What she was seeing was the double line of camels. The camel train at last, not more than a day out, surely. She would be going with it, she *should* be going with it, but how? How could she go to the T-One by herself? There was much to be decided. She needed to get back to the Camp.

37.

The man from the pools burst through the blue door, slamming it back against the wall in his haste. "Three white men! Three white men with the camel train! Mr. Hilenski sent me to tell you!"

They were sitting around the table: Janescz in Carnahan's place and chair, Bartosz on a bench beside him, Plietor and Ginna on the other side, Davik prowling behind. They had spent most of the day before sitting in this way, Hilenski with them. They had been talking since Ginna had returned in the glider, talking since she had told of Carnahan's fate, since she brought news of the camel train. So much to be decided.

Plietor's brain was spinning with choices. And with sleeplessness, now two nights. The same for all of them, except Davik.

They first had to think of recovering Carnahan's body. Should they mount an expedition? Davik was against it.

"Nah. Let the bloody eagle take care of him. He brought him down," Davik said.

But Plietor had said that body or no, the Camp ledgers were important. And Ginna had said more, that if the justice of their actions and of Carnahan's fate were ever to be decided in a court of law, the ledgers would be crucial evidence. An expedition must be mounted to try to recover the ledgers, at least.

But not before the camel train. No expedition could go and return before the camel train came. A ledger for the outgoing shipment was no difficulty. Hilenksi still had his production papers; he could make a new ledger for them. The difficulty was, even if they had all the ledgers, would they send them—send copies—with the camel train? Much else was to be decided before that.

Which of them would go? Davik wanted badly to go, to stand face-to-face with Gehlhausen. But Janescz said no. Shouting, or worse a fight, would be no good. What was needed at the T-One was to see all their production credited to them when the bags were loaded.

Davik had said, his voice hard, that he needed more than this. "How do we make the bastard pay for what he has done?" No one could say. Bartosz spoke up instead, following Janescz to talk of the credit of their production even at Oodnadatta when the bags were put upon the steam train. "Someone will have to go with the bags, all the way to Oodnadatta," said Bartosz.

"And how do they return?" Janescz asked.

No one could say this either. Or if anyone should go to Stuart-town. If they could recover the ledgers, should they be taken to Stuart-town to show to the Constable, proof of Carnahan's thievery? And Gehlhausen's? Was this the way to get at Gehlhausen? Who could deal with the Constable? Another thing no one could say. Ginna was quiet.

But Davik was not, finally said what was the first thing for him. "What about Ginna?" he said. "Does she go? Or does she stay?" He could not look at her as he asked it. Plietor felt his heart turn over too. The room had been quiet, Ginna looking at the floor.

That was when the man Hilenski sent from the pools

came, with the door banging, and maybe it was a good thing. *Three white men!* Who could they be?

"They have come for Ginna!" shouted Davik. "I know it!" Plietor tried to think, but there was no knowing for him. "We must hide her!" Davik still shouted. Plietor tried to object, thinking they could not hide her very well, and instead they should all stand together to see these men, Ginna with them. But Davik was frantic, overpowering. Ginna must go behind Carnahan's inner door until they knew what the men were, if they had weapons. Janescz must go down to meet the men.

Janescz went. And they waited. Ginna sat, but the others stood, walked about, Davik pacing like an animal, stopping at the blue door every time he passed to look out.

The pulled carts began to come out from the cleft one after another, all the Camp's supplies across the Shelf, moving towards the sheds, the Stack, the fob. And finally the men they all waited for, three white men in well-used khaki bush clothes, broad hats pulled down, Janescz behind them. The lead man was walking with authority, heading straight across the Shelf toward the Stack.

"Okay," said Davik. "Okay. Now it's in the back rooms for Ginna. Until we understand what these men are about. I will see to it." He looked at Ginna. "You know I will." Ginna looked at Plietor briefly, but she allowed Davik to lead her through the inner door. He returned in a moment, shut the door hard behind him. Bartosz and Plietor followed him out into the mist-dimmed sunlight.

The group stopped three paces before them, Janescz pushing forward. "This," he began, "I must tell you. This is—"

The man in front spoke. "I am Ian MacReedy, owner of this mine."

His words froze them all. Plietor heard Davik suck in his breath. The man who said he was Ian MacReedy was not as big as Carnahan, but strong and square. Of the other two, one was also big, but softer, with a brushy mustache. The other was short and hard, with a great squint.

"I understand from Mr. Boruski," said MacReedy, "that I am to be told of the whereabouts of my Overseer, Mr. Carnahan. Are you the ones to tell me?" He looked Davik over, moved his eyes to Bartosz, to Plietor last.

Janescz was looking at Bartosz, and at the look Bartosz stepped forward, holding his hat, fumbling, saying, "Yah, sir, we will that. We are the supervisors here, we are, save one, Anna Drowicz, who sees to the bunkhouse and the living stores, and..." he gestured, "and save these, Davik and Plietor Boruski they are, who are—"

He stopped, *Befuddled by his own speech*, Plietor thought, but even more by the look on the man MacReedy's face. Plietor had seen MacReedy jerk when Bartosz said Davik's and his names, and now MacReedy was staring, his eyes running to Davik's face, then Plietor's own. Plietor dropped his eyes, heard Davik shift his feet, but it was only a moment, and then MacReedy was going on.

"I am less concerned with the status of your group than with what information you can convey to me. Can we go inside here?"

"Oh, yes sir," said Janescz. "These are the Overseer's rooms, and this is the Gathering Room. We should go in there."

"Let me have your names, then," said Ian MacReedy, "and tell me what you do here." He sat behind the table as Carnahan had sat, in Carnahan's chair. They had pulled benches out for themselves. No one doubted MacReedy, doubted he was who he said he was. He had said the other men's names: Dolan, the big one, and Sheehy. These men sat on a bench along the wall. Bartosz sat to MacReedy's right, nearest the door; beside him, Hilenski. Janescz, Davik, and Plietor sat together on a bench to his left.

Janescz said his name again: *Janescz Boruski*. He said he had been supervisor of the gliders before…before— He did not finish the sentence. Davik and Plietor Boruski were his sons, grown up in the Camp. Janescz said he had a letter, from a Vice President of MacReedy Mining, from Perth long ago. Perhaps Mr. MacReedy remembered the two boys, from Perth? Now the boys were men, flyers, flying the gliders. Plietor fidgeted while Janescz spoke. Davik looked dark, his eyes on MacReedy.

The man did not change expression. His lips were tight. He looked only briefly this time at Davik and Plietor. No, he didn't remember. He might be interested to look at the letter, later.

The others gave their names: Gregor Bartosz, supervisor of the garden Terrace; Teodor Hilenski, supervisor at the pools. Plietor had never heard these whole names spoken.

MacReedy nodded as each man spoke, then took a breath. "Now," he said, "who will tell me of Mr. Carnahan? I have seen no communication from this Camp since Mr. Carnahan's last summary and accounts, which came out with the last camel train nearly five months ago. Mr. Boruski, will you speak?" He looked toward Janescz. Janescz grimaced, glanced at Bartosz, grimaced again.

"It is hard to know where to start," he mumbled.

"Speak up man," said MacReedy. "Start after the last camel train."

"There…there was things before that…" said Janescz, stopped, breathed, then looked up.

"To say after the last camel train. Things was good in the Camp then. We had all six gliders flying. Sixty sorties a day we flew, thirty on Midweek Day, three hundred ninety the week. We made our quota every day, every week. The gardens was good." He gestured to Bartosz, who looked at him a moment, then nodded. "The pools was good." The same gesture to Hilenski, who nodded too. "Carnahan...Mr. Carnahan was satisfied. He spoke well of all at the Gatherings."

Davik shifted, the bench creaking with his weight. Janescz turned his head quickly to look at him, just a glance. Davik tightened his lips but sat still. Janescz looked back at Ian MacReedy and spoke again.

"Things...things was so good that...after a bit, Mr. Carnahan raised quota, raised quota for chemical production. We...the flyers, met that, so he...he raised it again."

Now Bartosz was shifting, looking hard at Janescz, his own mouth tight. Janescz glanced at Bartosz, but didn't meet his eyes, drew a breath and spoke faster. "We met that, or we was meeting it, when we lost a flyer, a flyer and glider."

"Lost?" said MacReedy. Bartosz and Davik both shifted now. But Janescz was going on, leaning forward like he was reciting, his neck red.

"Now it was five gliders, and we was making that, with discipline on the Shelf, flying very disciplined, like Mr. Kemper taught us, flying only for production. And then we lost Karpiak to the coughing sickness—"

"Janescz! You leave out too much." Bartosz interrupted from his seat.

Davik stood, turning to glare at his father, his fists clenched at his sides. Plietor reached a hand up to Davik's arm. But Janescz was still talking, as though he could not, dare not stop.

"...And then the girl took Karpiak's glider. She said she

was a flyer and took Karpiak's glider and..."

"WHAT?!" shouted MacReedy. He was on his own feet, eyes blazing. And then all were, Davik reaching for Janescz, Plietor reaching for Davik, Bartosz moving toward them, Hilenski standing, gaping.

"STOP!" shouted MacReedy, bringing his fist down thunderously on the table. "I ORDER YOU ALL TO STAND!"

They all froze. "Everyone—take—his—seat," said MacReedy. They all did so, Davik looking wild, barely able to sit. MacReedy stood before them, a look as wild on his own face.

"What—girl?" said MacReedy, his head thrust forward.

"I found her!" Davik jumped to his feet again. "I found her at the Zeppelin. I brought her back—"

MacReedy's eyes were wide, his face filled with blood. He trembled.

"I told you!" Plietor found himself shouting. "I told you she should have been here from the first!"

"What—*GIRL!?*" said MacReedy again. "Where is she!?"

"She is here!" cried Plietor. "Just inside, in Carnahan's room with the electric telephone. We didn't want...they didn't want—"

MacReedy was past the table before anyone could react, before anyone thought how to react, past the Boruski bench, past the bench where Dolan and Sheehy had leaped to their feet. He wrenched at the inner door, pulled it wide. "GINNA!" he cried, in a huge voice. "GINNA, IS IT YOU!?"

"Pa-pa! Pa-pa!" Ginna's voice was a shriek from inside. The door slammed behind MacReedy of its own velocity.

They were all standing now, dumbstruck. Dolan and Sheehy moved out, as though to guard the door.

"He has come to find her. I said it," said Davik, breathing hard, his voice a croak.

"No!" said Plietor. "He did not know she was here.

Didn't you see it?" He looked at Dolan and Sheehy, but they only stood looking back. "How could he know? He thought she…He must have thought…" Plietor shook his head, clearing images he did not want to deal with. "He has come for some other reason." They all looked at MacReedy's two men, but Dolan and Sheehy offered nothing. Plietor looked at Janescz, then Davik. "This is new to him. To Ginna too. A high emotion. You saw it. We must wait to find what his other reason is."

Davik stood for a moment, then moved off across the room, toward the blue door.

"I think Mr. MacReedy will sure and want you all here when he comes back," said Sheehy.

"We'll stay. Be certain of it," said Janescz, looking at Davik, who halted near the wall. The rest of them moved towards him, to wait together.

Janescz said in a low voice, "Ginna will tell him, you know. She will tell him all the things we have done. And then…and then it will be as Carnahan said."

Plietor reached for Janescz's arm. "No. I am sure it will *not* be as Carnahan said. I don't think Mr. MacReedy came because Carnahan called him to come. Maybe…maybe he saw something in the production weights, something he didn't like. Maybe he came to look after Carnahan, to find an explanation of that. We must wait, only wait, that's what, to see what he says."

They stood and shifted, sitting on the benches and standing again, Davik pacing the length of the room and back, while Dolan and Sheehy stood silent before the inner door. Plietor tried to keep his mind from speculation. He didn't know what the others thought.

Finally Carnahan's door opened. Dolan and Sheehy stepped aside, and Ian MacReedy walked through it. Plietor saw that his eyes were puffy and red, and he seemed stooped from what he was before, like a man who has worked hard. Ginna was behind him, her own eyes red too, her hair coming down from the fabric that tied it. She did not look at them, but Plietor saw that she looked like her father, saw it right away when they came out together, saw it as he had not when he had first seen MacReedy. It was in the eyes, the nose, the chin. How could there be any doubt?

"This is my daughter, Ginna," said MacReedy, in a half-choked voice. "You can't imagine…" He stared at the group of them across the room, shook his head, closed his eyes.

When he opened them, he began to say, "You know how…" then stopped, reached for the end of the table and steadied himself with a hand on it, started again. "You know how she came here. I…I have just learned that." He took a deep breath. "What you can never know…never…is the depth of my joy that she has been returned to me." His eyes swept them. "What you may learn…is the depth of my gratitude that you have kept her safe so that she may be reunited with me this day." He looked at Ginna, and his eyes were glistening. Plietor felt water in his own eyes, a stop in his throat. "Let us sit again," MacReedy said.

He regained Carnahan's chair behind the table. Ginna joined Plietor, Janescz, and Davik on their bench, sitting a little away from them. When they were all still, MacReedy looked down at the table top for a moment, then sat up, firm again.

"There is much for me to discover here," he said. "Much more than I anticipated. I came…" He paused, looked at Ginna. "You will want to know that I came to investigate production ledgers on-site, to see production for myself. I hold this mine in high regard. I came to be able to understand certain patterns…" Again a look to Ginna. "But now, there is much more…to understand." Plietor met Janescz's quick look as MacReedy swept his eyes across them again.

"I will hear my daughter first, more than she has just told me. Then I will hear each of you, one by one. My daughter will make notes from those accounts, so that a record may be compiled which contains all the particulars. When we are completed, and in agreement as to what we know, and…" he tilted his head, "what we do not know, my daughter will prepare two clean copies. One will stay here at the Camp, as part of Overseer's records. The other I will take back to Perth. We must make haste. The camels wait. The other camps—" he smiled a grim smile—"wait on the camels.

"After my daughter, I will begin with Mr. Bartosz. Then, Mr. Hilenski." He nodded to each. "Then Janescz Boruski. I think I will speak to Davik and Plietor Boruski together. I hope a picture of Mr. Carnahan will emerge from this process. I understand…that he is not here to speak for himself." MacReedy's lips were a hard line across his teeth. "Mr. Dolan and Mr. Sheehy will attend the door, to see that we are not interrupted. If you are not talking to me you need to be working. The Camp must go on as always. Gardens must be tended, processing continued in the pools. Janescz, can you fly today, with such disruption?" Janescz nodded. "Good. But Ginna…I do not think Ginna will be flying gliders again here."

The late afternoon sun had tinted the mist-filled air a rusty ochre. Plietor walked the Shelf by himself.

He had flown six sorties after he and Davik talked to Ian MacReedy, flown them in Ginna's glider. Flying had been a struggle. His concentration was poor—from sleeplessness, from the distraction of events and thoughts. He had brought his quota, but now he needed to be by himself, to walk and think.

Ginna would not sleep with them in their flat again. She would be up into the night with her father, preparing the Record, the one story of what had happened, from all their separate stories. MacReedy wanted them all to read this Record, or have it read to them. He wanted each supervisor, and him and Davik, to sign with their names, both copies, as agreeing to the story. Then the Record would be final. Ginna would sleep in Carnahan's little room, the room where Plietor and Davik had been locked in. Her father would sleep in Carnahan's bed. Dolan and Sheehy would sleep in the bunkhouse.

Tomorrow they would go to look for the wrecked glider, for Carnahan's body, and most of all the wooden case with the camp ledgers. Four would go: Davik and Plietor, Musil and Karolyi, with a litter to bring back the body, if they could find it. Ian MacReedy was very anxious that they find the ledgers. "The final pieces of the puzzle," he said. They hoped that men from the T-One had not gone looking and found them first.

Plietor and Davik had told to MacReedy the story as they knew it, he—Plietor—telling, mostly, Davik breaking in. They told it from the beginning, with the Zeppelin. MacReedy let Davik go on, watching him very close as he talked and paced. They did not tell everything, not about the deep dives, not their fight after the rockslide, the night Ginna was taken off. Plietor led the story away from these things, and Davik was quiet when he did. Ginna was quiet too, the whole long time they talked, writing and writing, her head down. *It will be curious to see what the others left out*, Plietor thought, *what Ginna puts in herself.*

The final pieces of the puzzle. That's what MacReedy said the ledgers would be. Maybe they would be the final pieces of the puzzle of what Carnahan had done. But for Plietor they were hardly any pieces at all of *why* he had done what he did. Plietor wondered if he could ever understand Carnahan, a man of such force gone bad. Did Ginna understand him? Did MacReedy himself?

Plietor knew he should go to the Stack to sleep. But so much was to be decided on the next day.

38.

Six days. Six days they had been on the camels, Plietor by now firmly in the rhythm of the beasts and the desert sun. It was not so hot as Plietor remembered, out under that clear sun away from the mist. How many years before had it been? Nine years since the other camel train, he and Davik riding what seemed so high up, Janescz below walking with his satchel. That had been the sun of full summer. Now was the beginning of winter.

Plietor glanced over the line of twelve camels to his left. On the lead camel sat the head Afghan, lungeed, wrapped in his dust-colored robe. Behind him swayed Dolan and Sheehy. The camel behind Sheehy's carried the Afghans' gear, and gear for camping. The other eleven were trussed with bags, burlap bags loaded with threnium oxide powder. Same for the camels behind Plietor, except for one with all their luggage, precious little for Ginna and him, more for MacReedy and his men. All the jumble of bags, sacks, crates, tools, lengths of raw lumber and coils of wire the camels had brought out, everything three mining camps needed over the next four months, had been taken in by the camps, replaced with the chemical powder they now carried.

Ginna was on the camel in front of Plietor, Ian Mac-Reedy before her. The other Afghans walked alongside with their poles.

They had found Carnahan, thrown from the crashed glider among the rocks, but not far. His body had been worried a bit, but not bad, nothing like some of the bodies they had brought back from the Zeppelin. The wood case was nearby too, splintered but still closed up. Ginna had explained that her father would compare the ledgers with what weights had come to Perth from the Oodnadatta loading, to see with numbers what Carnahan had stolen, sold to Gehlhausen.

They had brought the body back along with the case. Davik would go again for salvage from the glider: wood and cable, metal hinges and linkages, the rubber wheel. They laid Carnahan out in the Camp cemetery, stones above him. MacReedy said a few words. "We must be ever vigilant to guard the production of our labor here," he said. "We must never lose sight of our proper goals." Carnahan would face the Perfect Judgment, MacReedy said, as they all would, when their times came.

Plietor had stayed in the camel camp at the T-One mine when MacReedy and Ginna had gone in with Gehlhausen. It had surely been hard talk. Ginna had told him only one thing about it. "It does not stop with Gehlhausen," she said. "It goes now to Wonthaggi Coal, in Brisbane."

Plietor would not be going to Brisbane, but to Perth, to the main place for MacReedy Mining. All the deciding the group of them had worried over had been done by MacReedy himself. He had said it when they gathered to hear the one Record read at the end of the second day after he came.

MacReedy had decided to read the Record to them himself. He read in a strong voice without pauses, sitting in Carnahan's chair. Ginna sat beside him on a bench pulled behind the table. The Record was not everything that had been told, but they all had known it was the Record MacReedy wanted.

He read a long time, then finished and looked up. No one said anything. They had signed, each, two copies written out by Ginna, "attesting to the veracity of the account." Then MacReedy had begun to say how things would be.

Janescz would be Overseer for the Camp. Davik would be supervisor for the gliders.

Davik had sat up when MacReedy said this, looked at Janescz beside him, who shrugged, then at Plietor. Plietor had only gestured to MacReedy, who was going on. Seven new workers would come on a special camel train, including a doctor. Two new gliders. Two flyers would be trained by Davik, one a man to be chosen by him; one, the woman Tiska.

Plietor had felt the bench shift as Davik tensed to stand, but Janescz had gripped his sleeve with a strong hand. Davik was pulling his arm away when MacReedy said that Plietor would go with the camel train.

Davik sat still then, his mouth open.

"What do you want?!" Janescz had spoken hard to Davik as he stormed along the wall in their flat. Did Davik want to go to Perth, to dress in starched shirts with collars, sit all day behind a desk for MacReedy Mining Limited in the stone building with marble floors? Did he want to trail MacReedy around like Dolan and Sheehy?

"I want to be with Ginna," Davik shouted from the wall. "I want Ginna."

"*Acch!*" had spat Janescz. Davik could not have her. He should know it, should have known it as soon as he knew what she was. If there had ever been any doubt, MacReedy had taken it away.

"Why Plietor, then?" Davik shouted. "Why him?"

Janescz did not know why. He had said this to Plietor, later, after Davik had banged out to go see to the gliders for tomorrow's flying. He did not know MacReedy's mind, but even he himself thought it might be best for the two of them, Davik and Plietor, to be apart. And what did Plietor think about a desk in the stone building in Perth? Plietor had smiled. *At least he could finally meet Angus McLoughlin,* he had said, then, more seriously, there had to be many jobs for MacReedy Mining, maybe in Perth, maybe at another mine far away. Ian MacReedy would say it, and that would be what was. Janescz had reached and held him on both shoulders. He would miss him, he said.

The why of Plietor's leaving had finally been told him by Ginna, though not until four days out. The camels were down in their evening double circle, chewing all around, the Afghans squatting with their tea before the fire. Dolan and Sheehy snored in their swags. MacReedy sat in a blanket on the far side of the fire, writing by the light of a candle. Plietor had stepped out of the firelight to lean against a red rock and look at the glittering sky. Ginna came from her own blanket to stand beside him. She stood close. He could feel her warmth. They stood looking at the sky for a bit, then she took a breath.

"Do you ever think of your mother?" she asked.

Plietor stifled a snort of surprise. She had heard him only once talk about his mother, Ginna said, with Janescz's Bible.

His mother. Yes, his mother had read a Bible. What about her mother? he had asked. Here was her father, but what about her mother?

Her mother had died when she was born, Ginna said. She never knew her.

Plietor said he was sorry, and when Ginna asked her question again he said some things. He described his mother as he remembered her: her hair long, brown like his, her voice with strange words, words he had heard Janescz use sometimes, her clothes bright, *always too tight,* she complained, her shoes tight too. He remembered their flat: two rooms, plain floors, a bed and cot, cooking shelf, privy corner, cold water. He remembered other women in similar flats in the building, other children, no fathers anywhere. How his mother often went out at night, he to flats with other children to sleep.

Ginna was silent while he talked, silent after he stopped. Then she asked, "When did Janescz come into your life?"

He had come one night, Plietor said, when his mother was at home. A dog was howling down in the street. A black dog, tied to a lamppost. Plietor dreamed about the dog sometimes. The dog howled and his mother called from the other room for Plietor to find out why. Then the door of the flat rattled and his mother came to open it, and there was Janescz. His mother and Janescz went into the other room and talked in low voices, while Plietor looked at the dog through the window. Then they came out and his mother told him Janescz was his father, and he was taking him to a better place. And they left. His mother sent him away with Janescz in just his clothes, carrying nothing more. They went to the steam train station and there was another man. Davik was with him. Janescz and the two of them—Plietor and Davik—got on the steam train and rode seven days.

"And when we came to Oodnadatta we got down, and took the camels twenty-five days, and came to Arltunga, and the rest...you know." He turned his head to look at her and saw she was looking at him. They held eyes for a moment, then she said, "What of Davik's mother?"

He had no idea, he said. He himself had never told what he had just said to anyone before. He was sure Davik had not either. There had never been any time for him and Davik to talk about mothers, not with Janescz riding on the steam train or with the camels, never after they had gotten to the Camp. When they came there Janescz had told his own story as their father to the Overseer, with the letter from Angus McLoughlin. And that had been the story they had lived by, all these years. Ginna was still looking at him. Then she had turned away, to look across the fire and the squatting Afghans toward her father.

"There is something you should know," she had said. She had taken a breath. "Janescz is not your father. Not Davik's father either."

Plietor stood stiff. "How is this?" he said.

Her father had told her, Ginna said. He had told her when they were making the Record. "It was hard for him," she said, "but he told me."

Plietor had looked across the circle at her father. "He wants me to tell you," Ginna said.

She breathed in, turned her face out to the dark of the desert. She knew, she said, that her own mother had died in her birth. What she had not known was that after her father's grief had passed, three years after, while Ginna was still small and in the care of a governess, her father had sought out other women. Not for marriage. Her father gave no details, only said that Plietor had come from this, and Davik. From different women. But both from him. That was what her father wanted him to know.

Plietor had felt dizzy. "Just that?" he said. "So simple?"

"Of course it's not simple," Ginna said. There were great complexities of feeling, complexities of situation. She was having to come to grips with it too. But those were the facts of it.

"Janescz always knew this, knew he was not our father?" said Plietor.

"Yes," said Ginna. "He always knew that. Nothing more."

Plietor looked across the campfire at MacReedy, his face down to his writing craggy in the candle light.

"Who will tell Davik?" Plietor said.

"Janescz will," Ginna said. Her father had told Janescz just before they left, just the facts as she had told Plietor. Janescz would find a time to tell Davik, maybe had already.

They stood, silent, the desert around them.

After a moment Plietor said, "What happened to the women? My mother? Davik's?"

Ginna breathed again. She had asked that, she said, and her father said they had been helped to return to their own countries, given money so that they would have some choice in their lives. That was the way he had put it.

They were silent again.

"You are my half-brother," Ginna said. He saw she was looking at him again.

"Is that what they call it?" he said

"Yes. And Davik too." And then she said, "That is one reason my father has brought you with us."

He looked at her for a moment, then said, "So I can be away from Davik?"

She shook her head, slowly, looking at him all the time. "No. So you can be together...with our father," she said. "He sees something of himself in you. That's what he told me. And..." She paused. "So you can be together with me, in some way." She made a gesture in the dark. "My father—our father—did not say that, but I think it must be so."

She put her hand on top of his, on the rock, and they were silent in the dark, the glittering sky all above. Somewhere out in the desert dingoes barked. A little wind swept through the camp, scattering sparks from the fire. Her father—their father—had put out his candle and slid down into his swag. Plietor had taken Ginna's hand, squeezed it between his own two palms, then released his grip. She had moved off then, around the edge of the camel rings toward her own swag.

His sister. Their father. Fifteen coming days the camels would walk. Maybe in fifteen days Plietor would come to a new way of thinking about himself, riding away from his brother and Janescz into his new life.

The wind swirled his lungee. The winter wind, hot and dry on his face.

ACKNOWLEDGMENTS

This novel was conceived and first drafted in Derek Nikitas' novel-writing class in the Bluegrass Writers Studio at Eastern Kentucky University in 2011. I am grateful to Derek and members of the class for perceptive reading.

Thanks also to Russell Helms of Greencup Books for an early reading of the whole manuscript and later astute editing. The Library Archivist at Girton College, Cambridge, helped me flesh out some details of my protagonist's education there.

Stephen Wiggins provided the cover image. I am grateful for his interpretation.

Thanks to Berea Writers Circle for their support of local writing and for opportunities to read and discuss my work.

Finally, I am grateful to my wife, Libby, for unwavering writing encouragement, astute reading, and a joyful spirit.

ABOUT THE AUTHOR

Roger Jones has always been fascinated by the way creatures move through the air, from insects to supersonic aircraft. He has spent his career studying, teaching, and writing about the history of science, particularly aerodynamics. In addition to academic writing, he has published short stories, non-fiction pieces in flying magazines, and a novella—a coming-of-age story about a vegetarian buzzard. He has drafted a monograph on Daniel Bernoulli, the founder of hydrodynamics, a textbook on its history, two flying-involved novels in addition to this one, and a memoir. He lives with his wife, flies powered planes and gliders, and writes in Berea, Kentucky.